SO-BEQ-619

THE MUSE

HUDSON AREA LIBRARY

HUDSON AREA LIBRARY

Praise for Meghan O'Brien

O'Brien "knows how to write passion really well, and I do not recommend reading her books in public (unless you want everyone to know exactly what you are reading). *Wild* is no different. It's very steamy, and the sex scenes are frequent and quite erotic, to say the least."—*Lesbian Book Review*

"Meghan O'Brien has given her readers some very steamy scenes in this fast paced novel. *Thirteen Hours* is definitely a walk on the wild side, which may have you looking twice at those with whom you share an elevator."—*Just About Write*

"Boy, if there was ever fiction that a lesbian needs during a bed death rut or simply in need of some juicing up, *Thirteen Hours* by Meghan O'Brien is the book I'd recommend to my good friends…If you are looking for good ole American instant gratification, simple and not-at all-straight sexy lesbian eroticism, revel in the sexiness that is *Thirteen Hours*."—*Tilted World*

"In *The Three* by Meghan O'Brien, we are treated to first-rate storytelling that features scorching love scenes with three main characters…She hits her stride well in *The Three* with a well-paced plot that never slows. She excels at giving us an astounding tale that is tightly written and extremely sensual. I highly recommend this unique book."—*Just About Write*

By the Author

Infinite Loop

The Three

Thirteen Hours

Battle Scars

Wild

The Night Off

The Muse

Visit us at www.boldstrokesbooks.com

THE MUSE

by
Meghan O'Brien

2015

THE MUSE

© 2015 BY MEGHAN O'BRIEN. ALL RIGHTS RESERVED.

ISBN 13: 978-1-62639-223-6

THIS TRADE PAPERBACK ORIGINAL IS PUBLISHED BY
BOLD STROKES BOOKS, INC.
P.O. BOX 249
VALLEY FALLS, NY 12185

FIRST EDITION: JUNE 2015

THIS IS A WORK OF FICTION. NAMES, CHARACTERS, PLACES, AND
INCIDENTS ARE THE PRODUCT OF THE AUTHOR'S IMAGINATION OR
ARE USED FICTITIOUSLY. ANY RESEMBLANCE TO ACTUAL PERSONS,
LIVING OR DEAD, BUSINESS ESTABLISHMENTS, EVENTS, OR LOCALES
IS ENTIRELY COINCIDENTAL.

THIS BOOK, OR PARTS THEREOF, MAY NOT BE REPRODUCED IN ANY
FORM WITHOUT PERMISSION.

CREDITS
EDITOR: SHELLEY THRASHER
PRODUCTION DESIGN: STACIA SEAMAN
COVER DESIGN BY SHERI (GRAPHICARTIST2020@HOTMAIL.COM)

Acknowledgments

I want to once again thank Shelley Thrasher for being such a kind and amazing editor. You've never been anything but supportive and amazing, and I appreciate all the ways you've helped me become a better writer. To my wife, Angie, for allowing me to retreat into my made-up worlds whenever necessary—I appreciate it, even though I know it must get lonely. To my sister Kathleen, because. And to my parents, again, who (again) should never, ever read this book.

To all the writers, and the readers who keep us going

CHAPTER ONE

Kate McMannis sat back in her office chair with an epic sigh of self-loathing. She'd stupidly checked the time after watching what had to be her thirtieth cat video in a row. Despite scheduling eight solid hours to write today, she'd already squandered half of them. Damn the Internet. How was she supposed to get anything done with an entire world of cuteness and hilarity at her fingertips? Not to mention news websites. Without sitting up straight, she reached for her mouse and clicked one of her permanent bookmarks. The day's headlines washed over her—most familiar from her previous twenty check-ins—and she almost longed for some catastrophe to shake up the boredom of her afternoon.

She should be working on her novel. Every minute her deadline drew nearer. She had less than two months to finish her latest work-in-progress. While it wasn't unprecedented for her to whip out a novel-length romance or erotica story in sixty days or fewer, she felt no closer to inspiration than she had the day before, or the week before, or even two months before. Paralyzed by writer's block, she couldn't manage to cobble together more than a few paragraphs in a sitting. She still had nine hundred words to go before reaching the twelve-thousand-word mark—and that had taken her months to achieve. Unfortunately, it represented only a fraction of the eighty thousand words she was obligated to deliver.

Kate glanced at the empty document titled "Chapter Four" that had been taunting her for days. Why the hell was this one so difficult? This wasn't her first novel. She'd published several others. Another unpublished novel-length work had poured out of her over the course of months—years, technically—and she'd never given up on it despite never receiving a dime for its completion. Yet now she couldn't seem to wrangle a seed of a good story out of her head and onto the screen despite the contractual obligation looming over her.

Why?

Grunting in frustration, Kate kicked back from her desk and walked to the kitchen. Maybe she needed a glass of lemonade. Or a snack. Granted, months of lemonade and snacks hadn't yet loosened the masterpiece lurking within, but who knew? Today a snack break might solve all her problems.

She surveyed her nearly empty refrigerator and let out a tired groan. No lemonade. No hummus, either. Obviously she needed to go to the grocery store. This was a legitimate excuse to run an errand, but she *had* been on the verge of actually accomplishing something. And now this. No wonder she was getting nowhere fast.

"Well, damn." A grocery run would obviously eat up at least another hour of her work time. Annoyed but resigned, she scooped her purse off the counter and left behind her dreams of whipping out a thousand words by lunchtime.

When she opened her front door, she couldn't stifle a gasp upon discovering an exceedingly attractive woman of apparently Mediterranean origin standing with her fist poised to knock. The stranger held a cloth grocery bag in her free hand. Another full-to-bursting sack of groceries sat at her feet, along with a zippered travel bag. She met Kate's no-doubt ridiculous expression of surprise with a wide, beaming smile.

"May I come in?"

Kate nearly stepped back to let her inside, no questions asked, before regaining some semblance of rationality. "Who are you?"

"My name is Erato." The woman bowed deeply, scooping up the bags at her side. "I come bearing lunch. And lemonade."

Erato strolled through the front door, and Kate moved aside as though she had extended an invitation. She was almost positive she hadn't. "I appreciate that, but…I'm sorry, who *are* you?"

Erato set the grocery bags on the wooden island in the center of the kitchen and began to unload items. She handed over a large container of Kate's favorite brand of lemonade. "I'm a muse. Put this away, would you?"

She did as the woman asked, trying to decide if she'd heard correctly. "A muse? You're *amused*?"

Erato chuckled. "I am now." She pulled out a container of hummus—once again, Kate's favorite brand—and set it on the counter. Then she took Kate's hands and squeezed them gently. "No, Kate McMannis, I'm *your* muse. You're blocked, in a big way. Worse than ever before." She broke into a grin so radiant Kate had to return it, her heart pounding that the most exquisite woman she'd ever seen was *holding her hands*. "And I'm here to help you finish that book."

Chapter Two

Help?" A horrible thought occurred. "Wait, did my publisher send you?"

Erato's laughter was as rich and warm as her touch. "No, don't worry. I'm a freelancer." She shot Kate a playful wink that weakened her knees. "This is between you and me."

Kate frowned. "That sounds expensive."

"Not at all." Turning back to the groceries, Erato opened a package of pita bread and turned the oven on low. "My compensation is the sensual, erotic story you'll create. The beauty of the words you'll choose." She poured one glass of lemonade, then another, then put the second container of lemonade inside the fridge beside the first. "The emotions you'll stir in your readers. That's all the thanks I need."

Clearly this woman was a lunatic. A strangely flattering idea began to form, one more than a little unsettling. "Does that mean you're a fan?"

"Your stories are lovely, Kate. Just lovely."

Hardly effusive praise, coming from an obviously obsessive stalker. Who else would track her down and present herself as Kate McMannis's own personal muse? Kate edged toward the knife block, images of Kathy Bates in *Misery* flashing through her mind. "Why do you assume I'm blocked?"

"Because it's my job to know these things and help those who need it." She put a couple of pieces of pita bread on a baking sheet and slid it into the oven. "And honey, let's be honest. You need my help, do you not?"

"Okay…" Now standing next to her full collection of cutlery, Kate wondered whether to brandish one and demand that the woman leave. She hadn't done anything overtly threatening yet—except be crazy, of course—and she *had* brought groceries. "Who told you I was having trouble?"

"Nobody had to tell me. I've felt it for weeks now—and I can't take it anymore!" Erato leaned against the counter and folded her arms under her generous breasts. "The angst, the self-loathing, the worrying about your deadline. If only you could channel all the energy that you put into self-flagellation toward your novel, you wouldn't need me at all."

Defensive in the face of such judgment from a total stranger, Kate said, "Who says I need you now?"

"If I walked out the door right this minute, you'd go back to your computer and write something?"

Kate didn't answer, somehow knowing Erato would call her out for lying. "How exactly do you plan to help me?"

"To start, by making you lunch." Erato pulled the tray of now-warm pita bread from the oven, which let Kate admire her form-fitting red dress. The skirt clung to her utterly delicious ass, tantalizing Kate with the promise of what lay beneath. Erato's dark hair came to just below her ears, cut in a bob that straddled the line between adorable and sexy with head-spinning ease. Standing in the middle of her kitchen fixing her favorite snack, the woman was heaven personified.

Had Kate fallen asleep or hit her head while showering? Whether this was a dream or a delusion, she just hoped it ended in sex. She drank some lemonade to hide her lascivious smirk.

Erato flashed her a white-toothed grin. "Let's wait until after we eat. You'll need your energy."

She nearly choked on the tart liquid. Surely she hadn't voiced her dirty thoughts aloud. "Pardon?"

"You want to make love with me." Erato cut the pita bread into wedges, then put them on a plate and pushed them across the counter. "It's a wonderful idea. That usually helps the creative juices flow. But you need sustenance before we begin."

For the first time in her life, Kate pinched herself to check that she was awake. And…she was. So either this gorgeous, free-spirited woman was a lunatic fan, or else she was involved in some shenanigans designed to make Kate look foolish. Who would pull such a stunt? Her best friend? Her sister?

She couldn't imagine any of her friends and family coming up with something like this to break her out of writer's block. Or to make fun of her for being mired in it. Kate frowned. She had to get to the bottom of this, because she was *way* too tempted to see if Erato would actually go upstairs with her. Sleeping with this woman was almost certainly a bad idea. But she had to know for sure before she would feel comfortable brandishing a knife or calling the police. *Or* turning her down.

"I *am* harmless," Erato said smoothly, once again seeming to pick up on her thoughts with ease. "Promise."

Kate tried to quiet her internal narrative, just in case. But Erato couldn't read her mind—could she? Covering, she ate a couple bites of pita and hummus while she searched for what to say next. "I just don't understand where you came from."

"Greece, originally."

She fought the urge to roll her eyes. "Yes, I get it. Muse. Erato. From Greece." Whoever this woman was, she was clearly stuck deeply in her delusion. Kate took another bite of hummus anyway, because damn, it was delicious. "So why visit me?"

"Why not you?" Erato scooped some hummus onto a piece of pita and took a bite. Her moan of pleasure sent the most obscene fantasies racing through Kate's mind, which she tried desperately to quiet on the off chance her visitor really could read her thoughts. Erato smiled broadly. "Listen, I'll leave if you want me to. Just ask. I'll walk out that door and never bother you again. But if you let me stay, I'll do my best to...*inspire* you."

Though this was absolutely insane, Kate was unable to eject Erato from her life. She seemed harmless enough, after all. And hot. *Very* hot. No risk in at least sharing a snack with her, right?

"I sense you're having second thoughts about making love." Erato tilted her head and regarded Kate curiously. "We can just fuck, if that's more your style. But one way or another, it's a good idea to end as many dry spells in your life as possible. It's how we'll get the words flowing again." She walked around the counter to stand within touching distance. "No reason to be shy."

Kate fisted her hands at her sides. Damn, she was tempted. Was

Erato unbalanced? Did it even matter if she was, when she was the hands-down sexiest woman Kate had ever had the opportunity to sleep with? "I've just never jumped into bed with someone so quickly."

Erato chuckled. "Your characters do."

"Because they're fictional."

"Surely you're projecting your own fantasies onto them." She traced her fingertip over Kate's wrist, then dragged a blunt nail up the inside of her arm. "Don't tell me you've never wanted sex with a stranger." Erato's fingers closed around her bicep, and Kate instantly became wet. "Or imagined being taken up to your bedroom by someone you aren't certain you should trust."

Kate shivered. "I don't even know you—"

"Take this leap with me, Kate. It'll be worth it."

Unsure whether it was the deep conviction in Erato's voice or simply the prospect of bedding a woman who put most supermodels to shame, Kate let go of her reservations and leapt. It wasn't like she'd get any writing done today, anyway. "Okay. Let's do it."

CHAPTER THREE

They had only to cross the threshold of her bedroom for Kate to lose her nerve. The incredible sexual fantasy she'd enjoyed downstairs in the kitchen evaporated into cold reality at the sight of yesterday's dirty panties lying on the floor beside her bed. What the hell was she thinking? She wasn't prepared to host a woman. Her legs weren't even shaved. She'd been holed up in her apartment for weeks, doing a whole lot of nothing while pretending to chase her ever-elusive word count. This had involved plenty of sleeping, masturbating, and eating, but not as much personal hygiene as she'd normally practice when actually preparing to have sex with another person.

And then there was the little matter of Erato being slightly south of sane—

"Would you like to freshen up?" A soft hand touched the small of her back, startling her. "I did just drop in on you suddenly."

This was the perfect opportunity to back out of the most unusual sexual encounter she'd ever considered pursuing. Sleeping with a most-likely mentally ill—but possibly supernatural—woman really was the kind of thing one of her characters might do. Unfortunately, for all the erotic adventures she'd imagined for her stories, she'd never come close to experiencing anything much out of the ordinary in real life. The wildest thing she'd ever done was a little public sex with her college girlfriend. And nothing *too* public—the threat of discovery had always been enough to get them off. She'd never even had a one-night stand.

Yup. Going through with this was insane. Kate cleared her throat. But instead of asking Erato to leave, she said, "Thank you. Freshening up would be nice."

Oh, well. Maybe insane really *was* what she needed. For the sake of her writing.

Erato sat on the bed. "I'll wait for you here?"

She stared at Kate with vibrant blue eyes that brought to mind cerulean skies and distant green meadows. The mental imagery stirred something deep within Kate, a desire to travel to that far-flung place in her imagination and then to stay a while. For the first time in months, she felt a mild pull toward her laptop. Writing had always been the best way she knew to escape her daily life and explore worlds more beautiful than her own. She loved taking those creative flights of fancy more than almost anything in *this* world.

So why the hell had she stayed away from it for so many months?

A quiet giggle broke her out of her musing. "That is, unless you wanted to work for a bit," Erato said. She raised an eyebrow when Kate shook her head swiftly. "You had that look you writers get. The gazing-into-the-distance-while-visiting-another-place stare. I don't want to interrupt anything."

"You're not!" She couldn't believe her immediate panic at the thought of not going through with this absolutely insane liaison. Five minutes ago she was ready to call the whole thing off. Obviously her libido had overridden her good sense. "I mean…I can write later."

"Are you sure?" Erato uncrossed her legs, offering a tantalizing glimpse of what lay between her thighs. "We could always do *this* later."

It had been almost two years since she'd had sex, and now that she had the opportunity, she realized she wanted to take it—*immediately.* Consequences be damned. "I'm sure. Just give me ten minutes to get ready, okay?"

Erato stood and pivoted in place, then shot a flirtatious smile over her shoulder. "Unzip me before you go?"

Feeling as though she were in a dream, Kate crossed the room to stand at Erato's back. Her hands hovered over the smooth olive skin between her shoulder blades for agonizingly long moments while she tried to convince herself that this was okay—and that it was really happening. Erato couldn't have been clearer about her intentions. She *wanted* Kate to touch her. With that thought in mind, she tugged down the zipper and exposed the tanned expanse of Erato's delicate flank.

Kate exhaled in a rush. "You're beautiful."

Erato giggled. "And to think, you've barely seen me." As though emphasizing her point, Erato turned to face her while allowing the top of her dress to fall down over her shoulders. Cleavage that had been merely hinted at before now spilled over.

Kate dragged her eyes away from the curves on display. It didn't feel right to ogle a half-naked woman while she was still fully dressed. "Ten minutes." She took a step away, toward the bathroom, before Erato caught her wrist. She stopped but didn't look back at her gorgeous visitor. She was too afraid of what she might see.

"Relax, Kate." Erato's low voice had an instant calming effect. "You don't need to be nervous with me. I'm here for *you*."

That didn't exactly erase all her doubts, but something about the woman was soothing. Kate drew in a deep, steadying breath, then met Erato's gaze on the exhale. She wasn't entirely certain what to say. *Thank you?* The whole situation felt strange. "It's…just been a while."

Erato gave her a sympathetic smile. "I know."

Of course she did. "And you have to admit, this is kind of a weird way to meet a woman."

The sweet smile never faltered. "I suppose so."

Kate made the mistake of allowing her eyes to drift lower, where she noticed that the very edge of one dark nipple peeked out over the top of Erato's unzipped dress. She licked her lips, aware of the action but unable to stop her instinctive response to the sight.

"Ten minutes?" Erato murmured, drawing Kate's attention back to her amused face.

"Ten minutes."

Ten minutes later, Kate returned to the bedroom showered, shaved, trimmed, and smelling of her favorite vanilla-scented lotion. She half expected to find the room empty and her visitor gone, but Erato was almost exactly where she left her. Except now she was completely naked—and Kate's bedroom was suddenly, *amazingly,* tidy.

"You cleaned?" Kate stood dumbly in her pajama bottoms and tank top, not sure whether she was more shocked by the spontaneous burst of housekeeping or the fact that Erato had apparently straightened things up in the nude.

With a beaming grin, Erato pivoted in place, arm extended. "Cleanliness breeds creativity."

Kate wrinkled her nose. She was almost positive *that* wasn't right. Still, she appreciated the gesture, even if she also felt horribly embarrassed that her new lover had sorted through her dirty laundry and discarded water bottles. "Well, thank you. You didn't have to."

"Sure I did." Perhaps sensing that she wouldn't make the first move, Erato closed the distance between them and took Kate's hand. "Like I said, I'm here for you. Whatever helps you meet your deadline."

Standing within touching distance of her supposed muse, she had no desire to think about that deadline. It was challenging enough to contemplate her albatross of a novel on a good day, let alone with a curvaceous, warm female body in the same room. Still, she couldn't ignore how very strange her current circumstances were. "So do you do this for many authors?"

Erato smiled beatifically and trailed her fingers up Kate's bare arm. "If that's your way of asking if you're my first, then I'm sorry to disappoint you."

Kate's nipples tightened into hard points, now visible beneath the thin cotton of her tank top. She blushed when blue eyes dipped to take in the sight. "Believe me, you're not a disappointment in any way," she said, then inhaled sharply when Erato hooked her fingertip under the strap of her tank top and pulled it down, baring her right shoulder. She watched, rapt, as Erato bent to kiss her clavicle. "At all."

"Nor are you." Erato straightened and pressed her lips against Kate's. Her fingers found the spot her mouth had just abandoned, caressing the still-tingling skin. After a brief kiss that literally curled Kate's toes, Erato whispered, "In fact, I can't remember the last time I was so excited by an artist—or her work."

Kate blushed. According to her worst critics, she wrote pornography. *Art* seemed like a pretty lofty description for what she did. Brushing aside the praise, she took a deep breath and curled her arm around Erato's waist, pulling her close. The soft firmness of full, bare breasts pressed against her own triggered an obscene rush of wetness. No matter how wet the characters in her stories were when engaged in the passionate, earth-shaking sex at which they were so adept, she couldn't help feeling embarrassed by the idea that Erato would soon see just how wanton and desperate *she* was.

Erato looped her arms around Kate's neck and went in for another kiss. Despite her lingering nerves, Kate immediately melted into it. Her hands settled on Erato's bare hips—triggering the startled realization that *she was holding a naked woman*—and her lips parted just as Erato's tongue asked permission to enter her mouth. Their first deep kiss was perfect. Storybook, even. Kate suspected this wasn't due as much to her own skill as it was to Erato's otherworldly instincts. She was so quickly lost in the bliss of what had to be the best make-out session in all of history that she felt completely disoriented when Erato pulled back moments later.

"Touch me." Erato followed up her sensual whisper by flicking the tip of her tongue against Kate's top lip. "Please."

Still in a daze, Kate struggled to understand what Erato wanted. She gently squeezed Erato's full hips and went back in for one more kiss, desperate for another taste of perfection.

Erato only allowed her a brief press of their lips before she moved her mouth to Kate's ear and whispered hotly, "Touch my body, Kate. I want to feel your hands on me."

The direct words startled her into action. She dropped one hand to Erato's bottom, curving her fingers so the tips teased at the crevice between her cheeks. With her other hand she reached for a perfect breast, and her gaze followed. Erato's nipple was dark brown and hard as stone, searing into the center of Kate's palm when she cupped the soft fullness surrounding it. Her caress drew out a throaty moan, a sound of unbridled pleasure that sent sympathetic vibrations straight to her clit.

"Tell me what you want, Kate." Despite being quite obviously aroused, Erato managed to maintain the calm confidence she'd projected ever since walking through the front door. "Anything you want to do—or that you want *me* to do—is yours. Any fantasy you've ever had, now is your chance to live it out. Just ask for it."

Kate wasn't sure what to make of the bold declaration. She'd never been with someone willing to give herself over so completely. The trust Erato seemingly had in her—unfounded as it was—was astounding. She didn't think she could muster enough trust of her own to reveal her most secret fantasies. Not to an almost complete stranger, at least. It was an ironic sentiment for someone accustomed to sharing plenty of lurid fantasies with thousands of readers, to be sure, but such was her contradictory nature. Besides, she couldn't fantasize about anything with her brain turned to mush.

"Uh, we can just do it the normal way." Kate wanted to smack her forehead as soon as the words left her mouth. *The normal way?* That didn't even make sense. "I mean…"

Erato giggled, and incredibly, the sound helped put her at ease. "I understand. How about you let me take the lead?"

Kate exhaled. "Gladly."

Stepping back, Erato slipped her hand into Kate's and pulled her toward the bed. "You're nervous." It wasn't a question.

"It's been a while. And…I'm shy."

Erato drew back the covers and gestured her into bed with a raised eyebrow. "You don't give yourself enough credit. I would have never guessed you were shy."

"Well, you didn't really give me a chance to be. I guess." Kate paused. She didn't feel shy around Erato. Unsettled, yes. Questioning her sanity, absolutely. But not terribly shy, considering that she was willingly crawling into bed with the woman less than an hour after meeting her. "I usually am."

Watching Erato slip into bed beside her was pure erotica in motion. Everything about her was so achingly feminine, from her full curves to the delicate softness of her skin. She scooted close, sliding an arm beneath Kate's shoulders and cradling her against the warmth of her ample chest. Most of Kate's apprehension melted away as she relaxed into the embrace. A warm hand stroked gentle circles over her belly, then trailed lower. Deft fingers teased the waistband of her pajama bottoms, scratching, tugging, just barely dipping inside.

"Is that why you came to bed fully dressed?" Erato bent to lick Kate's top lip. The contact sent a sharp spark of pleasure careening down between her legs. She gasped, and Erato held her closer as her fingernails continued to scorch a suggestive trail across the bare skin of her abdomen. "Because you're shy?"

Once again, her heart threatened to beat out of her chest. She could barely hear her whispered answer over the pounding. "Yes."

"How many lovers have you had?" Erato pushed her hand down the front of her pajama pants until searching fingers found the soft silk of her panties. She scratched at the fabric over Kate's clit, triggering a breathy moan that would have embarrassed her if she couldn't see the satisfaction on Erato's face. "And panties, too, my dear? You must really want me to work for it."

"I'm sorry, I—"

Erato gave a delighted peal of laughter. "Oh, sweetie, *I'm* sorry. I'm just teasing." She pressed her finger down against Kate's labia, stroking her lightly through the soaked fabric. "I'm happy to work for it, believe me." She drew a path from one side of her panties to the other, then played with the elastic leg band at the juncture of Kate's thighs. "Now tell me, how many lovers?"

"You're my fourth."

"And were you shy with the others?"

"I knew them a little better by the time we slept together." That was an understatement. All three had been friends first, then lovers. "I've never done this with a woman I just met."

Hungry eyes scanned the length of her body, and for the first time Kate lamented the mid-afternoon sun that streamed in through the windows. As much as she loved being able to gaze upon Erato's nude body in all its glory, she couldn't hide her own shaking hands or heaving chest. A look of compassion softened Erato's expression, and she flattened her palm against Kate's center, outside her panties. "I like crossword puzzles."

Kate couldn't help it. She bleated unladylike, thoroughly unsexy laughter. "Okay?"

Erato's forehead crinkled. "I'm trying to help you get to know me better. So you'll relax a little."

The sweet, quirky nature of the woman who cupped her between the legs *did* help her relax—degree by degree. Erato was like no one she'd ever met. In that way, she almost had no problem believing that this stranger wasn't strictly human, and for whatever reason, the thought filled her with a powerful sense of safety. It was better than accepting that the woman in her bed was mentally ill. "I'm all right, really."

"Just wound up tight," Erato murmured. Her hand began to move, slowly, barely applying pressure. "I completely understand that this must all seem strange. I assure you that I'm harmless."

Kate spread her legs, almost embarrassed by how *not* afraid she was. She bit her lip to hold back a gasp when a finger pressed between her labia, rubbing gently. She gazed at the full breasts that pressed against her side, then closed her eyes, exhaling through her nose. "And beautiful."

"Thank you." She could feel Erato smiling above her. "I'm also remarkably aroused, as long as we're cataloging my attributes."

Amused, Kate opened her eyes and looked up at Erato's face. She was stunned by the honest desire reflected back at her. Gaining confidence, she spread her legs wider, holding her breath when the fabric of her panties was finally pulled aside and a warm fingertip drew a line through her abundant wetness. "Me, too."

Erato seemed delighted. "Indeed." She circled her fingers around Kate's clit just long enough to establish a rhythm, then moved lower, causing Kate to whimper. "How long has it been since someone made you come?"

Intelligent thought was impossible with Erato's fingertip tracing around the edge of her opening. Kate threw an arm over her eyes, determined not to allow her hips to chase the teasing contact. She wanted nothing more than to impale herself on a long, slim finger or two, but pride dictated that she not appear quite so shameless.

"Do you want me inside you?"

She hoped her nod didn't look too frantic. "Yes."

Without teasing or hesitating, Erato pushed a single digit into her body, watching her face. "Personally, I don't think it's healthy for a writer of erotica to go so long without sex." She withdrew slowly, then penetrated her again with two fingers. "No wonder you're blocked."

"Well, it's—" She moaned when Erato angled her fingers and hit a spot that made her body sing. "It's not like I've gone that long without…" Exhaling, Kate focused on stringing together a sentence. "Without an orgasm."

Erato's thumb brushed over her clit, causing her internal muscles to tighten. "You know your body well, then."

"I'm an expert."

"Good. You can teach me." Erato's hand worked effortlessly within her pajama pants, coaxing wave after wave of pleasure from her hypersensitive body.

Kate cried out, startled that she was quickly climbing toward orgasm. She'd never been with someone so intuitive. "I don't think that's necessary." She nearly slammed her thighs shut on Erato's hand, overwhelmed by the mounting pleasure. It was nearly painful, and she wasn't ready to have it end.

Erato giggled and stopped. "Why don't you take off your clothes now?" She pulled away, leaving Kate torn between relief and painful anticipation. "As long as you're feeling a little less shy."

Kate sat up and tore her tank top over her head, then wrenched off her pajama pants and panties, kicking them over the side of the bed. She paused only when she saw Erato staring at her newly bared skin. "What?"

Erato raised her eyes with obvious effort. "You're as lovely as your stories."

"Thank you." Battling a fierce blush, she pressed Erato back onto the pillows. The genuine attraction in cerulean eyes emboldened her, and warm, supple flesh seared her own everywhere their bodies touched, driving her crazy. A surge of confidence allowed her to crawl on top of Erato, caging her with her body. "I'm definitely not feeling shy anymore." She lowered her hips and rubbed her wetness against Erato's belly.

Erato grinned sunnily. "Good."

Despite the throbbing insistence between her legs, Kate's own climax was no longer her foremost concern. When had she last gone down on a woman? Suddenly she was starving for a taste. "May I lick your pussy?"

An instant change came over Erato's face, eyelids lowering and becoming hooded, a pretty pink flush suffusing her cheeks. Her chest heaved. Clearly she liked the question. "I told you—whatever you want."

Kate lowered her face to Erato's slowly, enjoying the way her breasts rose and fell with her increasingly labored breathing. She kissed the corner of Erato's mouth, then her chin. "Yes, but consent is so sexy. Don't you think?"

Erato's hand landed on her head, stroking her hair as she moved her kisses lower, over the column of her throat. "*Very* sexy."

She licked a trail to the slope of one breast, then kissed a path to a rock-like nipple. Reaching for the unattended breast, she massaged lightly as she closed her lips around the turgid flesh. Erato moaned and arched her back, and Kate slipped her free hand beneath her, keeping her close.

"*Yes*," Erato breathed, and that was *exactly* the kind of consent Kate enjoyed. She smiled around the breast in her mouth, then bit the very tip. The fingers in her hair tightened, almost bringing tears to her eyes. The slight pain sent a lightning bolt of pleasure to her clit, causing her to release a moan to match Erato's. She seized the nipple beneath her fingers and twisted lightly, flicking its twin with the flat of her tongue. Erato's hips rose, no doubt searching for contact where she needed it most. "Kate, please."

She fought back a smirk. Erato didn't seem like the impatient type. Raising her mouth from Erato's breast, she locked gazes with the woman trembling in her arms. "It really feels that good?"

"You must be joking." Erato tucked a piece of hair behind Kate's ear, then put her hand on the crown of her head and encouraged her lower. "See for yourself."

She allowed Erato to guide her down the length of her body, dropping open-mouthed kisses on her belly along the way. When she reached the juncture of Erato's thighs, she used both hands to push them apart, then paused, stunned. Not only was Erato ridiculously perfect—impeccable in every way—but her gorgeous pink folds were swollen and slick like Kate had never seen. Erato's arousal surely rivaled her own, which relieved and empowered her. She opened her mouth to tell Erato, but nothing she had to say was more important than her first taste of her muse. Instead, she ran her tongue up Erato's soaked folds.

The soft, feminine form beneath her tensed, then trembled. Kate pulled back and murmured "Yummy" before going back for more.

Erato was wonderfully responsive. Her fingers tangled in Kate's hair, sharp nails scraping her scalp as she dug her heels into the mattress on either side of Kate's torso. Kate pressed one hand flat against Erato's belly and snaked the other between them, the tips of her fingers poised for entry.

"Yes!" Erato said.

"That's what I love to hear." Kate sucked languidly on Erato's clit as she penetrated her, delighted by her full-body shudder. *This* was what she'd been missing. Writing about it wasn't a substitute; she'd never go so long without again. She'd been starving and hadn't even known.

Erato shuddered and cried out—loud, throaty, and oh-so-sensual. Kate rose to her knees and spread her legs, arching her back as she licked and thrust. The lewd position was purely mental. She liked the idea of offering a wanton display, even if only to the wall. Unfortunately, her action brought forth a terrible yearning—for pressure on her clit, for penetration, for *anything* to soothe the painful ache between her legs. Yet she refused to budge until she brought Erato to orgasm. The quiet sighs and moans above her drove her on.

Moments later, Erato grabbed the hand that still rested on her stomach. "Oh! I'm going to climax."

Kate couldn't help but chuckle at the formality of the warning. She interlaced her fingers with Erato's and squeezed without stopping the motion of her tongue and other hand. She couldn't wait to feel the explosion, to taste every last drop. Heady with power, she quickened her thrusts, driving into Erato hard enough to make her entire body rock on the mattress. Both Erato's hands plunged into Kate's hair and held her securely in place as she came apart.

Fighting the urge to fist-pump, Kate continued the long, languid strokes of her tongue long after Erato regained her breath. As badly as she wanted to chase her own release, she hated to stop. Erato tasted so good and clearly loved the attention. Finally the hold loosened on Kate's hair, and Erato gently pushed her away. "As much as I hate to say it, I need a break."

Kate glanced up at her face, pleased to see her so unkempt. Her dark hair stuck up in a just-been-fucked coif that made Kate feel like the goddamn champion of the world, and she seemed dazed. Exhaling, she urged Kate to crawl up until they were lying face-to-face. Kate's lower body rested between Erato's spread thighs. She hadn't even met the woman before an hour ago, and now they lay tangled together, smelling of sex.

"You're perfect," Kate murmured.

The compliment earned her a playful kiss. "I could say the same. *Excellent* technique, Kate."

"Why, thank you."

"Shall I return the favor?" Erato gave her a wicked little

smile before nipping playfully at her lower lip. "I absolutely adore cunnilingus."

Caught between arousal and a giggling fit, Kate considered the request. Her body was on fire, and the idea of discovering what Erato could do with her tongue sent shivers to the tips of her toes. Yet she had a very different kind of desire—one she'd never felt before. None of her previous lovers had been as feminine as Erato, and something about her soft, full curves and pliant nature made Kate want to be *inside* of her when she came.

Erato ran her fingers up Kate's arm. "Whatever you want."

It wouldn't take much. She'd been close before taking off her clothes, and that was before she'd eaten out a Greek muse. Swept away by an errant desire—borrowed from a scene in one of her early novels—she placed her hand on Erato's throat and bent so their faces were inches apart. Stroking a pulse point on the slender neck with her thumb, Kate kissed full lips with tenderness. "Roll onto your stomach, please."

A moan further bolstered Kate's confidence. Erato swiped at her top lip with the tip of her tongue, then obeyed. She folded her hands beneath her head and tossed a playful glance over her shoulder. If she was uncomfortable being in a completely vulnerable position, she didn't show it. "What now?"

"Now I'm going to come." Kate climbed on top of Erato, planting her knees on either side of her thighs. She lowered her hips until she rested on top of the luscious body. As she'd hoped, the full, round backside she'd admired in the kitchen provided a perfect point of friction for her throbbing sex. She pressed her face into dark hair and ground herself into Erato's ass, delighting in the pantomime of penetration.

"Does that feel good?" Erato lifted her hips, angling herself so well that Kate's hips pumped faster automatically as she chased the orgasm she'd been denied earlier. "Don't stop fucking me, baby."

Kate reached between their bodies and spread herself open with her fingers, pressing hard against Erato's backside. Her clit glided across soft, warm skin, more swollen and distended than ever before. She imagined penetrating Erato with it, sliding into the slick channel of her pussy—or perhaps even better, the tight pucker of her ass. Aware that she was rapidly approaching release, Kate pushed the hair off Erato's cheek and kissed her ear.

"Careful," Kate whispered, "I think you've woken the sleeping beast."

"I'm glad to hear that." Somehow Erato managed to sound incredibly dignified even while being humped from behind. "Because it was my intention."

"Then well played." She slid both hands under Erato's chest, cupping her breasts. Lust like she'd never felt burned through her like wildfire, freeing her from any inhibitions. She thrust her hips wildly, mouth pressed against Erato's neck, inhaling her intoxicating natural perfume. "Because this feels incredible."

"Please, let me feel your climax," Erato murmured in a sweet, low voice. "Let go for me, Kate. *Use* me and let go."

An almost feral growl bubbled up in Kate's chest. She removed her hands from Erato's breasts and planted them on the mattress beside her head, using the newfound leverage to rock harder against the firm backside. Her hips began to jerk and she gritted her teeth, certain that her journey was about to end. Turned on by the sight of Erato, so submissive beneath her, Kate grabbed her fisted hands and stretched them out over her head, effectively pinning her down. She caught sight of Erato's exuberant smile just as waves of pleasure crashed over her, locking her muscles in place. Only her hips moved as she rode out every last bit of her orgasm, courtesy of Erato's incredible ass.

When she could take no more, Kate rolled off to the side and lay on her back, gulping huge mouthfuls of air as she fought to regain her composure. She couldn't remember when she'd come that hard. Had she ever?

Erato turned onto her side and tugged Kate into a loose embrace. She pressed their mouths together, her lips still upturned in perpetual cheer. "Well, that was delicious."

Kate giggled, then relaxed into a sensual kiss. "*So* delicious," she said when they broke apart for air. She put her hand on Erato's shoulder and pressed her down to the mattress before moving over her once again. "On that note, I seriously hope you're not expecting me to get any writing done now."

Erato shook her head, clearly amused. She tracked her fingernails down the center of Kate's back, going as low as she could reach. "No. I'll grant you a twenty-four-hour reprieve so we can get some of this sexual energy out of your system." She nudged her thigh between

Kate's legs. "It should take some doing to dampen this fire we've just ignited."

"I have no doubt that you're up to the challenge." By this point, it didn't even occur to Kate to feel embarrassed about the wetness she was leaving on Erato's skin as she rode her thigh. Everything felt *so* good. Already, she desperately wanted to come again. "On that note, is your offer still good?"

Erato lit up. "To perform cunnilingus?"

That phrase had no business sounding as sexy as it did falling from those full lips. Eager to get her mouth on Erato again, Kate said, "I'm happy to return the favor. You don't even have to wait, as long as you don't mind giving while you receive."

"That's perfect." Erato rolled them so Kate was on her back, then turned and straddled her face without any self-consciousness. Kate felt the soft tickle of hair against her inner thighs mere seconds before Erato's tongue touched her labia. It set her nerve endings aflame in the most painfully pleasant way. Breathless moments ticked by before she gathered the presence of mind to grab Erato's hips and pull her down onto her face.

Her muse tasted even sweeter the second time around.

CHAPTER FOUR

Hours later, they lay tangled in a heap with the sweat-dampened top sheet twisted between their calves. The comforter was off the bed after their lengthy sixty-nining session. Kate had lost track of the number of orgasms she'd had. They'd fucked in multiple positions until after the sun set, until finally they both collapsed in silent, mutual agreement to rest. Incredibly, though they'd just met, she felt comfortable cuddling with Erato. Marathon sex was a marvelous icebreaker.

"How do you feel?" Erato murmured.

"Great." Kate groaned as she rolled onto her back. "Like I'll be sore in unimaginable ways."

"Maybe that twenty-four-hour reprieve isn't necessary." Eyes twinkling, Erato pressed a kiss to her shoulder. "Have I worn you out already?"

"Hardly. I just need a quick break." Her stomach growled. "Are you as hungry as I am?"

"I brought a vegetarian pizza earlier. Shall I pop it in the oven so we can refuel?"

Erato really was the perfect woman. Kate grinned and stretched her arms over her head, luxuriating in the ache of her overtaxed muscles. She closed her eyes and exhaled. "That sounds wonderful."

"Why don't you jump into the shower?" Warm lips wrapped around her nipple, suckling gently. "I'll join you once dinner's under way."

Kate tangled her fingers in Erato's hair, loath to let her out of bed though she badly wanted food. "Only if you promise I can have you for dessert."

Erato left her with a playful nip on the slope of her breast. "Don't worry. I've got big plans for you."

Kate sat up in bed, awed by how Erato didn't cover herself, how wholly at home in her own skin she seemed. But why shouldn't she be? Not many people had her level of natural beauty and confidence. Kate certainly didn't. Climbing out of bed, she grimaced as she glimpsed her own body in the full-length mirror on her bathroom door. While she didn't think Erato had faked her attraction or her enthusiastic responses in bed, Kate was getting the better end of the deal. Even if Erato turned out to be certifiable, Kate would still be lucky to have had the opportunity to be with her.

Kate turned on the shower and waited until the water was hot before stepping beneath the spray. Like magic—and as it always had prior to the last year or so—her writing mind engaged as she luxuriated in the sensation of getting clean. Her thoughts wandered, but not aimlessly, and not about her grocery list or what errands she needed to run tomorrow. Instead she thought about her characters—Rose and Molly—and how she might try to make their erotic journey half as titillating as what she'd just experienced. She'd already written the beginning of their story, which was decent enough to present to her editor, if not her most skillful piece of writing. But now she was in the Chapter Four lull…too early in the story to introduce real romance, still mired in getting all the players into place, and not quite certain how to take Rose and Molly from A to Z.

She squirted a dollop of soap into her palm and smoothed it over her body, chuckling at how her muscles complained. The sedentary writer's lifestyle certainly didn't keep her well prepared for athletic sex. Not that she regretted one second. All the ways she'd taken and tasted Erato over the course of the day made her groan. Right now the thought of sex—hot, dirty, no-holds-barred *fucking*—completely dominated her thoughts and made contemplating story problems feel like a fool's errand.

Perhaps she should just write a love scene. Rose and Molly could have some adventurous sex—maybe something to introduce some drama and shake up their lives. When in doubt, why not add a little spice? Surely she was dying to write some exciting erotic scenarios.

The shower door opened and Erato poked her head inside, smiling in a way that lit up the room. "I can hear you working. Just nod if you need some privacy."

Kate shook her head, easily allowing thoughts of her book to slip away. She'd much rather focus on the woman who'd promised her more sex and was still naked and goddess-like. "No, please come in. I was just thinking. Maybe my characters need to have sex adventurous enough to excite me about writing this story again. Something that will introduce a story conflict...inject a little drama."

Erato nodded and stepped into the shower. She moved slowly, as if worried she might chase away emerging story ideas. "That sounds like a marvelous plan. What's an erotic romance without the erotic? And when an erotic scene leads directly to story conflict? That's gold."

"Well, I hope so."

Erato picked up the gentle cleanser and offered her the bottle. "Would you mind?"

"I'd love to." She squirted a line of soap across Erato's slim shoulders, then started rubbing it across her back and buttocks. Washing someone else was inherently relaxing, and Erato's quiet murmurs of pleasure made her forget her own sore muscles. She gathered more soap and moved her hands around to Erato's front, cradling and soaping her heavy breasts with a sigh of pleasure.

"That feels divine." Erato covered Kate's hands with her own and leaned back against her chest. The combination of the hot water and the soft, pliant flesh against her own stoked the dwindling flames of Kate's arousal. Suddenly she couldn't wait to be inside Erato again. Erato turned within the circle of her arms, an impish expression on her face. "I'll tell you what, my sweet bard. Dinner will be ready in less than ten minutes, so I'm quite sure we don't have time for whatever you're thinking. However, if you tell me the first sexual fantasy that comes to mind—and the sky's the limit—as soon as I say 'Go,' I promise to get you off at least once before we eat. Now go."

Panicked that she might have to wait for another orgasm until after dinner, Kate blurted out, "How about a threesome?"

Erato beamed at her like she'd just uttered the sweetest words of love she'd ever heard. "Now that wasn't so hard, was it?"

Kate opened her mouth to answer, but snapped it shut when Erato sank to her knees. That *had* been easy. She planted her foot on the edge of the shower, assuming that's what she was supposed to do. A gentle kiss to her inner thigh confirmed it. Kate tangled her fingers in the slick, dark locks of Erato's hair and pulled her forward so that her mouth pressed wetly against her puffy labia. "Your turn," Kate said, and closed her eyes when Erato licked her eagerly. "It shouldn't be too difficult, either."

She came after seven minutes and ten seconds, right before the oven timer went off.

Chapter Five

The problem with a threesome, Kate decided almost two hours later, was that it required a social acuity she simply didn't possess. Standing with Erato at the crowded bar of an even more crowded club, she questioned why this had to be the first fantasy of hers to spring to mind. She had others that might have been more embarrassing to admit—spanking, role-playing, exhibitionism—but they would have required far less courage to execute. Despite the glass of wine she'd ordered to steady her nerves, her hands were shaking.

Erato slid an arm around Kate's waist and pulled her close. "Don't be nervous. Nearly everyone is here looking for the same thing we are. It's prime time, Saturday night. You look amazing, and I happen to know that you're an exquisite lover. If you'd like, I can handle popping the question to the lucky lady. All you have to do is stand next to me and be exactly as enticing as you are right now."

Kate blushed, unable to meet Erato's gaze. "I'm pretty sure you'll need to. I can't imagine asking a stranger home for sex."

Giggling, Erato said, "Ironic, considering that you just spent an entire afternoon fucking a stranger."

"You're not a stranger." Or at least she hadn't felt like one for more than a few minutes in the beginning. Kate had to admit, that alone made her extraordinary. "You're my muse."

"True enough." Erato gave her a friendly squeeze. "So…do you see anyone who interests you?"

Kate scanned the crowd of people surrounding them. She discarded the men immediately, not ready to get quite *that* adventurous with their evening. Women of all shapes, sizes, and complexions danced and laughed around them, a veritable buffet of choices. She didn't doubt that any of them who had any interest in women would want to sleep with Erato, so that wasn't a concern. However, finding someone who felt right for *her* might prove slightly more difficult. She studied faces and bodies until they started to seem indistinct, no closer to finding someone she wanted Erato to approach. She downed the rest of her glass of wine in two gulps.

"I'm not sure," she said finally.

"How about her?" Erato gestured at a tall, pale blonde who danced in a small cluster of women on the dance floor. The woman's toned arms were covered in tattoos, and she wore the easy grin of someone who knew that everyone around her wanted her.

"Eh," Kate said. Confidence was sexy—cockiness was not. At the very least, it wasn't a personality trait that put her at ease about making herself vulnerable. "I don't know."

"You're right." The blonde noticed Erato checking her out just as she turned back to Kate, discarding her as an option. The disappointment that flashed across the woman's face was so obvious, Kate could see it from across the room. "She's rather cocksure, isn't she?"

Once again, Erato's word choice delighted. Smiling, Kate nodded at the wineglass in Erato's hand. "Are you going to finish that?"

Erato chuckled. "By all means. I think you need it more than I do."

"You've got that right." Kate tossed back the entire contents of the glass in four long sips. It was hardly proper wine etiquette, but she didn't care. This wasn't a tasting in Napa. It was a meat market, and she had to calm down to participate in it. Unfortunately, her bladder didn't seem keen to follow her lead. Moments after she started scanning the room for a second time, her drinks hit bottom. "Damn it," she muttered.

Erato kissed her temple and stroked the small of her back, somehow managing to make her feel like the most desirable woman in the club. "Let me guess. You need to visit the ladies' room?"

Kate blushed at her own predictability. "Yes."

"Want me to join you?" Erato nipped the side of her neck, drawing out a moan that captured the attention of the woman standing at the bar on Kate's other side. Kate met the woman's gaze briefly, then closed her eyes when Erato murmured, "If you've ever fantasized about fucking in a bathroom stall, we could start there instead."

Kate forced her eyes open, then flushed, embarrassed that the woman next to her was still at the bar and still watching her and Erato. Despite her secret exhibitionist tendencies, she didn't have nearly enough alcohol in her system to slough off her inhibitions and give anyone a show right now. The idea of a third participant was daunting enough, let alone a crowd. Turning so she could see only Erato, she steadied her breathing. "Maybe later. Right now I just really need to pee."

"Very well." Kind blue eyes searched her face. "Shall I keep looking?"

Judging by her one suggestion so far, Erato—for all her occasionally supernatural incisiveness—wasn't wholly in tune with what type of woman Kate would consider inviting home. Still, maybe she'd get lucky. "Sure. But don't extend any invitations until I get back."

"Of course." She lifted Kate's hand and kissed her knuckles. "I'll miss you."

Kate couldn't quite bring herself to return the sentiment, so she simply smiled and turned to make her way across the crowded dance floor. As soon as she left Erato's side, she felt as though she'd stepped out of a dream state and into her own personal hell. She hated clubs. And dancing. And crowds. There was a reason she never came to places like this. A pair of overenthusiastic dancers bumped into her, proving her point. No matter how uncharacteristic her behavior had been since Erato knocked on her door, she was still the same old Kate McMannis—much wilder with her characters than she could ever bring herself to be.

Sighing, Kate approached the restroom carefully, weaving in and out of the throng of bodies surrounding the entrance. She reached for the handle just as the door opened, and an attractive woman wearing black-rimmed eyeglasses spilled out. Literally. Without thinking, Kate held out her arms and caught the woman just before she fell onto the floor at her feet. The unexpected impact knocked her backward a step, and she struggled not to stumble and take both of them down.

"Oh my goodness," the woman in her arms said breathlessly. She struggled to right herself, stepping out of Kate's steadying grip to adjust her glasses with a nervous laugh. "I'm not drunk, I promise. Just clumsy, and a little mortified."

Kate lowered her arms only when she was certain the woman was safely on her feet. "No worries. I appreciate the opportunity to do something so gallant." She felt exposed on the heels of her attempt at humor, waiting for rejection, but she received an amiable grin instead.

"That *was* rather gallant." The stranger took a few seconds to look Kate up and down, and Kate mirrored the action. She tried to imagine how she would describe this woman if she were a character in her novel. She radiated intelligence. Her skin was a deep, rich brown, and her short hair framed a genuinely warm and stunningly pretty face. She looked like someone more at home in a bookstore than a nightclub, despite the red dress she rocked fiercely. By the time Kate's attention drifted back to her face, she was shuffling nervously. "My name is Olive, by the way."

"I'm Kate." She held out her hand, feeling a bit silly when Olive took it. She'd just copped a pretty decent feel on their way to the floor, so a handshake was probably a little over-formal. "Sorry." She shot a self-deprecating nod at their joined hands. "I'm still perfecting my social skills. Places like this make me nervous."

Olive's entire body relaxed and she seemed to brighten, if that were possible. "Me, too, obviously."

The bathroom door opened again and three women poured out, nearly colliding with them. Not ready to leave Olive yet, she gestured that they should get out of the way. They migrated to the wall next to the bathroom in unspoken agreement. "I haven't been to a bar or club since college. And then I *was* drunk. I had to be."

"You were adventurous in college. I was way too geeky for places like this. I met girls online instead."

Kate relaxed a bit, too. Despite Olive's natural beauty, she was personable and unassuming. The sheer radiance she exuded kept Kate only slightly on edge, afraid to lose Olive's interest to another woman in the club. That she wasn't already spoken for hardly seemed possible. "I've met women online, too. It's a lot easier to seem cool that way."

Olive put her hand on Kate's wrist, the touch as startling as it was thrilling. "Come on, now. You seem pretty damn cool to me."

It took Kate a breath too long to respond. She couldn't quite wrap her head around the fact that a perfectly gorgeous woman seemed to be flirting with her for the second time that day. This one even seemed sane. Olive started to pull away, a new air of awkwardness between them, when Kate finally kicked her brain back into gear. "You only say that because I didn't let you hit the floor."

"Give me a little credit." Olive paused with her hand inches from Kate's wrist, then lowered it back to her side. "Not letting me hit the floor means you've got good reflexes, strength, and balance. It doesn't necessarily mean you're cool."

"So you're making that determination based on some other factor?"

Olive graced her with another sunny grin. "Yeah, the fact that you dislike this place as much as I do."

Kate laughed. Her bladder forgotten for the time being, she leaned against the wall and folded her arms over her chest. "So why are you here tonight, if you hate it so much?" She could see Olive's internal debate about whether to tell her. That alone piqued her interest. "It can't be crazier than the reason I'm here."

A perfectly manicured eyebrow popped. "Color me intrigued."

"Yeah, well..." Perhaps too late, she tried to decide what to say. How would she explain Erato? And was she actually prepared to divulge their mission to a woman who might very well be scandalized by the thought of anything other than missionary-style sex? Trying to play it cool, Kate said, "Maybe you should be."

Olive hesitated, then smiled shyly. "So...if I tell you my reason, will you tell me yours?"

It was an offer she couldn't refuse. "Deal."

Exhaling nervously, Olive mirrored her pose, arms folded over her beautiful breasts. "I'm trying to check an item off my sexual bucket list."

Now Kate was intrigued. "Oh, really?"

"Yeah." Even in the low light of the club, Kate could see that Olive was second-guessing her decision to be honest. She searched Kate's eyes, biting her bottom lip. "I hope that's not TMI."

"On the contrary," Kate said. "You can't stop there. Which item?"

Olive managed to look downright bashful. "A one-night stand."

"Oh." Kate wished she had a drink in her hand. Taking a sip would buy her precious seconds to come up with something smooth to say. Unfortunately, she said, "Well. Good for you."

"We'll see, I guess."

She fumbled for a clever comeback, but her brain refused to offer any more attempts at charm. All she could manage was a self-conscious nod. "I wish you luck." Cringing at the thought that Olive might actually think she *wanted* her to go off and find a playmate because she wasn't interested, she said, "Not that you'll need it, looking like you do."

"I'm taking that as a compliment."

Olive's obvious delight made her stomach flutter. "You were meant to."

"Now what's so crazy about the reason *you're* here tonight?"

She'd forgotten she'd said that. Even though she definitely wanted to take Olive home for her threesome fantasy, she didn't feel comfortable revealing her intentions. But hopefully, given Olive's interest in women and sexual bucket lists— "Maybe it's not as crazy as I thought. It seems we're both here tonight to fulfill a fantasy."

"Oh, really?" Arching an eyebrow, Olive opened her mouth to speak before quieting abruptly, eyes gone wide. She stiffened, clearly no longer at ease. Before Kate could ask what was wrong, a familiar voice arose from behind her.

"There you are!"

Kate turned, surprised by the sight of Erato holding the hand of an undeniably sexy butch dressed in a tight black T-shirt that accentuated her toned upper body. "Erato, hi. I'm sorry, was I gone long?"

"No, not at all." Erato leaned in and kissed her on the cheek, eyeing Olive the whole time. Lips next to Kate's ear, she murmured, "I was eager to make introductions but didn't realize you'd met someone. Shall I say good-bye to mine?"

She had only an instant to answer before Erato pulled away. "Yes."

Giving Olive a warm smile, Erato said, "I'll be back." She walked toward the bar with the clearly enchanted butch in tow.

"Okay," Kate called after her. She almost felt bad about the brush-off Erato's admittedly delicious pick was about to receive, but not so bad that she wouldn't somehow muster the courage to invite Olive home with them. Even if this was only a one-night stand, it had been a long time since she'd met someone she clicked with so easily. Turning back to Olive, she said, "Sorry about that."

"Not at all." Olive gestured in the direction of the bar. "Was that your girlfriend?"

"No," Kate said quickly—a little *too* quickly, probably, when speaking to a potential one-night stand. She couldn't understand the feeling of guilt that overwhelmed her. Erato *wasn't* her girlfriend, but what was she? She couldn't explain the true nature of their relationship, so she decided to keep things simple and be as truthful as possible. "She's my editor, actually."

"Your *editor*?"

"I'm a writer." As it always did when she made this disclosure, her face flooded with heat.

Olive brightened. "Really? That's great! Fiction or non?"

"Fiction." Clearing her throat, Kate said, "Erotica and romance, mostly."

"Well, that's cool. Do you hang out with your editor a lot?"

"She's new." How, oh how, to frame this? "And she has an unconventional approach to curing my writer's block."

"Do tell." All of a sudden Olive looked like she was enjoying herself immensely. Maybe she got off on the embarrassment of others. "Does your writer's block have anything to do with the crazy reason you're here tonight?"

Kate nodded, studying Olive's face. She looked game, open to whatever Kate might say. She'd probably already guessed, given the context. Despite all that, Kate struggled to actually admit her goal aloud. "Let's just say that Erato feels that fantasy fulfillment will help spark my creativity." And calm her libido, in theory, though she couldn't imagine how that would happen. The prospect of being the center of an Erato-Olive sandwich made her weak all over. "I'm sure she would approve of your bucket list."

"What's a 'bucket list'?" Erato had returned, now carrying two glasses of red wine. "Also, I saw an open table over there. Why don't we all sit down?"

Kate glanced at Olive, once again tense with the possibility of rejection. "How about it?"

Olive gave Erato a shy smile, then met Kate's eyes. "Why not?"

Erato steered them through the crowd to a vacant table in the corner of the room. She pulled out a chair for Kate, then a second one for Olive. "I'm Erato," she said before Olive sat, and held out her hand in greeting. "It's a pleasure to meet you."

"Olive. And thank you." Unlike the butch, whose eyes had never left Erato, Olive looked at Kate as she shook hands. "I apologize for stealing your companion. She literally swept me off my feet."

"Not at all. I encouraged her to make friends." Erato sat down on Olive's other side, drawing her attention away from Kate. She placed one glass of wine in front of Kate, the other in front of Olive. "I'm pleased she did."

Lifting the glass, Olive took a small sip. Her hand was shaking. "Erato is a beautiful name. I assume you chose it for yourself?"

Erato gave Olive a bemused smile and tilted her head to the side. "No, my parents named me. Why?"

Olive's eyes flicked to Kate again, as though checking to see if Erato was pulling her leg. At Kate's polite nod, she said, "No reason. They couldn't have chosen a more appropriate name for an eventual editor of romance and erotica. You did say Erato, like the Greek muse of lyric poetry?"

"Exactly like that." Erato seemed to puff up with pride. "I'm flattered you've heard of me."

Terrified that Olive would judge Erato insane and leave, Kate interrupted them. "Are you a fan of Greek mythology, Olive?"

"Mythology?" Erato echoed, brows drawn.

Ignoring her, Kate said, "I'm just impressed you caught the reference. I doubt many people here tonight would."

"The benefit of being too geeky to do much more than study during college, I suppose." Though Olive seemed a little shy about the praise, Kate loved the way it made her squirm in her seat. "My head is full of useless facts, but they rarely earn me compliments from beautiful women."

Erato was staring at her with a question in her eyes. Eager to change the subject, Kate hoped Olive would forgive her for this. "Erato, a bucket list is a collection of experiences or achievements someone wants to have before they die."

Erato nodded with interest, then looked at Olive. "Kate thinks I would approve of yours. What's on it?"

Olive went wide-eyed again, and Kate quickly swooped in to rescue her. "It's a sexual bucket list. Basically she's already done the hard work of coming up with the fantasies she wants to fulfill. Before she dies."

"That's *fascinating*." Folding her hands on the table, Erato leaned forward, pushing her full breasts against the already straining material of her dress. Olive's gaze immediately dropped to her cleavage, which Kate took as a positive sign. If Erato noticed, she didn't let on. "So have you actually written all your sexual desires down on paper?"

It took Olive a moment to drag her focus away from Erato's breasts. When she did, her head snapped up like something had bitten her. "No, I actually…have an app for my phone. So I can password-protect it."

"Afraid someone might find your list?" Kate asked.

Olive looked at her, guilt in her eyes. Kate offered her an easy smile, trying to convey that it was okay for her to admire Erato. Relaxing slightly, Olive said, "I'm just private." She paused. "And honestly, some of the items are *pretty* racy."

Erato laughed in delight. "I *do* approve!"

So did Kate. "Do I get to hear any more of them?"

Olive shook her head, folding her toned arms over her chest. Now Kate was the one staring. The position accentuated Olive's breasts, which were smaller than Erato's, but perfect in Kate's imagination. She fantasized about unzipping Olive's red dress and helping her lower it to the floor, exposing the smooth expanse of her silky skin. How would she taste? Would Olive want to tick any other items off her list? Just how racy *was* she?

A warm finger caught her under the chin, gently moving her attention back to Olive's face. Mortified to see Olive staring at her expectantly, she looked to Erato for help. Erato released her chin and said, "Well?"

Kate glanced at Olive again, face hot. She suspected her cheeks were bright red, one of the curses of her fair complexion. "I'm so sorry, what was that?"

"I said not until you tell me what fantasy brought *you* here tonight."

"Oh." She nearly turned to signal Erato to take over but stopped. As easy as it would be to hand total control of the evening over, she needed to resist that urge. *She* was the one who'd hit it off with Olive. This was *her* fantasy. And frankly, she liked Olive too much not to assert herself as best as she could. Taking a deep breath, Kate said, "I want to have a threesome." She hesitated, then swallowed thickly before taking what felt like the biggest leap of her life. "With you."

Chapter Six

The next ten minutes were a blur.

Before Kate was able to fully wrap her mind around Olive's quick acceptance of her proposition, Erato had suggested that they relocate somewhere quieter. Olive looked visibly relieved to leave the club—though clearly nervous about the night ahead—and Kate had sympathized. They'd both tossed back the remnants of their half-full wineglasses, almost in unison, and shared a brief giggle at the awkwardness that had overtaken the evening. Then Erato was ushering them outside into the crisp evening and flagging down a cab while Kate stood next to Olive and did everything she could to avoid making eye contact.

It wasn't until she and Olive were settled into the backseat of the cab, Erato riding shotgun and talking the driver's ear off, that Kate managed to string more than two words together. "Thank you for coming."

Olive startled slightly but managed an easy smile. "Well…don't thank me yet."

Blushing, Kate considered her choice of words. She'd walked right into that one. "I still can't believe I worked up the courage to ask."

"Good, because I'm still marveling over the fact that I accepted."

Turning in her seat, she searched Olive's face, which wasn't easy when she was tipsy and stripes of shadow and light from passing streetlights kept illuminating and then obscuring her features. "You can change your mind, you know. Whenever you want."

A warm hand landed on hers where it rested on the seat between them. "I don't want to change my mind. But I appreciate the sentiment."

Kate forgot to breathe. All her senses were focused on the soft skin of Olive's fingers. She couldn't help but imagine how they would feel on her breasts.

Suddenly Olive's hand was gone. "Unless *you've* changed your mind. I don't want you to feel like you need to go through with something you're not feeling on my account. Seriously."

Bereft from the loss of contact, Kate reached for Olive and tangled their fingers together, then moved their joined hands onto her lap. "No, I'm feeling this. I promise."

Olive exhaled steadily. "I'm glad."

They sat in silence for a couple of minutes while Erato regaled their cabbie with tales of her time spent in his native land of Florida. Kate only half listened, but it was clear from the cabbie's enthusiastic laughter that yet another person had fallen prey to Erato's irresistible charms. Stealing a sidelong glance at Olive, she stroked a thumb along her slim wrist, delighted by the shiver the small caress elicited. Olive turned her head toward the window and closed her eyes.

Kate leaned in, not wanting the cabbie to overhear. "So is a threesome on your bucket list somewhere? Are we going to check off more than one item for you tonight?"

Olive took a breath, then opened her eyes. She turned to Kate, their lips now only inches apart. In just as low a voice, she said, "It's on there. And we're definitely going to check off more than just those two items tonight."

Intrigued by Olive's utter certainty and imbued with sudden confidence, Kate lifted Olive's hand and pressed her lips against the inside of her wrist. The strong pulse thrummed against her kiss, hinting at the same level of arousal currently running through her veins. "What's the third?"

"Fucking a white girl."

Kate blinked. "Kinky." She hadn't expected that but couldn't deny that being any kind of first for Olive was a *very* appealing prospect. "It sounds like this'll be a memorable evening for both of us."

Rather than answer, Olive licked her lips and erased the scant distance between them. Her free hand fisted loosely around the front of Kate's camisole as she brought their mouths together for a tentative first kiss. Her lips were soft and warm and tasted vaguely of gloss, a distinctly feminine flavor that made Kate's stomach flutter happily. She parted her lips and returned the kiss easily, pleased by how natural it all felt. Olive's hand smoothed over her chest, at first lying flat, then sliding down to ghost a trail between her breasts. Swept away by the desire that crashed over her, Kate brought her own hand up and brushed her knuckles against the side of Olive's breast. Her quick intake of breath only made Kate want more.

"Ladies?" Erato's amused voice broke through her haze and sent them flying apart. "We're home."

Humiliated to have completely forgotten herself in front of the driver, Kate opened her purse and fumbled for cash. "How much do I owe you?"

"I've already taken care of it." Erato opened the passenger-side door with a parting smile to the driver. "Thanks for the ride, Isaac."

"My pleasure, Ms. Erato." Dark, laughter-filled eyes met Kate's in the rearview mirror. "Ladies."

"Thanks." Olive quickly scrambled out of the car. Kate simply nodded before she followed, head down.

Once the cab drove away and they were left in front of Kate's building, the awkwardness she'd felt as they were leaving the bar returned. As though anticipating she would need the help, Erato took her hand and gave it a reassuring squeeze. Then she offered Olive her other hand, which she accepted. "I'm glad to see you two are hitting it off so well."

Blushing, Kate followed Erato inside. She glanced over as they walked, pleased to catch Olive shooting her a conspiratorial smile. "Me, too."

Kate unlocked the door to her apartment and let them inside. She stepped behind Olive and took her coat, glad for something to do as she hung it in the closet. She barely paid attention as Erato gave Olive a brief tour of the downstairs, her mind racing as she tried to decide how things would play out once they reached the bedroom.

Erato clapped her hands. "So. May I get anyone a drink?"

Not wanting to get any tipsier than she already was, Kate said, "Water?"

"Yes, water would be good." Olive stood at the bottom of the staircase, hands clasped in front of her. Kate recognized the mild panic in her eyes—like she was deciding whether she could truly go through with the evening, regardless of her bravado in the taxi.

"Three waters, coming up." Erato kissed Kate on the cheek, then captured Olive's hand and pressed her lips against her knuckles. "Why don't you two go upstairs and get comfortable? I'll be right there."

Kate checked Olive's face, relieved when she nodded. They made eye contact for only an instant before Olive glanced away. "Do you want to show me the way?"

"Sure." Her fingers twitched with the desire to take Olive's hand again. Anything that might help reestablish the comfort they'd fallen into more than once already tonight. Too chicken to reach for her, Kate started up the stairs instead. Neither spoke as they walked down the hallway, until Kate stopped in front of her bedroom. "I'm sorry if this is weird."

"It's not weird."

"You don't think so?" Kate pushed open the door. After a brief hesitation, she flipped on the lights. "It feels a little weird."

"To be honest, I'm mostly just excited." Olive's hand slipped into hers. "Nervous, but excited."

The knowledge that Olive was eager to play helped ease her lingering anxiety, but she still needed to ask. "And you're comfortable with Erato?"

Olive's instinctive smile made it clear that not even she was immune to Erato's considerable charms. "She's a bit of a character, but she seems very sweet, and I'm not going to pretend I haven't noticed that she's downright gorgeous."

An unpleasant twinge of jealousy seized Kate before she could talk herself out of the silly reaction. It was ridiculous to want so badly for their one-night stand to like *her* more, but she couldn't help it. Something about Olive tickled her imagination—not about her make-believe worlds but the possibilities for her own future.

Kate suppressed a groan at the direction her thoughts were taking. *This* was why she wasn't cut out for one-night stands.

Affecting as casual an air as possible, Kate said, "She *is* a character." She led Olive into the room by the hand, then stopped when they reached the bed. "But you're right, she's very sweet. She's also an amazing lover." She turned to face Olive, searching her eyes one last time for any sign that she wanted to stop. "I think you'll be very pleased."

"Have you been sleeping with her long?"

Unless she was mistaken, Kate thought she detected a hint of jealousy in Olive's question. Or maybe it was just wishful thinking to make her feel better about her own lack of emotional detachment. "This afternoon was the first time."

Olive's eyebrows popped. "Damn, girl. You're having quite a day."

"Tell me about it—and this was after a pretty long dry spell."

"So how long has she been your editor?"

Belatedly, she realized that the fewer details she disclosed about the nature of her relationship with Erato, the better. Olive could believe Erato was eccentric, but to get the wrong idea about *her*? "Not long." She lifted her hand, then carefully placed it on Olive's forearm. The muscles tensed beneath her fingers. "You know, I really don't want to talk about Erato right now."

"No?" Olive whispered. Her eyes were locked on Kate's mouth. She licked her lips.

Kate shook her head. "Nope." She stepped in to claim her second kiss of the night.

Olive wrapped her in slim, strong arms and held on tight. Kate groaned at the softness of the breasts pressed against her own. She let her hands roam Olive's sides and hips, engaging in a reverent topographical study of her body through touch alone. Then she swept her tongue into Olive's mouth, battling sensuously with its mate in a subtle war for dominance that absolutely set her on fire. Olive was ebullient, light, and possibly a little proper, but she would more than hold her own in the bedroom.

Which made her mostly just excited, too.

She smoothed her hand across Olive's back until she reached the zipper of her dress. Crossing her fingers that she wasn't being too presumptuous, she took hold of the tab and very slowly pulled it down. Olive broke their kiss with an excited gasp, then buried her face in Kate's neck.

"This all right?" Kate murmured. When she reached the bottom of the zip, she slipped her hand inside the silky material and caressed Olive's bare lower back.

Olive nodded and scraped her teeth over her throat, tightening her arms around Kate's waist. "Very all right."

The sound of a throat clearing sent them careening apart like nervous teenagers. Kate recovered first, stepping in front of Olive to protect her modesty. She realized how silly that was only when she saw Erato's amused smile and felt Olive put a hand on her waist as she stepped forward to stand by her side.

"I love that you're both so eager." Erato held up the bottles of water she'd brought with her, then walked to set them on the nightstand. She turned with a coy expression. "Am I still invited to play?"

"The more, the merrier," Olive said smoothly. She held out her hand, the strap that had fallen over her shoulder the only indication that she was partially undressed. It appeared she had found her confidence, because all traces of her shyness were gone.

Kate nodded, only a little surprised to also feel imbued with newfound courage. It was thanks to Erato's presence, she had no doubt. Whatever the woman was, she had the uncanny ability to lower a person's inhibitions while making them feel completely safe. That was as valuable a quality in a lover as it was an editor. "We're happy to have you back."

"Not that you weren't getting along fantastically on your own." Erato walked to the foot of the bed, standing within touching distance of them. "In fact, please don't let me interrupt you. Why don't you keep going?"

Kate blushed at the idea of making out for an audience. At the same time, she'd enjoyed exactly that kind of exhibitionistic fantasy for as long as she could remember. She checked Olive's reaction, prepared to go at her pace and within her comfort zone.

Olive slowly pulled the loose strap of her dress off her shoulder. Enraptured by the smooth skin she revealed, Kate had to remind herself not to stare. From the smile Olive directed at her alone, it was clear she noticed and enjoyed the admiration. "Actually, I'm feeling a little underdressed all of a sudden…"

"I can fix that." Erato presented her back and Kate immediately stepped forward to unzip her, too. With a murmur of gratitude, Erato turned to face them as she eased her dress down over her ample chest and past her hips before allowing it to drop to the floor. She wore a lacy lavender bra and nothing else. Olive failed to hide her surprise, which only grew when Erato quickly unhooked her bra and tossed it away.

"Better?" Now completely nude, Erato moved in front of Kate, whose palms itched to touch her bare skin. The muse winked at Olive, though their guest's attention had long since drifted southward. "Now Kate is *over*dressed, don't you think?"

Olive dragged her gaze away from Erato and looked at Kate, quickly zeroing in on her chest. Kate's nipples tightened under the scrutiny and the obvious anticipation in dark, desirous eyes. "Damn right she is."

"Would you like to fix that or shall I?" Erato asked.

"Let me." Olive stepped closer until they stood face-to-face, less than a foot apart. She hesitated briefly, then eased the gray jacket Kate wore down her shoulders, then off, leaving her in a black camisole. Rather than pull the top over her head, Olive raised her hands and skimmed her palms across Kate's hardened, sensitive nipples.

Kate whimpered, then fisted her hands at her side in mild embarrassment. So much for playing it cool.

"She's so very responsive," Erato said casually, speaking as though Kate wasn't right there. "Good with her mouth, her hands...her imagination. You should be *very* pleasantly surprised by the bad girl lurking beneath Kate's shy exterior."

Olive's lip quirked, and she made brief eye contact with Kate. "I look forward to finding out." She lowered her hands to the bottom of the camisole and hesitated. When Kate raised her arms, Olive got onto her tiptoes to pull the top off over her head.

Left in her bra—the cutest one she owned, black and lacy—Kate battled a mild tug of self-consciousness at being the center of attention. The wetness between her legs made it clear that she was enjoying the way Erato had taken charge, even if it meant all eyes were on her. Erato stepped to Olive's side and smiled, gazing at Kate with obvious appreciation. She stayed silent, though, probably because it was clear that Olive no longer needed any direction.

"May I?" Olive asked, tracing her fingers over the strap of Kate's bra.

Kate wished she could manage a more clever reply but settled for "Yeah." Taking advantage of their position, she slipped her hands beneath the loose shoulder straps of the red dress that had been driving her crazy all night. She said nothing as Olive reached around her back to undo the clasp, focused only on the softness of the skin beneath her fingers and her own excitement when the catch on her bra released and Olive pulled the fabric away from her chest. Olive's gaze locked on to

Kate's breasts and she licked her lips, then shrugged to encourage Kate to undress her.

Sometime before Olive's dress hit the ground, but after her quick hands began to work the zipper on Kate's pants, their mouths found each other again and they fell into another heated kiss. This time Kate reached out blindly in Erato's direction, smiling into Olive's mouth when a third warm body pressed against theirs. Erato wrapped an arm around each of their waists, and they broke apart to greet her.

Erato kissed Kate on the cheek, then Olive. She smirked. "So where should we start?"

CHAPTER SEVEN

K ate didn't even hesitate. "With Olive."

Erato nodded. "Good idea. She is the guest, after all."

They both looked at Olive, who could barely meet their eyes. For the first time, Kate really *noticed* that Olive wasn't wearing a bra. She'd vaguely felt bare breasts pressed against her while they were kissing but had been too overwhelmed with everything that was happening to truly appreciate what that meant. Now she took a good, long look, aroused by their perfect, delicate shape and saddened by the sight of a fairly major scar that lay in the valley between. Had whatever caused it also made Olive decide to compile a bucket list?

Olive cleared her throat. "Car accident."

Embarrassed to have been caught staring, Kate lifted her gaze. "I'm sorry," she said simply.

Olive gave her the sunniest smile she'd ever received. "I'm alive."

"Cheers to that." Erato released Kate and snaked an arm around Olive's waist. "May I?" She looked first at Olive, then to Kate, for permission.

Kate nodded, struck by the eroticism of the two of them together. Erato's skin was two shades lighter than Olive's, her breasts larger, her hips more generous, while Olive was one hundred percent sleek, strong femininity. Despite her rather delicate frame, she exuded power. The muscles in her arm flexed as she curled her hand around the back of Erato's neck, bringing their mouths together for a slow, exploratory kiss. Turned on by the way Olive refused to cede control even to Erato, Kate watched as they explored each other for the first time.

It was like viewing the best porno ever made reenacted live, just for her. In other words, it was everything she'd hoped for and more.

When Erato gestured her closer with a crooked finger, Kate obeyed as though in a trance. She stepped behind Erato and smoothed her palm over her gently rounded belly, excited by the heat she could feel pouring off Olive's stomach, only inches from her hand. Breaking the kiss, Erato tipped her head back against her shoulder as Kate dragged her fingers down through slick, hot folds.

Olive lowered her eyes and watched intently, then looked up, her full attention on Kate's face. "Please tell me she's as wet as I am."

Kate couldn't help it—she smirked. Moving so she was once again between her two lovers, she said, "But I don't know how wet you are."

Olive reached for her left hand, the one she hadn't used to touch Erato. Before she had time to react, Olive guided her down the front of her panties and pressed Kate's fingers against swollen, heated flesh coated with so much arousal it made her want to drop to her knees and have a taste. "Check," Olive whispered, biting her lip with straight, white teeth.

Kate curled her fingers inward and located the engorged knot of flesh that made Olive whimper in pleasure. She exhaled, taking a step closer. "You're both so very ready for this."

"You have no idea," Olive murmured.

"I might." She rubbed tiny circles over Olive's clit. "Do you want to lie down as badly as I do?"

Olive's legs wobbled. "More."

Kate removed her hand from Olive's panties, then rid her of them altogether. Mission accomplished, she took a step back and stared at the two naked, beautiful women who stood in her bedroom. Ready to sleep with *her*. Seriously, *had* she hit her head in the shower that morning? Surely she was about to wake up.

Erato brought Olive's hand to her lips. "Lie down, then. We'll join you as soon as I get Kate out of these pants."

Olive climbed onto the mattress without taking her eyes off them. "Please do. I've been waiting to see her naked since she prevented me from hitting the floor earlier."

"Really?" The thought that Olive had wanted her since nearly the first moment they'd met made her all goofy inside. Standing next to Erato, she would be an afterthought for most women. But she could see the sincerity in Olive's face—and heard the quiet, excited inhalation when Erato divested her of her pants and panties in one swift motion. Kate instinctively covered the juncture of her thighs with both hands for an instant before forcing herself to drop them and allow the appraisal.

"Are you honestly surprised?" Olive licked her lips as she scanned Kate's body, lingering over more than one spot. "I thought I'd been pretty obvious." She scooted back toward the headboard and gestured them closer. "Now come here, both of you."

Kate moved forward, aware that Erato was right beside her. They got onto the bed simultaneously, settling in on either side of Olive's prone body. Almost without thinking, Kate put her hand on Olive's chest so that her thumb touched the top of her scar. She traced it gently and searched Olive's face. "Tell me what you like." A glance at Erato confirmed her approval of the sentiment. "We'll do what you want."

Erato nodded eagerly. "*Whatever* you want."

Idly, Kate hoped Olive wasn't into anything *too* crazy. Erato's free pass could be a nightmare in the wrong hands.

Olive reached for Kate's hand, then Erato's. She gave them a smile that broke Kate's heart for reasons she didn't quite understand. "I just want to feel *good*."

"I think we can manage that." Erato squeezed the hand she held, then looked at Kate. "How shall we have her?"

Certain she could touch Olive for hours and still not get enough, Kate said, "Slowly." She stretched out alongside Olive, touching her stomach gently as she bent to place a tender kiss on her scar. "And thoroughly." Trailing her tongue over to a dark, erect nipple, she sucked as much of Olive's breast into her mouth as she could, languidly, yet with every bit of passion she possessed.

Olive moaned and her fingers tangled in Kate's hair. She tugged hard enough to send tingles throughout Kate, and Kate bit down gently around the nipple in her mouth. Olive's moan grew louder. Then it changed, becoming something closer to a strangled groan. Kate shifted to glance down the length of her body, unsurprised to find Erato rubbing her hand between Olive's spread legs. She could see and hear how wet Olive was, and her mouth watered for a taste.

Once again completely in sync with her desires, Erato pulled her hand away from Olive and offered it to Kate. "Care to try?"

Kate released Olive's breast and sat up to allow Erato to slip shiny fingers into her mouth. She sighed at the sweetness that coated Erato's skin, excited by the knowledge that it would taste even better direct from the source. Drawing away from Erato, Kate looked up at Olive. "May I have some more?"

Olive clawed the bedding at her sides. Her chest heaved. "Please, yes."

Erato put a hand on each of Olive's inner thighs and pushed her legs apart as far as possible. Enjoying the look of surprise on Olive's face, Kate crawled between her open legs and lay on her stomach. The view was breathtaking. Erato's long fingers moved inward, sliding over the dark, swollen labia to carefully spread Olive open so Kate could gaze upon her. Wetness poured out of her shiny pink opening, and the hood concealing her clit stood erect, begging for a kiss.

Kate wasn't about to deny her. She brought her mouth as close to Olive's pussy as she could get without touching, then simply breathed in and out until her hips began to squirm within Erato's grasp. Pleased by the shameless eagerness on display, Kate lifted her gaze and smirked at Erato.

Her muse gave her a mildly scolding smile. "Give the poor girl what she so clearly needs."

Kate parted her lips and planted a wet, lingering kiss on Olive's labia. The hips beneath Erato's hands jumped, smearing hot juices all over Kate's cheeks and chin. Like that, her restraint snapped. She slid her hands under Olive's buttocks and gripped her firmly as she buried her face in her pussy and began to explore everything her tongue could reach.

"Oh, God." Olive whimpered. Her hand found its way back into Kate's hair, gripping hard. "Don't stop."

The catch in Olive's voice hinted that she was already approaching her climax, though Kate couldn't imagine how that was possible. She'd just begun. Backing off slightly, she traced the tip of her tongue in wide circles around Olive's clit, coaxing it to stand tall and proud. Awed by the way she could wrap her lips around it and get an actual mouthful of throbbing, engorged flesh, she spent long, blissful moments sucking her off before pulling back with a happy groan. She kissed Erato's fingers, which still held Olive open. "Suck her clit for me, will you?"

"With pleasure." Without changing position, Erato bent and took

Olive's erect clit between her lips, very carefully working her mouth along the shaft as though it were a miniature cock.

Not content to simply watch, Kate reached between Olive's legs and swiped her fingers through her wetness. She made sure to brush against her entrance, studying her face for a reaction. Olive's mouth hung open and her eyebrows were furrowed. At the touch of Kate's finger to her opening, the corners of her mouth turned up and she rolled her hips, giving the sensual appearance that she was fucking Erato's mouth.

Cautious, Kate said, "Do you want me inside you?"

Olive arched her back and moaned, then spread her legs impossibly wider. "Please give me your fingers, Kate." Her nostrils flared as Erato bobbed up and down on her clit. *"Please."*

Heady with power, Kate traced two fingertips around Olive's opening. She dipped in, barely, noting the way Olive held her breath. Her fingers were tangled in Erato's hair now, and her thighs quivered around Kate's hand. She was clearly primed to explode. Kate crawled up Olive's body without moving her fingers, eager to watch her face when she finally pushed all the way inside.

Olive reached out with her free hand and pulled her in for a hungry kiss. Kate flexed her fingers as she kissed back, delighting in the velvety liquid heat beneath her. She moved her thumb and found Erato's jaw just inches away from her hand, the muscles working as she kept up her oral worship. Wanting to be the one to push Olive over, Kate broke their kiss and stared into unfocused brown eyes as she penetrated her as deeply—and as slowly—as she could.

Voice cracking, Olive released a deep-throated moan that seemed to reverberate throughout her entire body. When Kate curled her fingers upward and stroked with purpose, her lower half quaked, nearly dislodging Erato from her task. Erato's giggle elicited a quiet chuckle from Kate and a breathy apology from Olive.

Kate shook her head, kissing the corner of Olive's mouth. "Don't be sorry." She twisted her fingers, delighted by the way Olive couldn't seem to control the motion of her limbs. "Just let go."

She glanced down the length of Olive's body, beyond aroused to find Erato staring back at her. Cheeks shiny with juices, Erato angled her face so Kate could have a better view. Having received the best head of her life mere hours ago from that same pretty mouth, she had a very good idea of what Olive was feeling, a thought that drove her wild. She wanted nothing more than to add to the pleasure, so she bent to Olive's chest and laved a turgid nipple with the flat of her tongue. Olive's free hand flew to her head and tangled in her hair, trapping her in place just as she had with Erato. Pleased by the way Olive rocked her hips to move up and down on her fingers, Kate increased the speed and force of her thrusts, eager to make her climax.

She no longer wanted to draw things out. She wanted to make Olive come undone.

It took less than a minute more. Kate bit down on her nipple, curled her fingers, rubbed hard. Erato's hand flattened against Olive's abdomen, keeping her still as she buried her face in her pussy. Olive's limbs trembled and twitched and thrashed, until finally she threw her head back and yelled that she was coming. Kate didn't need to be told— she felt every contraction, every spasm, around her fingers, which didn't stop moving until Olive pleaded for mercy in a raw, hoarse voice. Kate stilled her hand and lifted her head from Olive's breast, touched by the sight of their guest gasping for air while tears leaked from the corners of her eyes.

Kate removed her fingers, careful to go slow and easy, and stretched out alongside Olive. Erato mirrored her action, closing her eyes as she kissed Olive's shoulder. Concerned by the emotion on display, Kate brought her lips to Olive's cheek and sampled the salty moisture there with the tip of her tongue. When she pulled away, she was relieved to see that Olive's gorgeous, sunny smile had returned.

"So do you feel good?" Kate murmured.

Nodding, Olive curled her hand around the back of her neck and pulled her in for a lingering kiss. Then she drew away and reached for Erato, giving her a somewhat briefer kiss. "I feel *wonderful*." She raised her hands over her head and stretched, then sighed happily before looking between Erato and Kate with a playful grin. "Now who do I thank first?"

Erato got onto her knees. "We ought to take care of poor Kate, I think. This *is* her fantasy, after all."

Olive also got onto her knees, crawling around Kate's other side to put her in the middle. She snaked her arm around Kate's waist as they shifted position and brought her mouth to her ear. "I was hoping she'd say that." Her free hand trailed between Kate's legs, gliding wetly over her trimmed curls and swollen labia. "Because I can't wait to fuck you as good as you just fucked me."

Kate nearly tipped over when Olive released her. Instead, she sagged against Erato, who quickly maneuvered her so she was flat on her back in the center of the mattress, hands pinned over her head. Kate's stomach flip-flopped excitedly at the forceful move and at the reality of being at the mercy of two gorgeous, horny women.

Erato bent and took her bottom lip between her teeth, then soothed the bruised skin with her tongue. "Your safe word is apple."

The introduction of a safe word—and a familiar one, at that—made Kate's breath catch. She wouldn't have thought it possible to be any more excited than she already was, but apparently she'd have been wrong. The knowing glint in Erato's eye confirmed just how easily her muse could read her. Kate nodded. "Okay."

Erato released her hands with a stern look of warning to keep them in place. She trailed her right hand down the inside of Kate's arm, to her shoulder, until finally she gripped her throat loosely. Then she looked over to Olive, whose mouth hung agape. "Have you read any of Kate's work?"

Olive shook her head. "I don't think so."

"I highly recommend it. She really has a marvelous way with words." Erato slid her hand down Kate's throat, between her breasts, between her thighs. "And her stories are rather revealing, I dare say. It's nice to know exactly what Kate wants, even if she's reluctant to ask for it."

Before Kate could wonder what that meant, specifically, Erato had planted her knees on either side of Kate's head. Not only did the position leave little doubt about her intentions, but it also made her choice of a safe word startlingly clear. Erato meant to reenact a threesome love scene from one of her early novels, in which the protagonist was made to pleasure one face-sitting lover while another forced her to orgasm again and again. Like many of the sex scenes she wrote, this one had started as a fantasy. In fact, it might have been the very fantasy behind her suggestion to try a threesome tonight.

Kate licked her lips, breathing hard as she stared at Erato's aroused sex hovering inches above her face. The thought of being smothered by that slick, fragrant flesh, of being rendered immobile and at the mercy of whatever Olive might want to do to her, made her so light-headed she couldn't speak. Her characters always talked during sex. A lot, actually. Yet in this position, with Olive pushing her thighs apart and settling between them, she couldn't think of a single thing to say.

Erato seized Kate's chin. "I'm going to sit on your face, and you're going to suck my pussy. Understand?"

It could have been a line from one of her books. Most likely it was.

Nodding, Kate looked down the length of her body and found Olive staring back. She wrapped her arms around Kate's thighs, an almost predatory grin curling her lips. "I'll just enjoy myself down here, if you don't mind."

Kate finally found her voice. "I don't."

Erato tightened her grip on her chin. "And Kate, I really want to *feel* you using your tongue. Please acknowledge that you understand."

"I do." Between her legs, soft lips pressed against her labia in a sensual kiss. Kate tipped back her head to moan only to receive a mouthful of Erato, who was wet and swollen and so very responsive to the first tentative swipe of her tongue. With her head supported on a pillow, Kate felt comfortable as Erato settled her weight entirely on her face. She battled a slight moment of panic at being rendered so totally helpless, and by the way she was forced to moderate her breathing, but the sensation of Olive's fingers and tongue exploring every inch of her sex helped distract her from the mildly claustrophobic experience of being sat upon. Eager to please Erato, she focused on licking and sucking the silky, sweet flesh in her mouth.

"In a moment I'm going to lift myself up." She assumed it was Erato's hands that caressed her breasts, then twisted her nipples until she moaned—but not knowing for sure was an incredible turn-on. "I want you to take a moment to breathe, and then you're going right back to work. Got it?"

Kate nodded and mumbled her agreement into Erato's wetness. When Erato rose onto her knees, she gulped for air and raised her head, desperate to take in the sight of Olive licking her pussy. As though she also knew exactly what Kate wanted without needing to be told, Olive shot her the same breathtaking smile that had entranced her at the bar, used both hands to spread her open, then very deliberately lapped her clit so Kate could see every last detail down to the string of wetness that connected her to Olive's tongue.

Knowing she was about to be silenced again, Kate locked eyes with Olive. She said only one word. "*Yes.*"

"All right," Erato purred. She lowered her body so her labia brushed against Kate's nose, then rocked her hips, painting her cheeks and chin with her wetness. "Get back to it." She settled her weight down again, so Kate had no choice but to lie back and do as she said.

A long finger slid into her, momentarily disrupting the rhythm of her tongue on Erato's clit. Both her nipples were pinched, then tugged, which she took as an admonishment not to abandon her work. But it was so difficult to focus, especially when a second finger joined the first and Olive's hot mouth engaged in a passionate kiss that threatened to bring her to orgasm already. Eyes squeezed shut, she worked her tongue in a furious attempt to keep up with the motion of Erato's hips. Her thighs trembled as the thrusts inside her increased in speed and depth. The pressure on her nipples also increased, causing her to cry out in pleasure-pain.

"You should see Olive right now. So beautiful with your pussy in her mouth." Erato's voice cut through her haze, the words jolting her with their eroticism. She was almost positive she could feel Olive smile against her. "In fact, take a look…and a quick break."

Cool air rushed over her face and she inhaled it greedily, aware for the first time of the slick juices that covered her cheeks. Worried that she wouldn't have much time to enjoy the sight of Olive fucking her so well, she lifted her head and sought out the woman between her legs. Olive gazed back at her, full of impish pleasure. Her fingers curled and moved faster, so that her knuckles slapped rhythmically against Kate's ass with each thrust. Kate dropped her head back onto the pillow and wiggled her hips, trying to meet Olive stroke for stroke.

Still hovering over her face, Erato played with her nipples as she watched. "How does she taste?" she asked Olive.

"Yummy." Olive shot her a playful wink, barely missing a beat. Her tongue went back to its exploration of her clit, and another of her fingers slipped down the crack of her ass to rest gently on her anus. Olive quirked an eyebrow, circling the fingertip cautiously around her tight opening. The unspoken question hung between them.

Kate didn't hesitate to nod her consent. Everything Olive was doing felt incredible and yet it wasn't nearly enough. What was missing was the sensation of being taken completely, and she was so grateful that Olive seemed to know exactly what she needed. "Fuck me."

"That's enough of a rest, I think." Erato lowered her hips a few inches, until Kate willingly lay back on the pillow. "Time to get me off."

Olive continued to tease her with just the hint of anal penetration as she attacked Erato's pussy with renewed vigor. Kate focused her efforts on sucking the distended clit in her mouth, hopeful that Olive would reward her for bringing Erato to orgasm by finally delivering the oblivion she'd been promising for what was starting to feel like forever. The tongue and fingers on and within her never ceased their pleasuring, even as that one, lone fingertip continued to toy with her slippery anus, all innuendo and no payoff. Kate grunted in frustration, triggering an amused giggle from the woman who sat on her face.

"Poor Kate," Erato purred. She dragged her lower half across Kate's face, so that Kate's tongue traveled the length of her sex before she settled back down in a new position. "She wants you in her ass." Realizing where her mouth was now, Kate poked out her tongue and searched until she found the tight ring of muscle, flicking gently. Erato moaned. "Fuck her ass, Olive."

The finger ceased its teasing and slipped inside her shockingly lubricated opening, deep inside, joining the steady, driving rhythm of Olive's thrusts. The motion was so skillful and smooth that Kate barely felt the initial penetration, just the sensation of her pleasure rapidly expanding beyond the limits of her body. She curled her toes and focused on working her tongue as Erato resumed the motion of her hips, riding her with abandon. Between her legs, Olive's hot mouth finally settled over her clit and sucked expertly. Kate's thighs quaked, her climax near.

The pressure on her nipples eased, and then her breasts were left cold when Erato's hands slid down over her abdomen. Already full of Olive's fingers and utterly turned on by Erato's dominant position, Kate nearly came undone at the sensation of Erato spreading her open for Olive's benefit. Immediately Olive's tongue brushed over a spot that made the muscles in Kate's stomach jump and her legs twitch. Erato's thighs trembled on either side of her face, indicating that she was just as close to the edge as Kate. With a groan, Erato raised up just long enough to allow Kate to gulp for air, then resumed her frantic rocking motion in an obvious last push to the finish.

Desperate to make Erato come before she was rendered boneless by the tsunami of her own release, Kate worked her tongue hard against the swollen clit in her mouth. She knew she was making progress when Erato's movements became jerky and uncontrolled. Hoping Erato wouldn't mind her bringing her hands into play, Kate grabbed her hips and held her in place as she worked on pushing her over the edge. With a breathy cry, Erato finally succumbed. She throbbed and convulsed and rewarded Kate with sweet, hot juices that made it clear just how good she'd made her feel. Kate wore a self-satisfied grin when Erato finally rolled off and collapsed beside her on the bed.

Without Erato above her, Kate was free to focus completely on the unbelievable pleasure Olive was creating with her lips and tongue and fingers. Her entire lower body was alive with sensation, hovering on the precipice of what promised to be a magnificent orgasm. And now a visual element had been added to the mix. As attracted to Olive as she'd been since the first moment she saw her, all it took was the freedom to enjoy a long, lingering look at her strong jaw working, her toned arm flexing, her eyes darkened with desire, and Kate was a goner. She grabbed the hand Erato offered and held on tight as Olive sent her flying apart.

She tried to ride out the wave for as long as possible. Her orgasm was so intense she forgot to breathe until Erato reminded her in an amused murmur, then took her hand to coach her through it. Olive never stopped what she was doing—never even seemed to lose focus— as Kate twisted this way and that, and clutched at Olive's busy jaw, and finally, reluctantly, pushed her away.

It took her long, agonizing moments to remember her safe word. "Apple!"

Olive left her with a final kiss on her hypersensitive clit. Kate gasped, then inhaled sharply when the fingers in her pussy were slowly removed, followed by the lone digit that had been buried deep in her ass. Then Olive was slinking up her body, hard nipples dragging across Kate's sweat-dampened skin. She settled firmly on top of her, claiming Kate's mouth in a passionate kiss that carried her familiar flavor. Without letting go of Erato's hand, she wrapped her free arm around Olive and kissed back eagerly.

Olive broke away with a contented murmur. She turned her head, grinned, then met Erato in a kiss far more tentative than the one they'd just shared. Kate lay back and studied their faces, turned on by the sight of her two stunning lovers exploring one another just above her. As much as she'd enjoyed the intensity of the sensory deprivation Erato had provided, now that she had her vision back, she had the overwhelming desire to *watch*. She slid her hands down Olive's back until she cupped her ass, massaging her round cheeks as the kiss deepened. Olive surged against her, shifting so that Kate's thigh nudged between her legs.

She was slick and scorching, and Kate wanted nothing more than to stare into her eyes the next time she came.

With that thought in mind, she gave Olive's bottom a gentle swat. Whimpering, Olive pulled away from Erato and shot Kate a playful glare. Her hips told a different story than her eyes, flexing against her thigh. "What was that for?"

She wanted to say *Making me want to fuck you again,* but she was all too aware that poor Erato hadn't yet been the center of attention. Because she was the one who'd made this encounter happen—who had, indeed, ended Kate's wretched dry spell with a resounding bang— she deserved it. Kate raised her hand and traced the line of Erato's jaw. "Shall we thank Erato for suggesting I go to that club tonight? I never would've gotten there myself."

Erato wore an expression of genuine delight. "I'm so glad you're enjoying yourself. And I have a *very* good feeling about this book."

Kate managed to refrain from rolling her eyes. Right now the book was the last thing on her mind. That said, a well-sexed Kate definitely wrote better than the self-starved version of herself. "I'm having a wonderful time," she said. "And I appreciate your help, believe me."

"I'm having a wonderful time, too." Olive smiled warmly. She gave a subtle roll of her hips, seemingly unable to keep still. Kate took that as a signal that she needed to come again. "Considering that I've just crossed three items off my bucket list, I'm happy to thank Erato in whatever way she pleases."

Inspiration struck. Kate helped guide Olive onto the mattress at her other side, leaving Kate sandwiched in the middle. Sitting, she planted a hand next to her hip and gazed down into Erato's eyes. "Do you like toys?"

Olive clapped in a girlish burst of excitement, then instantly looked sheepish when both Erato and Kate turned to stare. "Sorry," she said, sitting up to join Kate. "I *love* toys."

"I do, too." Erato nearly purred as she, too, sat up with a sensuous stretch. "Are you going to use one on me?"

"I'd like to." They hadn't played with anything other than their bodies earlier in the day. Thrilled that both her companions were so eager, Kate pointed at the dresser on Olive's side of the bed. "I have a harness and two different dildos in there. And some lube."

Olive scrambled to open the drawer, half-hanging off the bed as she searched its contents. "And a vibrator. And a bullet!"

Kate blushed at the recitation of her most personal collection. "I'm glad you're excited."

"You have no idea." Olive passed both dildos over to Erato, who studied them each in turn with an expression of serious contemplation. "My ex *hated* toys. So much that she made me feel guilty for even suggesting we try them."

Kate decided she didn't care for Olive's ex. She couldn't imagine not wanting to indulge whatever fantasy it would take to make Olive happy—especially such an innocent one. Thrilled to be the one to help Olive explore this arena further, she let the leather harness dangle from her finger. "Do you want to wear it or should I?"

Olive bit her bottom lip. "Actually, I'd like to watch you use it."

The naked desire behind Olive's request was intoxicating. Unable to speak, Kate simply nodded. Clearing her throat, Erato held up the bigger of the two dildos. "Fuck me with this one."

Olive grabbed the cock before Kate could. She sat back on her heels and beckoned Kate forward playfully. "Let me help you put it on."

Kate got onto her knees and crawled to Olive, thrilled by the plain hunger in her eyes. "That's very kind of you."

"A purely selfish gesture, I promise." Olive took the leather harness from her hand to help her into it, then fastened the straps carefully around Kate's hips.

The mere act of being outfitted to fuck was so deeply erotic that Kate's confidence surged. Emboldened, she brushed the back of her knuckles across the hard tip of Olive's breast, delighted when the caress elicited a quiet inhalation. She met Olive's gaze, unable to hold back her pride in having stirred a reaction. "Thank you," she murmured.

Olive adjusted the cock so the base rested flush against her and tightened the harness. Then she wrapped her hand around the dildo and pantomimed jerking her off, pressing the silicone hard against her still-sensitive clit. "You can thank me later." Before Kate could ask what exactly that meant, Olive turned to Erato. "Do you like it doggy style?"

"Ooh, I *love* it." Erato got onto her hands and knees facing away from them, then lowered her torso to press flat against the mattress. The position left her open and exposed, and so very vulnerable. She wiggled her bottom provocatively, knees set apart on the bed and back arched in clear invitation. Her pussy was shiny and pink and practically begging for Kate to sink into its depths. Glancing back, she announced, "I'm ready."

Kate checked Olive for a reaction to the absolutely pornographic sight in front of them. Wide-eyed, Olive glanced at her for what she assumed was the same reason. When Olive grinned broadly at the look on her face, Kate couldn't help but do the same. Without thinking much about it, Kate snaked an arm around Olive's middle and tugged her in for a lingering kiss. Then she patted Olive's bottom and nodded at Erato. "Check to see if she's *really* ready, will you?"

"Gladly." Licking her lips, Olive tore her gaze away from Kate's mouth with effort. She positioned herself behind Erato, then ran her fingertips through her sodden folds. Erato moaned quietly, then gasped when Olive penetrated her with two fingers. Kate watched the digits disappear into Erato again and again, transfixed by the display.

When Olive spoke, Kate had to shake her head and force herself to focus. "I'm sorry, what?"

"I said she's ready." Olive withdrew her fingers, amusement dancing in her eyes. "If you are."

"Very ready." Kate waited until Olive moved to Erato's side before she knelt behind her waiting body. Even as she tried her best not to let her confidence falter, she sent a quick plea to the universe to let her perform well. It had been years since the last time she'd played with a strap-on—and that time, she hadn't even been the one wearing it. All she could do was hope she'd muddle through based on sheer will and desire to leave both Erato and Olive completely satisfied.

Kate took the cock in one hand and used the other to hold Erato open. She rubbed the tip of the dildo over her folds, pressing in, then pulling back, content to tease while she lined herself up and steeled her nerve. The light pressure of Olive's hand against her lower back urged her forward, to carefully sink the first inch or so inside. Erato's satisfied moan reassured her that she was more than receptive.

A buzzing sound broke the taut silence. Confused, Kate went still and glanced around for the source of the noise, then laughed when Olive held up her silver vibrating bullet. One thing was certain—she officially loved the way Olive thought. She waited until Olive slipped the toy beneath Erato before pushing farther in. Erato grabbed onto the pillow with both hands and buried her face to muffle her cries of pleasure. She twitched and convulsed under the ministrations of Olive's busy arm, to the point where Kate had to grab her hips and drag her backward to remain inside. Olive pulled her hand away, releasing Erato from the sweet torment just long enough to allow Kate to drive the cock into her until she was buried to the hilt.

Erato cried out hoarsely. "Yes!"

Kate withdrew as slowly as she could manage, then plunged in again. She kept her thrusts measured and steady at first, too entranced by the sight of Erato wrapped around the thick shaft to rush. When Olive brought the bullet back to Erato's clit, Kate had to once again tighten her grip to keep control. Erato jerked wildly at a particularly pleasurable pass of the vibrator, and Kate picked up the pace. She hastened the motion of her hips, absolutely loving the sight of Erato's loss of control. She clawed at the pillow that muffled her cries and vibrated like she was about to explode. The knowledge that she and Olive together could bring this sexual goddess to her knees was potent and intoxicating and confidence-inspiring.

"Olive." She waited until hooded eyes met hers. "Watch me fuck her."

Olive lowered her gaze, then licked her lips. "I am."

"Is this how you like to take it?" Electrified by the mild embarrassment her question seemed to elicit, Kate searched Olive's face without slowing the motion of her hips. Erato moaned loudly, now rocking back to meet her thrusts. Raising an eyebrow, Kate glanced at the writhing body attached to hers, then back to Olive. "Hard like this?" She punctuated each word by driving herself inside so that her lower body audibly slapped against Erato's.

It took Olive a moment to drag her attention back to Kate's face. "I, uh…" Her embarrassment was clearly very real, and Kate faltered, wishing she hadn't pushed. Color rose in Olive's cheeks. "Actually, I've never, uh…"

"Oh." Suddenly aware that she'd stopped moving—and that poor Erato was squirming in desperation—Kate resumed her thrusting. She studied Olive, trying to decide whether to ask the obvious question and risk making things awkward. "Because of the toy-hating ex, or…?"

Olive nodded vigorously. "Because of that."

Erato pushed herself up onto her elbows and glanced over her shoulder. She gave Olive a playful wink even as her face contorted with pleasure on every stroke. "Would you care to join me? Kate really is quite good at this…it would be a wonderful first strap-on experience."

Kate tried not to laugh at how very proper Erato managed to sound even while being pounded from behind. Instead she caressed Erato's flank with every bit of the affection she felt for her in that moment, then checked Olive's face. A shiver of anticipation went through her when she realized that Olive was going to say yes. She reached beneath Erato's chest and palmed her breasts, teasing her nipples, suddenly eager for her to come. As though she had the same idea, Olive altered the rhythm of the hand between Erato's thighs, making her cry out breathlessly.

"Yeah," Olive murmured, and shot Kate a smile that turned her knees to liquid. "I'll take the next turn."

Between Olive's focused attention with the vibrator and Kate's vigorous race to the finish, Erato was crying out for mercy within moments. Instinctively, Kate shared a triumphant fist bump with Olive, who giggled in a way that almost made her forget the aching in her thighs and calves. After such a long period of chastity, her body was screaming at this full-throttle reintroduction to sex. Yet nothing would stop her from rallying with the prospect of fucking Olive in front of her. Finally coming to rest within Erato's sated body, she withdrew with a kiss to her sweat-dampened shoulder and rolled onto her back at Erato's side.

She would just take a moment to rest.

Erato patted her stomach. "That was lovely."

Kate laughed, swiping at her forehead with the back of her hand. "Yes, it was." Determined not to make Olive wait, she swiftly sat up and moved to kneel, but Olive stopped her with a hand on her chest.

"Let's give you a little break," Olive murmured. She pressed against Kate's shoulder until she had her flat on her back again. "I'll get on top."

Kate nodded dumbly. "Sold." She put her hands on Olive's hips once she clambered onto her body, glad for something to hold on to. Her heart had started to beat alarmingly fast. She felt somehow different being with Olive than Erato. Maybe it was the fact that Olive seemed like a normal, sane person, and therefore she cared more about what she thought. Maybe it was the bucket list and the strange responsibility she felt about ticking off its items in the most pleasurable way possible.

Erato propped herself up on her elbow and watched them with a peaceful half smile. "Oh, I like this." She touched Olive's thigh, smoothing her hand over the soft skin. Then she reached between their bodies and grasped the dildo in her fist. She rubbed the head over Olive's wet folds while Kate focused on her breathing. Olive hovered over her, a look of deep concentration etched across her beautiful face.

Kate took one of Olive's hands, warmed when the slim fingers interlaced with her own. "Go at your own pace."

Nodding, Olive angled her hips and sank down onto the cock with a quiet exhalation. Kate nearly came just from the sight of her, mouth open, face contorted with pleasure amid mild discomfort. Brown eyes locked onto hers, vulnerable and intense. Kate reached for her other hand, squeezing them both without breaking eye contact.

"Does that feel good?" Kate murmured.

Olive rolled her hips, biting her bottom lip as though trying to suppress a smile. "It's big."

"Do you want to use the other one?" Kate asked. Erato had chosen the larger of the two. She didn't want Olive to feel obligated to take on the same challenge. "I can switch."

Olive allowed a grin to overtake her face. She bent until their mouths nearly touched, only breaking eye contact at the last moment. "I think I can handle you." Dragging Kate's right hand between their bodies, she guided her fingers into hot, wet folds. "Rub my clit?"

Kate was already making circles with her fingertips. She raised her head the scant distance required to capture Olive's lips in a passionate kiss, delighted by the wetness she could feel on her thighs. Olive rocked back and forth atop her, slowly, her hips grinding sensuously against Kate's busy hand. Beside them, Erato watched in silence, seemingly content to stroke the backs of her fingers over the sides of their breasts, their flanks, their hips. Her presence lent an exciting air to sex that already ranked among the best Kate had ever had, if only for the novelty of knowing she was the first to have Olive like this.

Olive sat up, eyes screwed shut and nostrils flared. The new position allowed Kate better freedom of movement with her hand, and she took advantage by working her thumb and index finger along the rigid shaft of Olive's clit. Olive's thighs tensed, then quivered, as she matched the rhythm of Kate's caress with her lower body. Before long, her eyes flew open and she grabbed Kate's shoulder, jerking her hips erratically as her steady chant built from a whisper to a loud, throaty exclamation. "Yes, yes, yes…yes…*yes!*"

Kate realized they were still holding hands when Olive nearly broke her fingers as her orgasm hit. Wincing in pain, she didn't allow her other hand to falter in its rhythm even momentarily. Her plan was to overwhelm Olive with pleasure or die trying, despite the iron grip on her fingers and her shoulder. "That's right, baby, give it to me."

Hips moving almost violently, Olive rode her to a breathless climax that seemed to completely drain her of energy. She collapsed onto Kate's chest, hanging on to both shoulders as she fought to regain her breath. Kate slipped her hand out from between them and rubbed Olive's back while she recovered from her climax.

Erato broke the silence first. "That looked like a big one."

Kate felt Olive smile against her shoulder. "It was."

"Do you have anything left?" Erato's arm moved and, seconds later, Olive inhaled swiftly. "Or has Kate ruined you?"

Olive lifted her head. "It's very possible she's ruined me."

Kate tried not to read too much into Olive's words despite the very sincere, very tender gaze being directed at her. She mustered the cockiest grin in her arsenal. "You're welcome."

"How are you feeling, Kate?" Erato scraped a fingernail along her thigh. "Sated?"

"And sore." Despite the aches and pains associated with a day of marathon sex, she wished she had the strength to keep going. She wasn't ready for this to be over—or for Olive to leave. "Regrettably."

With a murmured apology, Olive pulled herself up with a subtle wince. Aching at the realization that they were no longer joined—and might never be again—Kate caught Olive's hand before she could roll off the bed. "Stay the night."

She wasn't sure Olive would agree. Then Erato said, "Yes, stay. It's too late to go home now, anyway."

Olive glanced at Erato, then Kate. She seemed hesitant, though Kate wasn't sure why. They'd been so comfortable together all evening. The last thing she would've expected was for Olive to attempt a hasty escape as soon as the act was done. To her relief, Olive's face softened and she nodded, then settled onto the mattress at Kate's side. "All right."

A wave of fatigue rolled over Kate along with the relief. "Good." Boneless, she gave Erato a grateful smile when her muse sat up to unbuckle the leather harness around her hips. "Thank you."

Erato returned her smile. "Wake up inspired and ready to write. That's all the thanks I'll need."

Kate nodded. She wanted nothing more than to be able to do exactly that. "I'll try." Aware she was still clasping Olive's hand, she turned her head and gazed into soft brown eyes. "Hi."

Flashing white teeth, Olive murmured, "Hi."

"So it was okay?"

"It was more than okay." Olive turned onto her side without letting go. Instead, she laced their fingers together and brought their joined hands to rest next to her stomach. "Thank you."

"My pleasure." Kate lifted her hips to allow Erato to take the harness and dildo away, then sighed in appreciation when her muse pulled the comforter up from the foot of the bed to cover them. Extending her free arm, she gestured at Erato. "Come on, lie down with us."

Erato turned off the lamp and curled up at her other side. She patted Kate's stomach fondly, then kissed her on the cheek. "Naughty dreams, Kate."

Olive vibrated with silent giggles. "Yes, mind firmly in the gutter, please."

Kate snickered sleepily but craned to return Erato's kiss. "Thank you. Really," she whispered.

"Just wake up ready to work."

Mumbling her agreement, Kate attempted to force her fuzzy thoughts to all she'd just experienced. She had so much to draw inspiration from. Her muse. Hours of nonstop sex. Her first one-night stand. A threesome. Olive.

Olive. Her smile. The way they'd hit it off so quickly and easily.

Tasting her. Being inside her. Without conscious thought, she squeezed Olive's hand—and felt a veritable surge of inspiration when the slim fingers tangled in hers tightened in response, seconds before she dropped off to sleep.

Chapter Eight

T he next day Kate woke up feeling like she'd been hit by a truck and left to die on the side of a desert highway. Her dry throat ached for a cool drink of water, but her muscles hurt too much to contemplate a trip to the kitchen without a serious gathering of willpower. The urgency of her need for sustenance led to a second, startling realization: despite having fallen asleep sandwiched between two naked, beautiful women, she was now all alone in the center of her very empty bed.

Groaning at the herculean effort required, she raised her head and forced her blurry vision into focus to read her digital alarm clock. 12:36 p.m. She collapsed back onto her pillow and closed her eyes, unsettled by the late hour. She'd always been a heavy sleeper—and never an early riser—so it wasn't terribly surprising that she'd slumbered past noon. What unnerved her was that she hadn't been roused by either of her bedmates disentangling themselves and leaving.

A terrible thought tickled at the back of her mind before exploding, full force, into panic. Kate's eyes flew open and she sat up quickly, cursing the agony of her protesting muscles. Her gaze darted around the room in a frantic search for evidence that she hadn't imagined the whole damn thing. *A muse?* Really? Despite the very real workout she'd had, perhaps she'd finally succumbed to the isolation and mental illness almost inherent in a writer's life. Could she honestly have hallucinated the entire day? Did Erato even exist? Her chest ached. *Or Olive?*

As though summoned by her rising distress, Erato walked into the bedroom wearing only one of Kate's T-shirts. She carried a tray upon which she'd balanced a bottle of water, a glass of apple juice, and a bagel, toasted and cut in half. A small container of cream cheese and a banana rounded out the selection. Dizzy with relief at the sight of breakfast and her not-so-imaginary friend, Kate sagged against the headboard and grinned. "Hey. I was just—"

"Starting to worry that your imagination had finally run away with you?"

Strangely reassured by Erato's uncanny ability to read her, Kate shrugged. "You have to admit, the past twenty-four hours have been *slightly* unbelievable."

Smiling, Erato climbed into bed beside her and set the tray on her lap. "Not from my perspective. But I do appreciate how you might feel that way." She tucked a lock of sleep-mussed hair behind Kate's ear, then gave her a gentle kiss that immediately woke up every part of her body. "Good morning, my sweet storyteller."

Kate returned the kiss, no longer concerned about her obvious physical limits. Instinctively, she put her hand on Erato's knee and slid toward the juncture of her bare thighs. She had no idea what it was about this woman that elicited such an unthinking, passionate response, but she liked it—and she was *damn* glad this hadn't been a product of her imagination.

"Eh-eh," Erato murmured, removing Kate's hand with a giggle. "Breakfast first. You need to replenish."

She wasn't wrong. Resigned to focusing on her other needs, Kate backed off with a nod. That's when she realized that her most immediate need was a trip to the restroom. "Actually—"

Erato gestured toward the bathroom while picking up the tray. "Go ahead, I'll wait."

"Thank you." As she scrambled out of bed, a pang of disappointment caused her to falter. The bathroom door was open, which had to mean—"Olive isn't in there?"

"No, she left a few hours ago." Erato tilted her head, clearly bemused. "She woke up around nine and left almost immediately. Said she had an appointment, and to tell you that she had an amazing time."

"Oh." The pang became an ache. What else had she expected? Olive's bucket-list wish had been a one-night stand, and that was that. Leaving without saying good-bye was the very definition of a one-night stand. "So she seemed okay this morning?"

"She was fine," Erato said, still smiling. "A little tired, maybe, but very satisfied." She paused. "Why?"

"No reason." Not entirely sure what she'd hoped to hear, Kate fidgeted, then pointed at the bathroom. "Anyway…"

Erato laughed. "Go."

Once alone, Kate tried not to notice how disappointed she felt about Olive's absence. What else had she wanted to happen? She wasn't old-fashioned enough to believe that having sex with someone equaled a relationship. Yet when she'd fallen asleep holding Olive's hand, she'd somehow expected to at least wake up next to her. To say good morning. Maybe even steal another kiss.

Kate sighed. A girlfriend was the last thing she needed right now. She had a deadline. She was supposed to be writing. That Olive had spared her the distraction of infatuation was a blessing, truly.

Besides, she had no idea if Erato was the jealous type—and she wasn't sure she wanted to find out.

When she emerged from the bathroom, Erato greeted her with a luminous smile. "So, are you excited about writing today?"

Kate suppressed the groan and the snarky retort that instinctively arose, not wanting to sink her mood even further. But it was too late… the fact that she would even react that way to a question about what had once been her favorite activity was depressing as hell. What was wrong with her? The thought of sitting down to work on whatever story she was telling didn't use to fill her with dread. Now she'd become so accustomed to linking writing with frustration that the response was Pavlovian—and that was a shame, when telling stories had formerly brought her unending joy.

Dropping down onto the bed with a tired groan, Kate said, "I don't know."

Erato offered her half of the bagel, upon which she'd smeared an ultra-thin layer of cream cheese—exactly how Kate would have prepared it. "Eat this. It'll help."

She took a tentative bite, unsure if she was even hungry. As soon as she swallowed, she realized she was ravenous. "Oh," she said, taking another bite, and then a quick drink of water. "Thank you so much for bringing this to me."

"You're welcome. Whatever you need, Kate." Erato touched her leg, drawing distracting patterns with her thumb. "Remember that. I'm here to make sure you can spend all your energy and focus on writing. I'm happy to attend to all your needs."

"You've already satisfied so many." She tore the rest of the bagel in half and offered a piece to Erato, who took it only when Kate gave her a pleading look. "Listen, I'm not going to treat you like my slave or anything. I appreciate the help, believe me, but—"

"My duties are to cook for you, clean for you, do the shopping, assist you with research whenever possible, talk through any story problems you want to discuss, reward you when you achieve milestones, incentivize your word-count goals to enable you to more quickly reach them, and keep you both highly aroused and sexually satisfied in ways that will take your creativity to places you've never even imagined."

It occurred to Kate that Erato was basically an author's ultimate erotic fantasy, apparently in human form. Once again, she wondered how she'd been chosen to be the recipient of such devoted servitude. "I know you said that my words are the only compensation you need, and that you think my stories are lovely, but come on…" She gave Erato a cautious smile. "Why me? What are you really getting out of this?"

Erato swallowed the bite she'd taken and set down the rest of her bagel with a dramatic sigh. "Would you rather I leave?"

"No!" Kate set aside the tray, her appetite gone at the thought of losing her muse before they'd even begun. "Of course not. I'm sorry." She hesitated, then searched Erato's eyes, afraid she'd hurt her. "I'm just…still confused."

"But that's all right to be confused sometimes." Erato took hold of her hand and laced their fingers together. "Isn't it?"

Kate wasn't sure she agreed. She hated not having a solid understanding of a situation. She supposed that was part of what vexed her about her current work-in-progress. So far, not only had the story been difficult to pin down, but even the characters and their motivations seemed nebulous. That wasn't normally the case, and it was driving her crazy. "I'm not comfortable with uncertainty."

"You seemed reasonably comfortable last night despite the uncertainty of how your first threesome would unfold." Erato raised an eyebrow. "Perhaps you should give yourself a little more credit when it comes to thinking on your feet?"

Silently, Kate mused that Olive's sweet and passionate nature— and not her own previously hidden talents for improvisation and going with the flow—had allowed her to be so comfortable during the previous evening's adventure. That, and her overwhelming desire to give Olive pleasure like she'd never experienced before. Her chest ached briefly as she tried to imagine what Olive had been thinking when she left the apartment. Had she been relieved to avoid an awkward morning-after? Maybe the tangible connection Kate thought she'd felt had been entirely one-sided, and Olive's hasty exit had simply saved her the embarrassment of believing that their one-night-stand threesome could become more. "Perhaps."

"Your new story is an erotic romance, yes?" Erato's earnest question pulled her away from her introspective thoughts. "Who are your characters?"

"Rose and Molly," Kate replied without thinking. She paused, uncertain she wanted to withstand the frustration of trying to discuss her unformulated ideas with a third party. Usually she wouldn't dare vocalize anything about a story at this stage of the writing process. She didn't crave outside interference in her creativity until editing had begun, but in this case—considering Erato's supposed credentials—she figured it was worth at least a brief conversation. "At the beginning of the story, Rose rescues Molly from an awkward blind date after noticing how miserable she looks. Rose is just about to leave the restaurant after a dinner with her ex, who used the occasion to break the news that he's going to remarry and move with his new wife to Alaska, along with the dog he and Rose had adopted as a puppy. So anyway, Rose is pissed off and upset and lonely, and that's when she notices Molly."

"I like this so far." Propping her chin on her hand, Erato seemed genuinely enraptured by her mediocre synopsis. "Go on."

Sitting up straighter, Kate said, "Well, Molly is out with a woman she met through a dating website, and it's a disaster. The woman has showed up to dinner tipsy and just keeps ordering more wine. As Rose passes her table on the way out, she notices Molly trying rather unsuccessfully to extricate herself from the situation, and their eyes meet. Seeing Molly's desperation, Rose takes her by the hand, tosses a few bills on the table, and informs the drunken date that Molly is needed elsewhere. Then she walks her out of the restaurant hand in hand. Once they're out on the street, Molly recovers from her surprise and thanks Rose for the save. She alludes to her poor track record when it comes to meeting women, and Rose sympathizes by alluding to her own unsuccessful history with relationships. They agree that dating sucks and that if they weren't driven by the need for companionship and physical release, they wouldn't even bother."

"I think I see where this is going."

Kate hoped Erato meant that—because she wasn't sure she did. "Well, naturally they end up making out after Rose walks Molly to her car. Then they end up *in* Molly's car, which leads to about eight thousand words of fucking that takes them from that evening through the weekend. Now I'm at a crucial moment in the story—the *what next?*—and I haven't even figured out what legitimate story problems I can use to keep these two having sex without succumbing to love until the end of the story."

"Well, they're both gun-shy after being unlucky with past partners." Erato stroked a thumb across her knuckle, the rhythmic caress helping Kate stay calm despite the familiar frustration of not being able to see how the rest of Rose and Molly's story should unfold. "That's one problem."

"But that's way too flimsy to be the *only* problem. If they're made for each other—and romance readers demand that they are—fear can only keep them apart for so long. I need something else. And I don't know *what.*"

"Personality conflict?"

Kate wrinkled her nose. "No. I want something they can reasonably overcome and still live happily ever after. A timing issue, maybe, or a question of propriety…Some circumstance that might realistically keep them apart but that they can choose to have the courage to confront."

Erato settled into the kind of thousand-yard stare that Kate knew she often wore when she was outlining a story in her head. "You mentioned that Rose has an ex-husband. Maybe she's not sure whether she could have a meaningful romantic relationship with another woman? Or Molly could be nervous about Rose's bisexuality. Perhaps she's not convinced that Rose truly wants to get serious with a woman."

"Ugh," Kate said, then shrugged in apology. "Sorry, I'm just not interested in writing about someone coming to terms with her sexuality again right now—or making Molly into a character who is judgmental about bisexuality. I guess I'm hoping for more of a real-world, through-no-fault-of-their-own obstacle."

"Well, what do they do professionally?"

Abashed, Kate admitted, "Actually, I'm not sure." She rushed to explain. "Normally I'd have a much better grasp of all these details by this point, but for some reason, with this story…" Snorting, she said, "They haven't done a whole lot of talking yet. I thought maybe Molly would work in the medical field, but I just don't know…" She sighed deeply. "Yeah, I don't know."

"What if Rose is Molly's new boss at work? Or maybe it turns out that Molly recently started working at the assisted-living home where Rose's aging mother stays and has a special knack with her. Perhaps the mother is suffering from the early stages of dementia, or some situation where Molly's presence in her life has become a tremendous comfort. Rose is afraid to pursue a relationship when the consequences of it failing might actually damage her mother's health and well-being."

"Except they just can't stop fucking," Kate murmured, almost to herself. "Especially as they get to know each other better, and Molly helps Rose become closer with her mother, and Rose sees how kind and compassionate Molly is…" She tried to judge how the proposed storyline would fit with the mood of the story so far. "That's a bit of a heavy plot for an erotic romance."

"Maybe." Erato shrugged. "Maybe not. Some readers want their erotica wrapped in fluff, but others enjoy a little real-world angst mixed in to the proceedings. Personally, I think it makes the moments of physical release the characters share have even more impact."

She *did* enjoy tackling weightier stories—and she agreed, dramatic tension only heightened the stakes of the erotic scenes. Kate nodded slowly, trying to decide how readers would perceive Rose's reluctance. Would she be seen as stubborn or afraid, merely making excuses to avoid happiness? Or would her gesture for her mother seem genuinely selfless? Unless…Kate clapped her hands as an alternative thought occurred. "Maybe it's not Rose who tries to put the brakes on a potential relationship. Maybe it's *Molly* who doesn't want anything to complicate this very special relationship she has with Rose's mother."

"Oh, that's *good*!" Erato kissed her on the jaw. "That's *perfect*. Molly gets to be good and noble by insisting they not pursue a relationship, and meanwhile, Rose could wind up mending a complicated relationship with her mother simply because her interest in Molly keeps her coming to the home for more visits than they've had in years. Eventually Rose can make the case to Molly that her presence in their lives has already led to so much good for both her and her mother that she refuses to accept the idea that they can't be together. After Rose's mother gives them her blessing—and indeed, makes Molly promise she will be there to take care of Rose once she's gone—Molly can surrender to the love she's felt from nearly that first moment Rose rescued her from that bad blind date."

"The end," Kate murmured. She sat in silence for a few minutes after Erato stopped speaking, stunned that for the first time since she'd conceived of these characters, they now had a story—and a pretty decent one, at that. She'd given her publisher very few details about how the novel would play out, so she had the freedom to take it in this direction, if she wanted. Amazingly, she thought she might. "It's not bad."

"It's good!" Erato brought their joined hands to her mouth and kissed Kate's fingers. "In fact, it could even be great. The premise will give you plenty of opportunity to plumb deep emotion, which you do well. Even though it's ultimately a story driven by all the great sex the characters are having—which leads them to the realization that they should be together, of course—"

"Of course."

"If you take it in this direction, you're offering readers the best of all worlds—hot sex within a story that has just enough realism to let them become genuinely emotionally invested. Plus, it will give you the opportunity to write more than just fucking, which I know you appreciate."

Kate smiled. Not everyone realized that about her. "I do, as a matter of fact."

"So what do you think?" Erato pulled her into a loose hug, reigniting the desire that had receded into the background during their talk. "Are you excited to write today?"

Now that she had a direction, she *was* feeling better about the prospect. "A little bit, yeah."

"Just a little bit?"

Kate leaned forward until their foreheads touched. It had to be an illusion, but she could swear her muscles no longer ached. She felt ready for round three—or thirty, honestly, she'd lost count—with Erato and her magical fingers and tongue. "Do we have time for a quickie first?"

To her surprise, Erato shook her head sadly. "Not until you write at least two thousand words. Two thousands words, and you can have me any way you want me."

Two thousand words? That was one-fifth of her total word count so far! Erato expected her to produce that in a single *day*?

She wasn't sure if Erato could read her mind or if her face conveyed her total dismay, but before she could say a word, Erato raised a placating hand. "First of all, two thousand words is hardly unprecedented. You've written twice that in an afternoon, many times."

"Not for years," Kate grumbled.

"So? Clearly you're capable of it. You've done it before, and now that you know where this story is going, you can do it again."

Kate opened her mouth, ready with a fast comeback, then hesitated. Attitude was everything. She knew that. This book would never get written if she didn't force away the pessimism that had been holding her back for far too long. "Two thousand words." It would give her body time to recover, she supposed. And if Erato kept the beverages flowing, a chance to hydrate. "Okay. I'll do my best."

"I know you will." Erato cuddled her closer. "As soon as you hit two thousand words, call for me. Deal?"

Clearly this was what Erato had meant when she'd referred to incentivizing word-count goals. It was a brilliant strategy, Kate had to admit. Already she knew she wouldn't be wasting her time with kitten videos and social media today. Not when the reward for her hard work was more naked time with a veritable sexual goddess. Kate exhaled, then kissed Erato's forehead before forcing herself out of bed to start her writing day. "Deal."

Chapter Nine

K ate hit two thousand words shortly after four thirty in the afternoon. Two thousand one hundred and seventy, to be exact, at the precise moment she finally stopped to check her count. But rather than call on Erato to collect her reward, she decided to keep going—just a while longer, as long as the words were still flowing. It had been such a long time since they had, she was fearful of breaking the spell, even for an orgasm.

True to her word, Erato crept quietly into her office every so often, refilling her drink, bringing snacks, clearing away plates—all in absolute silence, so as not to disturb Kate's progress. Often Kate didn't even realize that Erato had come and gone until she noticed that her glass was full or a new piece of fruit or veggie sandwich had appeared next to her. Without any reason to get up except to take bathroom and stretching breaks, Kate found it much easier to focus on the work. For the first time in far too long, she was able to completely immerse herself in the story of Rose and Molly.

She finally stopped when her daily word count reached four thousand three hundred and eighty-two. It was nearly half what she'd written over the past eight months, all in one afternoon. She didn't know whether to laugh or cry.

On cue, Erato came into her office as soon as she turned away from her monitor. "Ready to call it a night?"

Kate glanced at the clock, shocked to see that it was just after ten o'clock. "What the hell happened?"

"You wrote all day. Literally." Erato bounced up and down on the balls of her feet. "*So* exciting."

It was, actually. Jubilant, Kate went to stand and realized that she hadn't for at least two and a half hours. Her body was so stiff she nearly collapsed, and she had to catch herself awkwardly on the edge of her desk. "Oh, wow."

"Come on." Erato crossed the room and put an arm around Kate's waist, providing much-needed support. "I ran you a hot bath. Let's get you in there and start relaxing your poor muscles."

Hobbling down the hallway to her bedroom, Kate imagined that she must look about eighty years old. She felt it, too. "That sounds perfect."

Once inside the bathroom, she allowed Erato to undress her as though she were a small child, lifting her arms and legs when asked, but not doing much else to help. Though she'd promised not to treat Erato like a slave, she desperately needed the assistance right now. Marathon sex followed by marathon writing was as brutal a regimen as she'd ever experienced.

Yet she felt absolutely *divine*.

"I'm proud of you," Erato murmured as she helped Kate settle into the fragrant, steamy bubbles of the waiting bath. "You did twice what I asked. You even skipped the orgasm I promised." Once she'd settled against the back of the tub, Erato gave her a long, lingering kiss. "Now *that's* the sign of a real writer."

Kate laughed. "I have a feeling most literary critics would disagree." She exhaled, then moaned quietly as the impact of the hot water finally registered. "Oh hell yes, this is *exactly* what I need right now."

"And this?" Out of nowhere, Erato produced an expertly hand-rolled cigarette.

A joint. Kate was simultaneously startled and amused. "You really do have everything covered, don't you?"

With a flourish, Erato revealed the glass of wine in her other hand. "Choose your nightcap."

Kate didn't hesitate before plucking the joint from between Erato's fingers. "Wine upsets my stomach."

Smiling, Erato set down the glass and returned with a lighter. Kate leaned over the edge of the tub, touching the end of the paper to the flame and inhaling deeply. She took two hits in quick succession, then offered the lit blunt to Erato before once again relaxing in the water. Erato sat on the edge of the tub at her feet. She took a long drag, exhaling a tremendous cloud of smoke toward the ceiling.

"Good choice," Erato said. "Cannabis encourages creativity."

Already pleasantly buzzed, Kate giggled as she snatched the joint back. "You think *everything* encourages creativity."

"No, not everything." Erato dipped her hand into the water, swirling around idly. "Internet videos starring adorable kittens, for example." She arched a stern eyebrow, leaving no doubt that she'd peeked into Kate's browsing history at some point. "That rarely leads to good writing."

Too stoned and happy to feel seriously chided, Kate let her eyes roam over Erato as her libido flickered to life. Though she hadn't left the apartment all day—at least not to Kate's knowledge—Erato was once again every inch the Greek goddess. She was dressed impeccably, straight from the silver screen. "Why don't you take off that dress and get in here?"

Erato surprised her by shaking her head. Kate was momentarily stunned. Was she really going to be refused after delivering twice the required word count? But Erato softened the rejection with a tender smile. "You're exhausted. Let's finish smoking this thing and go to bed."

"But I want you," Kate whined. She handed over the joint with a mild pout. "And you still owe me one, right?"

Before she could cringe at her blatant manipulation, Erato plunged her free hand deep into the water and brushed against her inner thigh. Long fingers traced circles over her skin as Erato took another long hit. Instead of exhaling, she moved in close and pressed her mouth to Kate's. Prepared for the maneuver, Kate parted her lips and inhaled as Erato exhaled, greedily accepting the fragrant smoke. Erato left her with a nip on her lower lip and a sultry smile.

"I promise not to send you off to your dreams unsatisfied." Standing, Erato gave her the still-burning roach and turned to get a towel. "But I *do* want to get you to bed. For the sake of that beautiful body, all right?" She held open the towel in invitation, managing to make even that action seem painfully seductive. "Please just let me make you comfortable before I pleasure you."

Kate sucked deeply on the end of the joint, then stood up slowly to exhale. She stepped out of the tub, surprised by how much better she felt already. Erato knew how to deliver good medicine. Walking into Erato's waiting arms, Kate handed her the roach so she could dry off. She watched in amusement as Erato finished it in three more enthusiastic puffs. Turned on by the sight, Kate dropped the towel and pulled Erato into her arms. She flicked the roach into the sink behind her, nuzzled Erato's neck, and inhaled deeply. "Can we get rid of the dress now?"

Chuckling, Erato led her by the hand into the bedroom. Kate was surprised to see her bed made and the linens freshly laundered. She stopped and stared, almost overwhelmed by gratitude for just how thoroughly Erato had improved her life—in under thirty-six hours, no less. She'd just finished her best writing session in years, had eaten three home-cooked meals in a single day, and now was going to sleep on clean sheets. Not only that, but her totally lame sexual dry spell had been wholly vanquished. She opened her mouth to thank Erato again only to find herself caught up in firm but tender arms that guided her onto the mattress and beneath the comforter.

"Relax," Erato murmured. She straightened and reached for the catch on the back of her dress. Stripping down to nothing in just a few, fluid movements, she was pure poetry in motion, and despite Kate's deepening exhaustion, her body stirred to life when Erato finally slipped into bed beside her. Kate rose onto her elbows, straining to meet her lips in a kiss, but Erato pressed her back down against her pillow. "Relax," she repeated.

Surrendering, Kate lay back and exhaled. Her body seemed to melt into the mattress. The comforter was so warm. Eyes drooping, Kate struggled to stay awake. "No fair—"

Erato placed a finger over her lips, stopping her speech. "Let me." She grinned, then lifted the comforter and disappeared beneath the covers. Kate moaned in anticipation when Erato parted her thighs and settled in the space between. She reached down blindly, slipping her fingers into Erato's silky hair just in time for the first touch of her tongue against her labia.

The sensation was beyond description. She was already flying high. The post-writing euphoria mixed with the weed and the hot bath had her feeling as *good* as she ever had in her life—and the introduction of Erato's mouth instantly rocketed her to heights unknown. Her entire body was simultaneously alive with pleasure and soothed to the extreme. She felt safe and warm and like she was slowly building toward a climax that would undoubtedly leave her unconscious, if not outright kill her. But what a way to go.

One hand fell away from Erato's head, only to be caught and held with such tenderness Kate couldn't help but sigh dreamily at the gesture's romance. She resolved to have Rose catch Molly's hand during a particularly loving session of oral worship—maybe at the end of a long shift for Molly, during an encounter that starts out like all the others but ends with a tremendous dose of real emotion and feelings of love. Kate smiled at the absurdity of not being able to turn off her once-dormant writing brain in a moment like this, then arched her back and cried out as the pressure between her legs swiftly peaked and exploded into unrelenting, joyful release. She squeezed Erato's hand, glad to have an anchor in the blissful storm.

Erato continued to lick and kiss her labia long after the orgasm subsided, and although Kate was sensitive after such an intense climax, the sweet attention was far from too much. She felt like she could lie there all day—forever—if only she could always feel so content. When Erato finally left her with one last, intimate kiss, Kate struggled to open her eyes so she could thank her properly. Except she couldn't. Her eyelids were literally too heavy to keep open, even when Erato surged up from between her thighs to capture Kate's mouth in a sensual kiss.

Panicking a little at her sudden, all-encompassing fatigue, Kate felt her breathing hitch as she fought to stay awake. Soft, warm arms wrapped around her and pulled her into a gentle hug. "It's all right, my sweet Kate. Just let go. I'm right here with you."

Her sense of security in Erato's arms immediately lulled her back to total relaxation. Burying her face in Erato's chest, she inhaled deeply, then sighed. "Thanks, so nice." The sentiment came out much sleepier than it had sounded in her head. "Now I owe you."

A hand stroked down her back. "Three thousand words. You can pay up tomorrow." Soft lips on her forehead, then, "Sleep. Dream."

CHAPTER TEN

K ate snapped into consciousness the next morning with the rest of her chapter-in-progress already mapped out in her head. She'd dreamt the pivotal scene—after discovering that Molly is her mother's favorite caregiver during her first visit in months, Rose pulls her into an empty, private room at the assisted-living facility for an awkward conversation about what this newly discovered association means. A talk that begins as a breakup of their casual sexual entanglement ends in a hurried, frenzied coupling in a semi-public place. This would be the event that would set the rest of their story into motion. Though Molly would be consumed by guilt over mixing the personal with the professional, both of them were about to discover that they couldn't walk away from each other so easily.

Eager to dive into the messy world of her characters' sexual and romantic lives, Kate opened her eyes, surprised to discover it was still dark outside. She checked the clock. 5:14 a.m. Perhaps more surprising was the presence of a sleeping Erato curled up at her side. She was a veritable angel in slumber, sweet and gorgeous and apparently flawless. She didn't snore, or drool, or anything.

Kate shook her head in fond disgust, only barely resisting the urge to kiss Erato on the cheek. She didn't want to wake her. After all she'd done for her so far, her "muse" had certainly earned a little rest. Careful not to jostle the mattress, Kate slipped out of bed and went to her closet. She grabbed the first pair of pajama pants and tank top she could find, pulling them on as she left the bedroom and walked straight to her office. Pleased to see an unopened bottle of water on her desk from the night before, she pulled out her chair and sat down. Right now she didn't want to think about anything, not even sating her thirst or emptying her bladder. Already the images and dialogue from her dream were getting hazy, and the emotions stirred by Rose and Molly's encounter grew less immediate by the second. The sooner she could immerse herself in finding the words to describe this next chapter in their story, the better chance she had of capturing the intensity of the scene as it had existed in her dream.

So she typed. And typed. And typed some more. At first the words came haltingly. Although she knew what she meant to say, she wasn't yet *there* with Rose and Molly in that supply closet. But soon enough Kate found her way back into the theater of her mind, once again the omniscient observer, director, and choreographer of her characters' romance. That's when the words began to flow. She recorded their tentative attempts at a breakup, her heart aching along with theirs. She shared Rose's bewilderment at Molly's insistence that she couldn't be both Rose's lover *and* her mother's caretaker, even as Molly's stubborn loyalty impressed both of them. And when Molly—*not* Rose—finally initiated a searing kiss that sent them crashing into the wall for their passionate encounter, Kate was every bit as excited as both of them.

Driven by the need to exorcise this chapter from her brain all in one shot, Kate kept typing until her bladder burned. She forced herself to finish the last couple of paragraphs before she pushed away from the keyboard, groaning at the crick in her neck as she stood and dashed down the hallway to the bathroom. Using the toilet was an out-of-body experience, as was looking into the mirror while she washed her hands at the sink. Despite having gone to bed with wet hair and not having done a thing since waking, she was pleased by the woman who stared back. She looked happy.

Erato was waiting for her in the office when she returned. She stood next to the desk, gazing at the screen of Kate's laptop. Kate's first, irrational response was irritation at the thought of another pair of eyes on her unpolished work. She folded her arms over her chest, determined not to overreact. "Good morning."

"Almost twenty-five hundred words again this morning." Erato straightened, revealing the plate of pancakes she'd set next to Kate's computer. "Keep it up and you'll be done in just a couple weeks. Maybe three, if we account for your inevitable need for downtime and breaks."

"I woke up inspired." It was true. Whether Erato had literally sent her off to dreamland to retrieve that scene or not, she knew who to thank. "I'm really grateful for that, by the way. It was an incredible writing session."

"That's what I like to hear." Erato stepped away from the desk and ushered Kate back into her chair. Then she handed her a bottle of maple syrup and pointed at the stack of pancakes. "Eat up. Whole-grain blueberry—brain food."

"For creativity?" Kate poured a little syrup on her plate as Erato dragged over a second chair from across the room and sat down. Taking a bite, she moaned and shook her head at the perfect texture and flavor. "Is there *anything* you don't do well?"

"Of course." Erato crossed her legs and watched Kate eat with limpid eyes. "For example, sometimes I overstep when it comes to first drafts. I apologize for peeking. My only intention was to check your word count, although I must admit I *did* read a sentence or two. I hope you can forgive me."

Sheepish, Kate said, "It wasn't a big deal."

"It was, to you." Erato offered her an apologetic smile. "That's your book. Your baby. I shouldn't have even approached it without your permission."

No one had ever demonstrated so much respect for her work and her process before. Warmed by her sensitivity, Kate reached across the desk and squeezed Erato's hand. "If the book is my baby, you're basically the midwife. Right? So it's cool. Honestly." She meant it. Somehow, Erato had earned a trust she'd extended to very few people, if any—both in her writing life and otherwise.

"Still, I won't read another word without your explicit permission."

"Thank you." Kate chewed a bite of pancake, finally slowing down. She speared another bite and offered it to Erato. "Did you already eat?"

Erato leaned forward and took the square of pancake between her teeth. "A little."

Not sure she believed her, Kate said, "Have more." She fed Erato almost half a pancake, bite by bite. Erato waved away the last forkful, so Kate ate it instead. Then she pushed the plate aside and sat back in the office chair, taking her first deep, relaxing breath of the morning.

"So what's the plan for today?" Erato gestured at the bright blue sky outside her window. "You're welcome to keep writing, but if you're ready for a break, we could go on a little field trip. Get some fresh air."

Stunned that her harsh taskmistress would sanction time off—when she'd only had a couple of really productive sessions so far—Kate shook her head. "No, I'm still in a good space to write. I should keep it going as long as I can."

Beaming, Erato rolled her chair forward so that her knees fit between Kate's spread legs. She caught both of Kate's hands and squeezed. "Just a few days ago did you ever imagine you'd be saying that?"

"No." Kate snorted at how true that was. "No, a few days ago I was convinced that all my other novels were flukes. I wondered whether I should quit my writing career."

Erato seemed genuinely horrified. "What? No!"

Kate laughed. "Don't worry. I've backed away from the ledge."

"Good." A shudder ran through Erato's body, causing her breasts to jiggle in an extremely appealing way. "Nothing is more tragic than a writer who neglects that inner need to create. Even when it's not easy. Even when it hurts."

"Well, it's easy to agree with you now that the words are flowing." Kate fell silent. Then, seeing the way Erato's brow remained furrowed, she kissed her forehead. "I don't think I could ever *honestly* quit, no matter how much I may feel like it at times. I've never *not* written. Even when I was a little girl."

"That's because you're a writer."

Kate nodded. "I know." Sometimes it was easy to doubt that. When she listened to her harshest critics—external and internal—and when the words didn't come, she occasionally felt like she was fooling herself to believe she could earn an honest living as a writer. Right now she was on a sabbatical from work, one that had taken her ten years and many published books to save up to afford. Part of her acknowledged that a major source of her writer's block was likely her fear of failing this test of living wholly off her creative efforts. It had been her life's ambition to chuck her full-time marketing job and make a real go of being an author. Just last week, she'd seriously considered surrendering that dream for the safety and security of a regular paycheck.

Now, with Erato by her side, she was ready to do whatever it took to see her childhood dreams realized. Kissing Erato again, she said, *"Thank you.* Seriously." She wrapped Erato in a warm, entirely nonsexual hug, overcome with gratitude. How close she'd come to just giving up. She'd like to think she would have rallied eventually, but how much more time would she have wasted? Erato had rescued her in the truest sense of the word.

Pushing a hand under her tank top to rub her bare back, Erato held her close. "Don't thank me until the book is done."

Kate battled a mild wave of panic as she wondered what would happen then. Would Erato simply disappear from her life just as quickly as she'd swooped in? On to the next author? Even though she could hardly begrudge another lost writer the opportunity to be saved, just the thought of being left alone without her muse was enough to dampen her mood and put her off the idea of going back to her story. Why, when it would only hasten Erato's inevitable departure?

"Hey." Strong fingers seized her chin, forcing her to stare into vivid blue eyes. "I'm here as long as you need me. All right?"

She hesitated only momentarily before asking, "What if I always need you?"

Erato chuckled, then kissed her soundly on the lips. "My darling, you won't. I assure you."

Kate wished she could believe her, but writing was *easy* with Erato. *Life* was easy. How would she ever *not* need this, when everything had been so difficult before? "I'm pretty sure I'll always *want* you."

Erato's smile showed her pretty white teeth. "You might be surprised."

Unable to ignore her very real anxiety at the prospect of being abandoned by her muse—and therefore, potentially, her creativity—Kate silently vowed to put the brakes on her progress just a little. The *tiniest* bit. She didn't have a lot of leeway, considering her hard deadline, but she didn't want to let Erato off the hook any earlier than necessary. "We'll see."

"Hey." Looping her arms around Kate's neck, Erato shifted off her chair onto Kate's lap. She gave Kate a gentle kiss on the lips, then the tip of her nose. Soberly, Erato drew back and placed her hand over Kate's heart while she stared into her eyes. "Listen to me. I promise—*promise*—I won't leave until you ask me to. Deal? Even if that means I'm your bedmate for the next five years."

"That's a pretty big promise," Kate murmured. Indeed, the enormity of what Erato was offering stunned her. She didn't quite believe it. "You don't need to say that."

"I'm happy to say it—and mean it—because I'm confident you won't take me up on it. Eventually, you *will* decide that you don't need me anymore."

Kate wondered how Erato would feel if she proved her wrong. Would she turn bitter and resentful about being held captive by an overly needy basket case? What if Kate ruined her forever? "You hope I will." Unhappily aware of how vulnerable the confession would make her feel, she admitted, "Nobody has ever understood me or validated my work the way that you do. You make me feel good—in every conceivable way. You ask for nothing in return. Right or wrong, I plan to take everything you offer for as long as you offer it. I can't see a reason to stop."

Erato shifted on her lap, straddling her with a leg on either side of her thighs. Slipping her hands inside the back of Kate's tank top, she said, "You can't see a reason *now*." She rocked her hips against Kate's abdomen, subtle enough that Kate could ignore it if she were really serious about going back to work, which she wasn't anymore. "Later, you might."

Kate was done arguing the point. For now, she needed Erato. Like, *needed* her. She moved her hand between Erato's thighs, tickling her fingernails over the damp crotch of her panties. "Speaking of taking everything you offer…"

Erato tilted her hips and rubbed herself against Kate's hand. "Start with this."

Chapter Eleven

The rest of the week, and then the week after, went by in much the same way. Kate woke up at a reasonable time every morning, always ready to write, and she would go sit at her desk and type and eat the breakfast Erato always managed to serve at exactly the right moment, precisely when she was ready to think about food. She took breaks only to shower, use the bathroom, eat, have sex, and—a few times, at Erato's behest—take short walks around the neighborhood to get some fresh air. The result of her laser focus was undeniable. Her word count soared. The outline she hadn't been able to bring herself to put together was nearly complete, with only the very ending of the story still fuzzy in her mind. She'd even answered an email from her publisher without having an anxiety attack, confident that slowly but surely, this Damn Book was getting written.

That's why when she woke up on a Saturday morning with a total lack of desire to go to her laptop, she began to worry. "Something's wrong. I was on fire!" Seeing that Erato, who sat naked in bed beside her wrapped loosely in a sheet, seemed unconcerned, Kate tried to explain. "Before I fell asleep last night, all I could think about was waking up today and writing this scene between Rose and her mother. Dialogue was running through my head. I *knew* I should've gotten up and written it down. It was *perfect,* and now…" She gestured at herself, nude and lazy in bed. "Nothing."

Erato patted her hip. "You nearly tripled your word count in less than two weeks. Celebrate that, and relax."

Kate grumbled under her breath. At Erato's head tilt, she repeated, "I don't want to relax."

"Unfortunately, that's exactly what you need to do." Nodding decisively, Erato dropped the sheet and climbed out of bed. Kate was so distracted by the sight of her body—and her memories of all the nasty things she'd done to it the night before—that Erato easily caught her off guard, grabbing her hand and dragging her toward the edge of the bed. "Come on. We're going out. It's field-trip day!"

She only barely resisted the urge to groan out loud. Making her body as heavy as possible, she resisted being forced onto her feet. "Look, Erato, here's the thing. I'm kind of…an introvert."

Amused laughter met her confession. "You don't say?"

Kate rolled her eyes. She didn't particularly appreciate feeling like the butt of the joke. "Going out doesn't recharge me. It drains me."

"Going out wasn't so bad the other night." Softening, Erato stopped trying to pull her to her feet. "Kate, you need sunshine. And fresh air. But most importantly, you need a change of scenery. It doesn't have to be anything interactive, but you *do* need to pull back the curtain and remind yourself there's an entire real world outside these walls. It's good to visit it occasionally."

The problems her characters faced, albeit serious and realistic, were constrained to the limits of her plot and were nearly always resolved by the end of the book. If not resolved, they were mitigated by the love of a good woman. "I know…but *my* world is so much simpler."

"Even so, you can draw inspiration from even the simplest road trip." Erato tugged on her hand, gently. "You have before."

Kate remembered giving an interview once in which she'd attributed the inspiration for her first novel to her thoughts while on a road trip with her college girlfriend. She wondered if Erato had listened to it or if this was one of those things she just seemed to know. "You're right." She started to crawl out of bed, then stopped. "I'm not up for an actual *road trip* though."

"Don't worry," Erato said. "This is a brief journey out of the apartment and nothing else. We'll be back in a few hours, and I'm willing to bet you'll come home ready to write."

Kate sure hoped that was true. Erato hadn't given her a reason to doubt her yet.

❖

Once they'd driven about a mile away from the apartment, Kate had to concede the wisdom of Erato's plan. "You were right. This is nice."

The sun was shining—thankfully not into her eyes—and her favorite Fleetwood Mac song blared from the radio. Puffy white clouds dotted the vibrant blue sky, creating an afternoon so gorgeous it belonged in a painting. To top it all off, Erato sat beside her looking absolutely breathtaking in a lavender sundress that showed off her toned legs, and holding her hand tightly. The combination of the good weather, the even better company, and the low timbre of Erato's melodious voice as she sang along happily with Stevie Nicks filled Kate with a sense of absolute well-being. Nice was an understatement.

Pausing to reply only after she'd finished the chorus, Erato chirped, "Remember: your muse knows best."

Without a destination in mind, Kate decided to drive through the more scenic areas around town. She sang the next verse with Erato, happy to see the excited smile that elicited from her companion. One song led to another, then another, and then all of a sudden Kate realized she'd driven them right into the heart of the town square, where the weekend farmer's market was in full swing. Despite the bustling crowd, Kate actually felt a tug of desire to find a parking spot and check out the local fare. She rarely thought about coming down here, even though she always enjoyed it when she did. And she wouldn't mind having fresh fruit for her writing breaks over the next few days. She also remembered that the last time she'd ventured out to the farmer's market, a baker had been selling focaccia. Her stomach growled at the memory.

Erato chuckled dryly. "Should I take that to mean the pancakes didn't stick?"

"It's not that." Kate drove deeper into the throng of vehicles jostling for parking. "I was just reminiscing about a particularly good focaccia with red peppers and onions that I bought from a local baker here last summer. I wonder if he still has a stall."

"I'll cross my fingers." Erato gestured to their left. "There's a spot over there if you turn right now."

Kate reacted immediately, gratified when she slid into a recently vacated opening mere seconds before another car entered the row behind them. "Good looking out, parking pirate."

Erato's smile was warm but confused. "I don't know what that means."

Tickled not to be the befuddled one for once, Kate squeezed Erato's bare knee and gave her an affectionate kiss. "And that's okay." She opened the driver's side door and got out, rising on her tiptoes to stretch her calves. Truthfully, it felt good to be out and about. People-watching seemed particularly appealing. She smiled at two women who walked by hand in hand. They both slowed to stare at Erato as she climbed out of the car, then brought their heads together to whisper and giggle under their breath. She had no doubt that her muse had just starred in the couple's spontaneous, mutual sexual fantasy, a thought that thrilled her.

It was kind of fun to be out with Erato. Something was undeniably appealing about being on the arm of the prettiest, most popular girl in the room. She'd never envisioned finding out what that was like, certainly not in high school, when it would have mattered to her most. Was it awful to take such perverse enjoyment in it now?

Erato came around to her side of the car and linked their arms together. "Come, my sweet author. Let us find this focaccia that you seek." Her eyes sparkled. "And maybe ingredients for a fruit salad?"

"Once again, you're *perfect*." Kate kissed Erato on the cheek as they walked toward the first row of vendors peddling their wares from beneath tents and canopies. "I don't suppose you brought any cash?"

"I put some in your purse before we left." Erato bumped her hip. "Buy whatever you want."

Yeah. She was *totally* going to want Erato to leave at some point. Smirking at the ridiculous thought, she laid another big, wet kiss on her muse as they approached the first booth. "Tangerines to start?"

Erato urged her toward the farmers' generous selection with an encouraging pat on her rear. "Grab a few."

Thirty minutes and seventy dollars later, they had three bags of fresh fruits and vegetables, as well as an exceptionally delicious-looking artichoke-and-roasted-red-pepper focaccia, along with a few other interesting goodies Erato had insisted they indulge themselves by buying. Kate had grown hungrier with each purchase, and now all she wanted was to go home and snack. Unfortunately, Erato had managed to get caught up in *another* conversation—this time with the chocolatier from whom they'd just purchased a half dozen moderately overpriced truffles. They'd connected on the obscure topic of salmon fishing, of all things.

The only thing imperfect about Erato, Kate decided, was her tendency to strike up random conversations with total strangers. She seemed to hit it off with every person they met. Frankly, it was exhausting. That a variety of people fell all over themselves to interact with her—men, women, and children—made Kate feel better that she'd invited a total stranger to insinuate herself into her life. Erato was charm personified.

With only one row of vendors left to see, Kate was ready to call it quits. But she decided to do a quick sweep while Erato wrapped up her socializing. Touching the small of Erato's back, Kate murmured, "I'll finish up while you do the same?"

Erato nodded without missing a beat in her conversation or even breaking eye contact with the chocolatier. "Well, that's fascinating. I've always preferred the fishing in Iceland, myself—"

Kate walked away from the stall, relieved to be free from the interaction. She would never understand how some people could so easily strike up an easy camaraderie with complete strangers. Just watching Erato do it made her mildly uncomfortable. Undoubtedly, Erato would claim that chatting with new people was good for her creativity. Maybe that was true, but it didn't make the idea more palatable.

She was so caught up in her thoughts she almost didn't register the familiar face manning the final stall at the end of the last row of vendors. In fact, she noticed decadent-looking pies and muffins and other baked goods long before she realized that it was Olive—*threesome* Olive—standing there surrounded by the most delectable homemade pastries she'd seen in a while.

Olive. Staring at her.

Speak.

"Hi." It took every bit of Kate's willpower not to run. Embarrassed, she wished only for insight into the proper etiquette for encountering a one-night stand who had escaped your bed as soon as the sun rose. It felt silly and presumptuous to say much more than hello, and beyond rude not to. Kate held her breath as she waited to see what Olive would do.

Wide-eyed, Olive repeated, "Hi."

Kate stepped closer to the stall as though caught in an invisible tractor beam. Although the crowd was thinner at this end of the marketplace, she didn't want anyone to overhear whatever awkwardness was about to come out of her mouth. "You bake."

Olive blinked, then cracked a shy smile. "I do."

Not sure how to follow up that little gem, Kate dropped her attention to the case of baked goods on display. Her gaze immediately landed on a strawberry-rhubarb muffin, and her salivary glands reacted accordingly. "Oh, wow."

"The strawberry rhubarb?" Olive asked with a trace of amusement. When Kate nodded, she took the muffin out of the case and dropped it into a brown paper sack. "Take it." She offered the bag with a tentative smile. "On the house."

Kate shook her head, already reaching for her purse. "No, of course not. Please, let me pay you." She fumbled with the zipper, clumsy with nerves. "It looks delicious. I had no idea you were good in the kitchen, too."

She cringed the moment the words left her mouth. Smooth. *Really* smooth.

Olive flushed and her smile grew wider. "Hard to believe I didn't mention it, what with all the lengthy, intimate conversations we had that night."

"Point taken." Kate paused with her hand inside her purse. "Though to be fair, you *did* find out what I do for a living."

"Probably only because your job was why our paths crossed at all." Noticeably relaxing, Olive regarded her with a warm expression. "It's really nice to see you again, Kate. Now put your money away."

"*Very* nice, and thank you for the muffin," she said, then blushed as she zipped up her purse while trying to act nonchalant. "I'm glad you made it home all right."

Olive laughed, glancing around nervously. "I did. A little sore, but very all right." She hesitated. "I'm sorry I didn't get to say good-bye. I had to leave to meet someone for breakfast, and Erato insisted I let you sleep. She wanted you well-rested for a big day of writing."

Reassured that Olive hadn't actively tried to avoid her, Kate felt her walls come down a little. "No, I get it. And I appreciated the sleep. I actually had a really productive day, as it turned out. It's been a really productive two weeks, for that matter."

Olive's expression of pure happiness made her chest flutter in the most pleasant way. "That's fantastic news. I'm glad Erato's unconventional strategies are working."

"They seem to be." Emboldened by the way Olive gazed directly into her eyes, Kate said, "We can't give her all the credit, though. I found the time you and I spent together particularly inspiring."

She barely had time to register her relief over Olive's receptive smile before the expression changed as her attention shifted over Kate's shoulder. Expecting to find Erato standing behind her, Kate turned and instead came face-to-face with an elegant-looking man whose skin was as dark as his hair was white. Startled to find a stranger standing there instead of her muse, she scrambled for her manners. "Hello."

"Dad, this is Kate. Kate, this is my father, Howard." From behind her, Olive sounded adorably flustered as she made the vague introduction.

"Howard Davis," he said, offering his hand. "It's a pleasure to meet you. Do you and Olive know each other?"

Staving off an uncomfortable moment, Olive executed a skillful redirection. "Dad, what happened? I thought you were going to get a pulled-pork sandwich."

Howard's warm brown eyes sparkled as he gave Kate a careful once-over. "They sold out. Can you believe it?"

Kate shook her head despite the fact that she had no reason *not* to believe it, as Olive said, "You're kidding me. I'm so sorry. I know you were looking forward to that."

"My fault for not going sooner." Howard edged around Kate and joined Olive inside the stall. He kissed Olive's temple affectionately as he passed, then stepped to the far side of the table, ready to meet incoming customers. "Don't let me interrupt. You girls keep talking about whatever you were talking about."

Kate hoped she didn't look as embarrassed as Olive suddenly did. Content to let Olive spin a tale about how they knew each other and what they'd been discussing, Kate stayed quiet and waited to see what she would say.

It took Olive a few beats to recover her composure. She cleared her throat and said, "So, yeah, the strawberry rhubarb is a new recipe. Make sure to let me know how you like it."

Sensing an opportunity, Kate said, "I'd love to, but I may not make it back to the farmer's market anytime soon. With my deadline coming up and all." Her attempt to gauge Olive's receptiveness as she edged closer to the big question was frustratingly unfruitful. Now that her father had joined them, Olive's guard was up and her face nearly impossible to read. She might not even be out to her father. Asking for her number could be a major faux pas. With that thought, she froze.

"Well…" Olive's gaze traveled to a pair of elderly women who approached the stall and immediately began fawning over the selection of pastries. When her father greeted the women with a charming grin and a flirtatious comment that made both of them giggle, Olive rolled her eyes, looked directly into Kate's, and said, "If I gave you my number, maybe you could text me your review. You're an author…you understand the desire for feedback, right?"

In her peripheral vision, Kate could see Howard glance at his daughter with what looked like amused approval. Flattered that Olive would consider taking the next step with her father right there, Kate didn't hesitate to pull out her phone. "Lay it on me." She opened up a new contact record, entering Olive's number as she recited it aloud. Wanting to verify that she had it right, she created a new text message and typed *You look beautiful today*. Then she hit send.

Olive slipped her buzzing phone out of the front pocket of the blue jeans she wore so very well and briefly glanced at the display before beaming. "Got it."

"Wonderful." Kate jolted when something touched her elbow, turning sharply to find Erato standing behind her wearing a placid smile. "Erato. Hey. Look who bakes!"

Erato offered Olive a polite nod. "Olive, it's lovely to see you again."

"Likewise." Olive's gaze darted nervously to her father, who was still deep in conversation with their other customers. Kate could practically hear her panicked thoughts. Not one but two women with whom she'd had a torrid one-night stand, right there in front of her doting daddy. A nightmare scenario for any sane adult.

Taking pity, Kate said, "We should probably go."

Erato brightened. "That's a good idea."

"Yes," Olive said, although her face told a slightly different story. "Good luck with that deadline, Kate. You'll nail it."

"As long as I'm in charge, she will." Erato's sober pronouncement was indisputable.

Kate bristled at the suggestion that anyone was in charge of her in any way. The declaration suggested an ownership Kate didn't remember conferring upon Erato, muse or not. "Thanks, Olive. I appreciate that."

Erato waved at Olive as they walked away, then looped her arm through Kate's. "Did you know she would be here?"

"Of course not." Kate snuck a glance over her shoulder and caught Olive's gaze one last time before the crowd came between them. "That was a complete surprise."

"For her, too, it appeared." Giggling, Erato leaned against her as they made their way back to the car. "She looked terrified that her poor father would realize we'd used her as our plaything."

Not entirely comfortable with Erato's characterization of that night, Kate said, "I can't blame her. Nobody wants their father to glean the details of their sexual exploits." Just the mere mention of those exploits produced a stream of memories of her time with Olive, each more appealing than the last. That red dress. Her smooth, soft skin. The ardent flexing of her muscles beneath Kate's palms. How it felt to be inside her. With a pleasant shudder, Kate murmured, "Especially when it was as good as ours."

"Personally, I've never understood the point of being bashful about physical expressions of love and desire." Erato managed to sound slightly haughty, but her guileless nature tempered the inherent judgment in her words.

"No offense, Erato, but I have a feeling you don't understand a lot about us mere mortals." Kate gave her a fond squeeze, hoping to take any possible sting out of her words. "Not everyone is as evolved as you when it comes to practicing complete and total openness."

"That's true."

Amused, Kate tried to decide how best to approach her next topic. Having reached the car, she loaded their purchases into the backseat as she rehearsed the best way to ask for what she wanted. Finally she decided to say it as plainly as possible. After buckling herself into the driver's seat, she turned to Erato and took a deep breath. "Could we arrange to spend more time with Olive? If she's up for it, I mean." When Erato didn't immediately react, she added, "To help my creativity."

Erato regarded her seriously. "Do you like her?"

Kate's face caught fire—or at least it felt that way. "She's hot. Sexy. I had a great time with her the other night…didn't you?"

Patiently, Erato said, "We're not talking about me right now. *Do you like her?*"

It was difficult to discern whether Erato's dominant emotion was jealousy or concern. Either way, it wasn't approval. Disappointed by the lackluster reaction, she decided that partial honesty was the best policy. "I liked having sex with her—and I'd really like to try and see her again, if you're okay with that." She silently cursed herself for that last part. She didn't *need* Erato's approval. Did she? "You *are* okay with that, right? You're not—"

"I don't do jealousy," Erato said smoothly. "And we're hardly in a monogamous arrangement. I just want to understand your motivation for seeing Olive again. Is it sex? Or is it something more?"

Instinctively, Kate knew the right answer to give. "It's sex. Really fantastic, mind-blowing sex."

"All right." Erato waited until Kate turned on the engine, then said, "Because now is not the time for you to pursue something more. With anyone."

"Obviously." Kate backed out of the parking spot cautiously, uneasy about their conversation and how it made her feel. Even though she couldn't imagine ever wanting to lose Erato's presence in her life, she hated the idea of not trying to see where a friendship with Olive might lead. Or if not friendship, at least a casual sexual affair. As much as she loved and appreciated Erato and the role she played, she wasn't exactly ready to forsake all other options. After all, they'd only known each other for two weeks.

"Please don't mistake my concern over your deadline with a desire to control your romantic life." Erato put her hand on Kate's knee before sliding it higher up her thigh. "You will have time for a great love affair in your life—*after* you finish this book."

"Honestly, I'm not looking for some epic romance right now." That was true enough, though she wouldn't be devastated if she happened to find one. "I was just so inspired by our threesome with Olive, and when I ran into her today, it seemed like the universe was sending me some kind of sign. I can't tell you how free and open I felt after our last time together. The words poured out of me like I was possessed. I guess I wondered if lightning might strike twice or if the first time was a fluke." She paused, feigning a casualness she didn't really feel. "Maybe it's better to always wonder."

Erato sighed. "Fine. Give me thirteen thousand more words, and we'll talk about trying to arrange a playdate."

Caught between the urge to clap in relief and groan at her new word-count goal, Kate opted to simply act casual. "I can do that."

"I know you can." The hand on her thigh slid higher still. "Does this mean you're ready to go home and get back to work?"

Kate snorted. "Like I said before, you were right." The drive had been a *really* good idea.

Chapter Twelve

The new incentive worked its intended magic, as Kate went home and immediately sat down to write like a woman on a mission. Whatever thoughts she'd entertained of sharing a nice, leisurely lunch with Erato followed by raunchy sex vanished at the prospect of being able to ask Olive on another date. With only the slightly daunting word-count goal standing between her and the chance to recreate the single best sexual experience of her life, she had no problem dedicating all her energy to Rose, Molly, and their path to happily-ever-after.

Luckily, she'd left the story at a fairly crucial moment. Rose and Molly understood the complicated nature of their relationship, and although they'd tried to break up, they had just discovered that their undeniable chemistry wouldn't make that so easy. Now it was time to show Rose being persistent about staying in Molly's life and lay the groundwork for the story arc in which Rose repairs her strained relationship with her mother. Although she wasn't entirely sure what the source of their familial tension was yet, she couldn't let that hang her up. Not with Erato's blessing for another date with Olive on the line. No, she would simply start writing and see where the scene and the characters took her. She had a feeling she would uncover the source of the challenging parent-child relationship as soon as Rose and her mother started talking.

Hours later, she was deep into a conversation between Rose and her mother—and nearly three thousand words closer to her goal—when her cell phone buzzed with an incoming message. At first she ignored it, determined not to become distracted, but then it occurred to her that not only did she have Olive's number, Olive also had hers. The rest of the sentence she'd been composing in her mind vanished, the spell broken completely. Picking up the phone, she checked the display and then wiggled happily in her chair.

You looked beautiful today, too.

Glad that nobody was around to see her stupid grin, Kate leaned back and tried to decide how to reply to Olive's flirtation. She could either keep things on a purely sexual level, as she'd assured Erato she would, or tread more lightly to leave room for the possibility of more. She wished she knew what Olive wanted. The night they'd spent together was meant to be a one-time thing—and it wasn't as though she honestly had time for more than that, anyway. Her writing career was undeniably important to her, and now that it was finally back on track, it would be foolish to do anything to derail it again.

Playing it safe, Kate typed back.

Sorry we ambushed you in front of your father. I hope it wasn't too awkward.

She stared at the ceiling and rotated her chair back and forth while she waited for a response. Incentive or not, at the moment, thoughts of Molly and Rose were firmly out of reach. She was entirely occupied with wondering what Olive might say. Tapping her foot impatiently, she let her gaze wander over her desk until it landed on the brown paper bag next to her monitor. The strawberry-rhubarb muffin. She snatched it up, taking her first bite just as her phone signaled another incoming text.

As much as she was anticipating the reply that awaited her, Kate went still and paid attention to the symphony of flavor playing out inside her mouth. The muffin was blissful. No other adjective did a better job of describing the way eating it made Kate feel. She took another bite— moaning at the exquisite tartness of the rhubarb, the sweetness of the strawberry—then grabbed her phone, already mentally composing the praises she planned to sing.

Olive's reply made her smile.

I think it was mostly just awkward in my head. Dad said that you're very pretty and wondered if I planned to ask you out. If he only knew...

So that meant Olive was open about her sexuality. Good. Kate shook her head to clear away the thought as soon as it occurred. It didn't matter if Olive was out of the closet or not. The sex was incredible. *That* was what mattered. Anything else was just a distraction as long as her book remained unfinished. Determined to steer their conversation onto safer, more casual ground, Kate typed out a saucy response.

Knew what? That today wasn't the first time I sampled your muffin?

The reply came quickly.

Scandal!

Kate laughed out loud, then typed again.

In all seriousness, your strawberry-rhubarb creation is the second best thing to happen to me today. You're incredibly talented.

It took Olive a couple minutes to send a response.

Thank you. Is it lame to hope I also had something to do with the first best thing?

Her heart beat a little faster as she typed and retyped her next sentence a handful of times before gathering the courage to hit send.

You ARE the first best thing.

A soft knock on the office door startled Kate so badly she yelped and sent her phone clattering onto the floor. Scrambling to pick it up, she called out, "Come in!"

Erato opened the door partway, suspicion written all over her beautiful face. "Am I interrupting?"

Kate tossed her phone onto the desk, feigning carelessness, and shoved the rest of the muffin back into the paper bag. "Not at all. Is everything okay?"

"Everything is fine. Are you writing?"

Kate tried not to let any of her instinctive defensiveness seep into her tone. "Yes." Remembering that Erato had clearly seen that she hadn't been pounding away at her keyboard, she amended her statement. "Well, I was, but I took a moment to try some of the muffin I bought from the farmers' market. Would you like a bite? It's delicious."

Erato smiled. "Sure." She swept into the room breezily, crossing to sit on Kate's lap. "How's it coming?"

"Great." That wasn't a lie, at least. "I've written about three thousand words, and the conflict between Rose and her mother is starting to come together in my head. Dear old mom is a bit homophobic."

"Discovering that her favorite caregiver also loves the ladies will be a shock, then."

Kate didn't bother suppressing her evil grin. "Oh, yes. Especially the way I plan to write the discovery."

"Excellent." Erato kissed her on the temple, then reached inside the paper bag to break off a chunk of muffin. She took a bite, then closed her eyes, wiggling on Kate's lap in a way that made it clear that she appreciated Olive's baking prowess every bit as much as Kate did. "Oh, this *is* yummy." She paused to chew and swallow, then opened her eyes to stare directly into Kate's. "Olive really is something special, isn't she?"

Afraid she was being tested, Kate said, "She makes a kick-ass muffin."

Erato arched an eyebrow just as Kate's cell phone buzzed twice, vibrating obnoxiously against the wooden surface of the desk. "Texting someone?"

The question sent her heart crashing into her stomach—or at least that's how her writer's mind tried to put her sinking dread into words. She'd employed similar turns of phrase more than once to describe characters in tense situations, but before that moment, she'd never personally experienced the sensation so keenly. It was unpleasant, to say the least. She felt caught. By whom, she wasn't sure. Her girlfriend? Her writing coach?

She considered lying only briefly. That suggested she'd been doing something wrong. She wasn't positive she had. Perhaps more importantly, to lie would be to confirm that Erato possessed some level of authority over her—which simply wasn't true. No matter how helpful she'd been, or how much she'd done for her writing career, Erato wasn't in charge of her life and had no real say in how she spent her time.

Besides, she reminded herself, Erato seemed to be able to read minds. Or at the very least, to read people. If she lied, Erato would most likely see right through her. So Kate nodded. "Olive gave me her number so I could text her my review of the muffin. It's a new recipe and she wanted feedback."

"Ah," Erato murmured, and kissed Kate softly on the lips. "Let me guess, five stars?"

Kate smiled and kissed Erato back, struck anew by the softness of her lips and the happiness and creativity she brought with her every time she entered the room. The well-being she felt with Erato was *almost* enough to distract her from the fact that she had an unread message and that Olive was waiting for a reply. "Of course. Well deserved, don't you think?"

"Absolutely." Erato pulled back, and Kate realized that somehow she'd managed to grab the cell phone off the desk without her noticing. "In fact, I think I'll send my own review."

Kate forced herself not to react as Erato lowered her eyes to the screen and silently read their brief conversation. After a moment, Erato began typing a message of her own. Panicked, Kate craned her neck to read Olive's most recent text, but Erato angled the screen away and pinned her with a disapproving frown. "Kate, do you want to finish this book?"

"Of course I do." She tried not to lash out at such a ridiculous question. Of *course* she did. Finishing this book was integral to her career—not to mention her ability to pay her bills. If she *didn't* finish this book, she would be forced to return to her full-time job. Writing would become even more difficult than it already was. And even if it didn't always feel like it, she *loved* writing. So yes, *of course* she wanted to finish the goddamn book. "Erato, I wrote over three thousand words before taking a five-minute break to text Olive back after *she* texted *me*. You can't possibly fault me for that *or* suggest that it indicates a lack of motivation."

"I didn't suggest that you lacked motivation." Upon seeing Kate's gaze drift again to the cell phone's display, Erato turned it to rest facedown on her thigh. "I asked if you wanted to finish this book."

"You know I do."

Erato studied her for an uncomfortably long time before finally nodding. She dangled the phone between their faces, forcing Kate to summon all her willpower not to snatch it back. "Kate, *this* is a distraction. We both know it's true, so please don't pretend otherwise."

She *did* know it was true. And she *did* want to finish the book. Still, the thought of having her phone taken away—or worse, having Erato text Olive and tell her to fuck off—made her feel desolate. Bereft. Her desire to be with Olive again had already produced three thousand words she probably wouldn't have otherwise written, and she'd been confident that the next ten thousand would come just as quickly. If texting breaks spooked Erato into canceling the deal they'd struck, she was happy to lay off them. For now.

"All right, you win." Kate put on her bravest smile, hoping Erato couldn't sense how shaken she felt at the thought of jeopardizing whatever this thing was with Olive. "No more texting. I'm sorry. I wasn't trying to get a head start on my reward. She really did ask me to send feedback on the muffin, so I thought I owed her that much. And she *did* text me first."

"Mmm-hmm." Erato looked at the phone's display. "She wants to know if she can see you again."

Kate battled the urge to react to the revelation with the joy it naturally provoked. "How about I tell her that I need to isolate myself completely until I write ten thousand more words? Then we can set up a date."

Setting the phone down on the desk, Erato brought both hands up to cradle Kate's face. She stared at her soberly. "Kate, why don't we find some other way to reward you when you reach this goal? If you want another threesome, we can find a new girl. Hell, I could *hire* someone—a professional who will do *whatever* you want. Or *I* could do whatever you want."

Kate's stomach churned at the prospect of having the reward that had been dangled in front of her suddenly taken away. "We made an agreement, didn't we? Why can't we just stick to what we originally decided?"

Erato looked pointedly at the phone. "Because *this* wasn't part of our arrangement. I can't knowingly allow you to waste any more time, my darling. You've got less than six weeks left to deliver this manuscript to your publisher. It may be only a ten-minute break today, but believe me when I say it will quickly spiral out of control. Even if I take your phone away, I'm afraid thoughts of Miss Olive will hijack your creative energy. We can't have that. Not at this point."

Kate shook her head. "Won't happen," she said forcefully. "Let me prove you wrong. Our arrangement stands. You take away my phone *after* I respond to Olive and let her know that I need to focus right now, and I write my next ten thousand words *with* thoughts of Olive providing my primary motivation."

For a moment, she was afraid Erato would refuse, and she desperately didn't want them to come to an impasse. Though it was within her power to ask Erato to leave, she didn't even want to consider doing something so drastic. She wasn't sure she could. She *loved* Erato, in a way, even having only just met her. The woman had improved Kate's life immeasurably in the short time she'd been a part of it. Hell, if not for her, Kate probably wouldn't have met Olive. Asking her devoted muse to leave so she could have the chance, however slim, to pursue a relationship with Olive wasn't an easy trade-off to consider. On the other hand, forgetting Olive would be equally impossible. She didn't know what about Olive so intrigued her, but ignoring their mutual attraction hardly seemed like an option.

Luckily, Erato didn't force her to make a choice. "Fair enough. If you can prove to me that Olive is an inspiration and *not* a distraction, I'll honor our original agreement. But with *two* caveats."

Afraid to betray the full extent of her relief before hearing them, Kate said, "Okay."

"First, I'm resetting your goal to thirteen thousand words. Consider the three thousand you wrote this morning payment for being dishonest with me when I asked if I was interrupting, and if you were writing."

Kate searched her memory for the exact words she'd used. She'd been evasive but had tried not to outright lie. At least she thought she had. Then again, she *had* deliberately avoided mentioning that she'd been texting Olive despite being given two opportunities to confess. She supposed that was dishonest. Frankly, she wasn't going to disagree lest Erato call off their entire working relationship and walk out of her life forever. Or perhaps even worse, refuse to allow her any more contact with Olive. "All right. What's the second?"

Erato picked up the cell phone, erased the message she'd started to type, then handed it to Kate. "Tell her that you'll arrange a playdate with her once you hit your word-count goal. Then we'll get to your *actual* punishment for being dishonest about wasting time."

An extra three thousand words wasn't punishment enough? Not brave enough to voice the question, Kate accepted the phone with a grateful smile. "Fair enough. Thank you."

Erato gave her a stern, sultry look that truly confused her senses. Rising from Kate's lap to loom over her, she was the scariest, sexiest authority figure imaginable—the type of dominatrix she'd written about in more than one erotic story, pulled straight from her kinkiest fantasies. Fear and arousal battled for dominance within her, neither the clear winner. "Go on," Erato murmured. "Last text for now. Make it count."

Swallowing, Kate lowered her eyes, greedy to read Olive's most recent message.

I was hoping you'd say that. Now for my moment of courage: do you want to see each other again sometime?

Almost as soon as she'd finished reading, the phone buzzed and another message appeared. Her hesitation must have spooked Olive, because her courage seemed to be flagging.

Maybe?

Regretful that she'd left Olive hanging long enough to induce doubt, Kate quickly typed an explanation, followed by her good-bye for now. The pang in her chest at the knowledge that she would have no more back-and-forth flirtation to look forward to was a clear sign that Erato had been right. Escalating their sexual tension over text was a one-way road to an unfinished manuscript. She reread her parting message twice, then, in a show of good faith, turned the phone so Erato could offer her approval.

Erato shook her head without looking at the screen. "I trust you."

Nodding, Kate read over her reply a third and final time.

So sorry, didn't mean to leave you hanging. I just got busted for texting. Erato says we can make a playdate after I write another thirteen thousand words, as a reward, but I'm not allowed to get distracted again before then. Something about a deadline...ha! Wait for me?

She pressed send, then looked up to find Erato watching her, stone-faced. Kate tightened her grip slightly on the phone as she anticipated having it confiscated. "Do you mind if I—" Before she could ask permission to wait for Olive's reply, the vibration signaling a new message spared her the indignity. Kate took a quick, frantic look.

Don't waste any more time texting me, then. Go! Write!

Kate's grin faded when Erato placed her open hand next to the phone. Sighing, she dropped it onto her palm. Not only did she have to acknowledge that this was the best course of action for her productivity, but it was also obvious that in order to keep Erato and her magical writing juju in her life, she would have to play by a certain set of rules. So far nothing Erato had asked of her had been unreasonable, and the concerns about Olive weren't unfounded. For the moment, Kate had nothing to lose by just going with the flow. She exhaled steadily when Erato left the room with her phone in hand but didn't close the door, a clear sign that she intended to return.

What kind of punishment was she facing, exactly?

She barely had time to wonder before Erato walked back into the office to stand over her once again. "Your phone is in my possession until you've reached your new goal. If your publisher, parents, or sister calls, I'll let you know and you can ring them back during a break. Otherwise, it's off-limits."

She doubted her phone would be ringing much—she'd kicked off her official retreat into solitude by alerting her friends and family of her rapidly approaching deadline. Still, she appreciated the sentiment. "Understood."

"And before you even think about trying to look Olive up on social media, just know that I'm completely willing to cut off your Internet access. I haven't so far because you've avoided using it to procrastinate, and sometimes it's necessary for research."

Startled by the mere suggestion of no access to the Internet, Kate blanched. "It's *integral* to my writing process. You can't take that away from me, too."

Erato giggled. "Oh, Kate. Don't be silly. Human beings have been writing and telling stories for hundreds of years without access to a search engine."

If she hadn't already been skating on such very thin ice, Kate might've been tempted to defend her reliance on the digital world. Instead she said, "I won't give you a reason to turn off the Wi-Fi. I promise."

"You'll be a good girl?" Erato cocked her head, pinning her with a stern glare. "Is that what you're promising?"

Kate blushed. She couldn't remember the last time she'd been reprimanded like this, or if she even had. That such a beautiful woman was delivering the scolding made it equal parts shame-inducing, frightening, and exciting. "Yes. I'll be good."

"Excellent. Now stand up." Erato gestured with her head. "I want to leave you with a reminder of this conversation. Something to reflect on when the urge to get distracted—or to be dishonest with me—arises."

Kate stood. It didn't even occur to her to refuse—not until Erato took her place in the chair, straightened her skirt, and patted her lap expectantly. "Take off your jeans and lie over my knees. And don't look so scandalized, darling. I've read your stories. *All* of them."

That meant that despite the look of horror Kate knew she was wearing, Erato was perfectly aware of exactly how much the idea of over-the-knee spankings turned her on. Feeling utterly exposed by her past artistic choices, she shot back, "Hey, I'm allowed to be scandalized. There's a difference between writing something—or fantasizing about it—and actually having it done to you."

Erato allowed a brief, sweet smile. "Well, this wouldn't be much of a punishment, let alone a deterrent of future misbehavior, if you weren't at least a *little* scandalized." Patting her thighs again, she said, "Come on, sweetheart. Don't make me force you over my lap."

The threat made her clench pleasantly and caused wetness to trickle out of her and soak the panties she was being asked to expose. Blood rushed to her cheeks, setting her face aflame. "I feel…silly."

But silly was the last thing she felt when Erato captured her wrist and squeezed. "Don't. What I want you to feel"—she placed Kate's hand at the zipper of her jeans and gave her a pointed look—"is shame and regret for giving me a reason to confiscate your phone." She paused, staring at Kate until she finally gave in and undid her pants. "I want you to feel the sting of my hand on your ass. Not just once you step out of those jeans and I take you across my lap, but hours from now, when you're writing. I want you to feel horny. Desperate." By this point, Kate was moving on autopilot, and Erato beamed when she shoved her jeans to the floor and stepped out of them. "I want you to feel *inspired*."

❖

Kate had never actually been spanked before. Not for real, not like this. The closest she'd come had been an occasional smack on the ass during sex. Which she'd loved, of course. As Kate swallowed her pride and balanced herself over Erato's knees, palms planted on the laminate flooring in front of her face, she reflected that this wasn't exactly the unequivocally awful punishment she was pretending it to be. No matter how fundamentally embarrassing it was to be taken over someone's knee, she couldn't deny how wet the ritual had already made her.

Erato smoothed gentle circles over her panties-clad bottom. "This is the first part of your punishment." Her hand rose and came back down with startling speed, delivering a mildly stinging slap to one cheek. "You won't like the second."

Kate opened her mouth to ask why not but bit her lip when a slightly more powerful smack landed on the other cheek. She took a breath to compose herself but cried out when Erato spanked her twice more in quick succession. Each blow reverberated through her lower body and settled squarely between her legs. Squirming, she spread her legs in a silent plea for more.

"Still feeling silly?" Fingernails dragged over the cleft of her buttocks, and then her panties were yanked down, around her knees. Erato established a slow, deliberate rhythm, alternating between her cheeks, slapping with enough force that Kate had to concentrate on keeping her hands on the floor rather than reaching back to protect herself. "Answer me."

Kate shook her head. "Not silly. No."

"How about sorry?" The blows ceased just as they threatened to become too painful, allowing Kate a chance to catch her breath. As though sensing that she needed a moment to collect herself, Erato switched back to rubbing her bottom tenderly. "Do you feel sorry, Kate?"

"Definitely." Sort of. She was sorry she'd gotten her phone taken away, but she wasn't exactly sorry to be in her current position. She could *feel* how wet and swollen she was and knew Erato had to be perfectly aware of the effect this punishment was having. Hoping for a couple of fingers to soothe the ache between her thighs, Kate spread her legs as far as the panties that were still around her knees allowed. "I'm *really* sorry, Erato. Seriously. You're right…about everything."

Well, she hadn't meant to go quite that far. Still, if it got her fucked—

Once again totally in synch with her needs, Erato pushed her fingers between Kate's thighs and touched her slick labia, cupping her. "*This* doesn't feel very silly."

"It's not." Kate rocked her hips against Erato's hand, trying to force a more focused touch. "Please, Erato."

Without moving, Erato applied slightly more pressure to her labia. "I was right. This isn't much of a punishment."

Kate started to argue, but Erato cut her off with a renewed flurry of slaps. The last two were painful enough to bring tears to Kate's eyes, though she refused to let them fall. She was too proud to ask Erato to stop. As soon as the blows ceased, Erato's hand was back between her legs, once again checking her wetness.

"Luckily, as I said, this is only the first part of your punishment." A single finger traced up and down her slit, then pressed deeper to circle her opening. "So I still have the opportunity to leave a lasting impression."

Kate held her breath. Would she be penetrated hard and fast? Or would Erato drag it out, perhaps try to humiliate her a little more? She tried not to grin as she waited to find out. Regardless of what had gone down between them due to her indiscretion, the day just kept getting better.

"Want to know the second part?" Erato eased the tip of her finger inside, just far enough to *almost* bring relief. Kate raised her hips as best she could, hoping to draw Erato deeper, but the move earned her a sharp, painful blow across the center of her bottom. Balancing as best she could, Kate reached back with one hand to protect herself from another slap. Seemingly anticipating the move, Erato caught her wrist and held it behind her back, trapping her in place. "I'm sorry, but did you forget that this is supposed to be a *negative* consequence of your actions? Be good and stop fighting me *right now*."

With effort, Kate forced herself to relax completely. Total surrender was never easy, but her current position didn't leave her many options. Besides, she'd agreed to be punished. Sighing, Kate said, "You're right. I apologize. Again."

"Thank you." Erato released her wrist and returned her hand to its place between her thighs. She rubbed Kate's labia with her fingers while simultaneously easing her thumb between her buttocks to tease her anus. Kate braced herself on both hands, certain she was about to need the extra support. That's when Erato stopped moving her hand— and delivered a devastating blow. "Kate, the second part of your punishment is that I'm forbidding you to orgasm until you meet your goal. I want *all* your energy focused on these next thirteen thousand words. Obviously you aren't as motivated as you could be, so consider this me doing you a favor."

She removed her hand.

Kate groaned, unhappy about both the threat and the fierce hard-on Erato was leaving her with. "But you said—" *Smack.* She gasped, cursing her traitorous body for reacting with renewed arousal to the firm slap against her already-sore ass. Figuring that the worst possible consequence would be another deliciously pleasurable spanking, Kate dared to finish her thought. "I thought sex fueled creativity."

"So does desperation." Erato patted her bottom softly. "Now stand up. It's time to go back to work."

Kate wasn't positive her legs would support her. "Seriously?"

Erato's pats became increasingly hard slaps, which finally compelled Kate to her feet. Giggling, Erato gazed up at her with an altogether too-amused smirk. "Oh, did this finally become a punishment?"

"And a deterrent." Kate scowled, pulling up her panties before rubbing a careful hand over her sore bottom. "Remind me not to cross you again."

Erato's eyes sparkled. "I will."

Not for the first time, Kate wasn't sure whether to be frightened or aroused. The only feeling she was positive about was her frustration. No more orgasms for thirteen thousand more words? It seemed strangely impossible. She doubted she'd ever achieved such a feat before, even without a lover in her life. Writing erotic fiction made her horny—being horny usually seemed like an adequate excuse to seek release. Granted, it was a bit of a vicious cycle that often ended with her fully sated but lacking in progress. But to be cut off completely? And after getting worked up like this, with that spanking?

Kate waited until she was fully dressed to raise a final objection. "This is cruel and unusual, you know. I'm honestly not sure what it will do to my writing process. Like…really."

Erato stood and walked to the door, patting Kate's sore bottom one final time as she passed. "I have complete faith in you."

Shifting her weight from one foot to the other, Kate grimaced at the faint echo of pleasure that radiated from her wet center. She wanted so badly to coax the sensation to the front, to bring herself to the peak—

"And Kate?" The sternness in Erato's voice snapped her out of her fantasy, fast. "Touch yourself and the goal gets bumped up another three thousand words. I'm not kidding." After a beat, authoritarian Erato melted away, replaced by the sweet, sexy muse she'd come to love. "Now write! I'll make fruit salad."

With that, Erato swept out of the room as confidently as she'd come in, taking a piece of Kate's pride with her. Resigned, Kate returned to her office chair and sat down cautiously, all too aware of how deliciously sore she was. It took every ounce of her self-control not to clench her thighs together and rock subtly on the chair, *anything* for a little thrill. Only her fear of Erato's omnipotence—and a sense that her muse's creativity knew no bounds when it came to discipline—stopped her.

Kate inhaled deeply and stared at the monitor, willing her mind back to where it had been when Olive's first text came in. *Distracting, indeed.*

CHAPTER THIRTEEN

The next four days passed in a blur. Kate wrote all day long, stopping only to eat, visit the restroom, and take an occasional nap. Although Erato tried to convince her to take more frequent breaks, even attempting to get her to go for a walk in the local park, Kate maintained a laser focus on her goal. Nothing was more important than the next thirteen thousand words of her writing career.

She was able to knock out another two thousand words after recovering from her spanking, followed by another thirty-four hundred the next day. Day three of Operation: Olive floated by like a fever dream, and when Erato finally dragged her to bed at the end of it, she was thrilled to discover that she'd logged an astounding five thousand words. The fourth day was distressingly unproductive, as she spent most of her morning paying her monthly bills and answering important emails, but she still managed to write eleven hundred words by the time she forced herself to call it a night.

That meant she had only fifteen hundred words to go. A mere fifteen hundred, and she would be set free. She would have permission to contact Olive. She just hoped that Olive hadn't lost interest in meeting up.

Unfortunately, the chapter in which she would finally reach her goal started out with what she hoped would be a smoking-hot—albeit very secretive, and therefore hurried—sex scene between Rose and Molly in Rose's office. Molly had just dropped by Rose's workplace at the end of the day for an unannounced visit, armed with a plan to appeal to Rose's sense of propriety and get her to agree to make theirs a strictly professional relationship. She knows perfectly well that Rose's mother would flip out about a romance between them and doesn't want to hurt an old woman she's come to care about. What Molly didn't anticipate when planning this breakup, however, was the sexy, tailored suit that Rose wore so well—the one that weakened her resolve the moment she walked into her office.

So that meant that right now, on the morning of day five of her thirteen-thousand-word goal sexless writing marathon, Rose was *just* about to pull Molly in for a passionate kiss that Kate was almost certain would end with Molly laid out across the desk. There would be licking, sucking, fingering. As she considered all the wonderful possibilities, Kate gripped the edge of her desk and prepared for the challenge ahead.

Writing sex made Kate want to fuck. It was always difficult to propel herself mentally to the place she needed to be in order to craft a love scene and *not* walk away from her laptop to take care of business. Today was a million times worse than usual. She hadn't had an orgasm for over four days. Her whole body was coiled tight, and although her mind had remained surprisingly sharp despite her preoccupation with sexual release, the task of imagining all the different ways her beautiful heroines could bring each other pleasure was torturous.

She had no choice but to power through this and just write. A truly talented author would use her frustration—and the increasingly lascivious thoughts it triggered—to her advantage. If she could make her readers feel even *half* as turned on as she did, she'd consider the scene a masterpiece.

Kate closed her eyes, fingers on the keyboard, and placed herself in Molly's shoes. She was the point-of-view character in this chapter, so her perspective needed to dominate. Molly was there to end their sexual entanglement for good. She was determined, though weakened by the sight of Rose in business attire. The confident, powerful image Rose projects reminds Molly of the first night they met, when Rose rescued her from that blind date.

Confident. Powerful. Those qualities had attracted Molly to Rose in the first place. It made sense that those qualities should govern during this scene in which Rose easily persuades her not to end their sexual relationship. Kate had a flash of two women—one in a tailored business suit, the other in a light, flowing dress—locked in a heated embrace. Rose would initiate the kiss and escalate the encounter to the next level. They'd kiss, and then Rose would pull away to lock the office door.

Satisfied that she now had a little direction, Kate opened her eyes and began to type. She rocked almost imperceptibly against her chair as she did, enjoying the light friction on her clit. After testing the waters over the past few days, she'd concluded that this level of self-stimulation was permissible, bless Erato's vicious heart. The words poured out of her steadily, coming together like magic to create one of the most passionate kisses she'd ever written. Aroused by her own imagery, she had to stop and breathe with her characters when Rose finally broke away to secure the office door. She gave them—and herself—a moment of respite via an exchange of dialogue. Molly asks what Rose is doing. Rose: "Reminding you how good we are together."

Kate stopped typing and checked her word count. Only five hundred and two! Surely she'd managed twice that. How the hell did Erato expect her to churn out another thousand at the end of such a grueling stretch of abstinence? Annoyed, she took a drink of water, then a bite of tangerine, and tried to slow the rapid-fire fantasies burning through her brain. Rose could do *so* many things to Molly on a big wooden desk. First she should really decide if Molly would end up on her back, seated on the edge, or simply bent over the surface. And would Rose use her mouth, her fingers, or something else to make Molly come? If *she* were Rose, she'd fuck Molly *so hard*. If she were Molly, frankly, she'd *want* to be fucked hard. She'd take it any way it was given to her.

That probably all went without saying. *Fuck,* her clit hurt. If she didn't come soon, she might embarrass herself.

Closing her eyes again, she imagined Olive sitting on her desk in place of her laptop, legs spread, skirt pushed up over her hips. If she had the woman she wanted here with her right now, what would *she* do?

Taste her. Kate groaned as she imagined pulling Olive's panties to the side to expose her wetness. Though she'd like to think she'd take time to tease Olive thoroughly, in her current state, she wouldn't. She'd *devour* that pussy. That was most likely true for Rose, too. They were in her office, at her workplace. End of the day or not, Rose wouldn't draw things out. No, she'd dive right in and feast.

Shuddering at the visceral image of going down on a woman planted firmly at the forefront of her mind, Kate wrote Rose guiding Molly over to the desk and helping her sit on the edge. After she wrote the part where Rose pushed Molly's skirt up over her hips, then yanked her panties out of the way, she had to stop, plant her hands on the surface of her desk, and gasp for air. She had no idea if this scene would read back later nearly as smoking hot as it felt to her now, but she expected a lot of excited readers if it did.

Another word-count check revealed that eight hundred and fifty remained. Obviously she'd have to forge ahead into the thick of the action, even if thinking clearly was becoming more difficult. With a determined shake of her head, Kate hunkered down to decide how the rest of this coupling should play out. She could simply write a few more sentences detailing Rose's oral technique and Molly's quiet, enthusiastic pleasure, but if she had Olive in this position, no way would she stop at simply going down on her. Not with the woman she craved spread open right there in front of her. No, she'd slide at least one finger into Olive, maybe two. Maybe even sneak another down to tease her ass. If Olive were here, she'd want to possess her completely.

Swept away by the vivid imagery playing out in her mental movie theater, Kate fought not to forget the importance of realism in her love scenes. She didn't want to describe something that real human beings would have a difficult time doing—and enjoying—lest she yank savvy readers out of the erotic mood she'd labored to create. As she'd never actually performed oral sex on a woman while seated at her desk, let alone simultaneously fingered her pussy and touched her ass, she wasn't totally certain it was feasible.

Rolling back from her desk about a foot, she tried to imagine Olive sitting there in front of her. The height seemed okay for oral sex. Maybe. She bent slightly, as though performing cunnilingus on a make-believe friend, then raised her hand and extended two fingers. She moved them back and forth in the air, leaning down to where she *thought* Molly's pussy would be located. Could Rose even pull this off? All of a sudden, she wasn't sure this scene would work the way she'd wanted.

Kate growled in frustration. Eight hundred and fifty *fucking* words left, and she lacked the mental clarity to even choreograph a simple sex scene. She brought her hands to her face and released another enraged noise, pissed off that she was even dealing with this. Why the hell was she letting Erato deny her sexual release? For that matter, why allow her "muse" to dictate *anything* about her life and habits? She was a grown-ass woman, which meant she could masturbate if she wanted to, damn it. While she freely admitted that the denial thing had apparently worked for her for the first twelve thousand one hundred and fifty words of Erato's insane homework assignment, now that she was so close to her goal—and attempting to depict her characters getting laid—it just wasn't working for her anymore.

The quiet knock on her office door barely surprised her. By this point, she was well accustomed to the way Erato always seemed to appear whenever Kate needed her most—and, sometimes, when she wanted her the least. Shoving down her anger at Erato's extreme motivational techniques, she said, "Come in."

Erato set Kate's pulse racing by walking into the room wearing a light, flowing dress that matched her cerulean eyes. The style and cut were very much like the dress she'd imagined Molly wearing to Rose's office, and immediately, Kate focused on Erato's thighs. How would it feel to shove that dress up and expose her panties? To push them aside and see how shiny and pink and ready Erato was at the thought of her lips and tongue? She glanced at the surface of her desk, then Erato, trying to judge the realness of her scene now that she had an actual, live female body in the room. If only Erato could help her out and just—

"You seem frustrated. Do you need anything from me?"

Kate frowned. If she asked Erato for help with choreography, would she be accused of trying to circumvent the rules of their current arrangement? Given that she didn't plan to ask to be touched, she didn't think so. Still, she was frightened to incur another punishment, especially if it meant that the finish line would be moved back even farther.

Erato offered a sympathetic smile. "My darling, you've been doing so well. Honestly, you're moving faster than I expected—and I couldn't be happier with your progress. So please don't be afraid to ask whatever you want to ask. I promise that, at the worst, I'll say no."

Fleetingly, Kate wondered what would happen if she asked for an orgasm to help her finish this scene. Just a tiny one, to get by. If the worst Erato would do was say no...but Kate shook off the idea with a determined sigh. Her pride demanded that she ride out the rest of her sentence in silence. She would *not* beg. Not for this. Being taken over Erato's knee had stripped away far too much of her dignity; not pleading for a reprieve was one way she could protect what was left. Pivoting back to her original plan, Kate said, "I'm having a hard time picturing the mechanics of this sex scene I'm writing, and I'm worried it might involve contortions that will distract readers who are better than me at evaluating these kinds of logistics."

"Just to reassure you, I've never read anything you've written that wasn't entirely possible, given the right people and situation. That tells me you're just fine with logistics." Moving closer, Erato trailed her fingers along the side of Kate's neck, making her shiver. "That said, never hesitate to ask me for help blocking a love scene. I know how important it is to get these details right, and believe me, assisting with choreography is one of my favorite parts of the job." She clapped her hands and gazed around Kate's workspace expectantly. "Now where do you want me?"

Kate supposed that she shouldn't be *too* surprised by Erato's easy acquiescence. Before the texting drama and their disagreements about Olive's potential distraction level, Erato had fulfilled her every need with unprecedented eagerness. Using Erato as a living model for this crazy-making erotic scene—even if it *felt* opportunistic to her—met a legitimate writing need. It might honestly help her complete this last stretch of writing, and Erato obviously knew that. Otherwise she wouldn't have agreed.

Sagging with relief at the gift, Kate scooted her chair back to the desk and pushed the laptop, her plate, and her half-empty glass of water to one side. When she'd cleared a space large enough for Erato to sit directly in front of her, she rolled backward even farther and pointed. "Here."

Erato perched on the edge of the desk, knees pressed together, hands folded on her lap. "Like this?"

Kate scooted her chair forward a couple steps, unable to tear her gaze away from Erato's chest. Her breasts had always been divine, but either the dress or the cumulative effect of four days of total celibacy amid near-constant immersion in an erotic headspace made them appear particularly enticing. Kate yearned to bury her face between them, and so even though it wasn't part of her research, she did. Inhaling deeply, she kissed the side of one breast, then turned to acknowledge the other. She backed off with a sigh of longing and finally looked up into Erato's eyes.

Erato smiled. "Are you still upset with me?"

"I wasn't upset."

The lie earned her a pointed look. "Weren't you?"

"Well, all right." She shrugged, placing her hands on Erato's bare knees. "I was *frustrated,* yes." When Erato's skepticism didn't appear to abate, Kate decided to just come clean. So far dishonesty and evasion had gotten her absolutely nowhere. "Actually, I *am* frustrated. I've been locked in a room writing a hot love story for days while ignoring my own *extremely pressing* physical needs. It makes everything more difficult. I can barely think!"

"And yet you've written nearly sixteen thousand words in less than four full days. Before I met you, it took months for you to produce half as many words."

Kate rolled her eyes. "I'm not saying your methods aren't effective. Just that they're frustrating. As hell."

"Duly noted." Beaming, Erato chirped, "Now come on. Let's tackle this scene."

Excited, she squeezed both of Erato's knees. "Permission to act out my half? I just need to see if I'm in a reasonable position to multi-task. All you have to do is sit back and be delicious."

Erato planted her hands behind her hips and allowed her thighs to fall open slightly. "I can do that." Her gaze darted to the laptop, then returned to Kate. "How many words left to write?"

"About eight hundred and fifty." Kate slid her hands up the outside of Erato's thighs, taking her skirt along for the ride. She was delighted to find her actually wearing panties, pleased that Erato's choice of outfit so closely echoed Molly's. Tugging the already sodden crotch aside, she studied Erato's swollen, excited sex, memorizing every last sensory detail for future reference. "Once I get this problem sorted out, it should go quickly."

Erato cradled the back of Kate's head as she bent to kiss the gorgeous display in front of her. "Like I said, I'm happy to help." The end of her sentence turned into a whimper as Kate dragged the tip of her tongue along her folds before rolling the chair nearer so she could press her face deep into Erato's wetness.

Erato stopped talking, for which Kate was grateful. She wasn't in the mood to chat. She wasn't even particularly in the mood to focus on who it was she was pleasuring. All she wanted—the *only* thing—was to reenact the scene she'd been struggling to put together. First, because it would help her complete it, but more importantly, because concentrating so hard on the logistics of eating pussy had made her downright ravenous for it.

Fingers tightened in Kate's hair, nearly bringing tears to her eyes. "Oh! Oh my…uh, Kate!"

Gratified by the mild alarm in Erato's voice, which she somehow knew signaled disappointment about a rapidly approaching climax, Kate brought her hand up and found Erato's opening with relative ease. She had to angle her chair to find the proper position for her arm once she'd worked her finger deep inside, but was relieved to discover that she was able to juggle the task of sucking Erato's clit and pumping into her without any difficulty. Maybe this would work out, after all.

"So far…" Erato cried out and slammed her thighs closed around Kate's head. Gasping, she said, "So good. Right?"

Calmly, Kate used her free hand to push against Erato's knee. Once able, she pulled back far enough to speak. "Open your legs, my sweet research assistant. You're not done helping me yet."

Erato exhaled and relaxed her legs, spreading them even wider than before. "Of course." She took a shaky breath as Kate once again bent to circle her tongue around the swollen point of her clit. Kate scissored the fingers that still rested inside Erato, causing her mouth to drop open and her lids to grow heavy with pleasure. "So…what exactly are we attempting to determine?"

Kate's little finger glided easily between the cleft of Erato's buttocks, aided by the incredible wetness that coated her sex and her thighs. Unfortunately, she struggled to find the tight ring of muscle she so badly wanted to tease without removing the fingers that were buried deep within Erato's core. Cursing, she lifted her face and met Erato's hooded eyes. "Whether I can play with your ass while I'm fingering and licking your pussy. *Skillfully.*"

Nodding thoughtfully, Erato rested her head against the wall behind her and planted a foot on the desk for leverage. "Everything you're doing so far feels amazing."

Kate turned her hand, trying a different angle. She watched Erato's face as she penetrated her deeply, then set up a steady rhythm of purposeful thrusts. Although her face betrayed no discomfort, Erato's noises of pleasure seemed muted compared to before. "Not as good?"

"It's still *very* good," Erato reassured her. "It would be even better if you licked me again…"

Ignoring the not-so-subtle hint for now, Kate took advantage of a new position and sank her thumb between Erato's slippery cheeks. She sought out and found her anus with little effort, and celebrated by sharing a triumphant grin with her muse. Pressing the pad of her thumb against the tight opening, Kate enjoyed the way Erato's anticipation played out across her face. "You're so beautiful."

Erato's smile turned into a grimace of pleasure when Kate twisted the fingers inside her. "Thank you. Now *please…*"

As much as she loved making Erato come, she refused to miss this opportunity for a little payback. She'd been suffering for days. Erato could certainly withstand a few more minutes of teasing. Tickled by the wicked cruelty of her actions, Kate bent to kiss her labia before withdrawing both her hand and her mouth, leaving Erato wet, open, and alone in front of her.

Eyes widening in alarm, Erato grabbed for her wrist and missed. "Where are you going?"

Her appetite for revenge disappeared at the sight of her always-confident and in-control muse undone by a basic human need. Instead of telling Erato she needed to get back to her book, as she'd planned, she decided to take pity and grant her the sweet release she herself had been craving for days. But not without a little more teasing first. "This is about research, remember? I'm trying to consider the other possibilities."

Erato brought her hands up to her chest and, in a blatant attempt to do some teasing of her own, massaged her breasts with a groan of satisfaction. "But everything was going so well…"

Kate's inner muscles clenched at the sight of Erato pinching her own nipples through the fabric of her dress. "Yes, but there are *so* many ways to take a woman who's sitting on your desk. I'd be remiss to stop at imagining only one."

Nodding, Erato murmured, "True." She bit her lip and let one hand fall between her legs. "Just tell me how you want me."

Kate caught Erato's wrist before she could touch herself. "Turn over." She'd already made up her mind to finish her scene as they'd originally enacted it, so this part was purely for her own gratification.

After days of hard work and no sex, she deserved a little fun. "Show me your best, sluttiest pose."

Eagerly and without a trace of self-consciousness, Erato hopped onto her feet and turned around, bending at the waist so that her chest pressed flat against the surface of the desk. She hiked up her dress to expose soaked, askew panties, which Kate then pulled down around her ankles with a single, swift tug. Erato stepped out of her underwear so she could set her feet apart on the floor, back arched and ass thrust high into the air. Her sex literally dripped with readiness, the very definition of wanton arousal.

Kate grumbled, wholly defeated by her own needs. She simply couldn't deny Erato as she'd been denied. Not when she wanted her so damn much. Giving in, Kate gripped Erato's round bottom in both hands and spread her apart, using her thumbs to hold her slippery labia open. She was so very flawless, even photogenic—like the porn star you *wish* you'd see. Feeling once again like she was starring in her own fantasy, Kate buried her face between Erato's thighs and worked her tongue as deep inside her opening as she could go. Erato moaned and rotated her hips sensuously, smearing her juices all over Kate's face. Though she'd never particularly gotten off on messy sex, there was something delightful about knowing she was absolutely covered in Erato-come. She closed her eyes and tried to imagine how they might look to an outside observer, and the mental image made her own pussy clench in pleasurable anticipation.

Slipping her tongue from within the snug opening, Kate held on to Erato's ass and rubbed her face up and down, back and forth, luxuriating in the abundant sweetness that poured from her like the most delicious nectar. She felt almost drunk from it, happy and tipsy and, for the first time in four days, wholly present and concerned with nothing except the task at hand. *Hand.* Inspired and yet feeling as though she was struggling for lucidity during the hottest sex dream imaginable, Kate brought her fingers to Erato's clit and rubbed lightly. The caress elicited a breathy noise that sent a shiver up her spine and set her hips into motion against her chair as she once again indulged in the forbidden thrill of light friction.

"This…position…works…too."

Kate chuckled at Erato's weak attempt to maintain an air of professionalism, as though either of them was still concerned with blocking the scene. Using her free hand to smack Erato hard on the ass—a minor act of revenge—she then fondled the engorged clit beneath her slippery fingers with an almost exaggerated gentleness. As she'd hoped, the contradictory nature of her actions seemed to momentarily unbalance Erato. Her muse trembled beneath her, no longer in control.

Heady with a renewed sense of power, Kate pulled her mouth away without stopping the motion of her fingers. She grinned evilly at the way Erato's whole body twitched and jerked from the careful manipulation of her erect clitoris. It felt good to finally have the upper hand in their relationship. Literally. Eager to debase Erato, Kate feigned an air of disinterest. "Beg me for it."

If Erato had any problem submitting to a lover's will, she didn't let on. "Please finish me, Kate. I beg you."

Dissatisfied, Kate seized the hard ridge of distended flesh between her fingertips and milked its length with a touch that was too soft and unfocused to induce climax. Erato whimpered and thrust her hips, shamelessly attempting to coax Kate's fingers into more direct stimulation. Was it wrong to take such perverse pleasure in turning the tables? She hoped not. "Why should I? You worked me up and let me suffer for days. It would only be fair for me to do the same."

Erato exhaled, then planted her hands on the desk so she could push her upper body off the surface. She used her new position to glance back over her shoulder and meet Kate's gaze. "You're right, it would be fair. But if you're being honest with yourself, I don't think that would be as much fun for either of us. Especially now that you're so close to reaching your goal."

That was true. Kate drew back and delivered an even harder slap on her ass than the first one, delighting in the red handprint she left behind. She swore she could feel Erato's clit pulse beneath her other hand. "Lucky for you, I'm not as sadistic as my beloved muse."

"Your spanking hurt me just as much as it hurt—"

Kate cut off the cliché with another powerful smack in the same spot. Her hand tingled from the blow, and Erato's bottom turned a deeper shade of red. "Don't even."

Erato's breaths came out in quick, shallow puffs. Her thighs quivered, but whether from exhaustion or excitement, Kate wasn't sure. "*Please*, Kate. I apologize for reprimanding you. My concern is only for your art. I know the past few days haven't been easy—" Erato yelped as Kate swatted her again for the understatement. "But the art! Would you say I've helped it?"

When Erato caught her with those earnest blue depths, Kate had no choice but to be honest. "I'm not suggesting that I *ever* want to go through this again, but I'll concede that desperation is a powerful motivator." Moving her hand back into position without breaking their shared look, Kate renewed the careful motion of her fingers on Erato's clit. "I think I wrote some good stuff."

Erato positively glowed. "I know you did."

"And *that* is the only reason I'm going to bring you to orgasm with my fingers right now." Kate paused to watch her words land, then said, "Are you ready?"

"Yes." Bowing her head, Erato finally lowered her eyes. "Thank you."

"You're welcome." Kate licked her lips and returned her attention to the wet pussy in front of her. Enough playing—she was ready to dive back in. "Trust me, this isn't an entirely selfless act."

"That's the best part." Erato settled herself into her original position and thrust her ass high into the air. "Anyway, you know what they say…a happy muse makes for a happy author."

"Is that what 'they' say?" Snickering, Kate lowered her face and once again snaked her tongue into Erato's opening. Mumbling against the fragrant, engorged flesh that enveloped her nose and mouth, she admitted, "I *am* happy."

Then she made them both even happier.

❖

As soon as Erato caught her breath, she rolled over, then slid off the desk and sank to her knees in front of Kate. "I'm reducing the length of your punishment. You're only eight hundred and fifty words away… how about I take care of you so you can finish with a clear head?" She reached for the waistband of Kate's pajama pants with an apologetic smile. "You were right, after all. This crush you have on Olive didn't prevent you from meeting your goal—and exceeding my expectations. That deserves a reward."

Kate startled them both by knocking Erato's hand away. "No!"

Erato blinked. "Really?" She lowered her gaze and stared at the crotch of Kate's light cotton pants, which were so wet she could *feel* the size of the stain without looking. "As you said, you've been suffering. You're frustrated."

All true, but Kate had jumped into this love scene in a distinct frame of mind, and she owed it to herself to maintain that same mental state through to the finish. The scene wouldn't be as strong if she didn't. Besides…for some inexplicable reason, Kate didn't feel *ready* to come yet. Even after all her bitching and wishing for release, now that it was being offered, her pride refused to accept the idea of premature surrender.

"I can wait. Like you said, it's only eight hundred and fifty more words." Kate offered the bravest smile she could muster, which quickly faltered when she reflected on the fact that she was actually refusing sex. After wanting nothing *but* sex for days.

Granted, this wasn't exactly the way she'd pictured the big reward…

Erato pinned her with a playful, knowing smile. "All right. How about I give you back your phone so you can start making plans for your date instead? Would that adequately express my pleasure with your performance?"

Kate tried not to betray just how excited—and, frankly, distracted—the suggestion made her feel. "Yes, please."

She mentally composed and discarded at least ten different opening lines as she waited for Erato to return with her phone. She told herself that not much time had passed, and that she and Olive likely wouldn't have seen each other before the upcoming weekend even if she hadn't been chasing a word-count goal. That didn't erase her worries that her window of opportunity for pursuing the sexy, mysterious Ms. Olive had already slipped away due to the shenanigans her muse had imposed on her life.

Still: sixteen thousand words in less than four full days. It was among her personal best, if not *the* best, of the runs she'd ever had. And what she'd produced was definitely good. So maybe it was a fair trade-off: one shot at a potentially special romance in exchange for the unequivocal return of her writing mojo. Even if Olive had moved on, the effort of the past few days hadn't been for nothing.

When Erato walked back into the office with her cell phone in hand, Kate beckoned her over. She pulled Erato down to sit on her lap, wrapping her in a loose embrace. "Seriously, thank you. I'm approaching the halfway point on a book I'm not sure I ever honestly believed I'd finish. That is one hundred percent a result of your presence in my life, and I know that." Erato opened her mouth to protest, but Kate shook her head firmly. "Save it. Yes, my progress has also depended on my own efforts, but let's be honest…if not for you, I'd probably be watching Internet cat videos on a permanent loop right now. I may not always agree with your methods, but I can't argue with the results."

Erato melted into her arms. "I appreciate that *so* much. You have no idea."

Warmed by the obvious pleasure Erato took from her gratitude, Kate eyed the phone finally within her grasp with an unexpected degree of wariness. Erato had been right about so many things already. Was she also right that inviting Olive back into her life posed a danger to her productivity? It was entirely plausible. It had been a long time since she'd had a new relationship, but she remembered how all-consuming one could be. Even if Olive had understood about the thirteen thousand words she'd just written, would she be able to accept Kate's need for hours of total solitude over the upcoming month? And beyond?

In that respect, Erato was likely as perfect a mate as she would ever find. For her, the art always came first. Before her own needs, sometimes even before Kate's. If all Kate really craved was uncomplicated, guilt-free companionship, it really couldn't get much better than her sweet muse. She shifted her gaze from the phone to Erato's face, trying to decide how badly she would regret an impulsive decision to delete Olive's number from her phone and dive back into her writing full-force.

Erato tilted her head. "Really?" she asked, clearly surprised by her hesitation. "Darling, as long as you keep things casual, I have no problem letting you play with Olive again. It's what you wanted, what's been driving you. The whole point of the past few days has been to prove that you can handle the occasional diversion, no?"

"Yes." Unsure she wanted to admit the nature of her second thoughts—just in case she was about to change to a different perspective—Kate shrugged. "I just…" After days of forcing her mind away from memories of Olive, she made herself go there again. She pictured Olive's radiant smile, her brown eyes and smooth, delicious skin, that terrifying scar on her chest. The way she'd overcome her obvious shyness and nerves to throw herself into a night of adventurous sex with two complete strangers. How happy she'd been to see her again at the farmers' market and to discover that her crush was reciprocated.

Shit. She *totally* wanted to see Olive again. But if she chose to go there, how could she trust herself to stay on track?

The answer seemed obvious. Putting her hand on the cell phone without taking it from Erato's grasp, she stared into her muse's face so she would understand just how sincere she was in what she was about to say. "Swear to me that you'll keep me focused on the art. Whatever happens over the next month, however I might feel in moments of extreme pressure or punishment…even if I call your methods into question or beg you to leave me alone…promise you won't. Stay here with me until this book is done. *Force me* to see it through." She considered how embarrassing it would be to miss her deadline after having been granted more than one extension. Then to crawl back to her menial office job in defeat. *No.* Erato had to keep her honest. "Please."

Erato handed her the phone before taking her by the shoulders to give her a firm squeeze. "I give you my word, Kate. I won't let you sabotage this book. I'll make sure you finish on time, no matter what."

Equally reassured and frightened by Erato's solemnity, Kate took a deep breath and unlocked her phone. An entire battalion of butterflies wreaked havoc within her stomach, alerting her to the sad fact that most of her second-guessing about going ahead with this date was probably directly linked to a fear of rejection. Or worse, silence.

"Either you text her or I will." When Kate reacted to the threat with obvious surprise, Erato rewarded her with a peal of delighted laughter. "You think you're unsure, but you're not. Believe me, you want this. You want *her*. Enough that not having her again will most definitely be a real problem for you. The ultimate distraction. Trust me." She wrapped an arm around Kate's shoulders and pecked her on the cheek. "If you're worried about the art, don't be. I won't allow Olive to throw you off course. I gave you my word, and I *never* break a promise."

Kate shivered at the slightly ominous undertone in Erato's sunny words. "I'm not worried."

"Good." Erato held out her hand and wiggled her fingers. "Now who's going to make this date, me or you?"

Shielding the phone from Erato, Kate felt a surge of protectiveness. She would not allow her muse to interfere with whatever was happening between her and Olive. Even if they were just fuck buddies, she liked the something very real between her and Olive and selfishly wanted to keep whatever it was all to herself. "I'll do it."

"Would you like some privacy?"

They had no secrets—and shouldn't have, if her art was the priority. Kate shook her head. "No, that's not necessary." She opened her phone's messaging app, fighting mild disappointment at the discovery that her conversation with Olive was in exactly the same state as four nights ago. Her final request: *Wait for me?* Olive's response: *Go! Write!* A quick scan of their back-and-forth reminded Kate of all the excitement of their chance meeting at the farmers' market, which led to memories of the mind-blowing sex they'd had. Suddenly, the eagerness Kate had felt days ago returned. *This is what I want. Erato even said so.*

Erato turned her head to study the office window and the massive redwood trees looming in the distance. "Go ahead. Get the ball rolling so you can wrap up those final eight hundred and fifty words and take a well-deserved break."

Now that her writer's block had been vanquished, it didn't take Kate long to craft a brief missive to Olive—one that sounded more confident than she felt and would hopefully lead to enough erotic inspiration to carry her through the rest of her novel.

Still waiting for me?

She got her answer in under a minute.

Yes, but please tell me the wait is over.

Kate grinned.

CHAPTER FOURTEEN

It was a lucky thing Olive happened to be free for dinner and an extended round of dessert the very next evening after Kate met her goal. Once they agreed that the festivities would begin at seven, and Kate hinted that Olive should bring an overnight bag, a very curious thing had happened. Kate decided to keep waiting. She didn't want to orgasm until Olive was there with her—if not to actually do the deed, then at least to hold her hand while Erato finally ended her suffering. Since her desire to be with Olive had driven her recent massive writing effort, it only seemed right to wait until they were together to enjoy the other part of her reward.

With a strength of will that had clearly surprised both of them, she'd urged Erato out of her office so she could finish the final words toward her goal, and then she'd continued to write for the rest of the day. By the time she finally stopped at eight o'clock that night, she'd had just enough energy to eat dinner and enjoy a sweet but platonic cuddling session with Erato before dropping off to sleep.

She woke early the next morning energized and so painfully horny it took every ounce of her dwindling willpower not to reach for Erato, who slept peacefully a scant distance away. Instead, Kate rolled onto her side and brought her knees up to her chest, sending her mind far away from thoughts of soft, feminine curves and the hot, wet suction Erato's perfectly shaped mouth could deliver. With massive effort, she forced herself to return to her mental theater so she could listen to Rose and Molly talk about why they really, seriously, truly needed to stop sleeping together.

She'd been living deep in her characters' world ever since Erato had shown up and forced her to finally spend time there, and at long last, it was becoming much easier to hear their voices and understand their motivations. Now she was fully invested in their lives—yearning for Rose to reconnect with a mother who'd never been comfortable with her bisexuality, desperate for both women to find their happily-ever-afters together following a string of bad relationships in their pasts— and she couldn't wait to bring their story to a satisfying conclusion. She still had a ways to go, but at least the end was in sight. And most importantly, *she cared.*

Aware that she had hours to kill before Olive arrived for dinner, Kate decided to get up and write some more. It was the perfect activity to keep her mind off sneaking in a quickie with Erato. Thankfully, she'd gotten past the raunchy scenes of the prior day and now had to tackle the more delicate work of mending Rose's relationship with her mother while giving Molly an integral, positive role in the proceedings. As an author, she had quite a challenge, but now it hardly felt like work. It never did, when she was in the zone.

After a long day of progress, she finally stopped writing a little over an hour before Olive was due to arrive. That allowed her just enough time to shower, shave, and throw on the pair of jeans that made her ass look sexy even to her own eyes, along with her favorite V-necked top that revealed a strategic amount of cleavage. When she finally made it to the kitchen only two minutes before Olive was due to arrive, she was stunned to find Erato putting the finishing touches on the most delectable Greek feast she'd ever seen. She'd barely registered that Erato was cooking, let alone pulling off a spread that outshone the finest gourmet restaurant. To top it off, Erato wore a stunning light-blue dress Kate had never seen before. The flowing material matched her eyes and made her look so ethereal Kate was almost nervous to speak to her, just as she'd been the first day they'd met. Never mind that they'd fucked multiple times in all manner of positions. Once again, her muse was the popular girl and she was the shy geek.

Erato turned and flashed her a smile of such luminous happiness that it effortlessly elicited a matching one from Kate. "Welcome back." When Kate cocked her head in question, she giggled. "To this world."

"Oh." She shrugged, then nodded. Indeed, after days hunched over her keyboard living and breathing her characters' lives, she hadn't yet shaken the odd, vaguely unpleasant sensation of being firmly back in her own skin. "Yes, thank you. I'm still adjusting."

"Not everyone has the opportunity to enjoy the mild dysphoria of being able to move between different worlds at will." Turning off the burner where a delicious-smelling lentil soup simmered, Erato gave her a wink and wandered out of the kitchen. "Too many people lose the ability to immerse themselves in non-physical worlds once they leave childhood. Relish that you can and do, even when it's not a hundred percent pleasant."

Kate followed Erato into the hallway. "I do." Truthfully, writing was often unpleasant. Publishing only added another layer of potential unpleasantness to the equation. If she didn't delight in the entire process on some fundamental, soul-deep level, she wouldn't bother. It would certainly leave her more time to date—or do hundreds of other things that would lead to a more active social life. No doubt more money, too. "I love writing. It makes me who I am, literally. That's why when I can't—" Her throat went dry as familiar anxiety enveloped her. When she couldn't write, she felt worthless. Empty.

Erato abruptly stopped not far from the front door. She pivoted on her heels and rushed over to wrap Kate in a warm hug, stroking her back in a soothing rhythm. "Don't go back to that dark place. Hear me? You're not there anymore. I pulled you out. Now you're a traveler just returned from a long journey, ready for the girl of your dreams to give you a proper homecoming."

In a stroke of perfect timing, the doorbell rang.

"And here she is." Erato released her from the embrace and gave her a quick once-over. "You look absolutely adorable, by the way. *I'd* fuck you." With a wink, she went to answer the door.

Kate couldn't help but grin at the compliment, as she was sure Erato intended. When Olive stepped into her apartment for the second time, looking even more stunning in real life than she had in Kate's runaway imagination, she moved forward to greet her with renewed confidence. "Hey, Olive."

"Hey, yourself." Having given Erato a passing, mildly appraising glance, Olive took quite a bit longer to drag her eyes away from Kate's chest. "Congratulations on hitting your word count."

"And then some," Erato said lightly. She closed the door and stepped behind Olive to help remove her tailored jacket. "The prospect of inviting you over for another playdate inspired our sweet Kate to log nearly eighteen thousand words in one *week*."

Olive's eyebrows popped. "Even though I'll admit I'm not sure what a typical week's output might be, I'm impressed. At this rate, you should finish in no time, right?"

Kate struggled not to dash over to the banister so she could knock on wood. "I really hope so."

"She will." Erato gave her a meaningful look as she hung Olive's jacket in the closet. "As long as she stays focused."

Kate murmured her agreement, trying not to laugh as she recognized the irony in the fact that she was only half listening because she couldn't stop staring at Olive's choice of outfit. She wore a striking white dress like a second skin. The neckline plunged to a point just above where Kate thought she remembered the scar on her chest began, framing modestly covered and exquisitely proportioned breasts. Kate was transfixed by everything on display—Olive's narrow shoulders, the kissable expanse of her neck, her kind, flawless face.

Erato's voice snapped her out of her trance. "You'll have to forgive her. She hasn't had an orgasm since before we saw you at the farmers' market last weekend, and I'm afraid it's beginning to erode her social skills."

Olive seemed amused at the mortified look Kate could feel crawling across her face. "Honestly?" She closed the distance between them, hesitating momentarily before trailing a finger over Kate's clavicle. The light contact sent a pleasant shiver straight to Kate's clit. "Five days without getting off is enough to completely unhinge you?"

Kate parted her lips to reply but didn't trust herself to speak intelligibly with Olive still touching her.

Luckily, Erato swooped in for the rescue. "To be fair, I did tease her quite badly before imposing the no-orgasm rule. And then again a few times after that." She didn't attempt to conceal her delight. "Please understand, she's been thinking about touching you almost nonstop for the past week. Despite the fact that I gave her a chance to end this madness last night, she chose to wait for you." Erato came closer, kissing Kate on the cheek. "So I'm sure you can appreciate how she's feeling right now."

Thoroughly embarrassed, Kate found her voice only to shut up

Erato. "I'm fine." She scowled when Erato and Olive snickered together like a pair of obnoxious BFFs. "Whatever."

Erato squeezed her arm and moved past her to return to the kitchen. "I'll grab some treats I prepared. I figured we'd be casual about it and just lay out a few dishes that we can nibble on while we chat and get reacquainted."

Silently, Kate wondered how long they would actually keep up the pretense of having a polite evening meal together. Even though her stomach had been growling mere minutes ago, her appetite for food had all but vanished at the first sight of their guest. She gave Olive a sheepish smile. "Hi. Again."

Olive laughed. "Hi." She gestured at the door through which Erato had disappeared. "She really is a force of nature, isn't she?"

"Yeah." She held out her hand, delighted when Olive laced their fingers together. "Want to go sit?"

"Sure," Olive said, but when Kate started toward the couch, Olive swung them around and pressed Kate up against the wall. She pushed their lower bodies together, wrenching an embarrassingly loud groan from deep in Kate's throat. Clearly pleased by the effect she was having, Olive managed to look both seductive and bashful. "You really waited for *me*?"

"Of course," Kate replied automatically. She tilted her hips, seeking out friction against Olive's warmth.

"With *Erato* at your beck and call?"

Kate shrugged, hoping to seem nonchalant. "You're the one who's been inspiring me all week. It only seemed…fitting, I guess."

Chewing on her lower lip like she wasn't sure *what* to think, Olive looked so sexy Kate felt a sharp, throbbing twinge between her legs. Only the desire to stay cool kept her from humping Olive's thigh like a hormonal dog. Seemingly aware of how badly Kate was struggling, Olive offered a sympathetic smile before indulging in a deep, passionate kiss that nearly made her orgasm. She tasted vaguely of mouthwash, and her tongue danced expertly with Kate's as though they'd been kissing each other for years. Kate groaned and clutched at her back, delighted to touch so much exposed skin.

"Do you want to wait until after we eat?" Olive whispered roughly, breath hot against her ear.

It took Kate a few seconds to realize she wasn't certain what Olive was asking. That kiss had short-circuited her brain. "Huh?"

A warm puff of air blew against her neck, evidence of Olive's amusement at her lust-induced brain death. "To relax, Kate. Do you want to wait, or should I put my hand down the front of those sexy-ass jeans and get you off right now?"

She forced herself not to glance toward the kitchen, nor to wonder what Erato would want her to do. Already it seemed odd to have what felt a lot like a second date with Olive with her muse in attendance. She didn't want to give the impression that she honestly allowed Erato to make rules for her life or punish her for disobedience. That would be… too weird. Right? That sort of strange and twisted dynamic could easily chase a nice girl like Olive away. And right now, especially, the *last* place she wanted Olive to be was away.

Kate nodded almost frantically. "Now, please." In her head, she added, *Before Erato comes back!*

For all her talk of not wanting to lose focus on her art, it was amazing how quickly and thoroughly her entire existence had been reduced to the simple, fierce desire to be with Olive—just the two of them, together. Swallowing her worries about being interrupted, Kate tipped her head back and exhaled through her nose as Olive skillfully unbuttoned and unzipped her jeans with one hand. She prepared for what promised to be a searing first touch by thinking about baseball, and strawberry-rhubarb muffins, and how exactly she was going to write the pivotal upcoming scene where Rose's mother catches her with Molly. Whatever it took to prevent herself from coming too quickly. She'd waited far too long—and fantasized far too explicitly—for this encounter to end with a single stroke of Olive's clever fingers.

"Kate."

It dawned on her that Olive's hand had come to rest over the waistband of her panties, frustratingly far from where she was supposed to be. Confused by the lack of urgency, Kate sought out her eyes and pleaded without words. "Yeah?"

"Look at me while I'm touching you."

The command sent a shiver through Kate's whole body. This was a more confident version of Olive than she'd realized existed. Clearly, being the object of someone's unapologetic desire had infused her with a new sense of power, and Kate had to admit—she wielded it very well. Nodding, Kate murmured, "All right."

Without allowing her gaze to waver, Olive slipped her hand down the front of Kate's panties, deftly parted her already-slick labia, and rubbed gentle but firm circles around her swollen, sensitized clit. The caress sent ripple after ripple of ever-escalating pleasure through Kate's tense body, immediately sapping the strength from her legs so that she sagged perilously against the wall. Olive kept her upright with surprising ease, insistently holding their eye contact. She wore a sexy smirk as Kate's breathing devolved into gasps and moans.

"There. *Those* are the sexy little noises that have been keeping me awake every night this week." Olive snaked a finger down to tease Kate's opening, barely venturing inside. "The memory of them, and of how you *felt*...and tasted..." Blinking slowly as though emerging from a trance, she grinned and returned her attentions to Kate's clit. "But I have all night to reminisce, right? There's no need to draw *this* out any longer." She gave Kate a firm stroke to emphasize her meaning.

Afraid that they were mere seconds away from having Erato burst in and ruin the moment, Kate nodded in feverish agreement. "*Please.*" She whimpered as the circles over her clit increased in speed, bringing her to the very edge without sending her over. Through it all, she maintained eye contact, enjoying the feeling of connection. "Please, so I can *breathe.*"

Olive chuckled, her face softening in sympathy. "I'll take care of you, baby. Don't you worry." She curled her fingers, which made Kate feel like she was being touched everywhere at once. With a knowing grin, Olive kissed the tip of her nose. "Let go and come for me. *Just* for me."

The knowledge that Olive wanted them to share this moment alone as much as she did nudged her over the edge. But instead of the explosive orgasm she'd expected—generated by the inherent violence of a week of celibacy broken—Olive's hand coaxed from her the sweetest, most delicious symphony of pleasure her body had ever orchestrated. Toe-curling sensation rolled over her in gentle chords, building to a dizzying crescendo that seemed to last forever. She tried to keep staring into Olive's eyes as she rode out her climax, but it was too much. Something had to give, and vision was her only choice.

The instant her eyes closed, Olive's mouth covered hers in a deeply felt kiss. Kate grabbed her shoulders and tried pulling her closer, though they were already sharing the same space. Refusing to yield her position, Olive kept her fingers pressed atop Kate's clit, subtly pulsing them in time with the contractions of her inner muscles. Kate wasn't exactly sure how Olive managed to so precisely read and respond to her body, but the result was pure delight. She moaned into Olive's hot mouth, turned on by all the dirty thoughts running through her head, the various ways she planned to repay Olive for the gift she'd just been given.

Olive ended their kiss as soon as her climax subsided. "You are *so* sexy." She wore a cocky grin like a badge of honor, clearly proud of her feat. As well she should be.

Kate curled her hand around the back of Olive's neck and pulled her into another kiss. "*You.*"

In a stroke of timing that made Kate suspect she'd been waiting for the right moment, Erato came out of the kitchen carrying a tray full of food. She wore a cheery smile reminiscent of the stereotypical middle-American 1950s sitcom wife. Kate had no way to gauge its sincerity. "Kate, will you take this for me? I have another tray in the kitchen to bring out." She stood patiently as Olive backed away from Kate and straightened her dress with an embarrassed cough.

Kate zipped up her jeans with as much nonchalance as she could manage, then took the tray with a ridiculous little bow. "Of course."

"Olive, why don't you go ahead and wash your hands before we eat? The restroom is to your right." Erato winked, then looked at Kate as though gazing upon a beloved child. "Thank you for taking care of Kate's little problem. We appreciate it."

It's just casual sex, Kate reminded herself. *I nearly talked myself out of inviting Olive over just yesterday.* All true, but that didn't make her any less annoyed with Erato's possessive, condescending tone. Especially when she saw the subtle shift in Olive's expression that hinted at mild discomfort, even embarrassment. Kate glared at Erato, silently warning her that she'd just crossed a line. To her credit, Erato appeared to receive the unspoken message. After a wordless battle that lasted only a couple of seconds, Erato's expression softened and she exhaled.

"Rather, *I* appreciate it. I'm not exaggerating when I say that the fire you've lit in Kate has provided her with a lot of motivation, which is something she had in short supply before I took her on as a client." Erato regarded her with the fondness of a mentor who sees genuine promise in a favorite student, her gaze so earnest it set Kate's heart alight with deep respect and love while effortlessly sweeping away any lingering frustration. "These past few weeks have revived her as an author, and it would be dishonest not to acknowledge your role in that, Olive. You are truly an erotic inspiration. A veritable *muse,* if you will." She waited a beat, clearly enjoying her brief foray into humor, then waved Kate toward the living room. "Now go, set out the food. I'll be right back with the rest."

Blushing, Kate waited until Erato had once again disappeared into the kitchen to speak. "I'm so sorry, she—"

Olive cut her off with an amused snort. "Don't be. I'm not saying I necessarily want her to tag along on a *third* date, if it comes to that, but I like Erato. I especially like hearing about how much I *inspire* you." She brought the hand she'd used to touch Kate to her nose, inhaling with a quiet hum of approval. "You've inspired me, too, Kate. Not to write, obviously, but to read. All of your novels, I think, except the sci-fi one. I plan to start that one this weekend. The one about the call girl, though? I've read that twice."

As she always did when someone she knew in real life brought up her writing, Kate blushed. "Oh."

Olive's mouth curved into a sexy little grin. "Your stories, Kate…" She chewed her lower lip. Her nostrils flared—and Kate couldn't help but wonder which scene she was remembering. "Well, they inspired me to touch myself. More than a few times."

"So while I've spent the last week sexless and chained to my laptop, you've been reading my books and making yourself come over and over?" Kate wished she wasn't standing with a tray in her hands. Hearing that her words had gotten Olive off was a powerful aphrodisiac, one that made her want to eschew the idea of food and conversation altogether.

"I've lost track of how many times you've helped bring me to orgasm this week." Olive sashayed past her to the bathroom, then stopped at the door to pin her with a sultry smile. "The last one was only a few hours ago, before I showered to come over here. I didn't even need a book. I just lay on my bed, on my hand, and imagined you were there behind me. Took me just five minutes to call out your name." She paused, eyes sparkling. "Luckily? That won't make next time any less sweet."

The mental image of Olive lying on her stomach while masturbating to fantasies in which she played a starring role would likely sustain Kate sexually for the rest of her life. She didn't even try to hide how Olive's speech affected her. "I want you. Desperately, and as soon as possible."

"Then go put the food down." Olive stepped partway into the bathroom. "And I'll wash my hands."

Erato burst out of the kitchen with an exasperated sigh. The tray in her hands overflowed with just as many delectable goodies as the one Kate still carried, along with three glasses of wine. Lifting one shoulder in a defeated half shrug, Erato said, "Given how difficult you're both finding the task of stepping away from each other, it seems that I've grossly overestimated everyone's appetite for food and conversation. For that, I sincerely apologize." She waited a beat, then stuck out her lower lip in an exaggerated, undeniably sexy pout. "But will you two at least *try* my spanakopita first?"

❖

As it turned out, they ended up trying more than just the spanakopita. Out of respect for the time and effort Erato had devoted toward creating a romantic atmosphere for their second date, Kate once again ignored her libido to focus on the task ahead. Happily, eating Erato's delicious food while getting to know Olive better didn't present a real hardship. And actually, she decided as she finished her first glass of wine, taking the time to play out a real, respectable evening would only make the sex they had later even better. That was because everything Olive said only endeared her to Kate more.

"You'd earned an MBA from Stanford by the time you were twenty-two years old?" Kate repeated, stunned by the new layer her dream girl had just revealed. Nothing Olive had shared before now had hinted at a prodigious childhood, nor a background in business. It was startling to realize how little she actually knew about the woman who'd so easily captured her imagination. "Did you always plan to start your own bakery, or did you have another dream first?"

Olive took a slow sip of wine, perhaps mentally rehearsing her answer. Though only one sofa cushion separated them, Olive might as well have been in the next town over, for as far away as she seemed. Kate itched to touch her but stayed on her side of the couch, determined to sit back and enjoy the slow burn of their rising sexual tension. Erato had curled up on the love seat across from them, nibbling on a bite of pita with tzatziki while listening. While she'd contributed to the conversation a few times since they sat down, she seemed content to watch them talk.

Lowering her glass of wine, Olive revealed eyes that seemed almost haunted. "Actually, I used to be a high-level executive at a Fortune 500 company on the East Coast. They hired me right out of grad school and I spent the next six years climbing the ladder there." She snorted and shook her head. "In fact, that was my life—climbing the ladder. I'm not exaggerating when I say that I lived to work. So did my girlfriend at the time. We shared the same priorities, which at least meant neither of us pretended that our relationship was one of them. Nothing was, not even our families."

When Olive stopped talking to take another, nervous sip of wine, Kate realized her frown could be interpreted as disapproval. Softening her features, she said, "I'm sorry. It's just difficult to reconcile the Olive I know with the woman you're describing. You've clearly changed."

Olive set her glass of wine down on the coffee table and took a deep breath. "I had a pretty major wake-up call." Her hand fluttered to her chest, where she traced the expertly concealed scar with a trembling finger. "It's funny, but a near-death experience really does rearrange your priorities just like *that*."

Kate found it difficult not to react to the idea that Olive had almost left this world before they'd had a chance to meet. Her eyes burned with unshed tears that blurred her vision and made her feel pretty damn silly. Who cried over someone else's tragic backstory on a second date, for God's sake? *Not me,* she chanted to herself, a silent mantra. *Not me, not me, not me.* "I'm glad you're okay."

Olive nodded without meeting her gaze. She reached across the middle cushion and rested her hand on Kate's sock-clad foot, a point of connection that seemed to comfort them both. "A few years back, I realized I hadn't flown home to California to visit my parents in over three years. It took some begging and pleading, but I finally convinced Jasmine to take a weekend off with me so I could introduce her to them. We flew in late Friday night and planned to leave Sunday morning. After three years away, that was all of my precious time I was willing to spare. But I told myself they were proud of me and that they understood—"

Recognizing that Olive was falling victim to a nasty bout of self-criticism—clearly not for the first time—Kate wiggled her foot from side to side to jar her from that destructive line of thought. "Hey. You're a different person now," she said. "Obviously."

Olive shook her head, then covered her face with her free hand to muffle humorless laughter. "You guys, I'm going to bring our whole evening down with this tragic-ass shit."

"No, you won't." Erato spoke up forcefully in between sips from a cup of lentil soup. Despite continuing to feast, she came across as sober and deeply serious. "You're telling your story. Go ahead and get through the sad part. I promise our evening will recover." She offered Olive an encouraging smile. "Now go on and finish."

Olive stared across the coffee table at Erato—or more to the point, *away* from Kate—as she resumed her story. "We decided to spend Saturday driving around and visiting wineries. Jasmine insisted that we stay busy even though I would have been just as happy to sit at my parents' home and visit." She paused, then shook her head as though getting herself back on track. "Anyway, my mom and dad were in the backseat of our rental car and Jasmine was driving. I was sitting in the passenger seat, looking over my shoulder chatting to my parents between stops. At some point Jasmine got distracted by an incoming text on her cell phone, I guess, and she let the car drift over the center line…" A violent shudder overtook Olive, an ugly jolt of memory. "It was a head-on collision at roughly forty miles per hour. It's a miracle I'm alive. My father, too. Jasmine and my mother were both killed on impact."

Kate's hand flew to her mouth before she could stop herself. Worried that Olive would mistake her abject horror at the close call for judgment over the events of that day, she quickly put down her own glass of wine and scooted to the other side of the sofa. With a sense of reverence that arose from somewhere primal and deep inside her, she picked up Olive's cool, limp hand and brought it to her lips, pressing kiss after kiss into the palm. "I'm sorry," she murmured, and said again, "I'm *so* glad you're okay."

Olive brought her free hand to Kate's face, using her knuckles to stroke along her cheekbone. "Me, too." She managed to look into Kate's eyes for the first time since relating the story of her accident, and her face slackened in naked relief at whatever she saw there. "My father was in a wheelchair and had to do physical therapy for fourteen months before he was strong enough to get around on his cane. I had a spinal injury and over thirty broken bones. On top of that, I sustained a blunt-force injury to my heart. The scar is from the repair. I was in traction and then in a wheelchair of my own for almost a year."

Erato asked the question that Kate was too stunned to put into words. "How long ago *was* this?"

Olive smiled shyly, still staring into Kate's eyes. "Four years ago tomorrow."

"A miraculous recovery, indeed." Erato had assumed a decadent pose on the love seat, legs tucked beneath her, dress ridden up to reveal her tanned upper thighs. Kate barely noticed, unwilling to take in more than a peripheral glance lest she break the intimacy of the moment she and Olive seemed to be sharing. "It's little wonder you took the entire ordeal as a warning to reboot your life."

Kate raised an eyebrow, surprised and even a little delighted by Erato's astute and very modern word choice. She swept her eyes over Olive's body with a renewed appreciation for what she was seeing. "I would never have guessed that you'd gone through something like that."

Olive rewarded her with a genuinely sunny grin. "You have no idea how happy it makes me to hear that." With a tired exhalation, she rushed through the end of the story, clearly ready to conclude her tale. "I quit my job as soon as I was coherent enough to be sure that it was me and not a head injury that wanted to resign. I couldn't imagine I would want to leave my father even after I was physically capable of doing so, and with Jasmine gone, there was nothing else for me in New York. So I stayed here. The benefit to toiling away in your twenties as an overpaid workaholic is having greater freedom in how you spend time in your thirties."

She clapped her hands together as though announcing the

upcoming conclusion. "My father opened a bakery—his lifelong dream—when I was a child, but he struggled to keep the business afloat and it ultimately failed when I was away at college. We started baking together when we were both in rehabilitation, to combat the boredom. That's when we decided that I would help him reopen the business once we were healthy enough to make it successful. That became our motivation to heal." She paused, then sat back against the arm of the couch with a bittersweet smile. "It worked beautifully."

"To say the least." Kate squeezed Olive's hand. "And you're happier now?"

"Much." Olive's voice caught, but she waved a hand in the air and laughed off her rising emotion. "I mean, I'm single and motherless, but at least my life seems to have attained some deeper meaning."

"And you have a bucket list that's shrinking every day."

Olive chuckled. "Since I met you two, at least." She shot Erato a friendly smile before returning her attention to Kate. "Anyway, that's enough about me. Tell me something about you that I haven't already learned from your back-cover blurb."

Kate shrugged, never pleased to be the center of attention. "There's not much to tell. I'm the oldest of three, and my younger siblings are twins. My brother is a programmer at some start-up in Palo Alto, and my sister moved to London with her husband the banker last year. It sounds like she's carving out a career as a professional socialite, which is good, since her only real skill seems to be marrying up."

"And your parents?"

"They're retired and spend most of their time traveling. We get along well and visit each other when we can." She shrugged again. "Like I said, not much to tell."

"How do they feel about their little girl writing dirty lesbian-sex stories?"

Kate blushed. "I haven't really delved into that subject with them. Too awkward."

Olive laughed. "I'm sure they're proud of you."

"Well, I hope so."

"Have they read any of your books?"

Cringing, Kate tried not to think too hard about the potential answer to that question. "I asked them not to tell me if they ever did."

Olive snorted in amusement, which made Kate smile despite the fact that she was the punch line. "Fair enough." Turning her attention toward Erato, Olive asked, "How about you? I'll bet you had an interesting upbringing."

Kate barely had time to panic about the possibility of Erato being overly candid before she answered. "I'll say. But you don't want to hear about my family—even if they have been the source of enough drama and tragedy and comedy to inspire multiple tales." Erato shot Kate a conspiratorial little smile. If she was trying to be subtle about the fact that she thought she was being clever, she was failing. "Epic ones."

Olive smiled along with Erato. If she was at all perplexed about the response, she didn't show it. "Well, whoever taught you to cook did something right. The food is wonderful."

"Hestia, yes. She was a tremendous mentor in the kitchen." Erato's gaze went far away for a moment before she snapped back into the present. "Anyway, thank you. I'm so glad you're enjoying the food." Her expression turned wicked. "Even if it *is* keeping you from dessert."

Even a subtle allusion to sex was enough to bring Kate's clit to immediate attention. A quiet groan escaped her as she shifted on the cushion, positioning herself so the seam of her jeans pulled tight against her arousal. Instead of sating her overactive sexual appetite, Olive's little hand-job had achieved the opposite effect. Even after all the talk of grave injuries and catastrophic losses and guilt, she burned to reciprocate the sweet pleasure Olive had given her. And if the way Olive gazed at her now—all hooded eyelids and flushed cheeks—was any indication, the desire was very much mutual.

"Kate, since tonight is your reward for a job well done..." Erato waited until Kate dragged her attention away from Olive to finish her thought. She gave Kate an indulgent wink. "Go ahead and have your dessert."

Kate knew immediately what Erato was suggesting, and where she once might have felt shy, tonight she didn't even hesitate. Turning to face Olive, she carefully placed her hands at the hemline of her dress, over her knees. "May I?"

Olive blinked rapidly, her gaze fluttering back and forth between Erato and Kate for a second longer than Kate expected. Briefly alarmed that she was having second thoughts about another threesome, Kate squeezed Olive's knee and craned to look into her face. She didn't want to pressure Olive into something she didn't want. That would ruin everything.

It took obvious effort for Olive to meet her eyes, but her consent was clear even before she spoke. "You may. I *am* your reward, after all." She bit her lower lip, shy and sexy and, as Kate well remembered, even more delectable than Erato's best dish.

Kate leaned forward to kiss the piece of lip Olive had been worrying with her teeth. "Thank you," she whispered. "And please don't be shy about making sure you get exactly what you want from me." She flicked the center of Olive's upper lip with the tip of her tongue. "Deal?"

Olive nodded, already winding her hand into Kate's hair. Guiding her toward her lap, she murmured, "On that note, get your ass down there and take care of the mess you created earlier in the foyer."

Kate dropped to her knees on the floor in front of Olive. She'd barely registered the pain from kneeling on the laminate flooring when a pillow landed next to her, tossed by Erato. Startled, Kate looked up to find her muse contentedly sipping her glass of wine. Gesturing at the soft projectile, Erato said, "Be comfortable. I know you'll want to take your time."

It was true. With a murmur of thanks, Kate arranged the pillow under her knees. *Much* better. Prepared to go down for hours if that's what it took, Kate stared into Olive's eyes as she very deliberately pushed the hem of her dress up over her hips. Her desire to tease Olive outweighed the need for instant gratification, so rather than taking a long look at her prize, Kate instead held their shared gaze with an expression of feigned calm.

Olive, on the other hand, was the opposite of placid. Her chest rose and fell rapidly. She rolled her hips beneath Kate's palms, triggering an instinctive desire to grab hold of her tightly and keep her still. Gasping, Olive loosened her grip on Kate's hair as though acknowledging that she wasn't exactly in the position of power. "Don't you want to see what you've done to me?"

"Of course I do." Kate waited a full ten seconds before finally lowering her eyes. Delighted by the sight of silky red panties soaked with incredible wetness, she took a moment to savor the undeniable evidence of their electric chemistry. Olive's inner thighs glistened with it, and the sweet fragrance nearly sent Kate diving in. Drawing on the last of her self-control, Kate traced a slippery path to the edge of Olive's panties with her fingertip. She was getting off on the game they were playing too much to end it before Olive forced her to. "You want me to lick all this wetness up?"

With a rough nod, Olive pulled her hair almost hard enough to hurt. "I want you to eat my fucking pussy until I come all over your pretty face."

Kate raised her eyebrows. "Damn, girl. *That* escalated quickly."

Olive's aggressive demeanor melted away in an instant. "I'm so sorry, I thought—"

"Don't apologize," Kate murmured, then bent to kiss the side of Olive's knee. "I like it." She kissed the other knee. "And you *do* know my safe word."

"Apple?" A hint of steel crept back into Olive's voice. The fingers that had eased their grip tightened again.

"That's the one." She reached under Olive's skirt and grasped the waistband of her panties. "Lift up?"

Olive raised her hips to allow her to slide the panties off. Kate balled them up and threw them in Erato's general direction, which elicited a giggle and a murmured "Thanks" from their audience. Sensing Olive's comfort level dropping slightly with the reminder of Erato's presence, Kate pushed her knees apart and placed her hand over Olive's hot, noticeably throbbing sex. She flashed a grin, relieved when Olive returned it with apparent ease.

"Look at me while I'm tasting you," Kate said, deliberately echoing Olive's earlier words. She massaged the supple flesh beneath her fingers, delighted by how effortlessly she was able to trigger a blissful little moan. "Watch how much I love sucking on your pussy." Scooting backward on her knees so she could lower her head, Kate kissed one inner thigh, then the other. Licking her lips to sample Olive's flavor, she looked up into expectant brown eyes. "Will you do that for me?"

Olive dragged Kate forward by the hair, practically shoving her where she wanted her. Kate giggled until the second her face pressed into the succulent, juicy bounty she'd been dreaming about all week. Her amusement fled when she realized she was exactly where she wanted to be, doing exactly what she wanted to do. No longer capable of teasing, she explored Olive with her hands and mouth simultaneously—sucking lightly on her labia, rubbing one finger around her opening, batting at her erect clit with her thumb. She was every bit as tasty as she'd been the first time. More, even, now that Kate knew her better.

Loosening her grip, Olive nevertheless continued to hold her in place with a hand on top of her head. "Oh, fuck," she moaned, then, "Right *there.* Yes, and now—" Her back arched as Kate instinctively changed the rhythm of her tongue, painting quick, light circles around Olive's fat clit. The fingers in her hair pulled, nearly bringing tears to Kate's eyes and triggering an answering pulse of sensation between her legs. "Fuck, that's so *fucking* nice."

Thrilled by the praise, Kate stayed the course. When it seemed that Olive might be approaching the edge, she backed off just enough to allow her to recover. She was only slightly surprised when her actions didn't elicit a complaint but rather earned her a few grateful, trembling strokes of her hair. As she'd sensed, Olive didn't want this reunion to end any faster than she did. Lifting her head slightly, Kate smiled at the immediate groan of disappointment. She gazed up into dark, frustrated eyes with a playful smirk.

"Just wanted to check to make sure you were still looking." Kate kissed the inside of Olive's knee, as eager to get back to work as she knew Olive must be. Maybe even more. She moved to the other leg, pressing her lips to a spot higher on her inner thigh. A quick glance confirmed that Olive was staring at her with rapt, unwavering attention. Using her thumbs to gently spread her labia apart, Kate bent and covered Olive's clit with her lips, moving her head up and down as she sucked. She focused on creating a great visual that would enhance the pleasure she knew she was delivering, painfully aroused by the knowledge that more than one pair of eyes was watching.

Olive tightened her hand into a fist atop Kate's head, holding on to her hair as she pumped her hips against her face. "You want me to fuck your mouth, baby? I'll fuck your mouth. I'll even come inside it."

Vaguely, Kate mused that publishing one's sexual proclivities and turn-ons for the world—or at least for a potential lover—to read had benefits. The dialogue might as well have been lifted from one of her books, although she'd never written those exact words. She could have, for they swiftly and powerfully aroused her. Surrendering to the surge of dominance, she relaxed and allowed Olive to use her face and mouth as she desired. Eyes closed, she savored the hot, slippery folds Olive ground against her mouth and chin and cheeks and nose, licking and sucking on instinct and in response to Olive's specific, breathless commands.

This time when Olive neared her climax, she didn't give Kate the choice to draw things out. On the contrary, she rubbed herself against Kate's mouth with renewed vigor, begging for more tongue and harder suction in a voice made hoarse from so much unrestrained moaning. Even if she'd felt shy in Erato's company before, she'd clearly managed to shed her inhibitions now. Olive's raw enthusiasm—in tandem with the unrelenting grip on her hair—drove Kate to redouble her efforts. She chased Olive's impressively swollen clit with the flat of her tongue, then captured the rigid shaft between her lips and sucked hard. The reaction was explosive. Olive cursed loudly, grabbed Kate's head with both hands, and rode her face while hot, liquid satisfaction poured from her along with a stream of obscenities.

When the grip on her hair finally loosened, sometime around the twelfth "fuck" muttered from above, Kate sat back on her heels and beamed up at Olive. Once composed and elegant, now she was a well-fucked mess—dress askew, her pussy swollen and covered in come, the leather sofa below her bare ass stained with the same juices that continued to trickle out of her opening. Kate took a mental snapshot of the image for the next time she spent a lonely night with her hand. The expression of dazed contentment on Olive's face was the icing on the cake.

"That was worth the wait." Kate squeezed Olive's knee and pulled her skirt down to cover her nakedness. Then she crawled back onto the couch next to her, giving Olive a brief but heartfelt kiss on the mouth. "Did you like that?"

Olive wrapped her up in a hug that Kate desperately hoped was intended to be as intimate as it felt. "Couldn't you tell?"

Chuckling, Kate kissed Olive's neck. "I still enjoy hearing it."

"All right, well then, I *loved* it."

"So did I." Erato spoke up quietly, clearly aware that she was inserting herself into a moment they were trying to keep exclusive. Surprised by her uncharacteristic passivity, Kate glanced over to find her muse watching them thoughtfully. She had set aside her food and drink at some point during their encounter, and from the position of her own dress as well as the deep flush on her cheeks, Kate assumed she'd indulged in a little self-pleasuring along with her voyeurism. "You two are undeniably sexually compatible—and delicious to observe."

Ashamed that they'd so thoroughly left Erato out, Kate extended her hand. "Why don't you come over here and let me take care of you, too?" She tried to ignore the strange twinge of guilt she felt about touching another woman in front of Olive.

This is a threesome, for fuck's sake. Casual *sex. Fucking each other is why we're all here.* Even as she reminded herself of the supposed reality of the situation, she studied Olive's face.

To her enormous relief, Olive beckoned Erato over with an easy grin. "We'll both take care of you." She laced her fingers in Kate's, a gesture that felt entirely nonsexual yet enormously exciting. "Since this is Kate's reward, I'll even give her the first choice of holes."

Kate shivered at Olive's expertly delivered dirty talk. She had definitely gotten bolder since their first encounter. "I appreciate that, and I already know which one I want."

Erato batted her eyelashes at them, apparently enjoying the attention. "How do you want me?"

"Naked and across our laps," Olive responded immediately.

That was the moment Kate realized she was falling in love.

CHAPTER FIFTEEN

Somehow, with Olive, even the act of making love to another woman together felt intensely intimate. Once Erato had stripped off her dress—slowly, per their instructions—and assumed a facedown position over their thighs, Kate turned and captured Olive's mouth in a heated kiss. Not wanting to neglect the woman on their laps, she lowered her hand to rest on Erato's perfect ass, stroking the crevice between her cheeks with the tip of her middle finger. Erato wiggled her hips in anticipation but stayed quiet except for her audible, measured breathing. Because Erato's pelvis was positioned directly over her lap, Kate was very aware of Olive's hand as it snaked its way between them. She whimpered as Olive began to fondle Erato, causing her hard knuckles to brush against the seam of Kate's jeans.

Kate broke their kiss with a sigh of regret, all too aware that she could easily stay there with Olive all night. Turning her attention back to Erato, she moved her middle finger lower until she found wetness. A *lot* of it. Erato whimpered and spread her legs wider, pressing herself into Olive's busy hand while Kate gathered up the copious natural lubrication her muse never seemed to have trouble producing. Little shivers rolled through Erato's body with every one of their combined strokes, which made her plump bottom jiggle so enticingly it was difficult not to plunge right in.

Ever mindful of her manners, Kate circled the opening of Erato's vagina, gathering wetness. "Do you want me in here?" Then she trailed her finger up to massage her preferred hole. "Or here?"

Erato lifted her hips, chasing Kate's finger with her slick, eager anus. "Your decision."

Emboldened by the power she was being granted, Kate drew back and cupped a cheek in each hand, spreading them to expose Erato's ridiculously photogenic, hairless pink asshole. She glanced over to make sure she had Olive's attention before teasing the puckered opening with the pad of her finger. Olive half smirked, shot Kate an upraised eyebrow, and increased the motion of the hand that was trapped between her and Erato. Kate exhaled quietly through her nose at the increased friction against her own clit, while Erato's reaction to the new rhythm was much less subtle. Her arms shot up and she grabbed the side of the couch, using the newfound leverage to roll her hips against Olive's hand while still eagerly backing into Kate's questing finger.

"*Fuck me.*"

Kate blinked at the gravelly, demanding quality of Erato's voice.

"Damn, girl," Olive said, taking the words out of Kate's mouth. "Can we get a 'please'?"

Erato squirmed around for a moment, trying to force herself onto their hands. Catching Olive's eye, Kate smiled playfully as she backed off just enough to prevent Erato from achieving even a hint of penetration. "Manners," she scolded her in a singsong voice. In a stroke of pure inspiration, she followed up the reprimand with a firm smack on Erato's right cheek. Then the left.

Oh, that was *fun.*

"More revenge?" The huskiness of the question seemed to belie any resentment on Erato's part. "Is that what that is, Kate?"

"Maybe." At Olive's quizzical look, Kate mumbled, "When she caught me texting you, there was a punishment…"

"One that was ultimately pleasurable, I hope." Olive wore a smile as she spoke, but Kate read something else in her eyes. Concern? Maybe confusion. She assumed Olive was still trying to puzzle out the nature of their particular editor/author relationship—whether out of curiosity or because she was trying to determine if Kate was free for a girlfriend, she didn't know. She both hoped and feared it was the latter. Either way, she sensed that Olive was beginning to wonder how much control Erato exerted over her life. It was a fair question—one she'd asked herself more than once.

Aware of her audience, Kate chose her words carefully. "Ultimately, yes. More importantly, it helped me get a hell of a lot written."

Olive smiled. "I'm glad to hear that." The hand stroking Erato, having slowed considerably, picked up speed. "Please try not to punish her too harshly, Erato. Unless she asks you to."

Despite Olive then doing something to make Erato moan loudly, Kate recognized the brief moment of tension between them. Erato looked over her shoulder and met Olive's eyes, deadly serious. "I'm here at Kate's pleasure. I work for *her*." Resuming her former prone position, she murmured indignantly, "She asked me to help her meet this deadline, and so far, my methods are working."

"That's *very* true," Kate said. Although she understood why Olive was concerned, she had to give credit where it was due. "I've never been so prolific in my life. However unconventional her methods may be, Erato definitely knows what she's doing."

She remembered her moment of doubt about even making this date with Olive and the way Erato had encouraged her to follow through. Then the promise she'd extracted from Erato to keep her on track no matter what and not to let Olive become a distraction. Frustrated by how complicated everything suddenly seemed—and at a time when she wanted to focus on nothing but the two alluring, sexually available women right in front of her—Kate shook her head. "Ladies, as much as I love talking about my writing process, right now I'd much rather get back to what we were doing."

Nodding, Olive stared into Kate's eyes as she spoke. "I apologize, Erato, if it sounded like I was questioning your methods. I wasn't. I was just…" She quirked a wry smile. "Feeling protective of Kate's very sexy, very fuckable ass."

"Well, I can't blame you for that." Erato's light tone made it clear she wasn't holding any grudges. When she glanced over her shoulder at Olive this time, she wore a seductive little pout. "Now will you *please* put your finger inside me?"

Visibly relaxing, Olive grinned. "I can do that." Her hand shifted against Kate's crotch, and seconds later Erato let out a familiar gasp. "Better?"

Erato braced her palms on the arm of the couch and arched back with a luxurious groan. "Mmm, *yes*."

Kate craned her neck for a closer look. The sight of two fingers disappearing inside Erato's dark-pink opening, again and again, pulled a strangled whimper from her throat. Once more spreading Erato open with both hands, she savored the opportunity to watch Olive's masterful technique and tried to recall exactly how it had felt to be wrapped around those long, slim digits. Heavenly was the best word she could muster. It had been heavenly.

"*Please*." Erato moaned. "Kate, fuck me, too. I'm already so close—"

Olive leaned over, drawing Kate away from her observation like a magnet. "You heard her. Fuck her in the ass so we can thank her for all the fine editorial work. Tonight's reward is the result of a shared effort, after all."

Completely true. Reminded of her deep gratitude for all Erato had helped her accomplish, Kate very tenderly swirled her index finger in the incredible wetness that Olive continued to draw out. She brought the tip up to play with her other, tighter hole. Applying slight pressure, she checked with Erato. "Yes?"

"Yes!" Erato didn't wait for her to take action. She scooted backward onto Kate's finger, impaling herself up to the second knuckle before coming to a stop, her thighs trembling. "Slow," she whispered.

Kate moved her finger at a glacial pace, tickled to discover that she could feel Olive slowing her own thrusts through the thin wall that separated them. Closing the distance between their faces, Kate pressed a soft kiss to Olive's lips, moaning when Olive immediately deepened it. Their busy hands synched up as their tongues fell into a sensual dance that somehow felt comfortable and absolutely earth-shattering at the same time.

"Olive." Erato groaned pleadingly. "Not slow, all right? Olive, fast. Kate, slow…ish."

Amused by the typically verbose muse's loss of coherence, Kate began to giggle. Olive smiled without losing a beat, both hastening the motion of her fingers inside Erato and expertly wrenching control of the kiss from Kate before her laughter had died away. Erato and Kate released twin noises of pleasure, which widened the grin on Olive's face and finally forced her to pause in their kissing.

"You stud," Kate whispered, only seconds before Olive recaptured her mouth and Erato bucked against her hand, crying out.

The orgasm they coaxed from Erato was a thing of beauty. Her hips thrust jerkily against their hands, and she moaned and cried out in genuine, full-throated pleasure. Sensing that Olive was every bit as turned on by what they'd just accomplished as she was, Kate kicked up the intensity of their making-out a notch while Erato rode out a seemingly stunning orgasm.

Kate stilled her finger before Olive did, who waited until Erato begged weakly for mercy before she stopped pounding into her. Pulling away from their kiss with a quiet apology, Olive slowly moved the hand that was trapped between Erato and Kate, slipping out of Erato without abandoning her altogether. Kate followed suit, leaving Erato with a firm pat on the ass. "*That* was fun."

Erato stood with surprising grace, fixing her hair while wearing a demure expression that made Kate cough with quickly suppressed laughter. "Very fun, thank you." Seemingly at ease with her nudity— and being the center of attention—she planted her hands on her hips and looked back and forth between them. "So are we calling it a night or shall we move this to the bedroom?"

Kate tried to ignore the way her heart dropped at the suggestion that they end the evening. She was confused about why Erato would even make the suggestion, though she wondered if it had to do with the tension that had arisen between her and Olive earlier. Whatever Erato's intent, Kate wasn't ready to say good-bye. She had no idea what it would require to get permission to see Olive again, and that was a very bad, horrible, anxiety-inducing thing. Then again, no Olive in her life meant plenty of time and opportunity to write. And that was an extremely good, important, life-path-determining thing. Right? She reminded herself that last night, the book had been her top priority. So how come now she wasn't sure *what* was most important?

I'm so confused.

Olive looked at her hopefully. "I'm game to keep this evening going, if you are."

No deadline was worth shutting this down. Not when she hadn't even gotten naked with Olive yet. "Then the bedroom it is."

❖

Kate jolted awake sometime before the sun began to lighten the night sky, overcome by a powerful, sickening sense of déjà vu. Just like the last time she'd fallen asleep sandwiched between two naked women, it appeared she hadn't gotten lucky enough to wake up the same way. At the sight of the rumpled, empty sheets beside her, Kate's heart dropped as she silently lamented Olive's apparent habit of fucking and running. Was she doing something wrong? Or did she simply have unrealistic expectations for encounters that were never presented as anything other than one-night (or two-night) stands?

Rolling to face the lone warm body still pressed against her back, Kate felt her heart swell. *Erato* had stolen away, not Olive. Indeed, Olive was nude, looking breathtakingly peaceful with her features relaxed in slumber. Stunned to have been left alone with her crush, Kate didn't hesitate to touch Olive's shoulder, caressing the smooth skin as gently as possible. Olive grumbled and snuggled in closer, so wholly, unconsciously adorable Kate couldn't suppress a fond chuckle. She slipped a hand between their bodies, lightly petting Olive's bare stomach, and kissed her temple. Breathing into her ear, Kate whispered, "On a scale of one to ten, how awake are you?"

Not bothering to play possum, Olive smiled without opening her eyes. "Depends," she mumbled. "Why?"

Kate ran her fingers down Olive's spine, coming to rest only inches from the cleft of her ass. "Because we're alone."

Olive's eyes snapped open. Surprised by the suddenness of the reaction, Kate barely had time to process what was happening before Olive climbed on top of her. Instinct drove her to wrap her legs around the supple body that weighed her down, while Olive pinned her arms against the pillow next to her head. Kate moaned at the feeling of warm, bare skin pressed against her own, as well as the delicious friction of Olive's kinky pubic hair brushing her clit. All traces of exhaustion gone, Olive stared into her eyes as she shifted to slip her thigh between Kate's. "How long do you think we have?"

Shrugging, Kate raised her head off the pillow and captured Olive's lips in a kiss that rode a delicate line between hunger and restraint. Olive kissed her back, apparently content to live without an answer and make the most of whatever time they had. She ground her thigh back and forth across Kate's swollen sex, dragging the distended clit over her silky skin again and again. Shivering, Kate lifted her own thigh, eager to reciprocate. Olive rocked against her, a quiet moan rumbling up from her chest as she began to move in a rhythm every bit as sexy as the noises she made. Kate mirrored her motions, looping her arms around Olive's neck to keep their upper bodies in contact while their lower halves sought release.

Olive pulled out of their kiss to stare down at her with dark, glittering eyes. "Kate." She hesitated, mouth open and hips working. "Kate, I really like fucking you."

Kate bit her lip, afraid Olive would feel how much faster the words had made her heart beat. Feeling as though she were base-jumping off a skyscraper without a parachute, she opted to respond with complete honesty. "I *love* fucking you."

Lighting up with unself-conscious joy, Olive curled a lock of Kate's hair around her fingers without faltering in her driving rhythm. "I don't want this to be the last time we fuck each other."

"It won't be," Kate said, then pulled Olive down into a kiss that belonged in one of her hottest sex scenes. She didn't want to think about logistics right now, even as thrilled as she was to know that Olive wanted to see her again. There was Erato to consider, and her deadline, and, most importantly, the promise Kate had extracted from her muse not to allow her to become distracted by her very real feelings for Olive. Rather than worry about all that to the detriment of their lovemaking, she simply promised herself that she would finish The Damn Book as quickly as possible. That would solve all her problems, more or less. Luckily, Olive had just provided her with the greatest motivation in the world—what else did she need?

Olive ended the kiss and sucked in a deep breath as her whole body tensed and the cadence of her hips became sharper, more focused. Sensing that Olive was close, Kate dragged blunt fingernails down the length of her back, triggering a noticeable shiver and a renewed rush of hot, wet arousal against her thigh. In response, Olive tugged on the hair still woven around her fingers and grinned through her pleasure-induced haze when the slight twinge of delicious pain made Kate whimper. It was the grin that pushed Kate right up to the edge, so swiftly she literally gasped in shock that she was about to come. She grabbed Olive's ass and squeezed, encouraging her to go harder. She'd wanted Olive to climax first but was rapidly losing the battle to maintain whatever silly sense of pride fueled that goal.

Olive lowered her head and breathed into her ear. "I want to try all those things you've written about." She stopped talking, then moaned and shook as she ground herself against Kate's thigh. "With you."

Kate tightened her fingers on Olive's ass, closing her eyes as she fought not to orgasm despite the warm, slippery thigh she couldn't stop riding. Images flashed through her mind of all the sexual fantasies she'd written down and put out into the world—this time, with her and Olive as the players. That Olive was already intimately familiar with her proclivities and desires after only two nights together, and that she approved, was the ultimate turn-on. Made stupid by excitement and pleasure, all Kate could manage in response to Olive's suggestive words was a hoarse, "Yes."

"There's so much I've never done." Olive kissed her neck, then scraped her teeth over the spot where her lips had been. "But I already trust you so—" Her words died as she cried out. "*Fuck.*"

Even though she knew Olive didn't want their little interlude to end any more than she did, Kate wanted so badly to make her come before Erato interrupted them. It wouldn't be the same with an audience. This was the most intimate moment they'd had together so far, and she was desperate to see it through. Cradling the back of Olive's neck, Kate guided their faces together so that their foreheads touched. "Let go now," she murmured. "This isn't the last time…there's so much I want to do with you…and *to* you…" She groaned at the mental picture she suddenly had of her face buried in Olive's luscious ass, which quickly morphed into a full-motion fantasy of bending Olive over the desk in her office and fingering her from behind. A surge of predatory lust caused the hand still locked on Olive's ass to tighten—pleasurably, judging from the satisfied wince she elicited. Emboldened, Kate licked Olive's upper lip and murmured, "I plan to *destroy* your dirty little bucket list one item at a time."

Olive surged against her and then stiffened, her entire body trembling with the force of what was clearly a breath-stealing climax. Groaning, she buried her face in Kate's shoulder and shoved a hand between their lower bodies, stroking Kate's clit so that they were able to enjoy their moment of orgasmic transcendence together. Kate clung to Olive as she came only seconds later, and dug her nails into her ass, and kissed every piece of skin her lips could reach: temple, cheek, shoulder. She moaned as loudly as she dared, wanting Olive to hear exactly how good it felt to be with her like this—and how badly she wanted to do it again.

Her orgasm seemed to last forever, only subsiding when her body was at its absolute limit, but it was still over far too soon. From the mixture of satisfaction and loss in the smile Olive wore when she finally gained the strength to lift her head and look Kate in the eyes, the feeling was mutual. Olive wiggled the fingers still sandwiched between them, triggering violent, nearly painful aftershocks of pleasure. "You turn me on like *crazy*, Kate McMannis."

Despite her past handful of lovers, Kate wasn't used to feeling like a serious object of desire. Now both Erato and Olive made her feel like she was more than capable of backing up the passionate, sizzling erotic encounters she wrote about with real-life sexual bona fides, which was empowering, to say the least. But the two women, and how they made Kate feel, were so different. While Erato was never short on compliments and was clearly willing to do anything Kate wanted— for the sake of her art, of course—Olive's desire felt more real, and raw, and potentially messy. That was because *Olive* felt more real, as opposed to Erato, who seemingly had no aspirations, dreams, or even life of her own.

Kate experienced a strange moment of dysphoria not unlike the one she'd felt following her return to reality after being immersed in her book for days on end. From the second Erato had breezed into her life, everything had taken on an air of the surreal. She'd been seduced by the most picture-perfect woman she'd ever seen up close, then taken to have a threesome with the veritable poster girl for "exactly Kate McMannis's type." The days after that were a blur of food, writing, sex, flirting, punishments, and the occasional cannabis-induced haze. She'd been virtually cut off from her family and friends—with assurances that she wasn't dead, just writing against a deadline—so it had been easy to feel as though she'd relocated to a different planet altogether.

But she hadn't. This was the same planet, and the same life, where she'd always lived. And right now a beautiful woman lay on top of her, a woman she respected and admired and felt fiercely attracted to. And that woman wanted her, and trusted her, and might even be convinced to share a life someday, if Kate didn't mess things up too badly. The thought overwhelmed her.

Frightened by the intensity of her emotions, Kate adopted a playful air. "I turn you on, or my stories do?"

Olive removed her hand from between Kate's thighs, licking her fingers one by one. "Both."

"You said you wanted to try all the things I've written about." She'd penned a *lot* of erotic scenes. Depicting…a *lot* of sexual acts.

Enough to fill the sexual bucket lists of an entire small village. "*All* of them?"

Chuckling, Olive kissed her, leaving behind traces of a familiar flavor Kate recognized as her own. "Well, the ones *you're* interested in making a reality." She paused, taking on a faraway look that Kate assumed meant she was revisiting the numerous sex scenes she'd read over the past week. "There might be one or two things I'm not ready to do." Her eyes refocused, and she winked. "But I can't think of any examples off the top of my head."

With a groan, Kate tried to initiate another kiss. This time Olive stopped her, placing a hand on her chest and smiling at her. Nervously. "So…"

Curious about the source of Olive's sudden anxiety, Kate let her head fall back onto the pillow. She rubbed her hands up and down over Olive's sides, then her back, in an effort to soothe. "So, I definitely want to see you again."

Olive relaxed slightly. "Maybe we could have dinner? I know this amazing Mexican place I guarantee you've never tried."

"That sounds wonderful." Kate's mind raced. Exactly how much would Erato make her do to earn a dinner date? And how fast could she do it? "I'll probably need to meet another word-count goal, but—"

"Wait." Olive hesitated, once again showing her nerves. "Just to be clear, I'm not talking about another playdate. I'm talking about a *real* date. With you. And me." Her eyes darted to the side, as though she was afraid she'd discover they were no longer alone. "And nobody else."

Kate nodded to show that she understood. Unfortunately, as happy as it made her to know that Olive wanted to go on dates like two normal people might, that didn't change her answer to the original question. "I want the same thing, believe me. A real date." Silently, she wondered how Erato would react to the idea of an unchaperoned evening out. After all, she realized with a start, she and Erato hadn't spent any time apart—not for more than a few minutes at a time, unless she was writing—since the day she had arrived. How to explain all of that without sounding a little *too* eccentric? "I'm just not sure when I'll be available…exactly. With my deadline and everything."

"I don't even need you for the whole night. Just dinner." Olive's smile faded entirely at the uneasy expression Kate knew she was wearing. "Erato can't possibly expect you to write every minute of every day. I mean, she lets you stop to eat on occasion, doesn't she?"

Kate managed a humorless laugh. "Of course I stop for meals. And no, she doesn't expect me to write constantly."

"So surely she'd understand if you took an hour to meet me for dinner?"

Kate didn't know how to answer. She wasn't positive how Erato would feel about the idea, but she suspected that even if she were allowed to start dating before she finished the book, it wouldn't be until she'd written at least a few thousand words. Or ten thousand. Or even twenty, depending on how concerned Erato was that Olive might throw her off course. Stalling, she asked, "When are you free?"

"Pretty much any evening this week except Tuesday. We could even meet tomorrow, if that works for you."

So much for stalling. Hating that she was about to deflate Olive again, Kate tried to act casual about her inability to commit. "Let me just check in with Erato before we make a firm plan. I don't want to start things out by breaking any promises."

Olive's eyes narrowed, and then she rolled off to the side. Disappointed by the loss of the warm body over hers, Kate turned and pulled Olive into a loose embrace. She yearned for the closeness she'd felt while they'd made love, before she'd started this bungling explanation of why she couldn't commit to their first real date without checking first with her "editor." Olive allowed Kate to hold her, but a barrier had clearly gone up.

Not meeting her eyes, Olive said, "Is your relationship with Erato more than professional?"

Kate hesitated, totally unsure how to answer. "She's not my girlfriend." But that didn't begin to explain what the nature of their association actually *was*…not that Kate entirely understood it herself. "You know I have sex with her." She paused. "*Had* sex with her," she amended, watching Olive's eyes. "If it bothers you, I won't have sex with her anymore." Incredibly, she both meant it *and* felt at peace with the decision. Sex with Erato was amazing, but the emotional connection simply didn't compare. No matter how good it felt physically, continuing to sleep with Erato wasn't worth screwing up what might possibly turn into the best relationship she'd ever had.

When Olive didn't respond, Kate kept talking, hopeful she'd say whatever Olive needed to hear. "Erato is my writing coach, basically. And while I admit that her methods are a little out there sometimes, they seem to be working. I'm pretty sure she's single-handedly rescued the career I've spent the past year and a half sabotaging. So right now I'm feeling very grateful, and focused, and like I should continue to check in with her as far as what I do and how I schedule my days. Because even if it seems a little crazy, I'm not sure I can be trusted to manage my own time this close to a deadline."

Olive's expression softened. "I get it. I think." She petted Kate's hair, then sighed as she ran her fingers through it. "How about one dinner, the two of us alone, and then I promise not to distract you again until you call me—with Erato's blessing? No matter how long that might take." Her other hand found Kate's on the sheets. "Please, Kate. The time we've spent together has literally turned my life upside down. Even though I'm sure it's not only trite but also really uncool to admit that, it's true. I can't stop thinking about you, yet we've never spent more than a few minutes alone together. I'm pretty sure I want to *date* you, date you, and even if we can't start doing that for a month or two, it'll be okay as long as I know, *soon,* that this will become something more than just casual sex. Because if that's all this—"

"It's not."

With effort, Olive finally made eye contact. "Good, because that's not what I'm looking for at this point in my life." She quirked her lips. "I mean, don't get me wrong...I'm *definitely* looking for sex. I just want...sex *plus.*"

Sex *plus.* Kate liked that. Maybe even enough to borrow the term for a future book. She opened her mouth to ask permission to do just that, but the quiet creak of the bedroom door forced her to swallow the words and made her stomach twist in nervous anticipation. Their moment of solitude was over. Without letting go of Olive, she lifted her head and looked over her shoulder, surprised to discover enough light was streaming in through the windows to allow her to see Erato in all her glory, standing in the doorway dressed in lingerie with a tray of food and drink in her hands.

"Good morning!" Erato chirped. "Rise and shine!"

Incredulous, Kate glanced at the alarm clock on her nightstand. "It's six o'clock," she said, determined not to rise *or* shine. "In the morning. On Saturday." She paused to let the facts settle. "Are you *nuts*?"

Erato sat on the edge of the bed in the spot she'd vacated earlier and set the tray on the mattress. "I know you've suspected as much, once or twice."

"I'm not even remotely ready to think about food yet." Kate tried to snuggle closer to Olive but found it impossible to ignore the tension running through the body entangled with hers. Frowning at the change in mood, Kate decided to try to recapture a little of the fun they'd had together last night. "Seriously, Erato, you should go put that tray on my dresser and get back in bed." She stopped talking, suddenly unsure whether Olive would approve of her suggestion. Hadn't she just offered to stop having sex with Erato? Did it count if she and Olive did it together? "Or at least…don't make us get up yet."

Sighing, Olive held the sheet against her chest and sat up. "No, it's probably for the best."

Erato's smile turned distinctly chilly. "Yes, I think it is. Kate has a lot of work to do today."

Olive blinked. "Oh." Something that looked like embarrassment passed across her face, and she sat up straighter, then quickly leaned over the side of the bed and came back up with her dress. "Right, maybe I should just go."

"No!" Kate grabbed Olive's wrist, then quickly let go when she realized how inappropriate that was. "I mean, at least have breakfast first." She pinned Erato with a hard stare, silently urging her to make amends for her rudeness. "It's not like I'm going to start writing until after *I* eat, anyway."

"Please do stay and eat, Olive," Erato said, but her smile was forced and her voice made it clear she was being polite, but just barely. "Kate and I owe you that much after everything you've done for us."

Flushing, Olive rolled out of bed and quickly tugged her dress on over her head. The hurt in her eyes perfectly reflected the passive-aggressive ugliness of Erato's comment. "No, that's all right. I should go to the bakery, anyway. I'll grab something to eat there."

Shocked by Erato's not-so-subtle implication that Olive was nothing more than a whore who could be paid off with a continental breakfast—and that Kate and Erato were some sort of couple—Kate scrambled out of bed after Olive. "Wait." She glared at Erato, then pointed at the bedroom door. "Give us a minute alone, please."

Rather than leave, Erato lazily peeled a banana and took a bite. She fluttered her hand in the same general direction. "I won't follow you."

Confused, Kate turned just in time to see Olive rush out of the room. She followed close behind, trailing her as she navigated the stairs, but didn't speak until Olive stopped to search the living room for her shoes. "I apologize for her. I've never..." She searched her memory. "I've seriously *never* seen her act like that before. You didn't deserve to be treated that way, and she had no right to imply that your coming over was somehow a favor you did for 'us.'" When Olive didn't answer, instead perching on the arm of the couch to slip on her shoes, Kate walked over to stand in front of her. Sensing she was on the verge of losing something vitally important, Kate dropped to her knees and took Olive's hand, pressing her lips to the knuckles. "I'm almost positive she's overcompensating in an attempt not to let me get distracted from the book. Please don't take it personally."

Olive barely lifted her gaze. "Erato works *for* you, right?"

"She does." Kate swallowed, not liking the unspoken suggestion that her professional relationship with Erato could be easily severed. "I'll talk to her. She may have worked miracles as far as ending my writer's block, but that doesn't give her the right to interfere with my personal life." She rubbed her thumb over Olive's fingers. "It certainly doesn't give her the right to talk to you like she did. Believe me when I say it *won't* happen again. I'll make sure of that."

Nodding, Olive exhaled and buried her face in her hands. She waited almost a full minute to speak. "I feel like this just got complicated."

Terrified by what that meant, exactly, Kate said, "I've got a few weeks left before my deadline. Yes, things will be a little complicated until then—they always are when I'm pushing to finish a project—but I promise, *you* are my priority as soon as this book is done. In the meantime, I'll talk to Erato and tell her we won't be able to continue working together unless she loses the attitude—no matter *how* good she is at her job."

Olive sighed, then dropped her hands and tentatively met Kate's eyes. "I'm sorry. I'm not trying to upend your life *or* disrupt your working relationship with Erato. I'm happy to coexist with her, even if that means sharing you sexually...until this book is done, at least. We barely know each other, and I certainly have no claim on you at this point in our relationship. And I'm definitely not asking you to prioritize me over your writing. At all. That's your passion, and I respect that it's a major part of your life, believe me. I just..."

Kate took a chance and rose to kiss Olive lightly on the mouth. Without pulling back, she murmured, "You're just a human being with feelings—not a sex dispenser who deserves my attention only when I've met my word count." Pulling back, she made sure Olive could see how much she meant what she was saying. "Olive, you deserve a nice dinner where we can talk about this chemistry we're both feeling. Hell, we *both* deserve to take an hour out of our days to figure out if we might have a real chance together. I know we've had an unconventional beginning, but things aren't always this complicated with me, I promise."

She stopped, unsure whether to reveal how deeply she was falling. Would it undermine her sincerity if she appeared to be moving too fast, especially when they'd spent so little time alone? Maybe, but it was equally likely that baring her soul would make her vulnerable in a way that would reassure Olive about her intentions. Choosing her words carefully, Kate said, "Honestly, what I feel for you is incredibly simple—even though it's not like anything I've ever felt before. For anyone."

Olive cradled the back of Kate's neck and drew her in for a soft, lingering kiss. "When can we meet?"

"Tomorrow night." Encouraged by the renewed spark of intimacy, Kate trailed kisses from one side of Olive's full lips to the other. "I'll tell Erato I'll be away for an hour, tops. She'll have no choice but to accept my absence." With effort, she pulled away to look Olive in the eyes. "Now are you sure you won't stay for breakfast?"

She shook her head. "I know when I'm not wanted." Kate took a step back when Olive pushed herself off the couch and adjusted the hem of her dress. Gesturing upstairs, Olive kept her voice low as though afraid that Erato might overhear. "She may not have said it in so many words, but it's clear I've already overstayed my welcome this morning. I don't want to stick around while you issue an ultimatum or anything like that…" She hesitated, then took Kate's hand in both of hers and squeezed. "Talk to her. Please. Then text me and we'll work out the details about tomorrow."

"Deal." Stepping closer, she put her free arm around Olive and gave her a careful hug. "Thank you for last night. And this morning, especially."

Olive let go of her hand to hug her back. "There's plenty more where that came from." She tightened her arms around Kate's waist. "Thank you, too. Being with you has made me feel so incredibly, excitingly *alive*. More alive than I ever thought I could feel, even before the accident. I want to feel this way forever." She gave Kate a brief, desperate squeeze, then released her, turning to walk to the front door. "Text me?"

It was physically painful to watch Olive leave. Cursing Erato's obstructionism, Kate hurried after her, standing naked in the doorway as Olive stepped out of her apartment. "I'll talk to her right now." She caught Olive's hand before she could walk away. As far as she was concerned, they should still be in bed. Hell, they should have been able to stay there all day, fucking until they were physically incapable of going on. If not for Erato, that's exactly what they'd be doing. Complicated, indeed. "I miss you already."

Olive broke into a genuine grin. "I miss you, too." She stepped closer for a sensuous kiss, rubbing her hands up and down Kate's bare sides. Her touch conveyed so much more than mere words, full of the reassurance that despite whatever complications Kate presented, Olive was still interested. "Now go back inside before your neighbors see exactly how sexy you are. I don't need any more competition." She slapped Kate on the butt before stepping away.

"You don't have any competition," Kate called after her. She admired the way Olive's dress hugged her full ass, marveling at how inexplicably gorgeous she was even after a long night of sex and an unpleasant awakening far too early the next morning. And that was all while being a hundred percent human. It was strange, how erotic normality suddenly seemed. "No competition at all."

CHAPTER SIXTEEN

Kate's frustration flared anew when she returned to the bedroom to find Erato still nibbling on breakfast. Given Erato's barely concealed hostility toward Olive that morning and the anger Kate felt over having a woman she genuinely cared about treated like a prostitute, she figured it was inevitable that they were about to have their first real fight. She was sure as hell mad enough for one. It didn't help that Erato regarded her with an expression of placid calm that made her momentarily wonder if she'd imagined the tension of minutes ago.

But then, even before she made it all the way across the room, Erato said, "I hope you understand why I can't let you see her anymore."

Halting a few feet from the bed, Kate counted her breaths before she answered. She reminded herself how instrumental Erato had been in helping her take the book this far, and how certain she'd felt before last night that her muse's continued presence in her life was as vital to its completion as her own hard work. All true, but that didn't make it okay for her to pull rank when a future with Olive was at stake. With a deep breath, Kate said, "We need to talk about our relationship. Basically, what it is and what it isn't." She searched Erato's face for a reaction, and when she didn't get one, she added, "We need to set boundaries."

"The boundaries have already been established, by you. Our arrangement is the same as it's always been. I'm here to help you finish your book, nothing more and nothing less."

Annoyed by the carefully modulated tone of Erato's voice, Kate said, "Helping me finish my book doesn't mean being a bitch to Olive, whose only sin has been to accept both of my invitations home for sex. Regardless of our arrangement, or any previously established boundaries, you have no right to dictate who I date." She took a hesitant step, then sat down on the end of the bed and tried to interpret Erato's expression. "Look, I understood that one day, maybe even after I finish this book next month, you'll leave to be some other lucky author's muse."

"I told you I would stay as long as you need me."

Kate remembered her desperation when she'd imagined Erato disappearing from her life, and the peace Erato's promise had brought her. What had changed between then and now? Only a week or so had passed, yet somehow everything seemed different. She still didn't want to lose Erato, but with Olive newly in her life, more was at stake than just the future of her writing career. Why couldn't it be easier to have it all? "Yes, you did, and I appreciate that more than you know. But you also assured me that one day I *will* decide that I don't need you anymore, and I assumed you said that because, as far as you're concerned, this arrangement isn't forever. One day you *will* leave. Right?"

"But like I said before," Erato moved the tray of food from the bed to the nightstand, then stretched out on what had become her side of the mattress, "I won't leave until you ask me to."

"I'm not saying I want you to go." Kate covered Erato's bare foot with her hand. As angry as she was, she definitely wasn't there yet. "I'm just trying to establish that I'm not your girlfriend. That you don't think of yourself as mine, that you don't envision a future in which we grow old and die together. Therefore, we aren't in a monogamous sexual relationship, which means you have no right to decide who I see." She waited for a reaction, but Erato didn't give one. "Am I wrong?"

"You're correct that we aren't in a monogamous sexual relationship." Erato's intense stare burned through her, unwavering. "But that's irrelevant to the issue at hand, which is Olive's potential negative impact on your book."

"Her potential negative impact?" Affronted by the assumption that she would so easily allow her interest in dating Olive to derail a project she clearly cared about, Kate's frustration level ticked up. "My desire to see Olive again doesn't equate to a negative impact. I'm not planning to shack up with her for the next month, deadline be damned. I'm talking about one dinner date, *maybe* two, which will have zero effect on my writing schedule. Trust me, the book will still get done."

"That you actually believe that is the best justification I can offer for what has to happen next."

That…didn't sound good at all. Unsettled, Kate removed her hand from Erato's foot. "What's that supposed to mean?"

"Two days ago you admitted to me that Olive could become a distraction. Now she has."

"But we haven't even—"

"Believe me, this thing with Olive *will* distract you…even if you don't realize it yet." Erato sat up straighter as her calm facade began to slip. "Do you really believe you'll be able to leave things at one or two dinner dates? A few weeks apart might as well be a year when you're in the wild, hot, passionate stage of new love. Even if you aren't meeting in person, she will consume your thoughts. Can you honestly tell me you'll be able to concentrate on Rose and Molly and their happily-ever-after if you're busy daydreaming about the possibility of your own?"

Kate had fallen in love once before. Erato wasn't wrong. It was the most gut-wrenching, all-consuming experience life had to offer, and right now was the worst possible time for it to happen. But this was *love,* or it could be, and if that didn't come before all else, then what was she even writing about? "So I should let her go, have my heart broken, and somehow try to write Rose and Molly a happy ending despite my own miserable, loveless life?"

Erato clicked her tongue. "Your life is neither miserable *nor* loveless, so don't be ridiculous." Folding her arms over her chest, her frown brought to mind a petulant child. "You know, I'm only trying to keep the promise *you* asked me to make."

Too upset to recall specifics, Kate said, "I'm almost positive I never made you promise to forbid me from seeing Olive again. Or deny me a chance at happiness."

"*Writing* makes you happy." For the first time since they'd met, Erato raised her voice. "My dear, the night before last you made me swear I would keep you focused on your art, whatever it took. Even if you called my methods into question, you said, or begged me to leave you alone, I was to vow that I would *force you* to see the book through to the end. Not even forty-eight hours later and you're giving me grief about doing just that? *Seriously?*"

The exasperated incredulity in Erato's voice, reflected a thousandfold on her pretty face, triggered a rush of genuine shame.

Embarrassment colored Kate's cheeks and rendered her silent as she forced herself to calm down and analyze the current situation as objectively as possible. She had begged Erato to keep her on task. Less than forty-eight hours ago she had been so excited about her creative resurgence—and so *committed* in her newfound devotion to that Damn Book—she'd briefly considered not making a date with Olive at all. But Erato had insisted, literally *insisted,* even suggested that not seeing Olive again would prove to be an even bigger distraction than indulging in her favorite new addiction. Given that Erato seemed to read her mind ninety-nine percent of the time, hadn't she anticipated that a second date with Olive might lead to the desire for a third? What did she think would happen? That Kate would lose interest? That Olive would? Or had she simply planned that icy, passive-aggressive wake-up call from the start, hoping to establish ownership and scare Olive away once she'd served her purpose?

As her ire rose again, Kate forced herself to calm down. The more upset she became, the more she would bolster Erato's belief that Olive was somehow bad for her creativity. She needed to approach this disagreement as logically as possible.

Taking a breath to level out her emotions, she said, "You're right. I asked you not to let me get distracted. And yes, I *was* worried that inviting Olive back into my life might hurt my ability to meet this deadline. But I was questioning whether she could accept the demands writing makes on my life when the other women I've dated never seemed able to. Now that I've spoken to her, I'm not concerned anymore. She wants to meet me for dinner tomorrow—*one* hour, two at the very most—so we can talk, but beyond that, she understands that right now the book takes priority. She said that after tomorrow, she'll be happy to wait until you've given me permission to contact her again. If that's not until next month when I'm done with the book, then…" She wasn't really okay with that idea and was apparently unable to pretend that she was. "I hope you don't make us wait that long."

Erato huffed. "Absolutely not."

Kate tried to decide whether to be happy or upset about the vague answer for only a few seconds before asking for clarification. "Absolutely not *what?*"

"You're not meeting Olive for dinner tomorrow. Absolutely not. I forbid it."

She was *really* starting to lose patience with Erato's authoritative nonsense. "Actually, I am. I don't care *what* I made you promise— you're way out of line. One dinner is harmless and the least she deserves from me, especially after the way you behaved toward her this morning."

"After the way *I* behaved?" Getting up onto her knees, Erato suddenly towered over Kate, shockingly intimidating swept up in her righteous fury. "You're the one who's getting pissy with *me* for doing exactly as you asked—you wanted me to protect you from yourself, to act in your best interests, to not let you stray from the path you were on. Do you honestly think that falling in love won't hinder your progress on this book? As an author and therefore a student of human nature, you can't *possibly* believe that limiting yourself to one dinner date will insulate you from the emotional turmoil of wondering where Olive is, what she's doing, what she's *thinking,* and when you'll be able to touch her again. Do you?"

"And what about the emotional turmoil of blowing off a woman I really care about? Aren't you worried about the negative impact that will have on my writing?" She took a moment to consider how she would feel if Erato actually prevented her from seeing Olive again. The utter despair that accompanied the thought didn't bode well for the creativity Erato claimed to want to foster. "Believe me, issuing this kind of ultimatum won't achieve the desired effect. If you're such an expert on human nature, you'd realize that a broken heart is worse for my creativity than a mildly distracted one."

"Unfortunately, that's just not true." Erato's tone left no room for argument. "That your distraction would be mild, I mean, or that temporary heartache is the more impossible obstacle for you to overcome right now." She planted her hands on her hips, making Kate feel very much like a scolded child. "At this point we're in damage-control mode. I should have seen how dangerous Olive was from the very beginning, and I *never* should have allowed her to be used as an incentive more than once. That was my failure, and I apologize profusely for going down this road in the first place. It's not like you didn't try to warn me—you were afraid that seeing Olive again would derail you, yet I foolishly believed that what the book *really* needed was for you to scratch that itch once and for all. You'd assured me you wanted to keep things casual, that your writing was your top priority…

and I believed you." She exhaled, then sat back with a sweet smile. "Look, I'm not saying you can't date her. I'm just telling you that you can't see or talk to her again until you've finished a first draft you feel comfortable submitting to your publisher. That's all."

Kate searched her memory for her current word count, then extrapolated from there. "But that'll take me two and a half weeks, minimum!" And that was assuming she could write at the same pace she'd maintained for the past week without faltering—which seemed unlikely, considering how badly emotional turmoil tended to affect her ability to work and how burnt out she would be if she kept up this pace much longer. Even if she managed to finish the draft quickly, she was a perfectionist when it came to preparing her manuscripts for submission. She would almost certainly need the full month she had left to bring the story up to her standards.

It was one thing not to *see* Olive for that long, but to not talk to her, either? The whole point of the dinner date had been to discuss their feelings and process all that had happened so far. Olive was clearly shaken by her feelings and insecure about Kate's intentions. One hour at a Mexican restaurant wasn't likely to assuage all her fears about starting a relationship with an eccentric author like her, but it was the least Olive deserved.

Yet Erato wanted her to wait *three weeks*? Kate snorted. "She won't *want* to date me if I disappear that long."

"Then it wasn't meant to be."

Aghast, Kate got up onto her knees. "That's easy for you to say."

"None of this is easy for me." Erato scooted backward until her back was pressed against the headboard. She stretched her long legs out in front of her, then motioned Kate closer. "Now come over here and let's cuddle this out. I don't want you to be angry with me."

Kate didn't move. "I *am* angry. I don't want to have to choose between you and Olive. I really don't."

"The choice isn't between Olive and *me,* my darling, and besides, you've already made your decision." Erato's smile turned seductive, her hand fluttering to her chest only to run down the valley between her breasts. "And *I* made a promise to *you,* which I intend to keep. Just as I assured you I would." Her gaze drifted away from Kate's face to the juncture of her thighs, reminding her of her state of undress. Erato licked her lips, and when she spoke again, her voice was deeper. "Now why don't you come over here so we can get back on good terms?"

Kate actually considered going to her. Her body twitched as though compelled by a supernatural force, before her logical mind took over. "No. You're not going to appease me with sex. Not about this."

Erato released a long-suffering sigh. "Suit yourself." The hand that had come to rest over her stomach slid down between her legs, where she rubbed the crotch of her lingerie with gentle, confident fingers. "When you're ready to resume our physical relationship, let me know. Until then, I'm quite good at taking care of myself."

Kate tried not to look. She really tried—but it wasn't until Erato slipped her fingers beneath the elastic band of her panties that she was finally able to redirect her attention out the window. Despite the purely sexual—and admittedly enticing—display in front of her, Kate focused on only one objective: texting Olive to confirm their date before Erato could somehow manage to stop her. She stood up, ignoring the breathy moan behind her, and walked to her nightstand to get her phone. It wasn't on the charger, which didn't shock her. Last night hadn't followed her typical nighttime routine, to say the least. She checked the pockets of the jeans she'd worn for her date, then went downstairs to search the kitchen and living room. After a frustrating hunt, she tossed on a T-shirt and pajama pants, grabbed the keys to her truck, and went outside to check there. When she came up empty once again, her suspicions immediately turned to the woman currently masturbating in her bed.

She stomped back upstairs, telling herself she wouldn't get angry or make accusations, and would deal with the situation with the maturity and calm strength of character she needed in order to prove that her feelings for Olive weren't upsetting her sensibilities. Although she was prepared to interrupt a serious attempt at self-pleasuring when she returned to the bedroom, she still felt mildly taken aback at the sight that greeted her: Erato, lingerie strategically askew, lying in the center of the mattress with her hand between her legs and her back arched in pleasure. It was as though she'd walked into the middle of a scene from one of her stories, unrealistically beautiful heroine and all. The desire to join the woman on her bed was tangible, nearly melting away her fury despite her best attempts to hang on to the justified emotion.

Erato's vibrant blue eyes opened, full of affectionate longing. "I'm so close, Kate." She angled her wrist and penetrated herself with a slim finger, tilting her knee to the side to give Kate a better view. "Even if you don't want to touch me, will you stay with me while I come?" Her body shuddered, causing her breasts to jiggle appealingly. "Who knows? Maybe it'll help get your creative juices flowing."

A few weeks ago, she would have been skeptical about such a claim. Now she had no doubt that if she gave herself over to Erato's special brand of sex magic, she would almost certainly walk away inspired. Perhaps she would even forget that she wanted to text Olive, let alone meet her for dinner. Kate shook her head, resolved not to let that happen. It wasn't fair to Olive, to say the least, and would no doubt humiliate her after she'd gathered the courage to bare her soul in the immediate aftermath of Erato's rude dismissal. Keeping Olive—her smile, her warm eyes, her curvaceous, responsive body—firmly in mind, Kate wrestled with her brain to focus on the task at hand.

"Have you seen my cell phone?"

Erato stopped fingering herself immediately and, with a frustrated sigh, slipped out of her vagina, then her lingerie. She arranged the material over her crotch so that she was covered, as though girding herself for battle. Then she offered Kate an infuriatingly calm smile. "It's in a secure location."

"*Give me* my phone." Kate waited to see if the words had landed with the weight she'd intended, then held out her hand, palm up. "Now, please."

"I'm sorry, but no." Erato sat up. "We've played this game before, Kate. You know how it goes."

"That was different. This time she's expecting me to text her. If I don't, she'll think I've blown her off."

Erato's expression was patient and tender, which only stoked Kate's anger. "You can explain what happened once you finish the first draft."

Her resolve not to lash out slipped. "You're a smart woman, Erato. What don't you understand here? We're not in an exclusive romantic relationship, I'm only asking for the chance to spend an *hour* with Olive before the damn book is finished, and you sure as fuck don't pay my wireless bill, so you have no *goddamn right* to hold my phone hostage. I went along with it last time because your rules were somewhat reasonable. Now they aren't, so I'm done playing." She stopped, took a breath, and lowered her volume slightly. "Don't punish me for something I haven't even done. Let me take Olive to dinner tomorrow night, and if my writing falters in *any* way because of it...well, I'll accept that you were right and stop questioning your directives, once and for all."

Erato looked almost pained. "Must you make this so difficult?"

Sensing that they were at an impasse, Kate growled in frustration. She raked her fingers through her hair and pulled, welcoming the stinging pain and the way it released some of the pressure building within her chest. She didn't want to ask Erato to leave, but if pushed hard enough, she would do it. She really would. Maybe. "Must *you*?"

"I'm doing exactly what you begged me to do, and nothing more." Sighing, Erato got up off the bed and walked to the closet, where she'd hung the handful of dresses she'd brought with her. Kate caught a glimpse of her reflection in the mirrored door as she stripped off the lingerie and reached for a flowing blue garment that contrasted nicely with her olive skin and made her eyes look even more brilliant than usual. "Once the book is finished, you're free to ask me to leave, to disagree with the way I went about keeping you focused, and to hate me forever if things with Olive don't work out. Until then, I suggest that you put your energy into finishing the book instead of being upset with me."

Kate stood with her hands fisted at her sides. She literally had no idea what to do. She refused to give up on the idea of contacting Olive, if only so she could confess that Erato had decided to forbid her from dating until she'd produced a submission-ready manuscript. Like *that* would go over well. Still, it would be better than nothing— which was a pretty terrible thing for Erato to expect her to offer. Unfortunately, it was clear that Erato wouldn't change her mind based on whatever arguments, promises, or threats Kate came up with. She couldn't possibly finish the book before Olive's feelings were hurt from the lack of contact on her end, but maybe Erato would be willing to compromise?

Clearing her throat, Kate watched Erato in the mirror as she adjusted the hem of her dress. "How about I prove to you that I'm *still* not distracted? My feelings for Olive—which did *not* just develop last night—haven't prevented me from making progress yet. There's no reason to believe that one dinner date will change that—or at the very least, a few text messages to explain why dinner has to wait. If I spend all day and the better part of tonight writing, would that convince you there's no harm in letting me at least have a conversation with Olive to explain your point of view?"

Erato stepped out of the closet, ready for the runway. "I'd love for you to accomplish a lot today. The Olive situation has definitely rattled you, and it would certainly make me feel better if you're able to write through this."

It wasn't difficult to notice that Erato hadn't actually addressed the most important part of her proposal. "And when I produce *at least* three thousand words today, you'll let me use my cell phone to message Olive?" She hesitated, unsure whether to push her luck. Oh, hell. She'd promised Olive a dinner date, and she couldn't start an honest, healthy relationship by breaking her word. "All I want is one hour alone with her, one meal together. You could even wait for me in the car."

Erato arched an eyebrow and folded her arms over her generous breasts. "Oh, could I?"

Kate cringed. "I just meant…you know, to make sure I come straight home afterward."

Shaking her head, Erato regarded her without speaking for what felt like a long time. Kate bit her lip in an effort to stop the endless stream of bargaining and pleading that threatened to pour forth, anything to fill the silence and convince Erato not to jeopardize the trust and faith she had in their partnership. Finally, Erato sighed. "Let's revisit this discussion tonight, after you've written those *thirty-five hundred* words."

It wasn't perfect, but that was the best she was likely to get. Although she'd have preferred to text Olive before noon, she didn't think it would be a deal-breaker to wait until bedtime. Kate nodded vigorously. "All right. That's fair enough, as long as you promise you'll actually *revisit* and not just reiterate."

"I'll agree to that." Erato stuck out her hand and grinned when they shook on it. "Do you want to start writing now, or would you prefer to begin the day with a bubble bath and a cannabis cigarette?"

Trying not to smirk at Erato's formal word choice, Kate forced away the instinct to immediately dive into work and considered her options. She had a long day of writing ahead of her, but it was still early. Washing up was her next step no matter what, because frankly, she reeked of sex. A bath would take longer than a shower, but the joint would help calm her frustration and hopefully ease her into a creative space where she might actually be able to meet her word count. She would never admit it to Erato, but few things interfered with her ability to work like emotional upset. Today she simply *had* to produce good work despite the uncertainty of her romantic life and the inner turmoil that triggered. If she didn't, it would be all the proof Erato needed that Olive wasn't good for her creativity.

"Will you run my bath?" Kate managed a pleasant smile she didn't really feel. Staying calm about their disagreement while having a prolific writing session wouldn't be easy. Hopefully the decision to indulge in a little relaxation first would help.

"Of course." Erato winked as she passed her on the way to the bathroom. "I'll even roll your joint."

CHAPTER SEVENTEEN

B y the time Kate sat down at her desk an hour later, dressed in a tank
top and panties, hair still wet from the bath, she was sufficiently
calm enough to turn her thoughts away from Olive—who was no doubt
living her life and not yet worried about a lack of communication,
anyway—and back toward Rose, Molly, and their increasingly
complicated romance. When she'd left them the day before, Molly had
tried and failed to end their sexual relationship due to her misgivings
about keeping secrets from Rose's mother. After their office-desk sex,
Rose tells Molly they could just be open about being together. If her
mother has a problem with it, as she always has in the past when Rose
has dated women, then that's her loss. But Molly is insistent: she has
been Rose's mother's caretaker for far too long and has come to mean
far too much to a sick old lady to take careless risks with her emotional
state. Rose's mother is on the decline. Molly has no idea how much
longer she'll even be lucid, since for the past month she's been having
bad days rather than simply bad moments. The thought of ruining
whatever time she and Rose have left for reconciliation is unacceptable.
Even if Rose didn't resent her in the future, Molly is certain she would
never forgive herself. She suggests to Rose that perhaps they can be
together later, one day, but Rose points out that they have no idea how
long her mother has left, and life is short and unpredictable.

After reading through her chapter-in-progress, Kate put her
fingers on her keyboard and booted up her mental movie projector.
The scene she'd left off on was a sweet one between Rose and her
still-unsuspecting mother, who is thanking her for the more frequent

visits to the assisted-living facility. After Molly's speech in her office, Rose has decided that the best way to convince Molly to be open about their relationship is to try to patch things up with her mother. Though she's a little ashamed about the ulterior motive for her visits, she also recognizes that Molly has opened a real opportunity to reconnect with a woman whose approval she still craves, albeit grudgingly.

With her brain loosened by the morning wake-and-bake session, Kate had no trouble seeing the direction the story needed to take. First, she would build the bond between Rose and her mother. They would stay away from talk of her dating life and sexuality, as their initial scene together in the book had nearly veered into conflict when Rose's mother asked who she was dating. Now was the time to show the positive aspects of their parent-child relationship: Rose's mother would share a memory from her childhood, then Rose would, until eventually they ended up laughing together until they were in tears. The visit would end on a positive note, with a promise from Rose to return in a few days so they could spend more time together. The next visit, of course, wouldn't go as well. The dementia would be acting up. Her mother's mood would be unstable, to the point where she would make a derogatory comment about Rose's sexuality in front of Molly.

Kate grinned, already excited to tackle that scene. Ah, conflict. Honestly, she often found it easier to write angst than sex. That was a good thing, too. As she thought ahead, she realized she'd just entered the high-conflict portion of her story. Save for an interrupted romantic interlude a few chapters down the line, which promised to be a drama-filled treat to write, she wouldn't write another fully realized, intimate love scene between her main characters until the climax of the book.

She snorted. *Climax.* Cracked her up every time.

Once she'd established a tentative mother-daughter bond, then upset Rose by demonstrating anew just how sick her mother is—and how badly her mother's words still cut, dementia-fueled or not—she would have ample opportunity to bring Rose and Molly even closer together. Molly would have a reason to comfort Rose, and Rose would fully appreciate how tenuous her remaining time with her mother really was. That would perfectly position her to set off the bomb that would usher in the final act of the story: after a pleasant visit that includes an apology from her now-lucid mother, who mentions that her trusted caretaker Molly doesn't share her discomfort with bisexuality and has urged her to work toward acceptance, Rose goes to look for Molly and finds her cleaning the room of a resident who has passed away. Molly is emotional, and even more so once Rose thanks her for being the first person to talk some sense into her mother regarding her sexuality. Judgment clouded by grief, Molly embraces Rose and kisses her. Despite the risk of being caught, things quickly become heated. And then, Kate grinned evilly, she would cue the homophobic mother, stage left.

Opening her outline, Kate quickly jotted down notes to help her remember how the rest of the story would unfold. The horrified reaction of Rose's mother would be fairly delicious to portray. She would accuse her daughter of taking advantage of poor Molly, insinuating that Rose had essentially assaulted her. There would be name-calling. And then—yes, Molly coming to Rose's defense, which would only heighten the tension.

Clapping in anticipation, Kate quickly navigated back to her chapter-in-progress. Outlining was great, but Erato wouldn't count those words toward her daily goal. Luckily, she was pleased with where her story was going and excited to write one or two upcoming scenes in particular. Given the natural urgency she felt about earning the right to text Olive, she saw no reason she shouldn't have a banner day.

Two hours later, her optimism had faded. She'd managed only four hundred words. At that rate, she'd have to write for over fifteen more hours just to meet her goal, and she'd honestly hoped to exceed it. Things had started off well enough. Diving back into the scene between Rose and her mother, she'd lightly edited the previous two hundred words before forging ahead into new territory. At first the dialogue had practically written itself, as though she were merely transcribing a conversation overheard across the room. But as soon as she attempted to describe the complex emotions Rose was experiencing, specifically her gratitude for the opportunity to rediscover her mother and her regrets about their complicated history, Kate's mind had started to wander. Writing about the rebirth of a parent-child relationship and the fragility of life naturally made her think about Olive. She'd indulged the thoughts for a while, even convincing herself that wondering about Olive's childhood and whether her father would approve of their relationship—and her writing—would help her flesh out the interplay between Rose and her mother. But after the second time she caught herself staring sightlessly at her laptop, hands in her lap and her characters forgotten, she had to admit the obvious. She was distracted.

Worrying about whether Olive would accept a forty-five-minute phone conversation in lieu of dinner wouldn't increase her word count. She knew that. Yet her brain stubbornly refused to release its obsession with her sweet, brave new lover, which made it nearly impossible to inhabit the head of Rose, who was supposed to be in love with pale, Irish Molly. Every word she typed took deliberate effort, and more than once, she got stuck on a single sentence for so long she deleted the entire paragraph in frustration and had to start over. As the minutes ticked by and her word count failed to keep pace, Kate's frustration rose.

Had Erato permitted her to send one simple text message, this wouldn't be happening. Period. But even as she told herself that, she knew it was a lie. Even if she'd been able to confirm their dinner plans, she would still be thinking of Olive, wouldn't she? How could she not? Right now Olive was everywhere she looked. She was in everything Kate wrote. When she reached for Rose's feelings toward Molly, what she came up with was the elation she felt when she was with Olive. Though she'd rather die than admit it out loud, Erato was right. Olive had infected her, and the idea that one more hit of her new drug—or a text message, or dinner—would somehow hold her over or even sate her desire for the next month was downright ludicrous. The suggestion that Olive *wasn't* a distraction was so stupid that she had to give Erato credit for not laughing in her face.

The realization didn't change anything. She had promised Olive dinner, and she intended to keep her promise. As Erato had noted, the damage to her focus was already done. Even if Erato had been right about so many other things, Kate refused to believe it was better for her art to snub Olive and cause them both pain in the process. Dishonorable behavior was anathema to who she was, and she couldn't imagine anything more rotten than simply vanishing from Olive's life after sharing so much passion and connection. No creativity would flow from the wreckage of her heart if she hurt a woman who'd suffered far too much pain already.

Ultimately, it was her concern for Olive's happiness that enabled her to settle into a steady rhythm that, while hardly awe-inspiring, improved on the morning's word count. By noon, she'd surpassed one thousand words. Erato brought her a sandwich, which she nibbled on between bursts of typing. At a quarter past three o'clock, after she'd reached the two-thousand-word mark, she got up and walked around the apartment to stretch her legs. The idea of searching for her cell phone flitted across her mind, but she abandoned the notion as soon as it became clear that Erato wouldn't let her out of her sight. Aware that her muse was trailing her from room to room, Kate went out the back door and stepped into the sunshine, basking in its heat.

The screen door opened and closed behind her. "Would you like to take a walk?"

Kate turned to squint at Erato, then brought her hand up to shade her eyes. "No, that's all right. I need to get back to work in a minute."

"How's it going?"

Bristling slightly, Kate said, "Fine."

"Making progress?"

She was, albeit more slowly than in recent days. While she *really* didn't want to discuss her focus and motivation—or lack thereof—attempting to avoid this conversation would no doubt prove more detrimental to her end goal of seeing Olive than simply engaging in it. "I am. I've entered a fairly complicated part of the story, as far as the emotions and events I have to portray, so it's a bit of a slog, but I'm working my way through it."

Erato graced her with a warm smile. "Great." Her blue eyes sparkled as she gazed up at the similarly hued sky and inhaled with gusto, a move that naturally drew Kate's attention to her breasts. "Can I do anything to help? More food? Another joint? A little sexual relief?"

Kate felt bad about shaking her head. She couldn't imagine having sex with Erato right now. Even though Olive had given her permission, it didn't feel right—and not just because the woman was withholding her cell phone and threatening to sabotage her love life. Honestly, she was more than a little afraid of the power Erato had over her thoughts and emotions. What if she somehow persuaded her to abandon the idea of seeing Olive again? And then simply disappeared once the book was done, leaving her alone? The thought emboldened her to refuse. "I'm okay."

Erato raised an eyebrow. "Are we really done having sex?"

Kate exhaled in an explosive burst of frustration. "I don't know, Erato. For the moment, yes."

"Because of Olive?"

She wasn't sure what to say. The answer was yes, of course. If not for Olive, she would almost certainly be deep inside Erato right now. But the question felt like a trap she didn't want to willingly step into. So she deflected. "You know, for someone who didn't want me distracted by the drama of romantic entanglement, this line of questioning is starting to feel like exactly that. You've insisted that I stay focused, and that's what I'm trying to do."

Erato frowned. "You can't write to the exclusion of everything else. It doesn't work that way. If you don't take breaks occasionally and recharge, you'll quickly become useless. Think of your creativity as—"

"Erato?" Kate tried *very* hard not to sound annoyed. "I *was* taking a break. I *was* recharging—using the sun as my power source. If I need a little sexual energy at some point, I will most certainly let you know. But for now, the biggest threat to my creativity is having to deal with what *feels* like jealousy. From you."

Huffing, Erato planted her hands on her hips. "I told you, I don't *do* jealousy. I'm just aware of the inextricable link between your sexual satisfaction and your writing, so the fact that you've apparently decided to embrace celibacy alarms me."

Giggles erupted from deep within Kate, impossible to contain. "Oh, Erato. I had sex *this morning*. After a night of marathon fucking. Are you *really* concerned that I'm on the verge of drying up?"

"Fine." Erato stepped to the side and held open the screen door, head tilted in question. "Are you coming back inside?"

She was tempted to refuse, only to prove she could. But what was the point? She had fifteen hundred words left to write, minimum, and the afternoon was waning. It had taken her roughly eight hours to accomplish a little more than half her goal; unless she picked up speed, she wouldn't finish until after nine o'clock that night. Nodding, Kate approached Erato with caution. "Yeah, I should."

Before she could step through the door, Erato caught her by the arm. "Hey."

Kate stilled, then slowly made eye contact. "Hey."

"Are you *happy* with what you've written so far today?"

The expression of cautious hope on Erato's face frankly broke Kate's heart. In a moment of startling clarity, she understood that Erato was feeling both threatened and insecure about her role in Kate's life—

and no doubt about her usefulness—now that Kate was not only upset with her but also refusing her sexually. Erato had promised not to leave until this book was done, and Kate didn't doubt that she would honor her word even if it meant being treated with hostility every step of the way. Despite her lingering anger over the missing cell phone, Kate softened. Erato was only trying to help her finish the book on time. Even if she hated her methods, hadn't she willingly signed up for this *because* the results were so damn good?

This morning was no different. Even though it had been difficult to get started and her pace remained frustratingly choppy, she was almost positive she was producing some of the best writing of her career. Careful to keep it as platonic as possible—not an easy task with such a beautiful pair of tits pressed against her own—Kate drew Erato into a brief hug. "Yes. I think this book will be good. *Thank you.*"

Erato tightened her arms around Kate but didn't hesitate to release her when she backed away. "I can't wait to read it."

For the first time that day with Erato, she managed a genuine smile. "Me, too."

❖

She reached thirty-five hundred words slightly ahead of schedule, around a quarter of nine o'clock that night. Her fingers ached, but that was nothing compared to her brain, which had dissolved into absolute mush. She wasn't entirely positive that her last five hundred words were coherent—she might have to revise them tomorrow, but she'd told herself that was all right, that this was exactly what every one of her former writing mentors had meant when they'd suggested that she silence her inner editor during the first-draft stage. It didn't exactly leave her feeling comfortable, but with both her deadline and permission to contact Olive on the line, she was willing to let go of her silly expectations of rough-draft perfection and let the words fall where they might. She could either clean things up before she turned the manuscript in or address the issues during editing. Either way, what she wrote today wasn't set in stone.

Exhausted but triumphant, Kate rose from her chair just as Erato knocked on her office door. She stretched on tiptoe, flexing her fingers as she raised her arms above her head, before calling out, "Come in."

Erato entered the room like a beam of light. "Ready to unwind?"

"As always, impeccable timing." Kate spotted the joint and lighter in Erato's hand and frowned. She wanted to stay sharp and adversarial, if necessary, until they'd settled the matter of moving forward with Olive. "But no, I'm not ready to unwind quite yet. First we need to revisit this morning's discussion, like you promised."

"All right. Well, I'm still not giving you permission to contact Olive, and certainly not to have dinner with her."

"What the hell is wrong with you?" And just like that, the incredibly fragile hold Kate had on her control snapped. This wasn't a situation where she could tell Erato to fuck off, then go ahead and contact Olive despite the bullshit rules. Unfortunately, she hadn't had the foresight—rather stupidly, she acknowledged—to write down or even memorize Olive's number. That meant Erato was in complete control of her ability to communicate with Olive, short of waiting until next weekend's farmers' market. Kate's rage over her sense of powerlessness, which had been simmering for hours, boiled over. "You explicitly fucking promised to revisit, *not* reiterate! How the *fuck* is this partnership supposed to work if I can't take you at your word?"

Once again, Erato remained infuriatingly calm. "But I *did* revisit… in my head. This afternoon while you were writing, I realized that you were absolutely correct—it would be unfair and downright cruel to leave Olive wondering why you haven't contacted her when you told her you would. So I let her know what was going on."

Kate's stomach dropped. "*What?* What did you say?"

"That I wasn't comfortable giving you permission to date someone until you finish this book, and that you won't be free to speak to her until then. I also thanked her for understanding where your priorities lie and told her that if she wanted to talk through her feelings for you in the meantime, I'm available."

Kate winced. She'd literally *just* assured Olive that Erato was simply a writing coach with unconventional methods, and now Erato was talking about granting permission as though she held the keys to Kate's chastity belt. Or worse yet, as though she was Kate's partner in more than just writing. *Erato works* for *you, right?* If Olive had questioned that before, what must she think now? And just *how* small did Erato's offer to play therapist make Olive feel?

Yeah, this was bad. And if Kate couldn't figure out how to deploy some serious damage control by way of a follow-up text, if not ejecting Erato from her life altogether, this might spell the end for whatever she might have built with Olive. Shaken, Kate said, "Was she upset?"

"Maybe."

"What do you mean, *maybe*? Did she reply?"

"Yes."

Kate waited a beat. Then when it became clear that Erato didn't plan to share, she snapped, "*What did she say?*"

Erato shook her head. "This is exactly what I meant—instead of worrying about Rose and Molly and what they're feeling as they attempt to define their relationship, you're distracted by Olive. What *she's* feeling, how *she's* doing."

"That's because she's a real person!" Kate exploded. "With real emotions and real expectations about how a decent person acts after they fuck you and then promise they want more than just sex. And besides, *you're* the one creating the distraction! I wouldn't be distracted right now if Olive wasn't potentially furious with me!"

Rolling her eyes, Erato placed her hand-rolled cannabis cigarette between her lips and sparked up the lighter. "Well, we both know *that's* not true."

Kate waited until Erato had taken the first, harsh, mostly paper hit before snatching the joint from her mouth. She took a desperate puff, eager to calm her rising fury. Then she took another. When she felt able to speak without shouting, she ground out, "Seriously, why are you doing this to me?"

Erato took back the joint and enjoyed a long, lingering hit before answering. "You know why." When Kate opened her mouth to protest, she placed a finger against her lips. "Listen: *you* are an artist. So do what great artists do—take all the pain and frustration you're feeling right now and *use* it. As an artist, you must embrace all facets of the human experience wholeheartedly—good, bad, and indifferent—while taking mental notes along the way. If you're able to do that, then every difficult period of your life, every struggle, every adversarial roadblock becomes nothing more than potent fuel for future creations."

Snatching the joint from Erato's condescending grasp, Kate sniped, "*That's* the platitude you think will calm me?"

"Calming you isn't precisely my goal." Erato watched coolly as she took multiple, desperate draws on the half-smoked joint. "And there's a good reason for that. I suspect you're approaching the point in Rose and Molly's story where everything goes to hell for a few chapters until they can resolve the story conflict and declare themselves happily ever after." When Kate didn't respond, she cocked her head in question. "Am I right?"

In fact, she would be tackling the meatiest part of the story tomorrow, the chapter she'd been looking forward to writing for quite a while: Rose and Molly's interrupted make-out session, followed by Rose's mother's accusations and overreaction. But even if that scene demanded high drama, the presence of such in her own life had never helped her writing before. On the contrary, even minor angst seemed to leave her scattered and locked out of her mental movie theater. Seething, Kate said, "You may think you're helping me, but you're not."

"History will be the judge of that, I suppose." Erato nodded at the cold joint in Kate's hand, then produced a flame that she held steady in the space between them. "You finish the rest of that by yourself. You need it more than I do."

Kate didn't argue. She relit the end, then leaned against the edge of the desk and sucked desperately on the ever-diminishing source of good feeling between her fingers. Even pot wasn't taking the edge off the bitter disappointment and anger that festered within the blackest part of her soul, a frighteningly negative storm of emotion that rendered her wholly incapable of appreciating anything about what she'd actually accomplished over the course of the day. Irritated and eager to lash out, Kate grumbled, "This *fucking* worthless book."

Erato gave her a disapproving frown. "It's not worthless, and you know it."

It made her somehow angrier that Erato was right. After months of hating this novel on principle, Kate was beginning to recognize that it was one of her better efforts. The book might even have the potential to become something special. Her writing had never been more mature. She'd created high emotional stakes for her characters and was well positioned to deliver a uniquely satisfying ending. The erotic scenes were among the hottest she'd ever written, inspired by the very real, very earth-shattering sex she'd been privileged to enjoy with the two most alluring women she knew in the real world. So no, the novel wasn't worthless. It was the value of her wayward muse's draconian presence in her life that she was no longer sure about.

Sickened to visualize only one way forward, Kate said, "No, you're right. The book isn't worthless."

"I'm glad to hear you say that."

Without meeting Erato's eyes, Kate made a decision that, days ago, would have felt impossible. "Listen, I appreciate everything you've done for me. Really. But now I..." She hesitated, aware she might not be able to retract her next statement. "I need to ask you to leave."

Erato giggled. "Oh, sweetheart. You know I can't do that."

Kate looked up and pinned Erato with her coldest stare. "Excuse me?"

"I can't leave. Not even if you beg me, per your own words. Not until the book is done."

Kate had never before felt so close to flat-out losing her shit. She wanted to scream at Erato, to pick her up and physically remove her from the premises. Wary about her odds if she engaged in hand-to-hand combat with either a supernatural being *or* a mentally unbalanced individual, she counted to ten before answering. "You have no right to stay in my apartment if I tell you to leave. I'll say this plainly, without an ounce of ambiguity. I want you to go. Leave. Now."

Erato shook her head sadly. "Sweetheart, that's *not* what you want, and I honestly believe you know that, too."

"Well, there goes your all-knowing, all-seeing muse act, busted wide open." The madder Kate got, the nastier her tone and the words she burned to unleash became. She was tired of being told what she knew and believed and wanted, especially when it increasingly contradicted how she *actually* felt. "I want you the fuck out of my life, you meddling bitch. You think I don't want you gone? I'd call the police on you right now if you hadn't stolen my phone."

Inexplicably, Erato's pained expression tugged at her heart. "Believe me, you *really* don't want to do that."

She believed her. Honestly, Kate *didn't* want to involve law enforcement except as a last resort. Even if she managed to summon the police to her door, she had no idea what Erato would do or say to defend against her accusations. Somehow she sensed that her muse's gregarious, magnetic nature would easily charm the responding officers into dismissing Kate's complaints—or worse, suspecting *her* of some kind of wrongdoing. Still, she was happy to make threats if they got her point across. "Try me."

Erato pursed her lips. "Now you're just being ridiculous." She sighed, then arranged her hair with nervous hands. "Listen, the easiest way to make me leave is by finishing your book. Simple as that."

Kate tried to calculate her remaining word count. She was approaching the final act of her novel, but she still had a lot of work. The interrupted tryst would lead to a temporary breakup, a couple chapters of loneliness and soul-searching from each point of view, then a lucid conversation between Rose's mother and Molly in which the former homophobe offers her sincere blessing as she hates seeing her beloved caretaker so sad and her daughter not at all. Finally, the highly anticipated reunion between Rose and Molly, which would naturally involve a lengthy love scene. Wrapping up the story wouldn't take a lot more effort—maybe just a final chapter to hint at a happily-ever-after— but on the whole, the entire endeavor seemed incredibly daunting. Between her rising burnout from the furious pace she'd maintained for the past few weeks and the depression created by her muse's cruelty, she wouldn't be able to finish in less than two and a half weeks, minimum. After that she'd have to spend at least a few days polishing the manuscript for submission, which would lead to additional scenes and places where she would need to drop in character beats and flesh out the story.

She might very well need every one of the twenty-one days she had left to finish, and that was at least twenty days too long to wait for Erato to stop fucking up her life. Olive would have most definitely given up on her by then, and with good reason. No, writing her way out of this wasn't an option. Not if she wanted to win Olive back.

It was obvious that Erato had made up her mind, with an iron resolve. She couldn't talk her out of her decision. That left one possible course of action, which would require Kate to stop arguing and start thinking. Subterfuge. She had to pretend to throw herself into her writing—well, not *pretend*—while devoting her spare time to looking for opportunities and weaknesses to exploit. Muse or not, Erato *did* sleep on occasion. She might be able to find her cell phone and at least copy Olive's number—or else figure out *some* other way to let Olive know she was being held captive by her off-the-rails writing coach.

But before she could do that, she needed to accept her powerlessness over the current situation. She had to smile—and she did, as sweetly as she could manage with her hands still clenched into fists at her sides. Most importantly, she had to agree to Erato's terms, because to do otherwise was to invite more restrictions and a level of scrutiny that might be impossible to overcome. In this, with Olive's love and trust at stake, failure wasn't acceptable. She would do whatever it took to get out of the mess Erato had created for her.

So she took a calming breath and said, "You're right. I'll finish the book." Closing the distance between them, she gave Erato a friendly hug before swiping the lighter from her hand. She would need every bit of the roach she had left to get any sleep tonight. "Simple as that."

CHAPTER EIGHTEEN

When Kate sat down to work the next morning, both her anger and her sense of urgency had only grown sharper. She'd slept fitfully, plagued by anxious dreams in which Olive wouldn't accept her phone calls or texts and had apparently changed her number altogether. In typical dream fashion, everything had shifted and she found herself lost at the farmers' market, walking down endless rows of stalls looking for Olive and her father and always coming up empty. Then, back to her apartment, where the police had knocked on her door to deliver the message that Olive didn't want to talk to her and, in fact, absolutely hated her, and also that she was being sent to prison for being a terrible person. Then suddenly she *was* in prison, and Erato was her jailer...and so on, and on, and on until Kate couldn't stay in bed any longer.

She'd asked Erato to move into the guest bedroom after their discussion the night before, as cordially as possible, and had been relieved when her wishes were readily honored. As she scanned the final paragraphs of yesterday's efforts, making minor corrections along the way, she half listened to Erato walk around her new accommodations. The masochistic part of her couldn't wait to find out how things would play out today and beyond. Would Erato maintain their normal daily routine, minus the sex? Would she prepare and serve breakfast to Kate like everything was fine?

Kate got her answer almost thirty minutes and two hundred words later. That's when Erato knocked on the door and, full of breezy confidence, swept inside only after being granted permission to enter. She dropped off a glass of water and a plate of pancakes with maple syrup, wearing a wide, toothy, adorably sexy smile, then left with a chirped "Good luck!" and a brief squeeze of Kate's shoulder. The simple touch seemed to naturally loosen the tense muscles in Kate's back, helping her relax, and simultaneously sparked a fierce, focused desire to dive right back into her fictional world.

The worst part about Erato's maddening rules and restrictions and directives, Kate decided, was that they kept her from enjoying the genuine benefits of her muse's company. No matter who Erato was, or *what* she was, her mere presence inspired Kate to be at her creative best, always. Despite what she'd decided in anger the night before, the gifts Erato had to offer were far from useless. It was an awful, stupid twist of fate that she'd happened to meet Erato *and* fall for Olive all at the same time, because without her desire to maintain control over her romantic life, she would probably accept nearly any stricture Erato imposed. Even though she'd asked her to leave, Kate hated the idea of having to relearn to write without the clear-headed inspiration her muse provided.

"This sucks," Kate muttered under her breath, then took a grudging bite of pancake.

She let her mind wander as she chewed, thinking about Olive with all the defiance of an intentionally disobedient seven-year-old. It had now been over twenty-four hours since they'd last spoken, and no doubt at least twelve since Erato had decided to send those text messages. Where was Olive's head at right now? Was she devastated? Understanding? Pissed off? She wished for some way for her to check, to smooth things over as necessary.

As she'd predicted, writing through her anxiety about what Erato was doing to her and Olive wasn't exactly easy. But, surprisingly, it was apparently very possible. Even if her progress had slowed considerably, the words that did end up on-screen actually satisfied her always-harsh inner critic, with very little additional editing required. She was both surprised by how natural it felt to channel her own tumultuous emotion into the inner lives of her characters and irritated by the idea that, yet again, Erato's bullshit theories had some merit.

In the past, Kate would have allowed her current level of turmoil to yank her out of her characters' heads for the rest of the day. At least. With Olive's feelings at stake, that simply wasn't an option. If she couldn't devise some covert way to evade Erato's control, finishing the book could be her only ticket back into Olive's life. She had to plan for any eventuality, and unfortunately, it was possible—even probable—

that Erato would be able to predict and deflect any trickery or deceit on her part. That uncomfortable truth—along with the hard reality that her deadline cared not about her love life—would keep her honest about working even as she plotted in silence.

Besides, Erato might suspect the rebellion in her heart if she didn't continue to boost her total word count—and that wouldn't do. Her best chance at success depended upon preserving the element of surprise. If such a feat was even possible.

Kate finished her pancakes quickly, then waited for the knock that came almost immediately after she swallowed her last bite. "Come in," she called out, and mustered a pleasant but restrained smile. Too over-the-top with her affability and she'd arouse suspicion; too surly and she'd invite unwanted attention. She wanted only to hand off her dirty plate so she could bask in the two to three hours of solitude she'd have before Erato came to check on her again.

Erato took the plate with a small curtsy. "How were they?"

"Delicious." Kate placed her fingers on her keyboard, ready to type. "Back to work."

"That's the spirit!" Erato blew her a kiss, then flounced out of the room with an enthusiasm undeniably pleasant to watch. Especially as reflected in the subtle movement of her firm, round ass.

"For fuck's...stop looking, Kate," she grumbled under her breath as soon as she was certain Erato wouldn't overhear. "*Stop looking.*"

And that's when she had a brilliant idea, one she was embarrassed not to have landed upon last night. She might not have access to Olive's phone number, but why else did Internet search engines and social media exist, if not to solve conundrums exactly like this one? She knew from Olive's father that her last name was most likely Davis. They owned a bakery, and what business didn't have some presence on social media these days? Olive could even have a personal profile somewhere, which would offer an easy way to send her a message.

Forcing herself to stay calm—lest Erato feel the psychic vibrations of her anticipation through the walls—Kate opened a browser window for the first time that day. She navigated to her favorite search engine and spent a moment composing the most foolproof string of key words that she could imagine: Olive Davis bakery Sonoma County. Before she clicked the search button, she took a moment to send a silent plea to the universe to let this plan work. She might still have time to soothe

Olive's hurt feelings, but only if she got a chance to explain before another day of radio silence from her end destroyed whatever goodwill might remain between them. Taking a deep breath, she initiated her search and held her breath as she waited for the results.

The default search engine screen remained open, her criteria plastered across it. Kate shifted uncomfortably, glancing over her shoulder at every random noise she heard, terrified Erato might sneak up behind her and discover her transgression. After nearly a full minute of waiting for the results page to load, Kate frowned and stopped the page from executing. She tried again immediately. Her stomach twisted when the page instantly refreshed to display a cute ASCII graphic and the ominous message *Unable to connect to the Internet* emblazoned across the top.

At first she wasn't sure *what* to think. Until now, even with the threat of derailment via cute animal videos, Erato had allowed her access to the Internet. Truthfully, she hadn't been using it nearly as much as she normally did. Per Erato's advice, she'd been avoiding the news sites that only depressed her, along with social media and other forms of pointless distraction. She'd mostly stuck to checking her email during breaks and occasionally searching for research purposes. She had given Erato absolutely no reason to justify cutting her off now.

Maybe it was a coincidence. Maybe her provider was simply down, or she needed to reboot. She clung to her last vestige of hope as the computer restarted, then cursed when, after a few minutes of detective work, it became clear that this was no accident: it was sabotage.

Her gut instinct was to confront Erato, although that meant admitting she'd attempted to go online in the first place. But that wasn't exactly an admission of guilt, was it? Despite the light subject matter of her books, she had to conduct all sorts of research. Sexual positions, rope-bondage techniques, and BDSM best practices were frequent areas of interest. Depending on the tale she was spinning, she might need to look up details about weapons, surnames, the careers of her characters, real-world locations or events, as well as anything else she wanted to be accurate about. In fact, the more she thought about Erato's latest punishment, the madder she got.

With this, Erato had flat-out interfered in her ability to work. *The art is her only concern, my ass.* Simmering, Kate tried to decide if it would be better to pretend she hadn't yet noticed that the wireless router had been disabled. She risked alerting Erato to the real reason she wanted Internet access, which would surely make life even harder. Then again, Erato was most likely already perfectly aware of the way her mind worked, hence the blatant pulling of the proverbial plug.

As soon as she decided she had more to gain than lose at this point, Kate closed her browser (lest she leave behind incriminating evidence) and left the office in search of her muse. She found her in the guest room, sitting cross-legged in bed with the newest model of Kate's five-year-old laptop balanced on her knees. A pair of pink headphones obscured the sound from whatever she was watching, but judging from the smile on her face, it was pretty spectacular.

Erato lit up when she noticed Kate standing in the doorway. "Oh, Kate! You have to come watch this, seriously. This tiny, adorable kitten is *so* surprised, over and over again..."

Kate walked to the bed, craning her neck to confirm what she didn't want to believe. Apparently the Internet outage was limited to her computer alone. A familiar—and yes, spectacularly adorable—viral video was streaming in all its full-screen glory, evidence that what was good for the gander was apparently unacceptable to the muse. Kate watched until the end before speaking. "I came in here to tell you that our Internet connection was down, but apparently it's a fairly localized outage."

Clicking on to the next video, this one starring a baby goat, Erato didn't tear her attention away from the screen for even a second. "*Very* localized. Your computer, specifically."

This time Kate had to count to twenty before she could speak, which gave them both plenty of time to watch the exuberant cuteness of brand-new goat-hood. Finally, she raised her voice to make sure Erato would hear her over the sound of the video. "You cut off my Internet access?"

Erato snorted at the baby goat's antics, then clicked over to a different video before the current one ended. "I sure did. You tried to search for Olive?"

Wishing she'd prepared a cover story before opening her mouth, Kate blurted out the first excuse that came to mind. "No, I wanted to read more about..." She flashed on the scene she was just beginning to write: Rose visits with her mother, then goes to find Molly in the room of a dead patient. How did the patient die? What in the world did she need to learn about so badly? "Bowel cancer." She winced. "Or is that too much to even hint at in an erotic romance?"

Erato pulled the headphones from her ears and studied her intently. "What's your gut feeling?"

"Too much. You're right." She hesitated, then when it looked as though Erato might resume her viral film festival, said, "Even so, I really do need to be able to get online when the situation demands it. You may not think my silly sex stories require any real research, but I happen to take pride in being accurate about even the most minor details."

"Hey, hey." Erato touched Kate's wrist in an obvious attempt to soothe. "Believe me, I recognize that your stories—which are anything but silly, by the way—require serious thought and even some occasional nonfiction reading. The good news is, *I* have access to the Internet." She angled her laptop toward Kate, beaming. "If you need to get online, I'm happy to let you do it from here."

"While you watch over me like I'm some sort of prison inmate?" She covered her frustration over the ruining of her plans with a minor eruption of righteous indignation. That Erato had correctly guessed her true motivation had no impact on her ability to generate a healthy dose of legitimate outrage. "*Nice.* Really respectful."

"I don't see what the big deal is, if you weren't intending to try to contact Olive anyway." Erato set the laptop aside but remained seated on the bed. "Look, having limited Internet access is a *good* thing this close to your deadline. It removes temptation. *All* temptation."

"It also makes my job harder if I have to yank myself out of the story so I can come in here and talk to you every time I want to pursue a stray thought. Did you think about that?"

"I hear what you're saying." Erato's placating tone only heightened Kate's irritation. Where did the woman get off? "Unfortunately, this is a delicate case. I'd rather risk distracting you with longer research breaks than deal with the fallout of a well-placed search on social media for Olive or the family bakery."

Even though she'd anticipated that Erato would try to block any attempt she made to circumvent her missing-cell-phone problem, Kate still felt shaken to have been bested so quickly and effortlessly. "You're a real jerk sometimes, you know that?"

Erato responded by releasing a sweet peal of laughter totally at odds with the harsh comment that preceded it. "You're not the first writer to tell me so." She smiled pleasantly, then picked up her laptop and waggled it in the air. "Still need that search engine?"

Kate was too mad to care about keeping up her cover story. "Forget it. Too much, remember?"

Chuckling, Erato said, "All right, then." She slipped the headphones back over her ears, winked, and returned her attention to her screen. "Unless you need something else, I suggest you get back to work. The day is still young, and I know you want to get a lot more accomplished than you've managed so far."

Swiveling on her heels, Kate stomped silently out of the guest room. She started back toward the office out of habit, then stumbled to a halt as another thought occurred. Her truck. Out in the parking lot sat her ticket to the outside world. All kinds of places offered Internet-enabled computers for public use—she could find one. An even more earth-shattering realization set her heart racing. Of course! Her wireless provider's website would have a detailed list of her voice usage charges, each one identified by the associated phone number. Locating Olive's contact information would be easy, as long as she found a way to get online.

Kate dashed down the hallway and into the kitchen as quickly and quietly as possible. Thus commenced a frantic search: the hook where she was supposed to hang her keys, the bowl full of spare change where they usually ended up, the counter, her purse, then into the living room, the coffee table, beneath the couch cushions, by the front door—until finally she stopped, sweat dripping from her forehead, and accepted the obvious. Erato had anticipated this plan, too.

What other ideas had Erato already worked to counteract? For all she knew, the passwords to her online accounts had already been changed, including that of her wireless provider. It was possible, even probable, that Erato's devious, detail-oriented nature had enabled her to preemptively undermine even the most brilliant gambit Kate might think up. Perhaps she'd even found a way to remove every trace of Olive Davis from the Web. If anyone could, it would be Erato.

Kate returned to the kitchen, utterly defeated. Pouring herself a glass of now much-needed lemonade, she took a long drink as she analyzed her predicament. She was being held captive in her own home. So far Erato hadn't barred the doors to prevent her from leaving the apartment—as far as she knew—but she was otherwise cut off from the outside world. Short of trying to walk her way into town or flag down one of her rarely seen neighbors without Erato noticing, she could do little else but finish the book.

Walking for help *was* a possibility, although it meant a bit of a hike, and if Erato noticed she was missing within the first twenty minutes or so, she could easily hunt Kate down with the truck and force her to come home. Appealing to a neighbor might also work, but the other tenants in her small unit were nearly as quiet and reclusive as she was. She sometimes went days without seeing anyone, and even when she did, few people seemed to linger outside for much longer than it took them to walk between their outside-facing apartment door and the shared parking lot. If she wanted to get someone's attention, she would need to move quickly and stealthily the second an opportunity presented itself, without hesitation. And she would have to hope like hell that Erato wouldn't see her and interrupt, because she knew who would acquit themselves better in an awkward social situation.

Whatever she chose to do, she would need a high degree of confidence about her odds before she'd feel comfortable enough to act. She would probably get only one chance at escape. Any weakness she managed to exploit would no doubt be managed with brutal efficiency, and the potential consequences for her disobedience would likely be harsh. If she wasn't careful, she could wind up locked in her office—even chained to her desk. As much as she wanted to believe those fears were extreme, she was done underestimating Erato. The woman had made it abundantly clear she would do whatever it took to keep her away from Olive until she finished the book.

Dejected, Kate returned to the office, but not before very quietly testing the front door to make sure it still opened. To her immense relief, it did. Too frightened to run without a solid plan in mind, she closed the door and rushed to her desk. It was only after she was back where she belonged, in front of her laptop with her hands on the keyboard, that her anger resurfaced. Lashing out at Erato was clearly pointless, but as timing would have it, she happened to have another perfectly good target for her wrath.

Two of them, actually.

Aware that she was *way* too happy about the prospect of devastating Rose and Molly by forcing them apart via an interfering third party, Kate began typing—determined to do just that.

CHAPTER NINETEEN

The next five days passed quickly even as Kate's output slowed to a steady trickle. Almost as soon as she was finished writing the interrupted kiss and all the delicious angst that ensued, her anger toward Erato flattened out and her general emotional trajectory began to echo that of her characters. She had just broken up Rose and Molly, her perfect couple, and left them utterly destroyed by the unexpected turn of events. Their stark depression, their mutual sadness over what might have been, their shared anxiety and regret and the feeling of powerlessness they had about a situation beyond their control—it all perfectly reflected Kate's growing anguish over the inexorable march of time and her ever-diminishing hope that she would be able to find her own happily-ever-after.

Five days, a prisoner in her own home. She had promised Olive dinner. A chance to talk. A possible future. But all she'd given her was another reason to feel insecure, and no doubt heartsick. It really, really sucked—to put things in distinctly unliterary terms. She had never intentionally given anyone the silent treatment before, even those who'd probably deserved it. Being forced to give the cold shoulder to a woman she might actually love turned her stomach. Despite the delicious food Erato kept bringing her, every day it became more difficult to eat. Her mood sank lower and lower with the passage of each minute of her forced radio silence, as she imagined Olive's hurt and anger growing fiercer and more enduring.

So yes, while words continued to trickle out—each of them admittedly powerful and evocative of a turmoil she now knew all too well—wrangling them onto the screen felt like pure torture compared to the free-flowing ease of writing the chapters of passion, romance, and highly charged drama that came before. It wasn't simply the subject matter that was slowing her down. She was mentally and physically exhausted. After having spent nearly two years not writing much at all, this weeks-long marathon had pushed her to the absolute limit. Now that she was afraid and depressed on top of being overtaxed, every day required intense effort to keep going. If not for the slim possibility that Olive might forgive her one day, she probably wouldn't even try.

What really pissed her off was that before this Olive situation, she could have leaned on Erato for the energy, motivation, and sexual healing she needed to make it through the last third of the story. Now she didn't want to rely on Erato for anything—at least nothing more than absolutely necessary. Even if she had no choice but to depend upon her muse for access to the Internet and the world beyond her apartment complex, she could at least refuse to surrender to the comforts and pleasures Erato offered so freely. After all, if she gave in even a little, she might be persuaded to cave all the way—maybe even going so far as to voluntarily banish Olive from her thoughts until the book was submitted. Or forever. *No.* Her hypothetical future with Olive felt far too tangible to allow Erato even the slightest opportunity to make her lose focus on what was *really* important.

But could Erato easily revitalize her creative spirit and give her the push she needed to sprint to the finish? Could she end the torture of this final slog in the most pleasurable way possible?

Undoubtedly. *The jerk.*

What made the sixth morning of imprisonment different was that it was Saturday, which meant that for the first time, Kate knew exactly where Olive would be—for approximately five hours, at least. The farmers' market started at eight o'clock in the morning and ran until one. She had no idea how long it would take Olive and her father to pack up their booth and leave once it was over, so she would need to get to the town square by one o'clock at the very latest to ensure that the trip wasn't a waste. She would likely only have one chance to pull off such a bold escape, so she shouldn't try if she didn't think she could make it there in time to intercept Olive and have a face-to-face conversation. While she couldn't imagine deciding to delay contact for another week after the agony of the one she'd just endured, it would be better than waiting the two weeks it would take for her deadline to arrive.

By eight thirty that morning, Kate realized that writing just wasn't going to happen. At least not until after the farmers' market was over, and only then if she hadn't already dissolved into a puddle of bitter, mournful tears. It was impossible to focus when her window of opportunity was narrowing every second. Her heart wouldn't stop racing even though she sat perfectly still at her desk, hands motionless on the keyboard. Her gaze remained stubbornly fixed out the window, on the manicured landscaping that her apartment complex did such a nice job of maintaining and the sidewalk leading away from the building and toward the parking lot. If she was going to ask someone for a ride into town, it would need to be as they were walking to the parking lot or returning from their car. She had to be ready.

Unfortunately, by ten o'clock it became clear that her neighbors enjoyed sleeping in on weekends—or at least not venturing outside early in the day. Though she'd managed to write a sentence or two since first sitting down to work, her attempts at forward progress were cursory at best and specifically timed to coincide with those moments when Erato was due to check in on her. Although she never *saw* Erato glance at her word count or even look at her screen, she didn't want to call attention to her sudden, intentional drop in productivity and ruin her chances of escape.

"Stuck?"

Kate nearly succumbed to a heart attack when Erato's voice cut through the silence and interrupted the apologetic plea to Olive for a second chance that she had been mentally rehearsing while she waited for a potential hero or heroine to appear outside her window. She hadn't heard the office door open behind her. The single word, so evocative of her state of being at the moment, confused her as she tried to decide what, exactly, Erato was asking. Stuck here with a madwoman, forced to write like a literal slave to her muse? Yes, she was. Stuck within the narrative of her story? Maybe a little, as she hated the slog of writing post-breakup blues.

She turned to answer Erato but fell silent and stupid at the sight of her dressed only in a sheer white camisole and a pair of blue boy shorts. It took an embarrassingly long time to kick her brain back into gear, and even longer to tear her gaze away from Erato's visibly erect nipples. She answered without taking any additional time to think. "Not stuck as much as drained. I've been going-going-going, and now that my characters are just as depressed as I am, I seem to have hit a wall." As soon as she heard the words come out, she worried that Erato might use her confession as a reason to make her leave her post at the window—and maybe even spend the next few hours together. She hurried to add, "Well, not a *wall,* exactly, since I'm still moving."

"Maybe you should take a short break. We could go for a walk."

She doubted she could outrun Erato in a footrace, so even if the prospect of being outside was admittedly enticing, it would be foolish to accept the invitation. As long as she was with Erato, she couldn't keep trying to make it to the farmers' market in the next—she checked the time on her laptop as subtly as possible—two and a half hours. A walk would be a waste of precious time, as was *every* second she spent in Erato's presence. Shaking her head, she said, "No, that's okay. Honestly, I feel like I'm close to a breakthrough. Or something." Trying not to cringe at her frantic backpedaling, which felt so transparent she was certain she'd just ruined everything, Kate managed a weak smile. She had to come up with a way to keep Erato busy, *away* from her, stat. "Maybe I'm just hungry?"

She didn't realize how brilliant a diversionary tactic she'd just unleashed until Erato lit up with excitement. "Of course! It *is* almost snack time, after all." Clapping her hands together, Erato said, "Anything you want. *Anything* at all, I'll prepare it for you."

After almost a week of celibacy, which once again felt foreign following their month of near-constant fucking, Kate couldn't help but recognize the similarities between Erato's food-related promise and the one she made at the beginning of their sexual relationship. As angry as Erato made her, and as much as she missed Olive, Kate would be lying if she claimed she didn't miss sex with her muse. She did. It had been incredible: whatever she wanted, pretty much whenever she wanted it. And she knew—*knew*—that the wonders of Erato's sexuality were all still available to her. She just had to ask.

Kate realized two things simultaneously: despite her low mood, she was suddenly incredibly horny, and perhaps more startling, she was tempted to ask for the quickest of quickies. She didn't know whether to blame biology or witchcraft, but either way, it was clear she'd allowed this interaction with Erato to go on for far too long. The thought sparked an idea.

And it was *good*.

Kate racked her brain for a meal request that would keep Erato in the kitchen for at least the next two hours. Erato usually cooked while listening to music through her headphones, and if she also had the distraction of a complex, fairly involved recipe to keep her busy, Kate might be able to devise a bolder escape plan. Not being much of a cook, she had a limited knowledge of foods requiring lengthy preparations. However, she did have a single, horrific memory of a childhood cooking class that involved a pile of flour, eggs, and the complete loss of her pride. "You know, I'm really craving lasagna. But with fresh, homemade pasta."

"No problem!" Erato gave her a sunny smile that made Kate think she should have thought bigger. Much bigger.

"And could you make the pasta sauce from scratch, if you don't mind? I hate the stuff from the jar." When Erato's expression failed to change, Kate added, "With fresh tomatoes? Not canned?"

"Of course! How else would I do it?"

Shit. She made it sound so *easy*, and it probably would be, for her. In a final effort to complicate the request, Kate asked, "Veggie lasagna? With little chunks of onion, three different colors of bell pepper—but mostly red—zucchini, and squash? Maybe even some mushrooms or spinach?"

"Absolutely. Your wish is my command, darling."

Well, that was as complicated as she could make things without being totally obvious. But then another exciting thought occurred. "I hope I'm not forcing you into a trip to the grocery store. There's a big game on TV today…it'll probably be crowded." At least she hoped it would be.

"Actually, you're in luck. I went to the grocery store last night after you fell asleep—the twenty-four-hour one, downtown—so I could restock your kitchen. I bought a whole bunch of fresh fruits and vegetables, replenished all the staples—sugar, flour, eggs, milk—and pretty much picked up whatever else I could think of to satisfy your every potential need." Erato bounced a little, clearly pleased with her own foresight. "As it happens, I managed to get *everything* I need to make you the best lasagna you've ever had!"

Kate covered her disappointment with an over-wide grin. "Wonderful."

Erato tiptoed closer to plant a quick kiss on top of her head, then practically skipped out of the room, closing the door behind her. Glad to finally be alone, Kate sighed. All she could do now was sit back, wait for Erato to get busy, and hope she'd bought herself an opportunity for escape. She wanted to wait at least fifteen minutes before she attempted to step away from her desk, just in case Erato suspected the ulterior motive behind her very specific culinary cravings and was currently waiting outside the door. She turned back to her laptop, but her eyes refused to take in the half-written paragraph in front of her.

How could she possibly pay attention to her stupid book at a time like this? She had less than two and a half hours to formulate and execute an escape plan, find Olive at the farmers' market, and beg for her understanding and forgiveness. And then what? She had no clue. Sneak back here like nothing had ever happened? Or return with Olive so they could confront Erato together?

Glancing out the window, Kate groaned at the sight of the still-desolate sidewalk. She tried not to dwell on the twisting sensation in her stomach as she considered the possibility that Olive might not even *be* at the farmers' market today, or if she was, that she might be unwilling to hear any apologies. Instead she fantasized about how it would feel to hold Olive again. If she'd known last weekend that their parting embrace might also be their final one, she would have tried harder to memorize every detail. As it was, she'd already lost her visceral hold on the intoxicating sweetness of Olive's natural scent, the smoothness of her skin, and the absolute perfection of every line and curve of her miraculous body. Momentarily distracted from her mission of watchfulness, Kate closed her eyes to reminisce.

Their hushed, hurried morning sex had been altogether transcendent in a way that Kate hadn't fully appreciated at the time. Now that she'd had a week to examine her feelings for Olive, and to feel the pain of hurting her and the fear of losing her forever, she realized that last weekend was the first time the physical and emotional aspects of intimacy had truly come together for her the way it always did for her characters. She'd had amazing sex in the past, even genuinely tender sex with one ex-girlfriend, but last weekend was the first time she'd *made love* and actually *felt* it, as corny as that sounded.

Kate opened her eyes to briefly check the window—nothing—and the time—only five minutes gone, not long enough to start sneaking around—then closed them again, defiantly plunging herself into a fantasy of being naked with Olive. Holding her. Caressing her breast, then sliding her hand down between those inviting thighs to find the wetness that always seemed to be waiting for her. Without really thinking about it, Kate traced a similar path down her own body, only catching herself when her fingertips brushed against her clit and she unleashed an involuntary whimper.

It wasn't just that she hadn't been fucked in a week. She hadn't even given *herself* an orgasm. Frankly, she hadn't been in the mood. Given the current situation, she didn't understand how she could be now, but between Erato's sex magic and her thoughts of Olive, it was apparently possible. And since she had a few more minutes to pass…

Only slightly sheepish about her ability to be aroused while rapidly running out of time to escape, Kate bit her lower lip and forced herself to come up with a fantasy that would get her off quickly. As a general rule, the dirtier and more deliciously depraved the scenario was, the faster she would come. Sad, but true. So she settled almost instinctively into a storyline that involved Olive reacting to her apology with a burst of furious passion. Rather than forgive her, she would lead Kate by the hand to somewhere out of sight but still close to the bustle of the farmers' market, then "punish" her by pinning her against a tree and taking her roughly, all while whispering the most vile, depraved, shame-inducing words into her ear. A rush of wetness assured her that she was on the right track, so she added a spectator into the background—a man, for an extra dose of kink and depravity—who watched brazenly as Olive reduced her to a quivering mess. Then when she was done, she would drive Kate home so she could do it again, but this time she would force Erato to watch, and disciplinary spanking would be involved.

Both relieved and disappointed to already be at the brink, Kate cracked an eyelid to check the time and nearly fell over backward in shock. The only neighbor with whom she was on a first-name basis— Chad, the flirtatious, admittedly attractive firefighter—strolled by on the sidewalk not far from her window, headed for the parking lot. Thankfully his back was to her, but Kate snatched her hand from her pants anyway, feeling caught. Then her brain engaged. This was it. Her chance. It didn't matter that she was still wearing the camisole and pajama pants she'd slept in—*stupid,* she realized now—nor that she was poised on the verge of orgasm. Her *only* objective was to get to Olive.

Even as she launched herself out of her chair and toward the office door, she realized that she'd managed yet another spectacular failure in the planning department. Last night, she'd tried to come up with a couple of reasons to explain why she needed to get to the farmers' market quickly and quietly, without using her own truck that was clearly sitting in the parking lot, but she hadn't settled on anything specific and definitely hadn't rehearsed a story. There was an extremely high likelihood that she was about to thoroughly embarrass herself in front of a man with whom she'd only traded occasional pleasantries. Not exactly her preferred way to spend a Saturday, but…

"Shit." The muttered curse slipped out when she tried to open the closed office door and found it stuck. Or locked. Or blocked. *Or something,* except she wasn't sure what, since she knew of no way to actually secure the door from the outside. But somehow, naturally, Erato had managed to seal her in. *Why* was she even surprised?

Yet she was. Surprised, and wholly unprepared to improvise. Now she had no shoes—only her slippers—and no purse, which meant no money for the taxi she'd planned to ask Chad to call. Still, she had only about two hours before Olive would be lost to her for another week, so this was no time to worry about trivialities. Right now her most important problem was how to get out of the apartment. She could come up with only one possible answer. She dashed over to unlock the window, grunting as she wrenched the bottom half open with considerable effort.

Now only the window screen stood between her and the outside world. The stupid, flimsy, bafflingly impassable screen.

Kate stood and stared for what felt like five minutes, horrified that she wasn't *exactly* sure how to pop the screen free from the window so she could climb out. Meanwhile, Chad's broad figure had just disappeared from view, presumably into the parking lot. "Wait!" Kate shouted after him, then immediately cringed. He couldn't hear her now, but Erato sure as hell might.

Even if she'd lost her chance to flag him down, she still needed to figure out how to remove the screen. A parade of one hundred people could pass by and do her no good at all if she couldn't leave the room.

Unless one of them could tell her how to take out the screen, that was. That brilliant thought triggered a flash of hope when she realized the answer to her problem was only a web search away. Then she remembered her lack of Internet access. The fate of this entire endeavor rested on her own ingenuity.

Fantastic.

"Okay." She forced herself to calm down and focus. It didn't take long to locate two metal tabs on the bottom of the screen, which she assumed must be important. She pushed them in, then yanked up on both tabs. A jolt of excitement ran through her when the screen nearly dislodged, signaling that she was on the right track. She jiggled the frame back and forth as she continued to push up on the tabs, until suddenly, thrillingly, the screen came free and tipped precariously forward. Afraid of making a commotion, she held her breath as she fought to keep her grip on the tilting screen, then eased the awkward object inside the room as quietly as possible with her shaking hands and racing heart.

Once she had the screen tucked safely between her desk and the wall, she considered how to climb out of the window without injuring herself. Her desk partially blocked the opening, which meant she had to either shove aside the heavy piece of wooden furniture or move her laptop so she could crawl over her work surface instead. All too aware of the seconds ticking by, she decided to take the faster, easier route. She moved her laptop onto her printer, then scrambled onto the desk to perch at the edge of the open window. Despite the need to hurry, she paused to survey the relatively short distance to the ground, experiencing a healthy dose of trepidation.

Luckily, her office was located on the first floor, so this type of exit was totally doable, although she *was* facing a nearly six-foot drop. But she had no good place to land. Just below her window lurked a scarily overgrown bush full of sharp branches—probably bugs and itchy stuff, too. Despite her fear, she was totally committed, particularly because she wasn't certain she could get that screen back into place without a real struggle. If she was going to get into trouble, she might as well go all out. Besides, this was important. This was for *Olive.*

She intended to lower herself from the window slippered feet first, holding the sill with both hands until she felt confident enough to let go. Maybe she could even swing herself out and avoid the bush altogether.

But like so many of her plans, this one fell apart almost as soon as she attempted to put it into action.

As she shifted her weight to lower her second leg out over the edge, her slipper caught on something just long enough to disrupt her center of gravity. Her upper body pitched forward wildly, leaving her helpless to prevent her subsequent face-first tumble out of the window. Time slowed so she seemed to fall forever. The blue sky disappeared in a rush, replaced by the green of the fast-approaching bush that waited to swallow her up.

And then her forward momentum stopped, leaving her suspended upside-down.

Dangling precariously by one foot—which was still slippered, and still inexplicably stuck on her desk—Kate tried to figure out her next move. She *really* didn't want to lose that slipper to the office, as she couldn't exactly go to the farmers' market in pajamas *and* only one slipper, because...*that* would be too much? She would have laughed if her chest wasn't starting to hurt and if the flow of blood to her head wasn't making her so dizzy. Unsure what she would do even if she reached it, Kate swung one hand up wildly, scrabbling to grip the windowsill effectively feet away and obscured behind her hip. She definitely wasn't able to pull off such a dexterous move.

Then her stubborn slipper came loose, falling uselessly off her foot to send her crashing down into a very uncomfortable piece of foliage. Kate was grateful she'd covered her face with her arms and closed her eyes as she landed, so her only serious injury was to her already-flagging pride. As she lay there stunned and unable to move, legs sticking out haphazardly from the shrubbery, she sent a silent thank-you to the universe that her kitchen window was on the opposite side of the building. Hopefully Erato hadn't heard her.

"Jesus, Kate, are you all right?"

The genuine concern in the deep, masculine voice—which came from somewhere above her—unleashed a wave of embarrassment that instantly heated her face. Great. Now she was bright red as well as disheveled. Too humiliated to move, she silently cataloged the visible damage: her camisole had ridden up to expose her stomach (and maybe more), and her hair was caught in the dense, tangled brush, no doubt completely disarrayed. One of her feet was bare. Worst of all, she could feel the wet spot she'd created on the crotch of her panties, shameful evidence of her decision to masturbate instead of staying alert. She couldn't tell if her arousal had soaked through her pajama pants to create a visible stain, but wouldn't that just be her luck?

Mortified didn't even begin to describe her state of mind. Still, she managed to respond. "I'm fine!"

Strong hands grabbed her by the upper arms and lifted her out of the bush, causing her perspective to shift wildly once again, until finally Chad set her back on her feet and all she could see were his piercing blue eyes staring at her in confusion.

"What's going on?" His gaze flicked to the office window behind her. A hero by trade, it was unsurprising that he'd be all business. "Is there a fire?"

"No!" Kate said a little too loudly. She lowered her voice and straightened her clothing. "Nothing like that." She paused, not yet sure what alternative explanation to offer. "Thanks for the assist."

"Of course." Chad's eyes narrowed as he took in her disordered state. "Not an intruder, I hope. Are you hurt?"

Only her ego. She managed to smile as she plucked a clump of leaves out of her hair. "Just embarrassed. I know I must look pretty crazy right now…"

He matched her smile, relief flashing across his face. "Crazy is no problem, as long as you're okay."

"I'm…" The impact had apparently wiped her mind clean, because she couldn't come up with a plausible story to explain her inelegant tumble. As a professional tale-weaver, manufacturing one little white lie shouldn't be much of a challenge. But as a half-naked woman who'd just fallen on her head in front of a man so effortlessly handsome she could almost feel herself slipping one notch in the other direction on the Kinsey scale, she was thoroughly tongue-tied. "I'm okay."

He raised an eyebrow, obviously waiting for more.

Kate cleared her throat. When in doubt, she decided, stay as close to the truth as possible. She wouldn't sound so stupid that way. At least she hoped so. "I'm sneaking out."

Chad's grin widened. "Oh, *really?*" He paused as a thought seemed to occur to him. "Wait, you're not bailing on that gorgeous woman you've been seeing, are you?" Clearing his throat, he somewhat subtly swept his gaze over her chest—no doubt recalling Erato's own assets with the fondness they inherently inspired—before quickly reestablishing eye contact. "With the dark hair...I think she said her name was Erato?"

Of *course* she'd gotten to Chad. Why hadn't she anticipated that? Erato was a social butterfly who'd had a month of days to kill while she'd been busy writing. She'd have met at least a few of her neighbors. Worried that he'd agreed to do her muse's bidding out of appreciation for her fantastic tits alone, Kate could only manage a weak smile. "That's her."

He offered her his fist. "Way to go, Kate, seriously. You've got game."

It took her a beat too long to figure out that he intended for her to bump him. She made a fist and delivered an awkward attempt, feeling stupid. "Well, thank you. She's quite a woman."

"If the sounds from your bedroom are to be believed, apparently so."

The earth could swallow her up any time now. Really. "Yeah. So anyway—"

"Hey." Chad's concerned expression was back. "I'm sorry. I didn't mean to offend you. Or come off like a creep." He raised his hands as though to prove that he was harmless. "The walls are thin. And Erato mentioned that you wrote erotica, so I figured..." He shook his head, lowering his hands slowly. "It doesn't matter what I figured. I apologize. I promise I'm not *that* guy. You're just like my lesbian idol is all."

His bumbling apology allowed her to relax slightly, as his mild embarrassment put them on somewhat more even ground. Kate folded her arms over her chest—*why* hadn't she put on a bra this morning?— trying to adopt a casual air despite her state of undress. "Don't worry about it. That's what I get for being so good in bed."

Laughing, Chad visibly relaxed. He mirrored her pose, folding his toned arms over his broad chest. "So *why* are you sneaking out, exactly? And where in the world are you going dressed like that?" Clearly still worried about causing offense, he hurried to add, "Not that you don't look lovely."

"Nice save." She managed a smirk that she hoped made her look cool. "Well, I *did* have two slippers when I started to climb out the window. So there is that."

Chad looked behind her. "Want me to get the other one for you?"

Nodding, she said, "But Erato can't know I'm gone. She's supposed to be in the kitchen right now, cooking, but still..." She cringed, knowing how odd she sounded. "Can you do it quietly?"

He exuded cocky bravado. "Of course, ma'am. I *am* a trained professional." Then he winked, which only made her blush harder. "Give me a minute."

She watched, awed as he practically vaulted over the bush, pulling himself up into her office without seeming to sweat. Not until he'd disappeared did it occur to her to worry about what he might think of the mess she'd left behind. Had she left anything incriminating lying around? But it wasn't as though she had any pride left. Let him see a random vibrator or porn magazine or half-eaten candy bar. Like it mattered.

When Chad didn't reappear at the window immediately, she wanted to call up and ask what was wrong. A million possibilities flashed across her paranoid mind: Erato had caught him, he couldn't find her slipper, he was rifling through her desk drawers, he'd decided to betray her to Erato, or perhaps had been working as a double agent all along. Only her fear of alerting Erato enabled her to stay quiet and wait.

After what felt like hours, Chad's arm emerged from the window, her slipper dangling from his fingers. His head followed, then his broad shoulders, and before she could process how he did it, he had somehow managed to exit the window and land on both feet, clear of the obstacle below. He beamed as he presented her with the slipper. "My darling Cinderella."

"Prince Charming, indeed." Kate mustered a playful wink despite her unyielding self-consciousness as she finally completed her sleepwear ensemble. The guy was a flirt, so she would use that to her advantage. "Could you help me with just one more *tiny* thing?"

His chest honest-to-God puffed up, reminding her of a frigate bird she'd once seen in a nature documentary. Very dominant, very male stuff. Clearly she was on the right track. Chad flexed his muscles before answering, probably unconsciously. "Absolutely."

"So I'm not *bailing* on Erato." She surveyed their surroundings nervously, her paranoia belying her words. After confirming that her muse wasn't standing over them at the window, she gestured toward the parking lot. "Could we talk about it on the way to your truck?"

Chad's forehead furrowed. He wore confusion well. "Sure."

She started walking, trusting that he would follow. "I'm not bailing on Erato, but I do need to sneak away for an hour or so." Sensing that facts wouldn't work as well as fiction, she impulsively went with the first thing that popped into her head. "She's more of a writing coach than a girlfriend, see, and we're just about to wrap up our first big project together." That part was true enough. "I never thought I'd finish this particular book, so I owe her a lot." As was that. "Anyway, I thought I'd sneak down to the farmers' market while she thinks I'm busy writing and surprise her with…something. Like a gift."

Not her best effort, but hopefully it would suffice.

Once again, Chad seemed perplexed. "You didn't want to take the time to at least grab your shoes?" He gave her another skeptical once-over. "Or your purse?"

How would he react if she admitted that Erato had locked her in the office and that he was facilitating an escape? Not prepared to find out, she decided to veer far away from the truth. "I didn't want to risk being caught leaving, and it was sort of a spur-of-the-moment decision." She paused as the flaw in her story became clear. Without a purse, she had no money with which to buy the gift she claimed to be going to find. Thinking fast, she said, "A friend of mine is actually working the market today. I'm hoping she can help me out."

There. Not only did that make sense, but it was also sort of true.

Chad rewarded her with a real smile. "That's really sweet, to go to these lengths to surprise Erato."

Guilt twisted her insides—she hated lying, especially to someone so nice. However, she doubted he'd be as sympathetic to her cause if she admitted that she was actually slipping away for a rendezvous with another woman. "I try."

They arrived at Chad's truck, which happened to be parked only a couple of spaces away from hers. He glanced over at her ride, then back at her, grinning. "Let me guess. No keys?"

She patted the hips of her pocketless pajama bottoms. "Unfortunately, no."

"Need a lift?"

Her gratitude was so intense it left her boneless. "I'd love one, if you don't mind. I shouldn't be very long."

"No problem. I could stand to pick up some fresh vegetables, anyway." Chad unlocked his truck with the push of a button, and Kate scrambled into the passenger seat like she was entering the last escape pod to leave a self-destructing science-fiction starship.

Only after he'd backed out of his parking spot was she able to take her first deep breath of the day.

CHAPTER TWENTY

The drive to the farmers' market was the longest five minutes of Kate's life. Although she somehow managed to make small talk with Chad—he offhandedly mentioned, as so many people did, that he'd always dreamed of writing a novel—her mind raced as she previewed all the ways her reunion with Olive could play out. She mainly feared that Olive wouldn't attend the market today at all and that she had completely wasted her time and self-respect. Yet Olive might be there but turn Kate away without allowing her to explain. Or not forgive her even if she *was* permitted to apologize. She barely dared to imagine Olive actually listening to and accepting her apologies, then getting another chance to hold the woman of her dreams and kiss her sweet lips. It would destroy her to envision that potential outcome and then not see it realized.

Kate was relieved when Chad left her at the entrance of the market with the promise to meet her back at his truck in twenty minutes. Luck permitting, her conversation with Olive would go well enough that she could send him home without her, as long as Olive didn't mind giving her a lift back to her place. That would give them time to talk, maybe even have the chat they should've had over dinner a week ago. If Kate was lucky, maybe all it would take was one intimate, thoroughly honest exchange to satisfy Olive—and convince her that she was still worth the wait—until the book was done.

Unfortunately, whatever dim hope she had that Olive might actually be happy to see her faded the instant she spotted the bakery's booth at the far end of the market, verifying that yes, in fact, Olive *was* here—*and* she was angry. Kate faltered, suddenly a thousand times more self-conscious about her pajamas and slippers as she observed the steel in Olive's eyes at her approach. Her father Howard chatted amiably with an older gentleman who browsed their wares with the same level of scrutiny one might employ while shopping for the perfect wedding ring. He didn't seem to notice Olive's dark mood until she called out, "This isn't a good time, Kate," when Kate was still ten feet away from the booth.

Howard glanced sharply at Olive, clearly surprised by her icy tone, then turned his attention to Kate. His eyes widened slightly at her appearance, but he said, "I can hold down the fort if you want—"

"No," Olive said. She offered her father a brief smile but shut it down completely when she looked back at Kate. "A phone call would have been more appropriate at this point. And less awkward."

That was *definitely* true. Kate couldn't imagine feeling any more awkward. She'd never felt as silly, pathetic, cruel, and heartbroken. What a time to be in her pajamas. Her every instinct urged her to run away, to escape this humiliation and retreat to her writing cave before Howard's customer finally tore his attention away from the focaccia to stare at her, too. But she'd gone through too much—and the possibility that Olive was exactly the woman she'd always longed to find was too strong—to walk away now. Besides, this was her opportunity to make a grand gesture. Her characters did stuff like this all the time— albeit more smoothly and without making such asses of themselves. She stepped closer to the booth, off to the side, although she knew any sense of privacy would be illusory.

Lowering her voice, Kate said, "Please, Olive. I wanted to call, I promise." Her story was insane. Olive likely wouldn't believe it even if Kate chose to be completely honest. Even if she did believe it, she would almost certainly get angry. Either way, Kate didn't want to have this chat in the middle of a bustling marketplace. "Is there somewhere we can go? To talk?"

Olive folded her arms over her chest, face tight with anger. She didn't bother to keep her volume down. "You had your chance to talk to me a week ago. Now, I'm *working*, and this is unprofessional. I don't appreciate being ambushed in my place of business, so if you don't mind, *fuck off*."

Kate flinched as though Olive had just backhanded her across the face. Honestly, a physical blow would have hurt less. Even though she'd told herself Olive would be upset, and that she might not be forgiven, some part of her had believed she'd at least have the chance to explain. Deep down, she'd counted on the fact that the connection she'd felt—a connection Olive had also acknowledged—would be enough to earn her a second chance, no matter how ludicrous her story. To find out now that whatever feelings had existed between them hadn't been potent enough to persuade Olive to even hear her speak devastated her. After everything she'd gone through to get here, she couldn't bear to let things between them end so abruptly.

Mindful not to let Howard overhear, Kate murmured, "So that's it? All that stuff we said to each other, what we felt…it doesn't matter?"

She knew she'd said the wrong thing when fury flashed across Olive's beautiful face. "It didn't to you, obviously." Tears welled and threatened to spill over, and Olive cursed as she wiped them away. "I said fuck off, okay? Go back to Erato." She glared as though trying to burn away the lingering moisture in her eyes with her fiery gaze. "Just leave me the hell alone."

"*Olive*," Howard said sharply. His customer had finally left, the three of them now in relative privacy. "You're right. You *are* being unprofessional. Take five minutes and go cool down somewhere else. *Please*. I'll watch the booth."

In a huff, Olive brushed past Kate and stormed away through the crowd. Kate hesitated for only a moment before following. Relieved when Olive led them across the grassy lawn of the town square to a private spot under a large eucalyptus tree, Kate tried to calm the pounding of her heart while mentally rehearsing what she would say if given the opportunity to explain her week of silence. When Olive stopped under the tree and turned to look at her, extremely pissed off yet somehow still stunning, Kate took that as an invitation to speak.

"I'm so, *so* sorry. I wish I could say or do something to fix this, but at this point, all I can do is tell you that—I'm sorry, and I hope you'll let me make this up to you." When Olive just stared at her, seemingly unmoved, Kate kept talking. "Erato took my phone away last weekend after you left the apartment, or else I would have called you that afternoon. I *swear*. You're all I've thought about for the past week. I know it sounds crazy, but Erato went on this overly proactive rampage and took away everything she thought might distract me or prevent me from finishing my book on time." Wishing Olive would offer *some* kind of reaction, Kate said with a hangdog expression, "You were at the top of her list of threats to my productivity, unfortunately. So she did everything in her power to make it impossible for me to contact you."

To her surprise, Olive sighed—then seemed to soften slightly. Unfortunately, the decision to let go of her anger seemed fueled by defeat rather than actual forgiveness. "Listen, Kate…"

Uh-oh.

Olive's smile was anything but happy. "I really like you. You know that."

Kate's stomach clenched at the finality of the statement. "You said that being with me makes you feel alive." If she could make Olive remember what she'd felt that morning just by repeating the words, maybe she'd reconsider the breakup that now seemed inevitable. "And that you always wanted to feel that way."

Once again, Olive openly battled her rising emotion, wiping away the tears that fell before she could compose her features. "Yes, you absolutely make me feel alive. That's true. But after this past week, I realize it's not always in a good way. You clearly can hurt me deeply, and I'm sorry, but I've had enough hurt for one lifetime." She met Kate's gaze pleadingly. "There's just too much drama, too much complication. A lot of it seems to center around Erato, but this is just as much on you. She took away your *phone*? You're a grown woman and she's your *writing coach*—or so you claim. Despite the fact that you *promised* we'd meet for dinner and talk, all I got was a single, vague text message telling me you'd be in touch once the book was done. You want me to believe you had no other choice but to leave me hanging all week, sending unanswered texts to you like some sort of damn fool? Wondering what the hell I did wrong, if that morning, and the way we both seemed to feel, was all in my head?"

It wasn't difficult to imagine how the past week must have felt from Olive's perspective. "I'm so sorry." It was the only thing she could think to say. "It's hard to explain, and I know it sounds ridiculous, but I honestly tried my best to find a way to contact you. She's just…too clever. Today was the first real chance I had to get away."

As though noticing her attire for the first time, Olive frowned and gave her a careful once-over. "Wait, are you saying you literally had to *escape* from her to come here?"

Kate was stumped. Tell the truth and she might just win Olive's sympathy and forgiveness, but then what? Olive would want to confront Erato, or even call the police, if she knew Kate was actually being held against her will. For some insane reason, that still wasn't how Kate wanted to handle things. Erato was essentially harmless—but also because a police investigation would cause her to miss her deadline, not to mention totally complicate her life. And the entire endeavor would probably backfire. Law-enforcement officers wouldn't be magically immune to Erato's limitless charms and supernatural influence, and who knew how that might play out? All in all, complete honesty seemed like an unattractive option. Of course, she could downplay the reality of her captivity, even though it would make Olive doubt her claim that she'd genuinely tried to get in touch but couldn't.

Yup. No good answer.

Kate cleared her throat. "I had to sneak away. I have only two weeks until my deadline, so Erato has basically ordered me to focus on writing to the exclusion of everything else. She doesn't understand why it was so important to me that you and I talk before the end of the month, and I knew the only way I'd manage to see you was by not asking permission." She stopped, displeased. Was she making herself sound weak? Or like someone that others could easily manipulate and control, even to her own detriment?

Shit. Kate wouldn't want to date *herself* at this point. Unless she admitted that Erato was more than an average, overbearing human female, the fact that she was allowing a woman she was no longer even sleeping with to control her made her poor relationship material. Wishing she had the courage to explain why she felt so powerless to defy Erato, and that Olive would listen to that fantastical story with an open mind, she decided to shift gears and focus on what was really important.

"I like you, Olive, very much. I care about you and I desperately, *desperately* want to get to know you more. It kills me that I hurt you, and I fully acknowledge I don't really have a good excuse for my lack of communication over the past week—regardless of Erato's rules and restrictions." She paused, then decided to lay her heart bare, consequences be damned. "I think we could make each other very happy, if you'll just give me another chance."

Olive folded her arms over her chest, still guarded. "I need you to explain this Erato situation to me. Please." She waited a beat, then said, "Are you still sleeping with her?"

Kate shook her head emphatically. "No, not since that night the three of us were together. She's been staying in the guest room, and honestly, we're barely speaking. At this point things are strained, to say the least. I tried to sever our working relationship after she took my cell phone, but she refused. In fact, she says she won't leave until I finish the book, and it's easier to just put my head down and do it than try to kick her out at this point."

Olive's expression of concern deepened. "So, what, she's a squatter now?"

"In a manner of speaking, yes, I suppose she is."

"A squatter who has taken away your cell phone, attempted to isolate you from the rest of the world, and sabotaged a potential new relationship." Olive gave her a pointed look. "Have you thought about contacting the police?"

Well, damn. There it was, exactly the question she hadn't wanted to field. "It's...not like that." Kate struggled for a way to explain everything without trying to convince Olive that Erato was an honest-to-God muse that mere mortals couldn't stop, but she came up empty. This entire day was really crushing her storytelling self-esteem. Dumbly, she said, "I just think that would be overkill."

Once again, Olive's emotional state shifted before her eyes. Concern turned to wariness. "Fair enough."

Encouraged that Olive hadn't yet walked away, Kate said, "Look, I'm almost done with this novel. If I know you don't hate me—that maybe you're even willing to wait two more weeks and give me one last chance to show you exactly how important you are to me—maybe I'll be able to wrap it up even faster. Once I've submitted a manuscript to my publisher, Erato will leave. Then you and I will be free to get on with our lives...hopefully together, if I'm somehow able to make this up to you." Her heart threatened to pound out of her chest when she saw how unconvinced Olive remained. "Olive, I promise this isn't what life with me would be like—full of drama and complication. Usually I'm *way* more boring than my books, I swear. And fully in charge of my own life and decisions."

Olive nodded, but she radiated sadness. "I don't hate you, Kate. I was hurt, and upset, and honestly very angry, but I'm not anymore.

Now I'm just disappointed, and that's on me, not you. I accept your apology *and* I forgive you. I don't want to hinder your progress on the book, all right? So don't let me—we're fine, you and me, and God knows you don't owe me anything."

While she appreciated being let off the hook, that sounded a little too much like a brush-off. Olive hadn't offered to wait for her. Stomach turning, she searched Olive's face for a crack in her stoic facade. Didn't the thought of never seeing each other again hurt her, too? "May I call you?"

"You mean in two weeks?"

Kate hesitated. She couldn't make any promises that might be broken. "Unless I can figure out a way to do it sooner."

Olive gave her a humorless smile that contained absolutely none of the warmth Kate was used to seeing. "I really don't think it's a good idea. I'm sorry." For an instant, Olive's composure wavered. Kate could see genuine sorrow in her eyes and, if she squinted, perhaps even a moderate dose of second-guessing. But Olive was clearly committed to her course of action, because she didn't hesitate to say, "We had a lot of fun together, and nothing can ever change that. More importantly, you single-handedly reintroduced me to the land of the living, for which I will always, *always* be grateful. As much as I'd love to keep the good times going, I just…can't do this anymore. There's too much uncertainty for me, as much as I wish that wasn't the case." She paused, then as though anticipating a rebuttal, added, "You say now that she'll leave in two weeks, but what if she decides to stay? I wish I could trust you—and her—at your word, but I don't. Unfortunately."

She didn't drop onto her knees and beg Olive to reconsider because doing so would almost certainly make her look stupider than she already felt. Which was pretty goddamn stupid. Why *had* she let Erato bully her into submission? Now that she wasn't trapped in her apartment, it was easy to chide herself for not fighting back harder—physically, if necessary. By falling in line with Erato's totalitarian coaching style, she'd thrown away what might very well have been her only opportunity to experience the kind of love and desire that had until now been reserved only for her characters.

Even if Erato was supernaturally endowed with the ability to charm, persuade, and manipulate nearly everyone she met, Kate had fallen out from under her spell days ago. Sure, obstacles had littered her path, but surely she could have done more to reach Olive, and faster. And Olive had a point: if Erato refused to leave after her deadline had passed, Kate could have real trouble delivering on her promise of a more simplified life. What if Erato *was* lying about leaving?

Grief swelled deep inside her aching chest, followed by a breathless wave of regret. It was over. But didn't that mean she had nothing left to lose? Maybe she should just confess Erato's true nature, to explain how she'd gotten herself into this predicament and why it was so difficult to get out. Olive *might* believe her. But she rejected the desperate notion almost as soon as it crossed her mind. Olive already thought she was weak and easily manipulated; she didn't need to add mentally unstable to the list. At this point, her perceived sanity was one of the only things she still had going for her.

"I've got to get back to work. You should, too." Olive had gentled her voice, and from the tenderness in her eyes, it was clear she recognized the devastation she'd just wrought. Her full lower lip quivered briefly before she managed a weak smile. "Go home, Kate. Finish your book. I look forward to buying a copy."

Gutted by the new formality between them, Kate met Olive's pained gaze with tears in her eyes. "I'm happy to send you a free copy. You were my inspiration, after all. And I owe you for the muffin."

Olive closed her eyes briefly, then scrubbed her face with her hand and turned away. "Thank you, and good luck. I've really got to go now." She'd finally lost the battle with her own tears, evidence that she wasn't as unmoved as she clearly wanted to seem. Kate wished she could draw more hope from that than she did. Olive obviously cared about her—something real *was* there, for both of them—but without trust, they had nothing. No foundation to build on, no basis for a lasting relationship. Even if Olive were willing to give her another chance, she wouldn't be able to start earning her trust back until Erato had disappeared from her life, and by then it would be far too late.

It was probably already too late.

Utterly defeated, Kate said, "I apologize for ambushing you. Tell your father I'm sorry, too, for the scene." She paused, wishing she could conjure up a magical turn of phrase that would fix everything. Unfortunately, she wasn't nearly that clever with words. At a loss, she opened her mouth and spoke from her heart without trying to find the right thing to say. "I wish things had turned out differently. For a while

I actually thought you might be my happily-ever-after. At least I really hoped you would be."

Olive's shoulders hitched. Still facing away from Kate, she said, "Me, too." Then she made good on her promise to return to work, hurrying away toward the market without looking back.

As Kate trudged back to the parking lot to meet Chad, weighed down by regret and self-recrimination and soul-draining sadness, she realized that writing was literally the last thing she wanted to do— yet it was exactly what she *must* do, if she ever wanted to be rid of Erato. Necessary or not, she couldn't imagine spending the rest of the day at her laptop, engineering a happy ending for her characters when she'd just ruined her own. Erato might have taught her to write through adversity, but this was a whole different kind of obstacle. It seemed almost cruel to expect her to write a love story with a freshly broken heart.

How the hell am I supposed to finish this book now?

Erato was waiting for her in the window of her office when she and Chad returned to the apartment roughly forty minutes after Kate's not-so-great escape. If her muse was angry she hid it well, flashing Chad a radiant smile as she leaned over the ledge and proudly displayed her cleavage. "Well hello, you two. I was just wondering where my sweet Kate had disappeared to…"

Chad beamed up at her, then at Kate, wholly unconcerned that they'd been caught. "Busted."

Erato shifted her gaze to regard Kate with a bemused expression. Though her muse's cheerful facade never wavered, Kate sensed that she was in for a world of trouble once they were alone. In full flirtation mode, Erato said, "Should I be jealous?"

Kate was too mortified to answer, but Chad eagerly played along. "Are you kidding me? I can't possibly compete with what Kate has waiting for her at home." He winked. Erato giggled.

Kate barely suppressed the urge to roll her eyes.

Now entirely focused on Chad, Erato touched her collarbone in a way that seemed absentminded but no doubt wasn't, not-so-subtly ensuring that he couldn't possibly focus anywhere but in the vicinity of her infuriatingly amazing tits. "How are you, Chad? Making any headway on your first novel?"

He brightened, clearly excited that she'd recalled a key detail from their previous interactions. "A little, actually, thanks. The advice you gave me really helped."

Kate had heard enough. After having her heart ripped out and stomped on by a woman she'd fantasized about growing old with, she had absolutely no patience for watching Erato and Chad eye-fuck each other while chatting about craft issues. "On that note, I should really get back to work."

Erato gave her an approving, condescending nod. "Agreed."

Not eager to be left alone with an angry muse, Kate said, "But please feel free to continue your conversation. Maybe you two should go get coffee somewhere and talk about character development or plotting or whatever."

Erato gave Chad an apologetic smile. "Rain check, maybe? I really need to give Kate my undivided attention until she wraps her book up. Can't take our eyes off the prize now that we're in the home stretch, you know?"

Kate couldn't believe the litany of clichés that poured from Erato's full, pink lips. Her editor would slather her in red ink if she wrote dialogue like that. The small, silly observation helped dispel the notion that Erato was some infallible pinnacle of creation and served as a boon to her sanity.

"I get it." Chad bent to whisper to Kate, "Probably for the best, anyway. Didn't you have something you wanted to give her?"

With no idea what he was talking about, she nodded anyway. No point in resisting the inevitable now that Olive was lost. Two more weeks in her office prison—consisting of nearly fourteen full days of misery-fueled writing—and she would hopefully be done with Erato for good. Then she could move on and maybe even learn something from this experience. As long as the moral of this story wasn't "you had one shot at happiness and a crazy ancient Greek muse ruined it," that would at least be something. Looking up at Erato, she said, "Will you unlock the front door for me?"

She almost lost it when Erato shook her head and smirked. "No way. You managed to get out through this window. I refuse to miss the opportunity to watch you climb back in."

Kate had never wanted to slap someone across the face so badly. She gave Chad a helpless look, which he answered with a boyishly enthusiastic nod. "No problem." With a gentlemanly tip of an imaginary hat, he scrambled up the side of the building like the parkour artist he apparently was. Erato giggled in pure delight, which naturally inflated him even more. She moved aside coyly, allowing him entry into the office. Taking his place at the window next to her, he literally *flicked his nose with his finger* and said, "Beg pardon, ma'am."

Kate covered her face with her hand. She just couldn't. Could not *possibly* stand to witness the two of them in close proximity. Without looking, she called out, "Ready?"

After a slight hesitation, Chad announced, "Ready."

She removed her fingers from over her eyes and assessed the situation. Chad had ninja-warriored himself halfway out the window, anchoring himself to who knew what, one long, muscled arm extended far enough that she didn't even have to tiptoe to reach him. Unfortunately, she still didn't know how to avoid the carnivorous bush. Approaching it with exaggerated caution, she leaned against the sharp, wickedly uncomfortable branches and reached out for Chad's strong hand. He caught her around the wrist just as she lost her balance, once again crashing into the foliage with an ungraceful grunt. For a moment she considered just surrendering and staying where she lay, because really, how would she ever come back from today?

But Chad didn't give her a choice. In a feat of what seemed like impossible strength, he lifted her dead weight out of the clutches of the shrubbery and hauled her upright. His other hand beckoned for hers. "Grab on, Kate. We're almost there."

He really was a sweetheart. Without a trace of laughter in his eyes, he pulled her inside, handling her in a remarkably gentle manner considering the difficulty of the task. Not so for Erato. Although she allowed only a bare smile to show, her eyes danced with barely suppressed mirth. "Oh, you poor thing," she cooed when Chad finally set her down on blessedly solid ground. Erato stepped forward quickly, plucking a leaf from her hair while tugging up the side of her pajama bottoms that had ridden too low during her bushwhacking adventure. "Here, let me help you."

It was official. She wanted to die.

Stepping away from Erato, Kate resisted the urge to simply flee the room. A glance at the door confirmed that it was closed, so it might be locked and she couldn't, anyway. Even if she could, the only way to preserve any remaining dignity was to bid Chad a polite thank you and farewell. After all, it wasn't his fault that her grand plan had gone to shit. Or that a supernatural sociopath had hijacked her life. Or that she'd face-planted into the same bush twice in one day. Mustering up the very best smile she could manage—not as good as one of Erato's fake smiles, but it would do—she turned to address her savior cum co-conspirator in humiliation. "Thank you for everything." She intentionally kept her gratitude vague, because even if Erato would eventually drag the truth of what they'd been doing out of her, she refused to initiate that talk in front of their guest. "Sorry for derailing your day."

"Not at all. This was fun." Indeed, Chad was glowing. The guy nearly vibrated with happiness. And why not? He'd gotten to play hero more than once without having to risk life or arguably limb, had earned the gratitude and attention of two women whom he'd apparently enjoyed hearing fuck each other, and had borne witness to some of the greatest physical comedy performed since Lucille Ball was in her prime. Not bad for a Saturday afternoon. "Should I let myself out the window, or…"

Erato laughed and looped her arm in his. "How about I walk you out?" She led him to the office door and opened it, glancing back over her shoulder at Kate. "You should go shower. Lunch will be ready soon."

The savory aroma of baking lasagna filled the air. Why had she ever imagined that something as mundane as entirely homemade, from-scratch roasted vegetable lasagna would ever challenge Erato? She nodded, not wanting to say anything too revealing in front of Chad. "Fine."

She went into her bedroom while Erato showed Chad to the front door. She might never have a better opportunity to look for her cell phone than right now, even if she only had a minute or two before Erato returned, but her appetite for subterfuge had disappeared. She had nobody to call. Although things with Olive hadn't ended as acrimoniously as they could have, even a text message wouldn't exactly be welcome at this point. A fresh wave of pain rolled over her at the memory of how excited she'd been to receive that first text from Olive after they'd reconnected at the farmers' market. Back when everything had seemed so full of possibility…She stopped near the foot of her bed, awash in so much sadness she literally couldn't take another step forward. She just wanted to crawl under her covers and go to sleep and not wake up until Erato had vanished from her life forever and she'd forgotten how safe the world had felt in Olive's embrace.

"Care to explain?"

Startled, Kate turned to the half-open door of her bedroom to find Erato staring at her with a mixture of curiosity and amusement. She seemed almost playful, entirely devoid of anger or disapproval over Kate's afternoon excursion. For some reason, the apparent lack of concern over her whereabouts offended her more than any lecture or spanking. Fed up and full of self-loathing for letting this *asshole* ruin her life—this asshole who happened to look no less beautiful than ever, and into whose comforting arms she still longed to collapse—Kate couldn't stop the day's emotions from spilling over. "Just leave me alone. Please."

Erato took a tentative step into the room, her good humor fading away. "What happened?"

Kate huffed in disgust. "Like you don't already know." She steeled her gaze and took her own step forward, narrowing the distance between them. "Even if you can't actually read my mind, I'm sure you've got some other way to figure it all out."

"Is this about Olive?"

Kate closed her eyes and silently counted to ten. Her stark depression seemed to crave a more emotionally satisfying outlet in the form of abject rage, but whatever pleasure she took from lashing out would be short-lived. Nothing good could come of a knock-down, drag-out argument right now. "Let's just say you don't have to worry about me being distracted anymore." She counted again to five, slowly, then said, "I don't have anything left to be distracted about. I'm too complicated and untrustworthy, and your mere presence in my life is a deal-breaker. So…" Taking deep breaths, she opened her eyes only when she knew the sight of Erato's stupid, pretty face wouldn't undo all her careful self-soothing. "You win."

Erato stared at her with sad, baby-doe eyes. "I didn't intend to upset you—or Olive, for that matter. My only objective—as I told you on the first day we met—has been to help you meet this deadline. Now I don't want to say I told you so, but this is precisely why I warned you against pursuing a new relationship while we were working together. You swore that your fascination with Olive was only sexual, but clearly that's never been the case. Things were escalating quickly, and I had to choose to end the self-sabotage you were about to engage in."

When Kate opened her mouth to object, Erato held up a hand and kept talking. "I know, you only asked to go out for one little dinner date, but believe me, it wouldn't have ended there." She finally took a breath, challenging Kate with fearless eye contact. "You know where it would have ended? Eventually, with you crawling back to that full-time job you can't stand. It may not feel like it right now, but I've only ever acted in your best interest."

The beast inside her stirred, but she kept a tight rein and offered only a terse "Bullshit."

"I would never have chosen for you to have your heart broken. Certainly not while writing a romance novel." Erato reached out to touch her hand but drew back at the look of warning Kate offered when she got near. "I tried to be extremely clear that you wouldn't have room for anyone new in your life until you finished the book. You swore you understood. What you're feeling now, you chose to feel."

How could Erato inspire such passionate and introspective writing about love when she obviously knew nothing about its genesis? "My brain understood. Unfortunately, my heart doesn't work that way."

Offering a tentative smile, Erato said, "Well, if you and Olive are meant to be together, my interference can't possibly be enough to keep you apart."

Kate scoffed. "Don't be stupid. We're not living in some silly, unrealistic romance novel. In the real world, sane, stable women like Olive Davis run away from toxic dating situations like the one you helped create, and I, for one, tend to *applaud them when they do*. So I can't even tell you how offensive it is to hear you imply that if only we were 'soul mates,' we might have earned some sort of special protection against the cold-hearted, evil shit you've pulled to keep us apart."

Erato flinched, the color draining from her face. For the first time, she looked truly wounded. "I'm not evil."

"No? Well, it sure feels that way. I mean, *come on*. You've turned me into a prisoner in my own apartment. How do you justify that? It's not like I was planning to shack up with Olive and bang her for a month straight without stopping to write." Kate curled her fingers into tight fists, trying to control her rapidly building anger. "It's not like I don't take breaks throughout the course of the day, anyway. *Mandated* ones. What would've been the difference if I'd had a meal or three with her instead of you?" She shot Erato an icy glare, eager to cause pain wherever and however she could. "Except, of course, that you would have had to share me in some way other than sexually. Maybe that was the problem? Not enough control for you?"

The mocking attitude that had been on display earlier was gone. Erato stared at her with cautious regret. "You know that's not really the issue. At least I hope you do."

"Well, it doesn't matter now, does it?" Kate glanced into her bathroom, suddenly craving the sanctuary and privacy of a hot shower. "Could you please leave? I want to be alone."

"I'll leave the room, but I'm not leaving you. Not yet." Erato paused, making Kate wonder momentarily if she actually expected a thank-you for that. Luckily, she kept talking. "Soon, but not yet."

"Not soon enough," Kate muttered as she trudged into her bathroom, loud enough to make sure Erato could hear. She slammed the door behind her without looking back to check on the damage she'd caused. It pissed her off that Erato dared to act hurt about anything at all, considering all the crap she'd subjected her to over the past month and a half. Granted, the woman had also been responsible for some incredible highs—literal and figurative—and had also magically resurrected Kate's writing career, but still. She had a lot of nerve to get her feelings hurt about taking some blame for Kate's broken heart, basically, even if she *had* tried to warn her away from falling in love.

Maybe Erato was right and an entanglement with Olive *would've* sunk her already flagging writing career. She would've much preferred to find that out the hard way. Especially because right now, from where she was standing—sobbing beneath the hot spray of her shower while cursing the entire concept of sex and romance—she couldn't imagine how losing Olive wouldn't do exactly the same thing.

CHAPTER TWENTY-ONE

K ate was able to write during the next three days only because her characters were still mired in their own pits of misery and despair. Their moods matched hers. That helped keep her moving, along with the dim hope that Erato would actually leave as soon as Kate typed *The End* on a manuscript fit for submission. Erato did her part by delivering a constant stream of snacks and delicious meals—including the best lasagna Kate had ever eaten, the insufferable bitch—while also seemingly imbuing her with the improbable ability to push through her depression just enough to allow for the translation of her parallel feelings into the voices of her characters.

She was producing the most emotional work of her entire life. Even as she wrote, she wondered how she would stomach revisiting this part of the story, considering that she was attempting to grapple with her own sense of loss and regret perhaps even more than Rose and Molly's. Now more than at any other time in her life, writing served as pure catharsis, a way for her to take everything painful and torturous and messy inside her and project it onto her characters' lives. She had no trouble articulating how desperate they felt to go back in time and do things differently. Their misery was her misery.

Editing was going to be a nightmare.

Luckily for Rose and Molly, their change of fortune was fast approaching. Although Rose's mother had assumed her daughter had taken advantage of Molly—never imagining her beloved nurse might be a lesbian—Molly decides she needs to have a frank conversation with her charge and correct her assumptions. Kate had been looking forward to writing this scene: a heart-to-heart talk between Molly and

Rose's ailing mother, where Molly finally takes off the kid gloves she's used to wearing and confronts Rose's mother with three simple truths. First, that she is a lesbian and has been since she was ten years old, having had an early and at the time inexplicable crush on Lilith from the television show *Cheers*. Second, that her daughter doesn't limit her romantic choices based on gender, which was a quality Molly happened to admire—after all, it left Rose open to every possibility for happiness. And finally, that she has fallen in love with Rose and, while she'd love to have her mother's blessing, she's no longer willing to deny herself and Rose a chance at happiness to appease old prejudices or out of blind loyalty.

Because romance novels demanded a happy ending, Kate intended to write one. Rose's mother wouldn't experience a miraculous change of heart as far as her comfort with homosexuality (as her character repeatedly referred to it), but she would acknowledge that she has always adored Molly as a person, and her daughter could do—and had in fact done—a lot worse. After a little discussion, during which Rose's mother tries to convince Molly that both she and Rose are more than pretty enough to win over a couple of handsome, single men, Molly convinces her that the time she has left with her daughter is too precious to spend arguing about Rose's very nature, which hasn't changed despite years of her mother's overt disapproval. Molly is surprised but relieved when Rose's mother finally agrees and gives her blessing.

After that, she would have to write a reunion between Rose and Molly in which story problems are resolved and their relationship officially begins—topped off with some steamy, desperately needed sex. *That* chapter would be a problem. She knew it already. Hell, even the pivotal scene with Molly and Rose's mother was proving to be a problem, and it was the part she'd longed to write since she'd conceived of the characters and their story. Unfortunately, despite falling into a natural groove while navigating the doom-and-gloom section of the tale, she was finding it much more difficult to switch gears and channel a spirit of forgiveness and reconciliation into her writing.

If she wasn't feeling it, she wasn't feeling it. Period. Hadn't that sort of been Erato's point from the beginning? The reason she'd not only thrown herself at Kate, but also dragged her out for their ill-fated sexual adventure in the first place? Back then, Erato had understood that Kate was detached from her sexuality as it related to other people, and that the resulting emotional and physical deficit prevented her from truly connecting with her art. Now, however, she apparently thought it was reasonable to demand that Kate write the happy, emotionally satisfying conclusion to her fairy tale while drowning in an ocean of her own tears and regret.

Overall, Erato's performance as a writing coach had gone seriously downhill. Kate wished for a supervisor she could speak to—or maybe a performance evaluation to fill out. The thought made her smile a little, which was nice…even if it didn't help her write any more words.

A commotion that sounded like it was coming from outside in the hallway dragged her out of her silent musing. She heard a muffled thump. Then shouting. Another thump. Startled, Kate swiveled in her chair to face the doorway, unwilling to guess what madness lay on the other side. With Erato, who knew? Whatever was coming, she hoped like hell it wouldn't derail her mood even further. She had only nine more full days to complete her manuscript before her deadline arrived, which didn't feel like nearly enough time when she considered the arduous task in front of her. She was low on energy, patience, and inspiration, and she didn't want to write a fake happy ending when she'd just discovered firsthand that it took more than a genuine connection, great sex, and good intentions to make even the most promising of meet-cute relationships work.

"This had better be *really* good," Kate murmured under her breath. Her stomach twisted in anticipation of the chaos about to erupt before her. Seriously, how the hell did Erato expect her to work? It was hard enough to tackle the seemingly impossible without also having to fend off random, rude interruptions from the person who claimed to want to protect her productivity above all else. "No distractions, my ass."

"What the *fuck* do you think you're doing?"

Kate jolted upright at the very familiar voice right outside her office door. *Oh, shit.*

"Please don't make this any more difficult—"

"Difficult? Bitch, this is *kidnapping!*"

The sound of at least one—but most likely two—bodies slamming against the wall had Kate jumping to her feet, horrified by the fear and rage in Olive's voice. Clearly she had been brought to the apartment very much against her will, through force. What the hell was Erato thinking? Was she a lunatic or just totally out of touch with human nature? The police would definitely get called now. If not by her neighbors, then by Olive, and with Kate's blessing. As far as distractions went, being made to act as an accessory to the abduction of a woman she really liked—who no longer returned that feeling—was about as disruptive as it got. Certainly more disruptive than a few dinner dates would have been.

As she listened to the tussle in the hallway, Kate knew one thing: in forcing Olive here, Erato had almost certainly sabotaged whatever chance Kate had of actually meeting her deadline. Which meant that everything she'd done—to Kate *and* to Olive—had been for nothing.

That made her every bit as angry as Olive sounded. What an idiot she'd been to ever think Erato had some master plan, or that the torment she'd exacted like a malevolent child on a defenseless animal had a real purpose. With one bone-headed, impulsive decision, Erato had revealed herself as an impostor. No grand design was at work here. No deep psychological understanding of Kate's needs as an artist, or even the seemingly supernatural ability to meet them. Whatever magic Erato had seemed to bring into Kate's writing life had obviously been an illusion, a clever manipulation executed by a sexually available con artist with all-too-human imperfections. Kate no longer had any doubt about Erato's true nature.

A real muse would understand that this was just *too much*. Nobody could write through something this fucked up.

Horrified that she was about to face a justifiably irate Olive while once again scandalously underdressed—this time only in pajama shorts and a skintight camisole—Kate circled in place and hunted for an escape while the knob on her office door jiggled. Her only option was the window, and she didn't want to go that route again. When the door burst open and Olive and Erato tumbled into the room, she was still standing there. Still barely dressed. Completely mortified.

Olive regained her balance before Erato did and lunged at her wildly. "Let me the hell out of here."

Erato dodged Olive's attempt to grab her, slipping out the door and slamming it closed with a graceful pirouette. Kate's heart stuttered when she realized that Erato was going to lock them in. Together. Olive had been charitable to her the last time they'd spoken, but Erato had just destroyed any goodwill she might have felt toward Kate or the time they'd spent together. This wasn't going to be fun.

"Bitch, open the motherfucking door!" Olive grabbed the

doorknob and rattled it angrily before pushing away with a grunt of frustration. She raked a hand over her short hair, then turned and stopped as she seemed to notice Kate standing there for the first time. "Were you in on this?"

"What? No!" When Olive took a step forward, Kate took a step back, bumping into her desk. "I had no idea she was bringing you here." Olive abruptly halted in the center of the room. "Why did she?"

"I don't know."

No doubt coursing with adrenaline, Olive's entire body had started to shake. "You know this is fucking crazy, right?"

"Yes, of course." Concerned by her obvious distress, Kate gathered her courage and moved closer, but stopped when Olive held up a trembling hand. The confrontation with Erato had obviously rattled her, probably even traumatized her—a woman who had already faced as much trauma as some of Kate's most tragic characters. Even if she hadn't known what Erato was going to do, even if she *couldn't* control her muse in any meaningful sense, Kate still accepted that Olive's pain was entirely her fault. "Are you all right? What happened?"

Olive's hand drifted to her chest, settling over her heart as though trying to keep it from pounding its way out. "She grabbed me when I was getting into my car in the parking garage at the mall. Like she was in a goddamn action movie. Just wrapped her arms around me and started dragging me over to the truck." The anger that had started to recede flooded back full force. "A uniformed cop was standing right there! I called out to him for help, but she somehow managed to convince the guy she was just helping a drunk friend home. Despite the fact that I was *clearly* articulate and *clearly* begging for his assistance! I offered to take a breathalyzer to prove I was sober, but instead he *helped* Erato get me into the truck. Even put plastic zip ties around my wrists so I wouldn't put up as much of a fight." Glowering, Olive paced back and forth while rubbing the aforementioned wrists. "That was either the most straight-up racist bullshit I've ever personally experienced, or else your girl has the ability to manipulate absolutely everyone she meets. Except me, that is."

"She's not my girl." Kate cringed as soon as the words left her mouth. Of everything Olive had just said, that was perhaps the least important point. To Olive, especially. "But that doesn't matter. I'm absolutely horrified by what Erato did to you. I'm so sorry that cop fell under her spell, though I'm not surprised. He had absolutely no right to assault you like that, and neither did she. I swear I had no clue she was planning this. If I had, I swear I'd have tried to stop her."

"*Could* you have stopped her?" Olive studied her carefully, as though still trying to decide whether Kate bore any responsibility for what she'd just endured. "Based on the past half hour we spent together, I'd say Erato is used to getting exactly what she wants."

"That's certainly true." Kate considered her options, then sighed. She could be honest because Olive's opinion of her couldn't get any lower, even if the story she had to tell sounded absolutely batshit crazy. "You're right about her ability to manipulate. At the farmers' market, you asked if I'd thought about calling the police when she wouldn't leave my apartment. What happened to you today is *exactly* why I didn't want to. I knew she'd be able to convince the officers that everything was okay, somehow. Or maybe even that I was in the wrong."

Olive frowned. "*How* did you know that? I mean, who is this woman? What does she want from you? From *us*?"

Although Olive had given her the perfect opening to delve into Erato's dubious backstory, Kate still felt exceedingly silly. "I guess I should start at the beginning?"

Olive was clearly impatient. "Where did you meet her? Did your publisher hook you two up?"

"No, she just…showed up one day. On my doorstep, literally—with groceries."

"And you just invited her in? A complete stranger?" Olive tilted her head, clearly skeptical about her decision-making. "Because of the groceries or her tits?"

Blushing, Kate said, "I didn't exactly *invite* her in." Though she knew she deserved a firm chiding, she still wanted to defend herself in response to Olive's judgmental tone. For a woman who'd just been abducted in broad daylight, she had a lot of nerve criticizing other people's efforts to escape Erato's otherworldly influence. "She just sort of *came* in. And she said…" Here was the part that would make them both sound like lunatics. Resolved to get it over with quickly, Kate mumbled, "She said she was my muse."

When Olive didn't respond right away, Kate assumed she hadn't heard what she'd said—which was probably for the best. But then Olive confirmed her crystal-clear understanding. "So she wasn't fucking with me at the bar? When she said she was flattered I'd heard of her, after I recognized her name from Greek mythology?" Kate shook her head, and Olive said, "She thinks she's actually a real *muse.*"

"Yes."

Olive blinked. "And you...*believed* her?"

Kate shook her head, then shrugged. "Let's just say I was skeptical. But...I don't know. She was so beautiful and charismatic, and she almost immediately propositioned me with hot, anonymous sex, which definitely clouded my judgment—"

"You let a strange woman talk her way into your apartment, where you then allowed her to bed you. Got it."

Kate fell silent, hating the way Olive could make her feel so small with just a few words. She already felt stupid about allowing Erato into her life. She didn't need agreement from a woman she could still so easily love. "It sounds ridiculous, I know. While I definitely wasn't buying the muse story, I *was* extremely lonely. So yeah, I did something impulsive. She said that 'making love' would help get my creative juices flowing, and after almost two years of celibacy, I thought she might be right. It was insane, and out of character, and I still can't believe I went through with it, but yeah, I took her up to my bedroom and we slept together. Later that night she asked me to tell her the first sexual fantasy of mine that came to mind, and I said a threesome, and then all of a sudden she's got me at this club—"

"Where you met me." Olive's jaw tightened. "So that story about Erato being your editor, or your writing coach, or whatever...that was bullshit. You'd only just met her that same day. She was calling herself a Greek-fucking-muse, but you were okay with getting me sexually involved with a mentally ill person, because she told you it would help your writing."

"I don't think she's actually *dangerous,*" Kate said weakly.

"You didn't see her in that parking garage." Rather than belabor the point, Olive exhaled. Then she scrubbed her face with her hands. "Look...I'm sorry."

Kate shook her head. "You have no reason to be. You're the innocent party here."

"That's the thing." Olive looked around the office for the first time, as though finally taking notice of their surroundings. "I have a feeling you are, too—an innocent party. I mean, look, accepting Erato's sudden presence in your life was clearly a lapse in judgment. But then again, it's not like I didn't sleep with someone I'd just met that very same day, so…" She looked suddenly exhausted as she shuffled over to the futon across from Kate's desk and sank down to sit on its edge. "Two someones, actually, including a woman with an unusual name who gave me kind of a weird vibe." She shot Kate an embarrassed, begrudging almost-smile. "Yet I ignored that vibe because she was really very sexy, and I was horny, and I'd sworn to myself that I was going to check at least one item off my stupid bucket list—but most importantly, because I *really* wanted to fuck her friend. Which is all a long-winded way to say I'm sorry for taking out my anger at Erato on you, because I'd be a hypocrite not to acknowledge that sometimes desire can override good judgment."

Despite the awfulness of the situation and her lingering uncertainty that Olive could ever *truly* forgive her for bringing Erato into her life, Kate's heart soared. But it wasn't as though she was free from blame. "I appreciate you saying so, but it *was* selfish for me to involve you in any of this. The mutual decision-making of that first night aside, I chose to pursue you after we ran into each other at the farmers' market that day, even though I knew I had this major complication in my life. Erato warned me from the beginning that I didn't have time to date while I was finishing the book, and *definitely* not to fall in love—"

"Were you?" Olive finally made and held eye contact. She almost seemed to be holding her breath. "Falling in love?"

She had no pride left, and nothing to lose. "I think I might have been, yeah." Unable to read Olive's reaction, Kate looked down at the floor, embarrassed by the sight of her bare toes staring back up at her. Why hadn't she at least worn socks? "I know we'd barely spent any time alone together, but…I was looking forward to finding out if what I was feeling was real."

"That's why I wanted us to have dinner together," Olive said quietly. "So I could figure out what I was feeling—and if it was mutual."

"It was." Gathering her courage, Kate finally lifted her face. "It *is*." Worried that her confession might be taken as presumption, she explained. "My feelings for you haven't changed, although I completely understand if you don't return them."

Olive's eyes welled with tears, and she cursed under her breath as she carefully wiped them away. "It's not like I've forgotten our connection. How easy it is to talk to you, how perfect your body feels against mine."

Kate tried not to shiver at the mental imagery that Olive's suggestive words triggered. She'd spent days pining for this woman she thought she'd lost forever. To be locked in the same room with her, close enough to smell her distinctive scent, was enough to launch her into complete sensory overload. She didn't want to get carried away and make a fool of herself, even if that was her new specialty in life. She needed to help Olive out of their current predicament, she decided, forcibly turning her mind away from increasingly lurid fantasies and toward the goal of redemption. "Do you have your cell phone?"

Olive shook her head. "She took it when my wrists were bound. I tried to grab it from her when she cut the zip ties in the hallway, but I'm not sure she even had it on her anymore. I don't know where it is."

Kate sighed. "I know how that goes." Because it was the only option, she marched resolutely to the window. "I'll escape and go for help. You can come with me, of course, but there is a slightly treacherous drop—" She attempted to open the window and failed. She tugged harder, afraid she was simply growing weak from her time in captivity, then realized that Erato—*that horrible, awful demon's spawn*—had somehow rigged the window to no longer open.

"*Fuck!*" Kate roared, then kicked the wall below the sill hard enough to bring tears to her eyes. Instantly regretting her outburst and the additional pain it had caused, she sank onto the floor and squeezed her toes in her fist. "She must have sealed it shut after the day I escaped to go see you at the farmers' market." Defeated, she hung her head in shame. "I don't know how else to get you out of here. I'm sorry."

"Hey." Olive's voice was soft. Tender. The sweet sound brought fresh tears to Kate's eyes. "Don't worry about that right now. Why don't you come here and sit with me instead?"

Too embarrassed and sore to move, Kate shook her head. "You don't have to be nice to me."

"How would that make this any easier on either of us?"

Kate managed a miserable shrug. "I don't know." She took a shaky breath. "I just can't believe she did this to you."

"I can't believe she did this to either of us." Olive paused. "So did she actually help you to write? Beyond simply locking you in a room and forcing you to work, I mean?"

"Believe it or not, yes. But I didn't start writing until the morning after the first night we spent with you, so technically I suppose *you* could have been part of my inspiration all along." Although there might be some truth to her new pet theory, she also didn't want to underplay Erato's very real influence on her life. Olive had to understand that Erato had provided her with an actual service beyond sex, that she had a valid and not-altogether-dishonorable reason for keeping Erato around at first.

"Don't get me wrong. Erato is absolutely muse-like, if not an actual muse. She shattered over eighteen months of well-entrenched writer's block within the first twenty-four hours. Time and again when I've been stuck or lost motivation, just being in the same room with her has helped get me going again. I don't know how she does it, but she can help me let go of everything else and lose myself in my work. Or at least she did before she cut me off from the world—you, in particular." Staring hard at the floor, she said, "After that, most of my motivation has come from her promise to leave once I finish the book. Even now her presence still has some beneficial effect on me. It may be the only reason I've been able to keep writing at all."

Their long silence seemed to stretch into weeks, then months. Kate had nearly convinced herself that the last five minutes had been a hallucination and she was in fact alone in the room, when Olive suddenly murmured, "Kate, please come here."

Using every ounce of courage she possessed, she slowly stood up, turned, and walked to the futon. She kept her gaze averted as Olive moved over slightly, giving her ample room to sit at her side. Kate made sure to leave at least a foot of empty space between their thighs. She clasped her hands on her knees and stared at her laptop, swept away by a powerful wave of bittersweet longing. Right now she'd give almost anything to escape into Rose and Molly's world, where at least she could solve problems and deliver happy endings to the people she cared about. Miserably, she whispered, "This is so fucked up."

"Yes," Olive said in a quiet voice. She curled her fingers around Kate's wrist, pulling one hand free and tentatively lacing their fingers together. "But at least we're together."

Kate's vision blurred before she could attempt to suppress her visceral response to the simple touch. She'd never expected to be anywhere close to this intimate with Olive again. Not trusting herself to speak, she gave Olive's hand a gentle squeeze. Olive's other hand found her chin, urging her to turn and make eye contact. She couldn't. She didn't feel worthy. Trying to explain, Kate rasped, "You deserve better."

"So do you." Rather than continue to entice Kate to come to her, Olive angled herself so she could drop a kiss on the corner of Kate's mouth. "I'm trying to forgive you, dummy. Let me."

"I know what you're trying to do. I just don't know why."

"Because I'm tired of feeling hurt and angry, especially since it turns out that I've wasted a stupid amount of emotional effort being upset with the wrong person." Olive raised Kate's hand to her lips, kissing each individual knuckle. "I realize now what you were up against with Erato, and how our lapse in communication happened, and how you've likely never had *any* control when it comes to that woman. *I understand.* And honestly, I'm relieved. To know that what happened between us wasn't about me—or even about you. It's like I can breathe again for the first time in weeks."

Kate turned, a move that put her mouth mere inches away from Olive's. "I never, ever wanted to hurt you. I was devastated when she wouldn't let me call. We argued...I tried. I swear."

Olive nodded, her large, expressive eyes shiny with tears. "I believe you."

It wasn't exactly *I trust you,* but it was a lot more than she'd ever hoped to hear. A tangible weight lifted, lightening her mood for the first time since their last date. Kate managed a genuine smile. "Thank you. I appreciate that."

Olive shot her a look of desperation before grabbing a fistful of her camisole and pulling her forward until their mouths touched. "Now kiss me," she murmured. "Please."

Worthy or not, Kate had never felt anything as *right* as Olive's lips against hers. She groaned as the tight control she'd been holding over her body melted away. Without thinking, she scooted closer to Olive while simultaneously gathering her into a heated embrace. Their bodies fit together as easily as ever, and to Kate's relief, both the intimacy and the sense of connection she'd always felt with Olive was still there, strong and true. At least for her. Worried that the feelings of reconnection might be one-sided, Kate broke away from their all-too-brief kiss after considerable effort. She steeled her nerve and searched Olive's face for the truth, scared what she might find.

Olive shook her head as she chased Kate's mouth with her own in a playful attempt to resume their kiss. "Stop me if you don't want to do this, but let me be clear. *I do*." She pressed Kate back onto the futon, then climbed on top of her so that the entire length of their bodies was pressed together. Gazing down at her kindly, Olive said, "Do you?"

The last time Kate had felt this nervous beneath a woman, she'd been a twenty-year-old virgin. Why she would feel that way at a not-so-innocent thirty-four years old, and with a woman she'd already fucked a handful of times, she had no clue. But she did, and it made her blush. Aware that Olive was waiting for her enthusiastic consent, Kate nodded. "Yes, of course. But I just…my head's spinning."

Rather than reinitiate their kissing, Olive moved a lock of barely brushed, shower-dampened hair away from Kate's forehead. "Then maybe we should talk some more."

That wasn't *exactly* Kate's first choice. "It's just that I don't know how…" She paused, corralling her scattered thoughts. Totally unbalanced by her close proximity to everything she'd wanted for too many torture-filled days to count, she struggled to translate her confusion into a collection of words that Olive would understand. "You said you couldn't trust me."

Recognition flared in Olive's eyes. "Yes, but I didn't have all the relevant information." Olive traced a fingertip over one of her eyebrows, then the other, further disrupting her ability to think. "Now that I do, why don't we agree to go back to trusting each other until one of us gives the other a reason not to?"

As a first, tentative act of trust, Kate raised her hand and traced Olive's delicate jawline with the back of her fingers. "Okay. I'd like that."

"Good." Olive shifted her lower body, then smiled—almost smugly—when Kate bit back a whimper. "Now may I kiss you again? Because I really, *really* want to."

She couldn't think of a single reason to say no. So she didn't.

Chapter Twenty-two

Kate had no idea how long they kissed—just kissed, like teenagers, though intensely enough that Olive's glasses had to be set aside—before a hand landed on her breast, electrifying her with a firm squeeze. Her body reacted instantly, the slick wetness soaking her pajama shorts and probably Olive's tailored linen slacks, as well. Every instinct she had urged her to tear off Olive's clothes, then her own, so they could consummate their reunion. But they had just one problem, serious enough that she managed to push Olive away right before their heavy petting approached Kate's personal red zone. "Wait."

Olive rested her forehead on Kate's shoulder and took deep breaths. "Of course," she murmured, moving her hand from Kate's breast to her hip. "Too fast?"

"Under normal circumstances, not at all." Kate waited until Olive had lifted her head before nodding at the door. "But she could walk in any time. Hell, for all I know she could even be filming us."

Olive glanced over at the door as though evaluating it as well as their adversary. "She'd do that? Record us?"

"I have no idea what she's capable of. If she thought she could use a video as blackmail to force my word count higher, maybe." Unsettled by her paranoia, Kate propped herself up on her elbows and surveyed the room. She didn't see anything out of place or suspicious-looking, but these days cameras were tiny, and Erato had already managed to weld her window closed without her noticing. "Maybe we should wait." She didn't want to suggest it but felt almost unethical not doing so. Making love would leave them vulnerable in more ways than one and expose Olive to potential future harm. "We'll have enough time for that once we get out of here, right?"

Rather than the hurt she feared seeing, frustration and then sadness passed across Olive's face. In a tremulous voice, she whispered, "Not necessarily, no." Kate realized her faux pas immediately, but before she had a chance to rephrase, Olive continued. "Nobody has enough time, even when it feels like you do. Jasmine had no idea that morning when we woke up that it would be her last time to do that, her last time for everything. My mother, too. She and my father were scheduled to depart for their first Alaskan cruise a week and a half after the accident. Something they'd wanted to do since I was little. They had plans, and it didn't matter at all. It *doesn't* matter." Olive placed her hand over Kate's heart, the gentle touch soothing her in the aftermath of the jarring speech. "I don't want that woman to steal any more of our precious time together than she already has. Do you?"

Despite the sincerity of her plea, Kate still wasn't entirely comfortable letting Olive risk the potential consequences of a sexual encounter while in captivity—even if she *had* masturbated to prison- and hostage-themed fantasies more times than she cared to admit. Caught between chivalry, good sense, and unabashed arousal, Kate whispered, "You're sure?"

Olive seemed absolutely determined. "If she walks in while we're in the middle of fucking, I say we disentangle as quickly as possible and jump her tag-team style. Surely we can overpower her—or escape, at the very least. She'll never see us coming. And if she does, hopefully our nudity will distract her."

Kate doubted their chances of success, but Olive was so adorable while discussing strategy she didn't say so. "All right, I'm game."

Olive kissed the tip of her nose. "But I doubt she'll interrupt us. In fact, I'm almost positive she'll leave us alone for quite a while."

"Why do you think that?" Too impatient to wait for another kiss, Kate stole one instead, a quick peck on Olive's smooth cheek. She reveled in the heat of the skin beneath her lips. "'Cause she's such a sweetheart?"

"Because Erato's sole concern has always been your writing, and she seems to always have a plan. If she's gone from keeping us apart to kidnapping me and locking us in a room together, she obviously thinks that whatever happens in here will help you meet your deadline.

You said it yourself: you've been struggling to work since she broke us up. I could be wrong, but maybe Erato brought me here so we could reconcile."

Kate wasn't entirely convinced. "That's an awfully charitable interpretation of events from someone who was ready to kill that 'bitch' less than an hour ago."

Olive chuckled. "I suppose so." She lowered her head to bewitch Kate with another slow, deeply erotic kiss. When she drew away, she murmured, "I'm still pissed off about her methods—especially how she got that cop to manhandle me—but at this point I just feel like... all's well that end's well?" She giggled, suddenly bashful. "Excuse the terrible cliché."

A nearly overwhelming rush of affection—maybe it was even love—flooded Kate, making her entirely unable to continue her arguably misguided attempt to protect Olive's virtue. And it *was* misguided, wasn't it? After all, Olive was a grown woman capable of making her own choices. Tilting her head, Kate gave her a heartfelt kiss that quickly turned into a sensual wrestling match. But even as they fought for dominance with their mouths as well as their bodies, the occasional, unsettling thought intruded. What if Erato posted the sex they were about to have online? Would their fragile relationship survive? Not even an hour ago, Olive had said: *sometimes desire can override good judgment.* She didn't want to fail Olive again. She wanted to do better.

Then a brilliant idea—her first in what felt like far too long—occurred. Kate broke away from their kiss and rolled out of Olive's embrace, excited. "I'll be right back."

"I...what?"

Kate glanced at Olive as she made her way to the closet on the other side of the room. Sprawled across the futon, she looked flushed, turned on, unself-consciously lovely beyond words, and totally baffled. Offering her a smile intended to reassure, Kate said, "We deserve a little privacy, don't you think?" She opened the closet and scanned the slightly disorganized contents before zooming in on a neatly folded stack of spare bedsheets. "Perfect." She grabbed a khaki-colored top sheet from the pile, then stepped back and raised her prize into the air, triumphant. "Only the best for you, my darling."

Olive still seemed uncertain. "Why are you...what?"

Walking back to the futon, Kate unfolded the sheet and shook it out before carefully arranging it over Olive's body. Then she crawled beneath the thin material and into Olive's waiting arms, relieved that whatever they were about to share would now belong to them alone. "I'm not sure I'd have been able to relax otherwise. Sorry."

Olive's grin was both breathtaking and infectious. "Don't be. You're sweet." She pulled the sheet over their heads, enclosing them completely within its protective bubble. The sunlight from outside filtered through the cotton material, allowing them to see each other easily. "Besides, I want you to be relaxed." Using one arm, Olive tugged her closer and held her in a loose embrace. Her free hand played with the low neckline of Kate's camisole, a teasing fingertip tracing the valley of her exposed cleavage. "Now that you've taken care of the privacy issue, how about you let me take off this sexy little top?"

They'd already kicked off their shoes during their make-out session, but otherwise hadn't disrobed at all—Olive was very much *fully* dressed. Kate put her hand to the top of Olive's blouse, thumb poised to undo the first button. "I'll show you mine if you show me yours."

Olive dissolved into sweet laughter, then groaned when Kate brought their mouths together for another impassioned kiss. They went to work simultaneously, setting off a flurry of tugging and unbuttoning and muffled giggling, until finally they broke apart so they could drop their respective tops over the side of the futon and onto the floor. Naked from the waist up, Kate felt real disappointment to see Olive still wearing a bra. Ahead of her complaint, Olive unhooked the front clasp with a deceptively simple flick of her wrist, then pulled Kate's hands forward to rest on the cups. Her own hands found Kate's bare breasts and cradled them tenderly, her thumbs stroking the undersides.

"Go ahead," Olive murmured, and gestured with her head. "You *did* show me yours…"

Delighted by her playful tone, Kate peeled open the bra and gave an appreciative whistle. "Worth it."

"Glad you think so." Olive angled her upper body so Kate could remove her bra while they remained safely concealed beneath the sheet. She looked downright luminescent, alight with obvious joy and arousal and relief, all of it a perfect reflection of everything Kate was feeling.

But as Kate discarded Olive's bra somewhere behind her, she realized her own body was going to the opposite extreme. Tears stung her eyes, her heart thrummed in her chest. She'd nearly lost everything she was holding in her arms right now, but somehow she *hadn't*. As messed up as it seemed, she had Erato to thank for that.

Olive brought a hand to Kate's face and wiped away a tear just as it fell. "Shh, no. Uh-uh. Not now. Right now is for making each other happy. We'll have a really good cry together afterward." She gathered Kate into a warm, almost platonic embrace. Demonstrating her ability to pluck the perfect words out of the air, Olive whispered, "You're not alone anymore, Kate. We're in this together."

Although her nipples immediately hardened as they pressed against Olive's rigid peaks, Kate found nothing overtly sexual about the way she was being held. While her desire didn't ease, her melancholy lifted immediately, replaced by an overwhelming sense of peace and safety. Kate curled her hand around the back of Olive's neck and pressed their foreheads together, looking deep into expressive brown eyes. Olive was absolutely right—what was wrong with her? Reconnecting physically was far more important than dwelling on the past or engaging in any further self-flagellation.

Setting aside everything except thoughts of pleasing Olive, Kate murmured, "I want to unbutton your pants so I can slide my hand inside. May I?"

Olive giggled, clearly caught off guard by the direct question. But her hips surged against Kate's, signaling her approval. "I'd like that."

Kate pulled back so she could look directly into Olive's eyes. She'd never had a lover who'd read her books before, much less specifically enjoyed the sexual fantasies contained therein. Confident that Olive would enjoy the direction her thoughts had taken, she popped the button on Olive's pants open, then lowered the zipper with excruciating slowness. Enjoying the hitch in Olive's shallow breathing, Kate murmured, "Is it all right if I touch you through your panties?" Having already gotten permission, she didn't wait for Olive to answer her second question before easing inside the now-open pants. She let her hand hover over Olive's sex, making it clear she wouldn't go farther without another, specific yes.

Olive's mouth parted, her supple lips inviting a kiss that Kate desperately wanted to give. Hovering inches away, Kate whispered, "And may I kiss you?"

"Yes, to both." Olive sounded absolutely breathless despite the rapid rising and falling of her chest. She whimpered when Kate kissed her lightly, then moaned at the first brush of cautious fingertips against her sodden panties. Her legs fell open, which only served to pull the material of her pants tighter around Kate's wrist, trapping her in place.

Kate wiggled her fingers, a brief burst of movement to remind Olive what she had to offer. She broke the kiss and stared into Olive's eyes. "Maybe I should take your pants off. It would be so much easier to touch you like that—and I want to touch you more than you can possibly imagine, Olive. Will you let me?"

Her nostrils flared. "*Please.*"

Kate sat up beneath the sheets and slowly worked the form-fitting pants down Olive's shapely hips. She planted a trail of kisses on the delectably bare skin left in their wake, but only after receiving a nod in response to an uttered "May I?" as her lips hovered over Olive's upper thigh. To Kate's wholehearted delight, Olive didn't become impatient with her questions or simply offer unfettered access to her body. Instead, she actually seemed to understand and even get off on Kate's love of explicit, vocal consent.

When Kate crawled back up to lie at her side, Olive laced their fingers together, kissed each of Kate's knuckles, then set her hand back over the crotch of the panties. She appeared suddenly shy, meeting Kate's gaze as though uncertain how to react. Kate flexed her hand, startled by how wet and swollen Olive felt through the silky material. She longed to sink her fingers inside Olive's depths, to stroke her slick labia, to massage the rigid clit beneath the heel of her hand until Olive came all over her. But she wasn't nearly there yet. Mindful to stay within their currently defined boundaries, Kate dragged her fingers up and down the length of Olive's sex, then made wide circles around her concealed clit.

"I love how you feel," Kate whispered, holding eye contact. "So soft, so wet. So reactive to my touch." She moved her hand lower, pressing her index finger into the material so she could locate Olive's opening. "May I touch your bare skin? I won't penetrate you, not yet." She circled her fingertip, perversely delighting in the way her actions seemed to belie her words. "I could just pull your panties aside, play with your clit a little." She flattened her hand, rubbing Olive with her palm. "Will you let me feel how excited you are?"

Olive opened her legs as wide as she could, hips bucking as she chased a firmer touch. "Yes." She hissed when Kate tugged the crotch of her panties out of the way, then raised her hands to palm her own breasts, twisting the nipples harshly. "I'm so fucking wet for you."

Kate flattened two fingers along the length of Olive's labia, applying shifting pressure to the slick, swollen folds. Pleased by the shaky inhalation that her touch triggered, she drew back and swirled the pads of her fingers in tight circles, moving the teasing contact up to Olive's clit, then down again to her opening. Hot juices poured from her freely, the viscous fluid coating Kate with thick, fragrant evidence of her desire. Ravenous, Kate brought her hand to her mouth for a prolonged taste, reminded of exactly how much she craved Olive in every way. "I love the flavor of your pussy." She flattened her saliva-slickened hand against Olive's sex, grinding her palm against the hot flesh. "Actually, I love everything about it. The way it looks, smells, tastes…how it feels wrapped around my fingers." Rather than act on her words and tease about the possibility of penetration, Kate used her thumb to draw back the prominent hood peeking out from between Olive's labia, and her index finger to gently stimulate the engorged knot of flesh beneath.

Olive sucked in a quick, noisy breath. "Kate—" Her thighs were already trembling. "Wait."

Kate lifted her hand immediately. "I'm waiting."

"No, don't *stop.*" Olive was practically whining.

Amused, Kate put her hand back and resumed its former motion. The thighs that had ceased quivering started again. Transfixed by the sight of her hand moving between Olive's shaking legs, Kate murmured, "I want you to watch." She looked up into Olive's face. "Watch how I make you feel good."

This time Olive grabbed her wrist and slammed her thighs closed on Kate's hand. "*Wait*…which means, please don't make me come so fast." She poked out her lower lip in an exaggerated pout. "I don't want this to end too soon." After a pause, she slowly opened her thighs.

Although Kate would happily touch Olive all night long, coaxing orgasms out of her until one or both of them literally passed out, she wouldn't deny Olive's request to draw things out. Shifting her touch lower, she probed the intricate layers of delicate flesh that lay open and ready for her. "I'll make it last, my darling, I promise."

Olive gave an appreciative whimper, clutching Kate's bicep

as though reserving the right to take control of the action. Breathing hard, she pressed a flurry of kisses against Kate's shoulder as though attempting to distract herself, making Kate wonder if she was also thinking about baseball. Finally Olive exhaled in a rush, "My God, woman, why are you so good at this?"

Chuckling, Kate climbed over Olive so she could switch hands, then gathered a generous amount of wetness on her fingertips as she moved her touch away from Olive's most sensitive spots. "I was blessed with a very rich, very filthy imagination." Eager to keep her promise to slow things down, she angled her wrist to press her fingers deep between Olive's buttocks, rubbing the slick fluid around the tight opening of her anus. "So here's my dilemma. I *really* want to put my fingers in your pussy, but I'm afraid you'll end up coming all over them, and I know you don't want that. Yet." She gathered more wetness, until she was practically swimming in the glorious stuff. "Would you like a finger in your ass instead? To start?"

Olive whimpered, burying her face in Kate's shoulder. "You'll make me come just talking like that."

Kate laughed and kissed the corner of Olive's mouth. "Dirty?"

"Yeah." Olive wiggled her hips, urging the tip of her index finger barely inside. "No one has ever talked to me that way before."

Kate refused to play coy. She knew exactly what she was doing. "And you like it."

Olive wiggled again, maneuvering herself onto the first inch of Kate's finger. She was hot and wet and so snug, yet clearly relaxed enough to feel no discomfort. Moaning, she stopped moving to stare up into Kate's eyes. "I love it."

"And this?" Kate drew tiny circles with the fingertip that was firmly embedded in Olive's luscious ass. With her other hand, she gathered more wetness to ease the way. "Should I stop here? Or slide in all the way?"

Shivering, Olive whispered, "Don't stop." When Kate didn't move, she released a shuddering sigh. "Go inside, Kate, please. I need to feel—" Her voice broke as Kate withdrew, lubed up, then worked her finger back inside to the second knuckle. "You."

Kate paused. "Keep going?" The tight muscle gripped and released her in time with Olive's heartbeat, which echoed through her own body as though they shared its ancient rhythm. Gazing deep into

Olive's eyes, Kate couldn't fathom ever feeling more connected to another human being than she did in this moment. "Or is this good?" At this point, she was only asking for the pleasure of hearing Olive answer.

"All the way," Olive murmured, keening quietly as Kate eased the full length of her finger inside. She banged the mattress beside her hip with a closed fist. "*Fuck*, everything feels so good."

"Then my evil plan is working." Kate lowered her mouth to Olive's breast and sucked the erect tip between her teeth. She bit down cautiously, gratified when Olive's body jumped and then contracted around her. "Excellent."

Olive let out a laugh that caused her inner muscles to tighten around Kate's finger. "It's definitely working, because I'm starting to forget why I wanted to draw this out..."

Kate bit down harder on the nipple, then dragged the flat of her tongue in wide circles around the tender flesh. She lifted her gaze, hoping to catch Olive watching, pleased when she did. She spent a few moments fucking Olive in the ass with her finger while studying her face, excited by every twinge of sensation that registered there. Leaving her breast with a final lick to her shiny, turgid nipple, Kate rasped, "Are you saying you want my fingers in your pussy? Because you can have them."

Olive hesitated, her internal conflict playing out across her pretty face. "I do..."

Banking on the idea that Olive *really*, genuinely loved dirty talk, Kate put her mouth against her ear and whispered, "A little butt fucking and you're ready to give it *all* up for me, aren't you?" She eased her finger out of Olive's ass before slowly forcing it all the way back in. "Ask me...whatever you need, I'll give to you."

Olive hooked a trembling arm around Kate's back. "I need you inside me."

Pleased at being given ample opportunity to tease, Kate sucked on the nearest patch of skin as she established a slow, driving rhythm with her finger. The shallow thrusts caused Olive to quake uncontrollably, as though she might actually climax from anal penetration alone. "I *am* inside you."

Growling, Olive reached between her legs and grabbed Kate's wrist. "You know what I mean."

"Do I?" Kate withdrew from Olive's ass, once again reversing their positions so she could switch back to her dominant hand. But before she settled down, she stopped to tug saucily on the waistband of the panties she'd left in such disarray. "You mean you want these off now?"

Olive lifted her hips. "Yes."

As committed as Kate was to her role as semi-bad cop, she was in no mood to mess around. She yanked the panties down and off before retaking her place at Olive's side. Reaching out, she pulled their bodies together as tightly as she could, wishing like hell for some way to get closer. She traced the delicate column of Olive's throat, then the valley between her full breasts, her belly, before drifting to a contented stop at the juncture of barely parted thighs. Kate petted the short, wiry hairs beneath her fingers and murmured, "Will you open your legs for me?"

Olive's thighs fell open as though Kate had uttered the secret password. "That's exactly where I want you."

"Here?" Kate ran her fingers through the unbelievable wetness coating Olive's vulva and thighs.

No longer shy, Olive took hold of her hand and positioned Kate at her opening. "I want you to slide your fingers inside me," she said, and helped her do just that. "*Deep.*" Holding tight to Kate's wrist, she fucked herself with the two digits on offer. "God, Kate, you have no idea how much I've missed you."

Moved by the palpable emotion in Olive's voice, Kate closed her eyes and murmured, "I think I might." She thrust in and out of Olive slowly, burying her fingers as deeply as she could. "Have you spent the past couple weeks feeling like you'd lost something you'd just discovered you needed? Something you were terrified you might never find again?"

Olive's blunt fingernails dug into her back. "I guess you *do* have an idea."

Bracing herself for a no, Kate moved her thumb to brush lightly against Olive's swollen clit. "Would you let me make you come if I promise to do it again just as soon as you recover?" She withdrew her fingers until only the very tips remained, then brought a third to join the two Olive had been enjoying so well. A raised eyebrow earned her a fervent nod, which emboldened Kate to ease back inside. She kissed Olive's neck, pleased by the way the muscles beneath her lips tensed as she stretched her fingers slightly apart. "I want to hear those sexy little noises you make and feel the way you tighten and convulse around me." She paused, then admitted in a whisper, "I need to remember what it's like to make you feel *good*."

Olive caressed the side of her face. "*Yes*."

Kate drew a light path around Olive's clit, testing her readiness. Her body jolted in reaction to the careful touch, clearly on a hair trigger, thrillingly close to detonation. Eager to bring on the explosion, Kate pulled Olive into a deep kiss, increasing the speed of her thrusts until her knuckles slapped rhythmically against Olive's ass. She groaned, pleased by the lewd sound of their fucking, doubly pleased when Olive grabbed a handful of her hair and tugged hard enough to bring tears to her eyes. Nipping Olive's lower lip, Kate finally brought her thumb in to join the action, rubbing precise circles designed to elicit the fastest, hardest, messiest climax possible. She wanted Olive to soak the futon, to fall apart completely all over her hand.

"Oh, fuck." Olive stiffened. Arched her back. Spread her legs impossibly wider. "I'm gonna come."

Excited, Kate kissed a path down Olive's throat to her chest, sucking on the nipple closest to her mouth while redoubling her efforts between what seemed like perpetually shaking thighs. She closed her eyes in anticipation, dedicated for the first time in days to something other than writing. And damn, did it feel *good*.

Olive's orgasm hit hard and wrenched a hoarse cry from someplace deep inside her, so loud that Kate knew it signaled a genuine loss of control. She surged up and covered Olive's mouth with her own, swallowing her delicious moans in case Erato was listening at the door. She didn't slow her hand until Olive's taut body went limp, and it only went still after Olive grabbed weakly at her arm, mumbling, "Please, no more."

Kate pulled out slowly, relishing every aftershock that rolled through the supple body pressed tightly against her own. Flattening her hand over Olive's aroused sex, she bent and kissed each of her nipples in turn. "You. Are. *Magnificent*."

Olive managed a breathless chuckle. "Only with you." Encouraging Kate to rest her head on her chest, she took deep breaths in an obvious effort to calm herself. "Wow. That was even better than your books."

Kissing the skin closest to her lips, Kate murmured, "I try." Then she closed her eyes and enjoyed the thrum of Olive's rapid heartbeat beneath her ear. After a moment, she added, "I'm choosing to accept that purely as a compliment of my sexual prowess and *not* as a subtle panning of my love scenes."

Quiet laughter rumbled through Olive's chest, making Kate smile even harder than she already was. "As it was intended."

Kate sighed at the mindless scratching of blunt fingernails between her shoulder blades. "It just feels so easy with you—Erato's interference aside."

"Who will henceforth be referred to as She Who Shall Not Be Named whenever we're postcoital. Or precoital. Or midcoital, for that matter." Olive stretched to give her left butt cheek a sharp pinch. "Deal?"

Yelping, Kate rolled away while using her hand to shield her bottom against further assault. The sheet dislodged slightly, sending a welcome, cool breeze over their sweat-dampened bodies. "Deal!"

"Excellent." Olive beckoned for her to return. "Now get back on top of me, but facing the other way."

The mental image that accompanied the invitation unleashed a renewed flood of wetness to coat Kate's already sodden folds—so much that she felt almost awkward about accepting. Face hot, Kate admitted, "You'll drown."

"I won't." Olive tugged lightly on her arm. "I'll feast." At the realization that Kate wasn't going to budge, she reached between their bodies and nudged Kate's thighs open. Locking eyes, Olive dragged her whole hand through the abundant wetness coating her sex before lifting it to her mouth so she could suck each finger clean. She finished her lengthy, deliberate display by licking every last drop of juice from her palm. In a low, huskier-than-usual voice, she murmured, "Believe me, wet—even messy—can *never* be a bad thing when your pussy tastes *this* yummy."

With both her ego and her libido boosted, Kate was able to let go of her insecurities and resume her position on top of Olive. But before she reversed direction, she paused to cradle Olive's face in her hands so she could cover her cheeks, nose, forehead, and chin with kiss after feather-soft kiss. As much as she burned to come, she wanted Olive to know without a doubt that this—that *they*—were about more than sex. She whispered, "On that note, I haven't forgotten that I owe you a very fancy, *very* private dinner date."

Clearly pleased by the comment, Olive caught a lock of her hair and gave it a playful tug. "As much as I appreciate that, right now you're all I want to eat."

Mindful of the rule against mentioning her muse, Kate declined to point out that she happened to be Olive's only option as long as they were locked in the office (save for the half-eaten bag of M&Ms next to her laptop). Instead, she groaned at the sensation of yet more wetness seeping from her body, drawn out by Olive's blunt language and the slight pain of having her hair pulled. She ducked out of Olive's grip, shooting her a mock dirty look. "Keep doing that and you'll really have a mess to contend with."

"Promise?" Olive's eyes flashed with pure, sinful mischief. "Now will you *please* sit on my face already?"

Turned on by Olive's total lack of inhibition, Kate gave her a final, passionate kiss, then maneuvered herself onto her hands and knees until she hovered above Olive's eager mouth. Drawing upon her newfound confidence that with this woman, sexually she could do no wrong, Kate snaked her right hand down to fondle herself. Her clit was so sensitive she didn't dare touch it, not wanting to bring on her own climax when a far superior source of release was mere inches away. She stroked her labia instead, imagining that Olive was not only watching but thoroughly enjoying the show. "Is this what you want?"

Olive let out a quiet growl before grabbing Kate's ass and pulling her down onto her waiting mouth. Overwhelmed by wet, sucking heat that threatened to send her swiftly over the edge, Kate forcibly lifted her hips so she could at least remove her fingers from the overwhelming mix of sensation. Olive delivered a firm swat to the fleshiest part of her bottom. "Brat."

Not in any real mood to play hard to get, Kate lowered herself back onto Olive's mouth with a seductive wiggle of her hips. The moan that greeted her sent pleasant reverberations through her lower body, setting off tiny explosions that stole her breath and left her clinging to the futon. Wanting to distract herself from the way Olive's skillful tongue sought out her most sensitive spots with unerring ease, she brought her now-unoccupied hands to Olive's fragrant, slippery sex—laid out so temptingly right below her face—and spread her open.

The sight that greeted her was absolutely mouthwatering. She wasn't sure she'd ever seen a woman so beautifully aroused, in real life *or* within her shamefully extensive history consuming visual pornography. Olive was dark pink, swollen and heavy and coated with droplets of milky white fluid, practically begging to be kissed. Obliging what she hoped was a shared desire, Kate gave in to temptation and dipped to have a taste. As soon as her tongue made contact, the driving suction against her clit faltered, offering her a welcome reprieve from her own fast-approaching climax.

Grateful to have found a way to buy herself a little breathing room, Kate moved her hands to Olive's thighs and pressed them apart to pin her down against the futon's mattress. At the same time she rolled her hips, dragging her pussy from Olive's chin to her nose, trying to stay away from her searching mouth. Whatever embarrassment she'd felt about her copious wetness was long gone, a testament to the trust and comfort she felt with her new lover. The enthusiasm that met her every action— from grinding her pussy into Olive's nose to the near-theatrical way she bobbed up and down on Olive's clit in an exaggerated pantomime of giving head—reassured her that with Olive, even her kinkiest instincts were worth following. Best of all, they were probably shared.

As though privy to her thoughts, Olive slipped two fingers into her vagina, then ran her other hand through the slick crevice between her buttocks, pausing to tease her anus with the barest indirect pressure. Aware that now *her* focus had slipped, Kate rocked herself on the fingers inside her briefly before redoubling her own efforts, penetrating Olive once, twice, three times, then withdrawing altogether, reaching down to grab and spread her ass instead. She moved her tongue in fast, tight circles around Olive's throbbing clit, feeling suddenly competitive about who would make who come first. Olive seemed to pick up on the new game, because the hand on her ass lifted only to return seconds later, landing low on her cheek with a resounding *smack*. Kate moaned against Olive's clit, feeling her own jump in response. That earned her another slap, which caused her to contract around the fingers inside her—which, damn it, was the beginning of the end.

Cursing, Kate did her best to keep licking despite the thunderous pleasure she could no longer hold back. The grip on her ass tightened, keeping her firmly attached to the wet suction of full lips and at the mercy of an expertly controlled tongue. At the same time, she could feel the fingers inside her fighting to keep moving even as she clamped down around them. The result was a friction so divine it rendered her momentarily useless, unable to do anything except be present and *feel*. She kept her tongue pressed against Olive's clit, her entire body quivering as she flew apart with a muffled shout. Olive squeezed her butt, then slapped it, moving her head back and forth as she milked wave after wave of ecstasy from Kate's absolutely exhausted body.

Acting on instinct alone, Kate sank her fingers into Olive once more, as deep as they would go. She sought out and found a spot she recalled drove Olive crazy and rubbed hard against her walls as she suckled the swollen bud beneath her tongue. Though Olive managed to continue the blissful torment of her clever mouth, she also began to tremble in what was by now a familiar pre-orgasmic ritual. Encouraged, Kate moved her hands back to Olive's thighs, pushing them open in a thoroughly lewd pose. She pinned one of her knees to the futon and held it there, then very carefully forced three fingers into her until she was buried to the knuckles. Olive moaned loudly, prompting Kate to push up onto her knees, away from her greedy mouth.

"Kate." Olive whimpered. Her fingers slipped out of Kate, and she hooked both arms around her thighs for leverage. A wet kiss pressed against the side of her knee, followed by warm puffs of air from Olive's rapid panting. "Yes, baby, lick me. I'm so close."

Kate used the movement of her tongue and fingers in lieu of her words to let Olive know exactly how much she'd missed her and how glad she was to be here with her now. Olive was crying out and biting at the tender skin of her thigh before she'd even said half of what she wanted to say, but that was okay because even if they didn't have unlimited time, at least they had the rest of the night. It was more than Kate had any right to expect.

Olive rode out the intensity of her release for an admirably long time before she finally patted Kate on the hip. "Kate, get up here."

All Kate heard were the tears. Frightened by the quiet sobs that suddenly overtook the body beneath hers, she scrambled off Olive and struggled to turn around without disturbing their increasingly disarrayed cover. She swore as her ankle got tangled up in the sheet, pulling it off their bodies to expose her bare ass and Olive's presumably weeping face. Panicking, Kate fought to cover Olive while rushing up to lie at her side. Instead she managed to roll off the futon and land on the hard laminate floor. Thankfully, the sheet stayed behind. At least one of them could preserve their modesty—and dignity.

Olive's gorgeous face peered over the side of the futon, caught in the no-man's-land between laughter and concern. Yet her cheeks still glistened with evidence of the tears Kate knew she'd recognized. Eyes wide, Olive said, "Are you all right?" Then, before Kate could answer, "After all that fucking, I can't believe the dismount is what did you in."

Despite her lingering concern, Kate couldn't help but dissolve into giggles. She'd faced a lot of humiliation over the past few weeks, so this barely registered. Olive's two-pronged response of concern followed up by a perfect one-liner reassured her before the notion of shame could even occur. Accepting the hand offered, Kate allowed Olive to pull her back onto the futon and beneath the sheet. She arranged the cover over their bodies so their heads remained out in the open and drew Kate into a thrillingly intimate embrace.

Kate kissed the corner of Olive's eye, sampling the saltiness of her tears. When Olive let her eyelid slip shut, she pressed her lips against one closed lid, then the other. "You were crying," she said. "So I kind of panicked."

Olive slid her thigh between Kate's and settled a hand on her hip, rubbing with her thumb. "I was just keeping my promise." At Kate's raised eyebrow, she said, "That we'd have a good cry together afterward." She smiled, brightly, then sobered a bit, looking down at Kate's collarbone as she traced it with her finger. "Honestly, it just hit me all of a sudden. What I'd nearly lost. How good this is—how good *we* are."

Kate placed her hand over the scar at the center of Olive's chest, feeling her own emotion rise again. What she'd nearly lost was staggering. How good they were seemed almost improbable. In a way, she still wasn't sure she could accept that this was real. What about when Erato let them out of this room? Could she and Olive honestly build a lasting relationship out of a beginning this strange and tempestuous? She had no idea, but—she reminded herself as the tears threatened to flow again—at least for right now, in this room, she wasn't alone anymore.

"Hey," Olive whispered, and caressed her hip, then her inner thigh. She kissed away the lone droplet that had managed to escape from Kate's eye, capturing it on her tongue with a murmured, "Shh." Her hand crept between Kate's thighs and stroked her soothingly. "I'm here now. We're in this together, remember?"

Kate nodded, then muttered, "Shit," when two more tears slipped out. She laughed when she saw Olive had restarted her own waterworks, a similar curse falling from her lips. "We are *such* girls."

"We *so* are," Olive said, and hugged her tight as she laughed and the tears seemed to flow harder. The hand between her legs continued its caresses, further confusing Kate. As though sensing her shift in mood, a single finger parted her labia and slid wetly over her highly sensitized clit. "The good news is, I love girls."

And then—for the moment at least—Kate had nothing left to cry about.

CHAPTER TWENTY-THREE

Olive fell asleep after the sun went down, worn out from at least five orgasms and hours of hushed conversation between rounds of making love. She fought to stay awake until the very last second, hanging onto consciousness as though succumbing to her exhaustion was tantamount to abandonment, but Kate reassured her again and again that it wasn't and that, in fact, Olive's nap would give her the perfect opportunity to write. After all, their freedom might very well depend on her ability to keep making progress. Olive was only able to let go after eagerly accepting the idea that Kate should write, which actually compelled Kate to drag herself away from their little love nest, get dressed, and return to her laptop for another round of trying to finish The Damn Book. Within minutes, she was glad she had.

The words flowed. No, they *poured* out of her, tumbling onto the keyboard one after the next, filling up the formerly blank pages of her document as though she were simply transcribing the end of a preexisting tale. The heart-to-heart talk between Molly and Rose's mother materialized on the screen just as she'd envisioned in her head, the fragments of dialogue and action she'd imagined for so many weeks finally coming together in a scene she was immediately and immensely proud to have written. Incredibly—and despite her increasingly unhappy bladder—she blazed through the entire thirty-five-hundred-word chapter with energy and motivation to spare, leaving her poised to tackle the very scene she'd dreaded less than twenty-four hours ago, but which she now felt completely prepared to write. The reunion. Complete with red-hot sex! Like she'd just enjoyed with Olive!

Humming to herself, Kate plunged into the literal and figurative climax of her novel. She was so engrossed in crafting the buildup to a perfect love scene she didn't realize Olive had risen until a cautious hand landed on her shoulder. Deep in her fictional world, she gasped, nearly falling out of her chair as she was jerked back into reality.

Olive stood there in her half-buttoned blouse and panties, tousled and sexy from sleep. She was grinning, legs crossed in a manner that suggested she was mere seconds away from doing the pee-pee dance. "I'm so sorry. I tried calling your name."

"No, it's okay." She reached for Olive and tugged her onto her lap but immediately regretted it. Her bladder screamed for relief from the pressure that had been building all day. "Uh-oh."

"Yeah," Olive said, and grimaced. She looped her arms around Kate's shoulders and leaned in for support. "She has to let us out to pee, right?"

"If not, things between us are going to get really intimate, really fast." Rubbing a hand down Olive's back, she sat forward to indicate that they should stand. "Because I've got to *go*."

"Me, too—at the very least." Olive got to her feet, shifting in discomfort as an increasingly petulant frown took over her face. "I also need a shower, desperately. You do, too."

Kate's muscles screamed as she straightened her legs for the first time in hours. She could feel their mingled juices dried on her skin, along with lingering wetness mixed with fresh arousal from having Olive on her lap. Her hair was a mess, and she tried to flatten it with a hand that smelled distinctly like Olive's pussy. "You're not wrong."

Olive bobbled from foot to foot. "Okay, so…unless you have another idea, I'm going to go knock on the door and tell that crazy bitch to let us out."

Kate winced. "I'd leave out the 'crazy bitch' part if I were you."

Olive left her with a peck on her cheek. "Don't worry, I've got this." She walked to the door, took a deep breath, then pounded with her fist for a good three seconds. "Hey! Erato! We need a bathroom break."

Silence greeted her request.

Now Kate had to hop back and forth, all the talk of using the bathroom working against her self-control. "She could be sleeping. Probably upstairs—"

Olive banged some more, so insanely loud Kate couldn't imagine it not waking the neighbors. "I mean it, Erato! We're in serious pain here. You can take us one at a time, if you want. Put bags over our heads, or whatever it is that sadists do to their *fucking prisoners*—"

"Shh." Kate cautioned her, alarmed by both the volume and the increasingly hostile tone. "You'll wake the whole building."

Olive turned and gave her an incredulous look. "Would that really be a bad thing?" At Kate's nod, Olive whipped around and grabbed the doorknob, rattling it noisily. "Listen, bitch," she yelled, before yanking the office door wide open with a force that caused her to stumble backward a few steps. "If you don't—" The threat ended as the reality of her role as the engineer of their escape seemed to sink in.

Kate was caught between feeling unsettled and immensely relieved. "Well, that's kind of weird."

With a fleeting backward glance, Olive shot out of the office. "Totally agree, and also, dibs on the bathroom across the hall!"

The sound of a door slamming in the hallway jarred Kate out of her temporary stupor and sent her jogging toward the master bedroom, shouting to Olive as she passed by. "Going upstairs!"

"I'll meet you there," Olive said, voice heavy with pleasure. "Enjoy—it feels divine."

Kate giggled the rest of the way upstairs, even as she battled a serious case of nerves over the prospect of suddenly facing her jailer. Where *was* Erato? She'd never been a heavy sleeper, so it was difficult to imagine she would still be tucked away in bed after all the commotion downstairs. Half expecting to find her muse waiting for her in the bedroom, Kate exhaled audibly when she found her private domain unoccupied. She wasted no time visiting the toilet, which—as Olive had promised—was simply exquisite. Though she was tempted to turn on the shower, hopefully for her and Olive to share, she wouldn't be able to relax until she knew where Erato was and *why* she'd decided to release them.

Hands and face washed, Kate left the bathroom and went to the place Erato was most likely hiding: the guest room. But it was empty. Oddly so. Erato hadn't come with much, but the bag that had carried her extra clothing was gone. As was her fancy new laptop. Fresh linens were on the bed, which had been made with military precision. Kate stood in the center of the room and turned in a circle, searching for *some* sign that Erato hadn't simply vanished.

"Kate?"

The sound of Olive tentatively calling out from the hallway sent an unexpected flood of relief surging through her veins. Even if her muse had disappeared, Olive hadn't. "Right here," Kate said, and walked out into the hall. "I think she might be gone. Like, *gone*."

Olive held up an envelope with *Kate* handwritten on the front. "This was on the office door."

She stepped forward to take the envelope, nervous about what might be inside. "She said she wouldn't leave until I finished the book. Why would she have left?"

"I thought you *wanted* her to leave," Olive murmured, not unkindly. "Maybe she decided to respect your wishes."

Rolling her eyes, Kate unfolded a piece of stationery covered in impeccable, flowery script. She skimmed the first couple lines, then blinked. At first she could only state the obvious. "It's a letter."

"I see that," Olive said in a gentle voice. "Do you want to read it out loud or would you prefer that I give you some privacy?"

Kate looped her arm through Olive's and steered them into her room. "No need for privacy, but let's sit down first. I'm exhausted."

"I'll bet." Olive disentangled when they reached the bed, guiding Kate to sit beside her. She enfolded her in strong arms and encouraged her to lean back for support. "I have no idea how you're still awake after all those orgasms."

Kate yawned loudly and rubbed at her eyes, hoping to sharpen the blurry words on the handwritten page. "Me neither, all of a sudden." A brisk shake of her head brought everything into temporary focus. She cleared her throat, eager to read Erato's missive so they could clean up and then crash for a few hours. "All right…"

My dearest Kate,

If everything has unfolded according to my design— and it always does—then you and Olive are snuggled up, reading this letter together. Good! Contrary to what you've grown to believe, I am the veritable captain of Team Olive (that's the proper usage of the idiom, isn't it? "Team So-and-So" to denote support for said so-and-so? At any rate, I think she's a doll).

Ironically, I'm not much of a writer, and this letter is a particularly challenging one to compose. I wish I could've told you good-bye in person, as I've always expressed myself better in real life than on the page (more irony), but this will have to do. You've wanted me gone from your life for a while now, so I suspect the heartbreak you once feared you'd feel at my departure is no longer a concern. I'm glad. That, too, is by design. After the suffering and torment I've forced you to endure, now that you have the woman of your dreams firmly at your side, how could you possibly mourn the loss of such a terrible pain in your ass?

First, an apology: I told you I wouldn't leave until you finished, but obviously that wasn't quite true. I know you have two and a half more chapters left to write, but whether or not you realize it yet, this book is as good as done. The rest will practically write itself. Enjoy the ride.

I think it's important for you to understand why I made you experience everything you did, why I let you agonize over the possibility of losing Olive despite knowing your own happily-ever-after was all but guaranteed. The reason, dear Kate, is because you were stuck. Not just in writing, but also in life and love. Two years without sex? It would be one thing if you'd chosen celibacy deliberately, but let's face it—you were simply mired in complacency, the simplicity of a life spent mostly interacting with other human beings online, if at all.

You are an author, *Kate, and a storyteller—one who excels at transcribing universal human emotions and experiences into sexy little distractions from the sometimes-painful grind of daily life. Some artists are able to draw inspiration solely from their imaginations. You could isolate them in a cave at the top of a mountain and they would still produce magnificent works of beauty. Unfortunately, you are not one of those artists. Your creativity needs to be fed. It needs to be challenged. It needs to be informed by real-life experience, because it is when you're able to tap into your own emotions that your prose really soars.*

And let's not forget, your creativity desperately needs to be fucked.

Blushing, Kate stopped reading and gave Olive a sidelong glance. "You're sure you want to hear the rest of this?"

Olive patted her arm, then kissed the crown of her head. "Baby, I know your creativity needs to be fucked. And I know Erato took care of that before me. I'm all right."

Nervously, Kate forged ahead.

The reason you were struggling to write Rose and Molly's romance is because your own heart had become so hardened toward the entire concept of true love. You've written about passionate, all-consuming romances for years without ever experiencing one of your own. And yes, your work has been outstanding, but believe me when I say it's about to get even better. After all, you've just lived your very own romance novel.

Think about it: girl meets girl, girl has a one-night stand with girl only to discover the existence of an indefinable spark hinting at the possibility of more, and then, unexpectedly, life throws girls back together. Girl fucks girl again, things start to get serious, and then life (or the antagonist, which I suppose was me) interferes, throwing the happy ending into doubt. As a crafter of romance stories, you know very well that there's a direct relationship between the severity of conflict and heartbreak the characters suffer and the sweetness of their eventual reconciliation—and after enjoying your own reunion with Miss Olive, I suspect that now you truly *understand on a whole new level. Do you not?*

No matter what anyone tells you, you don't have to write what you know, but it's almost always easier when you do.

This time Olive interrupted by scoffing under her breath. "Neat trick, great for your writing, but she's lucky we played our roles the right way or else she could've ruined everything."

Having skimmed ahead a couple of sentences, Kate murmured, "Sounds like she didn't consider it a risk." She kept reading.

I suspect that one or both of you are thinking that I was taking a big chance with your hearts by manipulating the unfolding of your brand-new relationship the way I did. All I can do is assure you I wasn't. For one thing, you're too well matched for me to easily keep you apart. Believe me—even if I hadn't locked Olive in that room with you, unimpeded, you two would have found your way back to each other eventually. Besides, I played the perfect villain, able to wreak havoc on your budding romance while simultaneously serving as a target for your collective rage once Olive discovered the lengths to which I would go to enforce my will. The enemy of your enemy...well, let's just say I was certain you would eventually bond over your mutual anger toward me, which would enable Olive to see clearly that the hurt she experienced was at my hands alone.

On that note, this paragraph is addressed to Olive: Hello. I sincerely apologize for the way I grabbed you in that parking lot and for the way I embarrassed and—let's face it—dehumanized you in front of that very handsome law-enforcement officer. My need to help Kate in a very specific way trumped your right not to be terrorized—at least according to my own internal code. I hope that the outcome of my endgame will be enough to convince you to forgive me. If not, I understand. If I'm able to make it up to you some day, I will.

"Shit," Olive murmured, and took Kate's hand between both of hers. "I forgive her."

Kate gave her a subtle squeeze.

So, about that endgame. Let me explain.

I always make it a point to jump-start the separation process well before my relationship with an artist comes to its natural end. Unfortunately, that usually means turning myself into the enemy. Harsh, but necessary. My policy is to never stay with a writer for more than one project, out of concern that he or she might grow dependent upon my presence to work. That can't happen for a number of reasons, least of all because my job isn't to inspire. Not really (although I have been told I have some talent in that department). No, my job is to find my client's perfect inspiration—their own personal muse. For some it's a new lover, for others a new passion or even just a new perspective. I am a filler of empty spaces, to attempt a slightly lyrical turn of phrase.

Kate, Olive is your muse. Treasure her (and take her out for a nice dinner, for goodness sake! On me...I left some cash on the kitchen counter...along with both your cell phones!).

All right. In conclusion, I just want to say that I hope I imparted some lasting lessons, such as

- *Write through the turmoil of your own life. From adversity flows poetry!*
- *Make sure to have a life. Your art demands it.*
- *Nobody ever achieved her dreams by watching kitten videos on the Internet (except the woman whose dream it was to watch kitten videos on the Internet).*

I'll leave it to you to suss out the rest—there's more, trust me, but I'm guessing that you're exhausted right now (after hours of frenzied writing, I hope?) and would like nothing more than a shower and a nap. You have my blessing to enjoy both.

However, consider this a warning: I expect you to hit that manuscript hard after you wake up. The book still needs to be ready for submission within the week, and if I even get slightly nervous that you're not on track, I may just have to come back and oversee your efforts until you're done. Thankfully, I'm confident that you no longer need—or want— my services. So be a good girl and work hard, won't you?

On a personal note, I thoroughly enjoyed every bit of the time we spent together (admittedly, the parts where you liked me and/or made love with me were my favorites). Thank you for sharing your home, your body, and your fantasies with me. I will never forget you or the time we spent together.

Never stop creating other worlds, especially when this one proves difficult,
Erato

Kate stopped reading and stared at the letter sightlessly before folding it up and tossing it on her nightstand. Olive tightened her embrace and stayed silent while Kate processed everything she'd just read. Or tried. Now that the adrenaline of her sprint for the bathroom had worn off and she knew they were alone, her bone-deep exhaustion was finally overwhelming everything else. She yawned and closed her eyes.

With a gentle squeeze, Olive pulled her to her feet. "Come on. I'll run us a quick shower so we're not totally rank when we wake up."

Kate groaned. "While I'm sure future-me will be incredibly grateful, right-now-me just wants to curl up in bed with you and fall asleep." Despite her protest, she followed Olive into the bathroom and watched as she turned on the water and tested the temperature with her hand. "What do you think of the letter?"

Olive unbuttoned her blouse and shrugged it off. "I think the important thing is what *you* think."

"I think…" Drifting off at the emergence of more and more bare skin, Kate took a minute to gather her thoughts. "I think that right now, at least, I'm happy. And I *am* writing again—better yet, I actually like a lot of what I've written. So I guess while I'm still not one hundred percent sure whether Erato is a supernatural being or just a diabolically manipulative madwoman, I can't deny that she's made my life better for having walked into it."

Now fully nude, Olive began to undress Kate with careful patience. "But as far as wanting her to come back?"

"Nope."

"Good, then we're in agreement. We'll nap, spend an hour, *maybe* two, waking up, and then I'll bake some muffins while you head straight back to work. I'll text my father to let him know I'll be in late today, so I can make sure you get off to a good start. Because I'm telling you right now, you *will* finish that book in a timely manner. Understand?"

Vaguely unsettled by Olive's no-nonsense tone, Kate sensed that she really *had* just traded one muse for another. Her slight unease lasted only seconds before turning into a warm, gooey feeling in the pit of her stomach. Who was she kidding?

This was the happiest of endings.

CHAPTER TWENTY-FOUR

Exactly four weeks later, as she walked hand in hand with Olive around the farmers' market while Howard minded the bakery's booth, Kate stumbled over her feet, gasping, as the crowd parted to reveal Erato standing not five feet away. Radiant as ever, she lit up at the sight of them, even as Kate shrank back in fear. Olive's fingers tightened around hers, though she couldn't say whether it was out of fright or in an effort to reassure.

"Kate! Olive!" Erato swept in to greet them, taking Olive by the shoulders to plant a not-quite-platonic kiss on her lips, then giving Kate the same treatment. She released Kate and stepped back with a happy, friendly smile. "I've been expecting to run into you. Frankly, I can't believe it didn't happen sooner."

Unsure how to feel about the sudden reappearance of a woman who had genuinely traumatized both of them while also helping bring about all the best things currently happening in her life—including her amazing girlfriend, the glowing feedback her editor had emailed just that morning, and two brand-new short stories written within two weeks—Kate struggled for the right greeting. *Hello* seemed inadequate. So did *thank you*. *What the hell is wrong with you* was certainly too harsh, considering that everything had turned out so wonderfully.

Olive stepped in to break the silence. "She turned in her manuscript. The editor loves it. Why are you here?"

Straight to the point. Kate drank in the sight of her girlfriend, vibrant and confident and alive, aglow under the mild warmth of the autumn sun. She loved this woman, beyond a doubt. Olive really was her happy ending.

Erato giggled. "Don't worry. I'm not here for your lover. I actually just forced my current artist to leave his place for a bit, to get some air. He has the rest of the month off from work to finish his novel, so I understand his intensity and focus, but the quality of his work is directly proportional to his exposure to the outdoors. He's always been a nature guy. We decided to stop off for a few snacks before hiking out to the river for a picnic." She clapped her hands, elated by a sudden thought. "You two should join us. We could make it a double date."

Kate opened her mouth to decline what was sure to be an incredibly awkward afternoon, then gaped in shock as Chad strolled up to Erato with a loaf of sourdough bread in one hand and a bag of local meats and cheeses in the other. He leaned in to kiss Erato on the cheek, then froze as he registered who she was talking to.

"Kate!" Chad straightened, looking painfully sheepish. "Hi. I haven't seen you around lately."

She'd been busy writing, fucking Olive, and generally falling in love, so Kate hadn't seen much of anyone over the past four weeks. Clearly Chad had also been consumed by plenty of writing and fucking of his own. "I've been busy." Hoping to reassure Chad that she wasn't jealous of his new muse, she lifted Olive's hand to show him their entangled fingers. "Chad, this is my girlfriend Olive. Olive, my neighbor Chad. He's the one who drove me to the farmers' market the day we more or less broke up."

Olive reached out with her free hand to shake. "It's a pleasure to meet you. Thanks for helping Kate. I know she appreciated it."

"It was no problem at all!" Chad visibly relaxed, reaching out to tentatively wrap his arm around Erato's middle after a prolonged pause. "Actually, it was fate, I think, because it led me to this amazing creature." He stared at Erato with moon eyes. "Now I'm almost halfway through my first novel, which is something I *never* thought I'd say."

Oh, boy. Kate caught Erato's gaze, tipping her head at the silent admonishment not to reveal anything about her methods. She didn't want to spoil the surprise for Chad, anyway. If Erato was as good as she seemed to be, his life was about to change for the better—even if he had to suffer a little to get there. Beaming at him, Kate said, "That's amazing, really. Congratulations."

"Thanks." Chad bounced up and down on the tips of his toes. "It's the craziest thing, but I just can't get enough lately." His gaze slid over Erato, and then he quickly looked back at Kate and Olive, red-faced. "Of writing."

Kate smirked. "Of course." She cleared her throat and gave Erato a polite smile. "As much as we appreciate the invitation, Olive has to get back to work, and I should really go start on some edits. You two enjoy yourselves, though."

Erato seemed pleased with her answer. "We will. I hope you two have something exciting planned for tonight? It *is* Saturday…"

"Bucket-list Saturday," Olive said, saving Kate from having to decide how to answer such an inadvertently personal question. "In which we make it a point to try something new."

That delighted Erato even more. "To whittle down any potential regrets?"

Olive startled so subtly Kate was sure she was the only one who noticed. "Exactly."

With a nod, Erato stepped out of Chad's loose embrace and went to Kate for another hug. She whispered into her ear. "She's exactly what you need."

Overcome by a powerful sense of well-being, Kate returned the hug without hesitation. Whatever lingering hard feelings she might have had melted away at the realization that Erato really *did* have her best interests at heart. She always had. "I know. Thank you."

Watching Erato and Chad walk away, Olive wrapped her arms around Kate and kissed her on the cheek. "You okay?"

"I'm wonderful." She turned to initiate a slightly more playful kiss. "You?"

"The same." Olive nipped her lower lip, then pulled away to stare after the muse and her new artist once again. "That dude is in *so* much trouble."

"And he has no idea." She smiled as the two distant figures finally disappeared from sight. "I'd feel sorry for him if I didn't think there was a damn good chance Erato will figure out a way to give him the same ridiculously happy ending she gave me." She thought back to the low points of her time with Erato. "At least I hope so."

Olive put a hand on her ass, briefly, as a tease. Voice lowered to a throaty whisper, she breathed into Kate's ear. "And I hope you're ready to make that amateur film you promised me tonight. Lights, camera, action, my little exhibitionist. We're going to have some *fun*."

Kate shivered and melted into Olive's arms for a long, lingering kiss—fully prepared to live happily ever after.

About the Author

Meghan O'Brien lives in Northern California with her wife, their son, and a motley collection of pets. She is the author of six previous novels and various short stories, mostly of the romantic/erotic variety, and is a two-time recipient of the GCLS Award for Lesbian Erotica. Meghan is a native of Royal Oak, Michigan, but can't say she misses the snow. You can connect with her on Facebook or Twitter (@meghanobrien78).

Books Available From Bold Strokes Books

Searching for Celia by Elizabeth Ridley. As American spy novelist Dayle Salvesen investigates the mysterious disappearance of her ex-lover, Celia, in London, she begins questioning how well she knew Celia—and how well she knows herself. (978-1-62639-356-1).

Hardwired by C.P. Rowlands. Award-winning teacher Clary Stone and Leefe Ellis, manager of the homeless shelter for small children, stand together in a part of Clary's hometown that she never knew existed. (978-1-62639-351-6)

No Good Reason by Cari Hunter. A violent kidnapping in a Peak District village pushes Detective Sanne Jensen and lifelong friend Dr. Meg Fielding closer, just as it threatens to tear everything apart. (978-1-62639-352-3)

Romance by the Book by Jo Victor. If Cam didn't keep disrupting her life, maybe Alex could uncover the secret of a century-old love story, and solve the greatest mystery of all—her own heart. (978-1-62639-353-0)

Death's Doorway by Crin Claxton. Helping the dead can be deadly: Tony may be listening to the dead, but she needs to learn to listen to the living. (978-1-62639-354-7)

The 45th Parallel by Lisa Girolami. Burying her mother isn't the worst thing that can happen to Val Montague when she returns to the woodsy but peculiar town of Hemlock, Oregon. (978-1-62639-342-4)

A Royal Romance by Jenny Frame. In a country where class still divides, can love topple the last social taboo and allow Queen Georgina and Beatrice Elliot, a working-class girl, their happy ever after? (978-1-62639-360-8)

Bouncing by Jaime Maddox. Basketball coach Alex Dalton has been bouncing from woman to woman because no one ever held her interest, until she meets her new assistant, Britain Dodge. (978-1-62639-344-8)

Soul Selecta by Gill McKnight. Soul mates are hell to work with. (978-1-62639-338-7)

Same Time Next Week by Emily Smith. A chance encounter between Alex Harris and the beautiful Michelle Masters leads to a whirlwind friendship and causes Alex to question everything she's ever known— including her own marriage. (978-1-62639-345-5)

All Things Rise by Missouri Vaun. Cole rescues a striking pilot who crash-lands near her family's farm, setting in motion a chain of events that will forever alter the course of her life. (978-1-62639-346-2)

Riding Passion by D. Jackson Leigh. Mount up for the ride through a sizzling anthology of chance encounters, buried desires, romantic surprises, and blazing passion. (978-1-62639-349-3)

Love's Bounty by Yolanda Wallace. Lobster boat captain Jake Myers stopped living the day she cheated death, but meeting greenhorn Shy Silva stirs her back to life. (978-1-62639334-9)

Just Three Words by Melissa Brayden. Sometimes the one you want is the one you least suspect…Accountant Samantha Ennis has her ordered life disrupted when heartbreaker Hunter Blair moves into her trendy Soho loft. (978-1-62639-335-6)

Lay Down the Law by Carsen Taite. Attorney Peyton Davis returns to her Texas roots to take on big oil and the Mexican Mafia, but will her investigation thwart her chance at true love? (978-1-62639-336-3)

Playing in Shadow by Lesley Davis. Survivor's guilt threatens to keep Bryce trapped in her nightmare world unless Scarlet's love can pull her out of the darkness back into the light. (978-1-62639-337-0)

Twice Lucky by Mardi Alexander. For firefighter Mackenzie James and Dr. Sarah Mackenzie, there's suddenly a whole lot more in life to understand, to consider, to risk…someone will need to fight for her life. (978-1-62639-325-7)

Shadow Hunt by L.L. Raand. With young to raise and her Pack under attack, Sylvan, Alpha of the wolf Weres, takes on her greatest challenge when she determines to uncover the faceless enemies known as the Shadow Lords. A Midnight Hunters novel. (978-1-62639-326-4)

boldstrokesbooks.com

Bold Strokes Books
Quality and Diversity in LGBTQ Literature

 victory
EDITIONS

 *Drama*

 MATINEE BOOKS

 E-BOOKS

SCI-FI

MYSTERY

 HE erotica

 BSB SOLILOQUY

YOUNG ADULT

 BOLD STROKES BOOKS

EROTICA

 LIBERTY EDITION

Romance

W·E·B·S·T·O·R·E
PRINT AND EBOOKS